The Collier's Daughter

by

John Little

Illustrated by Claire Ball

Preface

This is a tale of what might have taken place. It is fiction, though it is shot through with many historical facts. I came across a real story in a real photograph which forms the frontispiece of this book; or rather two real stories that interwove into a tale worth telling, and in both stories most of the people were real. They lived, they breathed, they walked under the sun and saw out their lives as we all do. But beyond that I have put words into their mouths, ascribed actions to them that they probably never took and made them interact in ways they may never have done. On the other hand, they may have done all of these things and the fact is that no-one alive today knows whether they did or not; their lives are mostly a blank sheet. So in telling their story I set them as far as I could into the world of their day and made the detail of their everyday lives real, though I have tried to treat them with respect. If my characters go to a shop, then be assured, that shop existed. In the visiting of a theatre, that also existed; the playbill is composed of acts of the time. If they catch a train at a station, though closed for 100 years, that station was there; many of the small details in my book may be searched for and found in books and on the internet should anyone care to do so.

Not all of my characters are real, for it was necessary to invent some for story purposes. Nonetheless, they are of their time also; I have tried to make it so that my audience can enter into the age in which this story is set, even in minutiae, and in some way, though through a glass darkly, to see the world as it was then. It is my hope that the reader enjoys the result.

I wish to thank my wife, Ruth, and David Banks of Nova Scotia for their careful editing and proofing of this book and Margaret May for her assiduous genealogical research and edits. I am delighted with the deft artistry in the illustrations of Claire Ball, which have enhanced the text considerably. More thanks must go to my sample readers; Sylvia Smith, Val Smith, Eunice Small, Irene Martin, Claire Ball, Jane Storey, Betty Telford, Dave

Adams and Margaret Way. I am grateful to Mr and Mrs Chesters of West End Farm Edderside for allowing me to visit and see where my protagonists lived. I am similarly obliged to Mr and Mrs Carter for allowing me to see where John and Nancy Adams lived for nearly 60 years.

The book was partly inspired by HE Winter's *History Of Dearham*, and his excellent account of events during the Dearham Miners' Co-operative which allowed me to merge real events into my fictional synthesis. I obtained much valuable material from the splendid books of the Holme St Cuthbert Local History Group; *Plain People* and *More Plain People*. Finally, my work was much eased by the British Newspaper Archive, which is an invaluable resource.

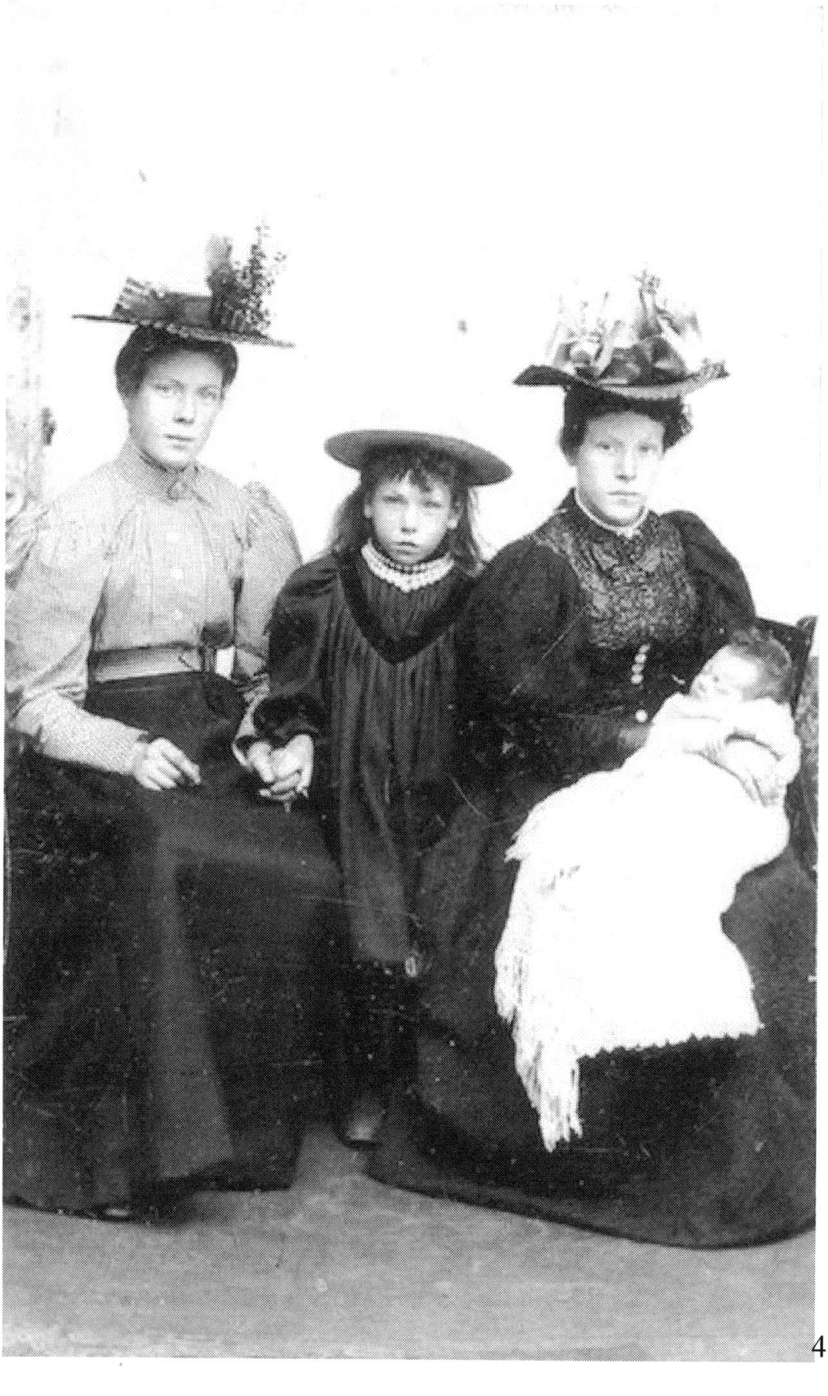

4

The Collier's Daughter

Chapter 1

Easter 1894

Margaret heard the church bell toll out and paused momentarily in pounding the shirts in their old wooden tub, but she did not join the groups of people hurrying down the road and up again towards the churchyard. Though it was just after Easter, there was a slight warmth to the afternoon air, and the clear bright weather was tempting her to go to what she knew would be an important meeting. This temptation was resisted sternly as the steel in her character reminded her that it was Monday and whatever else happened, the laundry had to be done. She was soon to be 19 and still living at home, which was very late by the standards of most in the neighbouring households, but her mother wanted her to be able to command a good wage when her time came to take service. She had left school at thirteen after completing Standard VI and had become a day scullery maid at the local vicarage where she had earned one shilling and six pence a week, with her lunch and evening meal. The money went straight to Mother, and her getting of two meals a day elsewhere helped the family budget considerably. The rate of pay had risen now to two shillings a week, which was not over-much, but her father wanted her at home to ease her mother's work as well. Early in the morning she rose at six o'clock to help with breakfast and other household duties; her day work commenced at nine o'clock when she washed dishes at the vicarage, a task that was repeated after lunch, and after dinner; she was usually home by nine o'clock in the evening. Between dishwashing she assisted round the kitchen and learned a lot from cook and the parlour maid about the running of a house.

As was normal practice, she had half a day off a week and had elected to take it after lunch on Mondays so that she could help her mother with the washing, a strenuous and time-consuming task. She also worked fewer hours on Sunday, it being a day of rest, so she was allowed the afternoon off. She was a girl who was very used to hard work, and consoled herself with the thought that at least when the time came for her to leave home and enter service, she would be able to ask at least £5 a half year instead of the £3 to be expected by someone of no experience at all. The fact that she had left school with the higher exam gave her hopes of perhaps rising to be a housekeeper in a large establishment; she was not without ambition. At any rate, there was nothing she could do about the situation she was in, and since Omega had left home her mother relied on her help for washday and other household duties.

Her elder sister had followed a similar course to her own, save that she had managed to become a day scullery maid at Dovenby Hall at age twelve when she had reached Standard V, then at sixteen the good character she had obtained enabled her to get a resident place as a general maid in the house of a solicitor in Maryport where she was content, but they only saw her for a half day a week when she was allowed to walk home to keep Sunday with her own family. Omega was three years older than Margaret, who had been kept home later than her because the three younger siblings, Thomas, John and Alpha, were significantly younger and Mother sometimes found herself struggling. She might not be able, as a miner's wife, to afford a maid, but with an older daughter at home she could manage very well. The two boys were getting older now, and Margaret knew that soon she would have to go and look for a job to make her own living. Even if she had been inclined to stop her work and go to the meeting, her mother would not have countenanced the idea. Nancy Adams was a good and caring parent, but a firm believer in duty, prayer and good order. Father would go to hear what was said and would report back for good or ill, but she hoped that it would not be ill. She liked living in Dearham where she had been born, and the word was around the village that families who had been here for generations might have to move to Flimby, even Workington or Whitehaven if the pit closed. Some people had already left, but these first-flyers were mostly those who had not been long in the village and whose emotional roots in this area were shallow. There were many other coal mines dotted round the region and work could be had for those who wished to move.

On the whole the Adams family did not wish to move, for they liked where they lived. Up the steep hill from Townhead was a row of terraced houses incorporating the Ship Hotel. About two thirds of the way along the row was a small opening where a stone and dirt track led to a lonning that ran behind the houses. The track also ran steeply down as a ramp or to a tiny flat area backing onto the small stream called Row Beck where in 1878 a local speculative landlord had built a red brick house, divided in semi-detached fashion, into two small cottages. Behind each of these was attached a scullery, a cubby hole for an earth bucket, and tacked onto the side of each cottage was a lean-to that could be used as a shed but which was quite weather proof, to be used as a place to lodge any workman who was accustomed to roughing it. John Adams had watched it being built, and with a growing family he knew that sharing a house with his parents as they had been doing, would not answer his needs. Upon inquiry, he found that the place was to be rented out for three shillings a week, struck a deal on it there and then, and they had moved in shortly afterwards. Margaret had been two years old then and could remember no other home.

'Margaret, we're almost out of soap. Run up to Saul and get another bar. Oh and some Borax too.'

Margaret dried her hands on a rough piece of towel and walked through the cottage, straight out of the front door and up the slope. They lived 'down the Dib' though they did not know why it was called the Dib. A Dib as all knew, was a ramp of earth leading up or down in the precincts of a colliery. Calling the little lane down to their house 'the Dib' where there was no coalmine, always struck her as bit odd, though it had to be admitted that coalminers did live in both cottages. Turning right out of the lane she walked up a few doors and into the small grocery shop of Saul Serginson. The musty smell of provisions tickled her nose with a deft appeal and she sniffed it with a long-held appreciation. Mr Serginson's shop was small and so was his stock, but it took less than a minute to get from their door to his so that is where they went most often for minor purchases. The shop was really the front room of a house with a counter across it, but dotted round it were tins, a bacon slicer, boxes of biscuits where whole or broken could be purchased singly, or in any number you wished, in brown paper bags. Two containers of loose tea and one of ground coffee gave much of the piquancy to the smell of the shop, but it was underlaid with the tang of carbolic laundry soap. Saul was not there; he must be out back doing something so she picked up the small bell on the counter, noting as she always did, that it had a number '5' on it and wondering why it was so. Ever since she could remember she had puzzled over that 5 but had never dared to ask for fear of being thought ignorant. Although Margaret could be very forthright on occasion, she did not like to parade the fact that she might not be aware of something obvious to others. This form of shyness did not manifest itself often though. She rang the bell and its silver clang had the desired effect as Saul came bustling through the door from the back, slightly red and sweating, wiping his hands on the white apron that he always wore for work.

'Sorry, Maggie. I hope I haven't kept you. I was packing some eggs and that straw cutter is hard work.'

Margaret winced inwardly, though it was not perceptible to the grocer. People would call her Maggie, but she always hated it. To her, Margaret was her name and Maggie was something else. Maggie was a diminutive, a belittling, a shortening and a taking of a liberty. The trouble was that in this community, if you insisted on such a detail they might think you a snob, or trying to be posh, or getting above yourself, and the last in particular was a social solecism. As ever, she ignored it.

'No Mr Serginson, I just got here.'

'Well, that's good. So what can I do for you this lovely afternoon?'

'I'd like some laundry soap and some borax please.'

'Right - there you are.' So saying, Serginson handed over a paper bag with half a penny's worth of borax crystals already weighed out, then moved towards the side counter where a huge block of soap stood on what looked like a cheeseboard. There was a cheese wire attached to the back of the board and he cut a slab off it about an inch thick.

'I had some ready of course, but it's all gone. Busy day for soap is Monday.'

Margaret nodded because Monday was washday for everyone and as far as she knew, for all the world.

'A ha'penny's worth please.'

Serginson nodded and carefully used the wire twice more to cut across the slab, before wrapping the resultant tablet of soap in a square of greaseproof paper and handing it to her.

'There you are young lady. That's one penny please.'

Margaret handed over the brown copper coin and turned to go with a thank you.

'I don't suppose you've heard anything have you?' said the grocer. There was an undertone of anxiety in his voice that Margaret understood. She had heard much of that tone among her friends and neighbours lately. The closure of a mine in such a small community would signal the loss of 260 jobs, all men, and behind most of them stood a wife and family, all bereft of income. Such families could not afford to buy what shopkeepers offered and Mr Serginson was quite right to be worried about his own income. He was a fair man and his prices were reasonable; he was also willing, as some were not, to allow goods on tick to those with less ready cash than others, but there were limits and he needed to live.

'I haven't, Mr Serginson,' said Margaret, 'but I expect they'll be back soon and then we'll all know. Why didn't you go to the meeting?'

'Shop won't mind itself. Thanks lass; I guess I'll have to wait like everyone else then. I'll see you again.'

Bidding the grocer a good afternoon Margaret walked back down the Dib. Often she skipped along this path, but not today. There was work to be done, and besides, a mood hung over the street that did not dispose her to be cheerful. Back in the scullery all was steam and heat.

'Half the borax into the tub,' said her mother, 'then get a bucket of water to top it up. Put a few bits of coal on the fire, then get busy with that posser.'

Washday was hard work. Obedient to her instructions, Margaret took the metal washday bucket and walked to the stream. Carved out in the bed of the shallow beck was a hollow that John Adams had cut many years before to make easy the dipping of a bucket to fill. In theory, they used water from a tap up the hill that served several houses, but for the scullery the stream was easier. The beck rose from a spring a couple of miles upstream and the water was clear and clean. Kirtling up her long black skirt, she leaned out from the bank and drew a bucketful before standing up and walking back to the galvanized metal tub or barrel, leaning sideways to balance her load, the muscles of her abdomen straining under the weight. This was what they called the 'set pot' even though, unlike the built-in copper pots of olden days, it was not set in place. She had been helping her mother do this, and indeed much else of heavy housework, for years and her arms could well cope with the load as she lifted it to the top of the tub and tipped half of it in. The boiling water ceased to bubble and she threw a shovel of coal on the fire underneath it. With great energy she took the metal plunger, universally called a 'posser', and agitated the clothes up and down vigorously in the tub.

'Right now bring the rest of the water here, because this is a bit hot, even for me.'

Margaret did not know how her mother could stand the heat of the water in the wooden tub after she had reached into the metal one with the wooden tongs to grab garments out and transfer them. Most of the dirt came out with the boil, but collars and cuffs were persistent in remaining grimy so it was here that she or Nancy had to rub the laundry soap onto them, twist the garment to get most of the water out then rub it on the washboard or hit it with a dolly stick to persuade the grime to leave.

'Now change the rinse and get busy on that.'

Once again Margaret collected water from the beck, and this time poured it into the rinsing tub. The clothes that Mother had finished with were now hers to slosh about until there was no soap left in them, then to mangle them in the corner of the yard. The cold water bit at her hands painfully, but the rinse had to be done; she ruefully reflected that she seemed to spend half her life with her hands in water. After a few minutes, satisfied with what she had done, and seeing that the clothes were clean, she began to put them through the mangle. They had had this device for about four years and it had made her mother's life a lot easier. Father had bought it in the Maryport Co-operative shop in Dearham Main Street that sold all kinds of groceries, meats and household goods. It was where Nancy Adams went for most of her shopping for being a Co-operative store its goods were cheaper than most of the other grocers in town. The mangle was made of cast iron with two wooden rollers and a handle, and what Margaret liked most of all was that on each side there was a likeness in cast metal, of General Gordon, the hero of Khartoum. Before this acquisition, Mother had had to wring the clothes out by hand, but this simple machine squeezed out most of the water before Margaret pegged them onto the clothesline that ran across the yard. Some could go on the airer that hung from the ceiling above the small range in the back room of the house, but there was not room for everything, which was especially true of their linen sheets.

These sheets were a source of special pride for Margaret because she had made them. Of itself, making this was not exceptional, because everything she now wore was made by her, and when she was younger, by her mother. Most women in this society were used to making their own garments, knitting, darning, following patterns impressed in their heads and hand stitching to the highest standards possible. Mr Joseph Hodson up in Dearham Main Street was a draper, and that was where she had got the black material for her skirt, while Mr Waugh held a warehouse supply of good quality cotton from which she had made her blouse. The linen was a different matter because she had made it. Margaret's maternal grandmother had come over from Belfast where, as a young woman, she had been involved in the treatment of flax and its transformation into linen. She knew the arts of drying flax from the fields in the wind, then steeping it, stripping out the fibres, drying them, then spinning them into thread using a distaff. Margaret had used a distaff for as long as she could think, and watched her mother doing it so much that she thought of it as a womanly craft, desirable to learn. Some of the local farmers grew flax and were quite happy to sell to Mrs Adams. Tucked in the corner of the back room, leaning against the wall, was a hand loom strung with warp and weft; whenever any of the Adams women had time to spare, which was not very often, then Mother would tell them to weave. Omega had done it, Margaret did it, and in her turn Alpha Nancy would have to do it, though the latter, being only five, was excused at the moment. The Adams family often wore linen shirts and blouses cut from cloth made by their womenfolk. Everything had to be put through the mangle and hung on the line. Just then a train puffed northwards from the halt at Railway Cottages heading for Bullgill along the Derwent Branch line.

'At least the wind's from the west, eh? No sooty marks on the washing today,' said Mother.

Margaret paused from her work and looked at the train just across the valley not 200 yards away and saw several children waving at her from the carriage windows. With a bubbling enthusiasm she waved back, for it was a dream of hers that one day she would travel that line and go all the way up to Dumfries and back, across the Solway viaduct that she had heard was a sight to be seen. One day she would cross the Solway to Annan and see the sights of Dumfriesshire, which was in Scotland. She had seen Scotland across the sea from Maryport, but had never yet been there, Dearham forming the boundaries of her world for most of the time. One day!

Just at this moment, Thomas and young John, known as Johnny to differentiate him from his father, came into the yard with much attendant noise, quickly quelled by their mother.

'I'm glad to see such energy! You can take over the mangle from your sister if you've got so much.'

Thomas grinned and relieved Margaret at the mangle. He was fond of mangling because as a boy he liked the muscular effort it took, and the palpable result as the water streamed down the chute of the machine and into the yard gutter, bubbling towards the stream. This was man's work to him, and at eleven years old, he was beginning to feel his strength.

'Thomas got the stick today!' squeaked the eight year old Johnny.

'I told you to say nothing about that,' hissed Thomas, the smile vanishing from his face.

'Well you did anyway,' said the sneak.

'Oh,' cooed Mother. 'What did you get the stick for?'

'Nothing.'

'Mr Marshall hit you for nothing? That doesn't sound like him. In fact, that doesn't sound like him one little bit. Do I have to ask him at church?'

'He wouldn't do the German drill.'

'The German drill? What on earth is that?'

'It's a new thing we have to do,' explained Johnny. 'We have to bend and jump, and hop and hold our arms out like this.'

So saying he held his arms out straight from his shoulders and continued in that pose, circling his hands until his face turned red with effort.

'Goodness me,' said Mother. 'Why on earth do you have to do that?'

'Mr Marshall says we've been told to do it by the guvment 'cos it's good for us.'

'I see. The government and Mr Marshall told you to do it. Did you all do it?'

'Yes. The whole school in the yard. Except Thomas. He wouldn't do it until Mr Marshall hit his bottom…' Here Johnny broke off for a snigger, 'Then he did it quick enough.'

Thomas's face was red with anger now and he said softly, with a voice full of menace, 'Just you wait…'

His mother broke in, 'No. Just you wait. You are getting a little ahead of yourself Thomas. The whole school does this and you refuse instructions. Why did you not do as Mr Marshall told you?'

'I ain't doing German drill.'

'Because it's German?'

'Yes.'

'What have you got against Germans, Thomas?'

'Well, they're not British.'

'And so?'

'Well everyone knows that one British person is worth ten dirty foreigners!'

'Do they Thomas? Do they?'

'Yes – we should be doing British drill, not German.'

'You do talk nonsense. It's called a German Drill because it's a kind of exercise invented in Germany, I suppose?'

'Yes.'

'Well if your teacher says to do it, you should do it. As for one person being better than another because of where they were born, you can just think again Thomas Adams. Read your bible and show me where it says that. All men are created equal.'

Thomas looked sulky and muttered that he did not wish to do any German drill.

'Your father will have opinions on this and you can explain yourself to him when he gets home. Now get on with that or I'll belt you myself.'

Thomas knew better than to argue and Mother did not dream for a minute that he would, so without a pause she turned to Margaret.

'Time to start work on your father's dinner. You know what to do.'

She did indeed. This was washday and that meant rissoles. Johnny went with her to the kitchen, for it would be his job to turn the mincer. On a shelf in the pantry, covered over with a dish were the remains of several cuts of meat that had provided the meals for the last several days.

'There you are, now get busy,' she said to the small boy and he set to with a will. He liked feeding the lumps of fat and meat into the mouth of the mincer and pushing them down, seeing the grey mince pour out of the other end.

'And watch your fingers. I don't want to be frying bits of you for dinner.'

Into the mincer went meat, then an onion, and then stale bread. Margaret had been preparing vegetables from the garden, and by the time she had finished peeling potatoes, chopping cabbage, of which they ate a lot, and carrots, Johnny had a full bowl to which she added salt and sage, also from the garden and an egg from one of their hens. Digging her fingers into the bowl she commenced to knead the mixture to mix the ingredients well, and after a while began to form patties that she put onto a plate at the side.

'Stir up the stove Johnny and when you've stoked it, go and find Alpha.'

This, too, was man's work so the eight year old poked the fire in the range energetically, raking the ashes and shoveling one load of coal onto it. Then he ran off to get his five year old sister, as he knew well where she would be.

'Mother. Shall I start the vegetables yet?'

'Yes. Your father knows well enough what time dinner is. If he's late it's his lookout. And do the gravy.'

John Adams worked hard and he expected a large meal when he came home. His 'bait' or lunch was usually bread and cheese, but that did not sustain him for long. He was a man used to hard graft and like all the other miners he was thin, larding the tunnels of the mine with his own sweat, so he needed a lot of fuel. To him, dinner without gravy was simply not a dinner and this was a household standard.

Young Johnny went up the Dib and turned left into the lonning behind the terraces fronting the road. Sure enough there was a crowd of little girls about halfway down, some skipping, some sitting on back steps playing with dollies, and all wearing the uniform white pinafore that was supposed to keep their dark dresses clean. Among them was the small person that he was looking for.

'Alpha. Come and wash your hands. It's nearly dinner.'

The little girl picked up her own dolly from the group of them who seemed to be having a tea party and trotted along with her brother.

'Is Father home yet?'

'No, but it's almost dinner so he will be. You must come and wash your hands.'

Contentedly, she skipped down the slope to the front door, holding his hand.

In the house was the smell of cooking meat as Margaret had commenced to fry the rissoles in the big pan that usually hung above the range when not in use. On one side the pans containing vegetables were also simmering, and the table had a cloth on it.

'Now lay the table Johnny.'

This was another 'man' job that Johnny was quite used to, so he set out knives and forks in their usual positions, and in the middle a wooden board, a square loaf of white bread and a dish of butter. Bread went with every meal in this house, for it had a vital function. Margaret was mixing meat stock with flour and whipping it to gravy ready to simmer.

Mother came in announcing that washday was done, the clothes were hanging on the line and the tub was empty and hanging up.

'Now all we need is Father.'

It was curious how she habitually referred to her husband as 'Father' as indeed he always called her 'Mother' or 'my dear,' at least in front of the children. When they were alone, or tucked up in their own bed they were, as ever, John and Nancy to each other, but it had something to do with status. John was a good earner and a coal cutter, an undergoer; something of an aristocrat in the hierarchy of the colliery. His work and his wage conferred a dignity which would not have quite the ring to it that it should have if their offspring called them 'Mam' or 'Dad' as did most of the neighbourhood children. This was also a Christian household and both parents read only one newspaper, which was the Christian Herald. In each edition of this weekly there was a well-written and moral short story in which parents were referred to as 'Mother' and 'Father.' That was quite good enough as far as John Adams was concerned and that was how their children addressed them.

'Where is Father?' asked Thomas, not without a certain apprehension. 'The pit's shut so he can't be at work.'

'You must have heard the bell Thomas. He's gone to the meeting with the vicar. He'll be back soon. Only I hope it's not too long or the vegetables will be overdone.'

Chapter 2

The Miners' Meeting

The subject of her thoughts had been gone for two hours since he had left the house and gone striding down the road, then up the hill past Townhead, directing his course to where a gathering crowd was waiting outside the church gate beside the new Mission Hall, built two years previous for £600 and a visible sign of their local prosperity. The bell tolling out had been an expected signal and a crowd of men had gathered there who would normally have been at work at this time of day. Not surprisingly, the conversation was anxious and subdued for every man there stood to lose his employment if the mine stayed closed. It was a singular group of men who stood around waiting for the Reverend Melrose because these were not ordinary miners, but kings among the working class, the third generation of colliers in their village. Under their feet were seams which were world renowned as the source of the best steam coal in the world. From the Senhouse Dock in Maryport hundreds of thousands of tons were shipped each year to bunker Britain's merchant fleet, the might of the Royal Navy, and to feed the needs of the huge liners built just across the North Sea in Belfast. The miners of Dearham had grown used to a certain level of prosperity and it showed in the appearance of their group. John Adams was typical in this style with his dark suit and waistcoat over a white shirt and a watch chain of massive silver stretched across his middle, bought before his marriage to sport his wealth among his peers. On his head was not the flat cap of an ordinary labourer, but the soft felt brimmed hat of a man of substance. This is not to say that he cut a figure among his fellows, because they all wore similar garb in a kind of uniform. Many who stood there waiting owned their own houses or land, had money in insurance funds or savings, and the news that the Lonsdale Pit was to close could herald a change in their circumstances which, to many of them, would be disastrous. Thus, the mutter of conversation was of a rather subdued note, but many men preferred to roll and smoke cigarettes whose fragrant smoke drifted through the sunlight, or simply to continue what they did down the mines, and chew tobacco, which occasioned a lot of spitting. This was normally something considered ill-mannered, but there were no ladies present and the rules were different.

The door of the old Norman church opened and a group of men came out, headed by the Reverend Melrose, and they walked over to the churchyard gate and came through. Someone brought a chair out of the mission hall which the Vicar stood on to see over the crowd gathered in the wide lane leading to the vicarage gate. He was much respected in the village and attendance in his congregation had increased markedly since the commencing of his tenure, even though he was not the most striking of men. To look at him was unremarkable, because all that the observer would see was an average clergyman in black, with a dog collar and a spare sort of face, a pointed parson's nose, and a bald head; in short he was a Church of England 'type'.

However, his eyes betrayed him; to be sure they were brown and friendly, but a closer look revealed a fire burning behind their pupils and this in turn demonstrated why he had become a priest. The Reverend was a staunch believer, but he was no Tory vicar concerned with rank and station; his style was to involve himself in the affairs of his flock in every way that he was supposed to, and he had done this from the very onset of his ministry. He visited the sick and the dying, he encouraged and gave to charity, he organised events to help the less fortunate, was a prominent local advocate of Temperance, and gave downright interesting sermons. He was also very direct and with a habit of getting straight down to business, so without any preliminaries or clearing of throat, he commenced saying what he had to say in as unvarnished a way as he could. A respectful hush fell, because the Vicar was well liked even by those who did not share his faith.

'As you know, Alderman Patterson, Mr Cameron and myself made an appointment this morning to go and see Mr MacIntyre Walker and Lord Lonsdale to ascertain what their position is regarding Mr Ormiston's desire to close down the Lonsdale Colliery. Their position at the moment is understandable in that they feel that they can do nothing with it. The closure is a commercial decision by Mr Ormiston because he is losing money by the winning of coal in that pit. In his view, it must close and for reasons you are all familiar with.'

Here he paused and looked round to allow his words to sink in, as a low murmuring broke out and heads were nodded or shaken. Each man was a professional collier and they well knew why Mr Ormiston, who ran the pit, wished to pull out. The ground under their feet held several seams of the best coal it was possible to find anywhere on earth, but the strata it lay in were so faulted, so fractured and so unpredictable that it was difficult to pursue modern long-walling. Any attempt to do so would end in the seam disappearing up or down, so consequently the coal was hewn in the old way, by hand, and in a very labour intensive way. The expense of it was making Ormiston reluctant to continue even if he could. There was a lot of coal left, but the fractured geology also meant that there was a lot of water ingress and as the levels were dug deeper there would have to be a heavy investment in new pumps just to keep the mine dry. It was easy to see why closure could be desirable for any operator who was losing a lot of money already and did not wish to throw more into this hole would wish to walk away.

'Lord Lonsdale and Mr Walker cannot influence Wood's decision on the future of the Dovenby which it was thought might amalgamate with the Lonsdale, and therefore the mine will not be reopened. We have to accept that last week's closure was final and that the Lowca Engineering Company will be moving into the site next week to dismantle and salvage all they can to sell off and re-use, and within a month or so the shaft will be capped. That is the situation as it stands at the moment.'

The Vicar looked round at the 300 or so faces that stared at him attempting to comprehend what he had just told them, and saw in their faces the dawning realization that they were in trouble such as they had never been in during their lives. Wood of Glasgow were the operators of the neighbouring pit in the village, the Dovenby Colliery. The Vicar and his two companions had approached Wood and asked if they would be interested in taking over the Lonsdale Pit, but they had declined on the grounds of expense. There were a few subdued groans around the crowd, for hope thrives on faint threads, but most of the reaction among the men was stoic. They were colliers, and many of them were cutters of coal in an area where cutters of coal were many. Up and down the Cumbrian coast between Whitehaven and Maryport, even up to Lambley near Hadrian's Wall there were dozens of mines and thousands of men who made their livings from them. Colliers, trolley men, coal sorters, shaft men, rock men, shot-firers and a plethora of other jobs. Certainly many of them would be able to find other places, but many could expect a drop in their wages. There was no standardization of wages across the coalfield and the rich steam coal of Dearham had paid good money. Inferior bituminous coal such as was found in most other pits would not pay as well. For some there would be a drop in their standard of living, for the older there may be no jobs at all, and for many a journey down to Flimby Pit three miles away, or further just to get to work. The community would lose money and people; a few might find employment in the village's other colliery, the Dovenby, but not by any means all.

The Reverend Melrose continued and his message contained hope.

'Lord Lonsdale and Mr Walker as royalty holders for this land, have no objection at all to the mining being continued, but as the matter stands at the moment there appears to be no other party to step forward and take over the colliery as a going concern. This is an avenue that we wish to explore further with the representatives of Lord Lonsdale and Mr Walker. We shall do our best to keep you informed of further developments. This being Monday 9 April, I hope to speak to you again with further developments so I would ask you to please attend us at the Boys' Board School at six o'clock on this coming Friday, so that we may apprise you of anything you need to know, and discussion may occur. Thank you for coming and for your attention.'

A voice from the crowd cried out,

'And thank you Vicar for all you've done. Champion it is!'

The Vicar smiled half-ruefully, shook his head slightly disparagingly and turned to go back into the church with his companions as a low growl of approval broke out at the speaker's words. In small groups the miners drifted back down Church Street towards Main Street, except John Adams. The Vicar's words had tipped him into a long suspended decision and he hung back to speak to him; the Reverend Melrose listened to what he had to say, nodded his head in understanding, shook John's hand then turned and went through the Vicarage gate. John then turned to go down towards home, accompanied by Bill Gannon, who had waited for him.

'What do you think John? What'll we do now?'

John Adams looked at his friend who happened also to be his lodger and thought for a few seconds, weighing his words carefully. His blue eyes were thoughtful in a brown tanned face surrounded by a thick beard rapidly assuming a snow white colour.

I'm not sure Bill. It depends on what the Vicar manages. He's not a man for idle words and he says something then does it. Something will happen I'm sure and hopefully it won't be too long. You're worried about rent aren't you?'

'Well I'd be fibbing if I said I wasn't.'

'You're a good marra, the best I've had. I'd be sad to lose you, so if you've got a bit stashed then I'm sure we can make out a few weeks, say till the end of May, but then you know how things stand.'

Bill Gannon knew how things stood. He had a bit of cash put by, but he did not, like John, earn enough to rent a house and had no family. In some ways it would be cheaper for all of them to live through hard times if he contributed what he had to the communal household pot, but he could not expect the Adams' to support him once his money run out. They would have quite enough to do in keeping themselves in that way. John's daughter Omega was out to service, and Margaret would soon follow, but there were three other children to think about. The little house they lived in was crowded enough, but Bill valued the comfort he had in his place in the little lean-to built on the side of the house. As a bachelor he appreciated the chance he had to live in a family where he was liked, relied on, and thought much of. This status was enhanced by the fact that he was very good at his job as John Adams' marra or mate. Adams appreciated how good Bill was because he himself was an undergoer and had been since he was 21, and before that he was a putter, pushing loaded trolleys of coal along underground tracks assisted by a younger boy, his 'foal'. When he came of age Adams had graduated to the dangerous job of going to his allotted station at a coalface, lying on his side and undermining a mass of coal in front of him so that eventually it would fall. This was a skilled job, for if the undergoer went too far then the mass of coal might fall on him and kill him or break limbs or worse. A man crushed but living would then have to eke out the life of a pauper unable to support himself or his family. Adams had a natural aptitude for this work and had never had a dangerous fall occur. A cautious and reflective man by nature, he never tried to do too much which younger men were often inclined to do. Men were paid by the amount of coal they cut, each tub, as it was taken away, having a wooden token or tab placed on it to indicate who had won it. Taking short cuts by undergoing deeper than might be safe meant more coal to load, thus more money. Adams was not tempted to do this, preferring to go home safe and intact. In this way he bore none of the bluish scars that disfigured many undergoers where they had been gashed by falling coal, and had been able to take home five shillings a day from the age of twenty-one though he could have earned more by taking risks. Now in his forties he was earning a regular seven shillings a day in a rich coal seam and taking home £2.2s a week, which had made him one of the better off in the Cumbrian Coalfield until the mine closed. He could have earned more, as he well knew, but he did not take risks and spent time propping and packing his stent as it should be done, holding that it was fools who did not do that who did not make it home to their wives and children.

Bill Gannon, as John's marra, did not hew under the coal so did not earn as much. He had once been an undergoer, but had suffered several falls and consequently had lost his nerve for the work. He was quite happy to use a shovel to load or to break up what John cut onto a truck to be dragged away by one of the putters. When John decided that he had undermined enough coal he would haul himself out from where he had been hewing and take a long broad three foot chisel or wedge, putting a wad of waste cloth over the striking end to avoid sparks, and hold it to the top of his stall. Then Bill would hit the wedge hard and repeatedly. If they were lucky it did not take more than a few blows for the coal mass to fall and fracture, after which it could be broken up and taken away. Sometimes the overhang did not fall as planned and in that case John and Bill had hard work on their hands, with a large manually cranked drill with which they bored holes into the coal face. Then they had to place small 'shots' of dynamite, light the fuse and retreat well down the tunnel. This was a dangerous task and men were killed regularly in the neighbourhood while carrying out this work.

If timed correctly, this would end the shift, for on either side were two pillars of coal which now held up the roof between them and the men in the next stent. On either side were two other undergoers with their marras who had been similarly engaged and between them they had moved the coal face some ten feet forward if it was a good day. John knew he could rely on Bill to get him out of trouble if it happened but so far nothing had. His marra worked hard and well, went to church, and did not drink. Like John, he was pledged and a teetotaler. It was quite natural in a village where miners took in lodgers to ask his own marra if he wanted to lodge with him, and it was natural for Bill to accept. Really good marras were hard to find, and John had known a few. He was one of the best, and if keeping him meant going easy on the rent for a few weeks then he was quite happy to do so; at least he would be once he had squared it with Nancy, his wife.

The two men now made their way back towards Row Beck and down the Dib, sniffing appreciatively as the savoury odour of rissoles replete with sage and onion caressed their nostrils.

'I love the smell of frying onion.'

'So do I,' replied John Adams. 'I think everyone does, and Margaret is a dab hand with rissoles. I'll be sorry to see her go.'

'Is she going soon?'

'I think she must. I'm going up to see Mr Nixon tomorrow, but from what I gather it'll not be riches.'

John Adams led the way into his house, opening the front door straight into the living room where the folding table had been set out in the centre with six places round it.

'Hello, my dear. I see it's ready so please let's eat when you're set.'

'Before you sit down Father, there's something you might want to attend to. Thomas had the stick at school today from Mr Marshall.'

'Oh yes? And why was that?'

John turned his gaze upon Thomas who went pink and tried to avoid his eyes.

'Look at me Thomas. Why did you get the stick today?'

Thomas had to tell his father of the German drill and his refusal, and his face dropped in shame as he told it.

'So you refused instruction from your teacher who wished you to carry out some exercises required by the Board of Education?'

Thomas nodded miserably.

'What else have you done?'

Thomas had been down this route before and he knew well what he had done.

'I have shamed you Father.'

'And how have you shamed me?'

'By letting people think that you are a bad parent who has brought up a disobedient child.'

'Indeed. And you knew this all along yet still did it. How many strokes did Mr Marshall give you?'

'One Father.'

'He's a very humane man. Go and fetch my belt, and meet me in the yard.'

Fetching the belt was part of the punishment because of the anticipation it created. Thomas did not cry, but dragged his feet unwillingly to the cupboard in which the belt hung, and followed his father outside.

'Bend. Now there's one for making Mr Marshall beat you.'

Thomas winced as the belt hit his rear end.

'And there's another for shaming my good name. And a third for forcing me to do this in the first place. I will not have a son whom people think willful, disobedient and spoiled. Do you understand me, Thomas?'

Thomas nodded; he still did not cry for he had been brought up in a hard culture which taught that it was unmanly for boys to weep.

'Very well. Don't do it again. You have taken your punishment, and now I want my dinner. Put the belt back and this matter is behind us.'

Both now joined the group and John took his place at the head of the table whilst Margaret served the food. The plates were piled and the reception was quietly enthusiastic. All looked at John whose eyes twinkled as he put his hands together, bowed his head and said;

> *'Give us, O Lord, a bit of sun,*
> *A bit of rain and a bit of fun;*
> *Give us, in all the struggle and sputter,*
> *Our daily bread, and a bit of butter.'*

'Amen!' they all said, laughing, even Thomas. The Cumbrian grace was always useful to lighten a mood.

The family and their lodger set down to eating their meal. There was no talking for it was a rule in this house as there was in many houses, that a table was not the place for talking. Food was for eating and was something to be taken seriously. Talking at the table gave rise to spills, spluttering, choking and other accidents that were not desirable, so it was considered bad manners. It also showed disrespect to the cook who had put effort into the making of the dinner. No one asked Father about the meeting, because there would be plenty of time for that later. Rissoles, cabbage, carrots and mashed potato covered in a rich floury gravy might well have satisfied many, but each member of the family in turn reached into the middle of the table, buttered the end of the loaf of bread, then cut a generous slice, placing it on the side of their plate. Some of it was eaten with the meal, but each family member left about half, and when the food was gone this was used to sop the gravy from the plate until each was clean.

When the meal was over all eyes looked at John Adams with an expectation that he would give them the news that they had been waiting for, but he did not.

'Margaret. Your mother and I are going for a walk. Please get this place tidy and do the dishes. You'll have help of course.'

He looked at the boys with expectation and they nodded. Mother, who had not been consulted about this, looked surprised but rose from the table. Usually John liked to sit for an hour or so to let digestion proceed, and this was a great departure from the normal practice.

'I'll get my shawl.'

As they went up the Dib Nancy said, 'What's this about John?'

'Hold on a moment or two, I want to be out of earshot and then we'll talk.'

At the road they turned right and strolled up towards Row Moor. There was a chill coming on as the evening advanced, but the sun was still bright and the fields glowed in the April sun.

'The mine will not be reopening, so I will not be going back to work there.'

Nancy caught her breath, for she knew the implications of what had been said.

'I know that you don't want to move from here any more than I do, so I'm minded to stay. It might be possible to find a place in the Dovenby. I saw John Ashton the other day and he intimated that there's always room with him for another good undergoer. It's not a bad idea, but if a manager takes on a man it's likely he would let another go, so I'm not altogether attracted by the idea of gaining a job while another man loses his place. The Vicar seems to think he can get something going with the Lonsdale workforce and I'd like to lay off for a few weeks to see what he can do.'

'Can we afford it John? I mean I know we've put a bit away but with you off work it'll eat into our savings and things will get tight.'

John Adams smiled, 'You know Nancy, we eat well and compared to many we do alright. Are you forgetting the Pearl? I'm an unemployed man.'

She paused in her steps and looked at him, 'Yes, I had actually forgotten the Pearl. How much would you get?'

John, like many of his trade, was a prudent man. Coal mining was a risky and hard business, and he worried about what would happen to his family if he were killed or injured at work. In common with perhaps the majority of his workmates, he had taken out insurance with the Pearl Loan Company back in 1872 when his wife had announced that she was pregnant with their first child, Omega. His insurance cost him a shilling a week for life assurance plus another sixpence to cover unemployment. He also paid a further shilling into a pension fund that would pay him a weekly sum when he attained the age of 65. In theory he would get, in the event of his losing his job, ten shillings a week for six months, and five shillings a week for six months after that. It was not munificent, but it would pay the rent and more. With seven shillings surplus, the produce of the garden and their small savings, they should be able to tide over until John could find a post.

'I'm going to see Lowry Nixon tomorrow, but I think I have it right that we should get ten shillings a week. If what the Vicar said is true then I should be back in employment well before the end of the year.'

'I see all that, but why have you brought me out here to talk about this?'

'Margaret.'

'Oh. I see.'

She understood. Margaret was an expense, a mouth to feed and she was quite capable of fending for herself.

'I know she's your pet and I know she's a great help to you. But she'll be nineteen on the 19th of this month. Omega had a place at sixteen. She's ready enough I think, and although her earnings at the Vicarage help, they don't cover the cost of keeping her.'

Nancy thought very hard, for it was true that her middle daughter was a dab hand at all the work to be done round the house and she would miss her sorely. John earned good money so, although most girls went into service at sixteen or younger, pushing her daughters out so young had not been a matter of necessity. Having them at home took a great deal of strain off her and enabled her to run a neat well-ordered and well provided for sort of household. On the other hand, Margaret was old enough and it would not be fair to the younger children when times were straitened if they went shorter on food than they need do.

29

Margaret was quite able to earn her own way and her mother knew it.

'Yes, she is ready. I will miss her and I was hoping to have her at home a little but longer, but you are right. Will you tell her?'

'Yes. I'll see Mr Nixon tomorrow and I'll tell her after. I've spoken to Mr Melrose and given her notice in so he'll be looking for another scullery maid. She's a canny lass, so when she sees things as they are I think she'll take it well enough.'

'When shall she go?'

'Whitsun Fair next month. You can take her down to the hirings. James Gibson will be going down there to sell stuff, so I'll ask if he can take you at the same time.'

The business being agreed between them, they turned for home. Nancy then brought up the matter of Thomas, for although his refusal of instructions had been dealt with, the sentiments expressed towards Germans were troubling her. In a few words she told her husband about it and it set him to thinking.

'You're right of course. It's not a healthy attitude and I have no doubt that he's been listening to some jingo somewhere waving a flag and going on about the Empire and glory. I don't want a son of mine thinking that way if he can be guided away from it.'

A silence fell between them as they strolled back towards the Dib, broken only when they turned down the slope.

'Look Nancy, I do not want to bring this up again with Thomas. As far as he is concerned he's taken his punishment and it's ended, but I will do something about it. Just leave it with me eh?'

In this community tradition directed that in most affairs of daily life Mother instructed her daughters and Father instructed his sons. The responsibility in this case was clearly John's, so in agreement Nancy caught his arm as his went round hers and they walked down to their house in perfect harmony. It was twilight and out of the windows of the little cottage a soft yellow light showed.

'They've lit the dip,' said John, 'But I fancy a bit of a read, so I think we can do better than that. We've got enough paraffin for a while, haven't we? Well let's have the big lamp on.'

In front of the range the family spread out and John took to his chair with 'The Memoirs of Sherlock Holmes', and Thomas with 'Kidnapped' courtesy of the Dearham Reading Room in Main Street, and Nancy with some darning. On the mat Alpha Nancy played with her dolly, while in the corner Johnny bounced marbles off each other and Bill Gannon sat with an old newspaper, cradling a cup of tea. Margaret Adams, if she had seen into the future and identified this picture of contentment as the last night of her childhood, might have drunk it in more than she did, storing it up in the eyes of her mind for future memory. No-one has such prescience, however, and the night before her world changed forever was spent knitting a pullover for Johnny.

Chapter 3

Changes down the Dib

Margaret and her father walked past the Old Mill, over Janet Bridge and up the rise heading for Dearham Main Street. Her father had said nothing of importance since getting up, save to change his custom of many years and order that breakfast from now on would be different. As a hard manual worker John had always insisted on the importance of a full breakfast and to him that meant bacon, egg and black pudding in a good amount, with toast and tea. Many people who thought of themselves as working class could not possibly have afforded to eat so well, but an undergoer's wages could well support this, and indeed it was necessary to sustain the physical effort needed at work. John had directed that he would have the same breakfast as the rest of the family and had sat down that morning to pobbies. In some parts of the country this was called 'slops' being composed of stale bread broken up and soused in warm milk. To this could be added whatever the person consuming it desired, be it sugar, raisins, jam or nothing at all. That the head of the household should condescend to eat pobbies did cause a hush, but all knew why it was necessary and why Bill Gannon elected to do the same. For the moment they were out of work, economies were necessary and belts may have to be tightened though both men were thin enough anyway because what they ate they used up in labour.

'Tattiepot Nancy. I think we'll be having quite a lot of tattiepot for the next few weeks.'

Nancy nodded. This traditional Cumbrian dish, a favourite at their table, was also a good standby in hard times, and though the money was not yet short, it would be best to husband what they had. The basic ingredients of tattiepot were scalloped potatoes, sliced carrots and onion placed in a shallow dish and roasted. Of course it could be argued that chunks of lamb and black pudding should be added, and they usually were; some people even made a case that it should be topped with cheese, but if money was short it could be done without meat. In really hard times a community could pool their resources and meet in a hall where the women would cook up a tattiepot supper and all comers could get a nourishing meal at a low cost. The Temperance Society often did this and indeed had run several during the winter just past, which had been very hard indeed. That John Adams was resorting to frequent tattiepots was not just a sign that he liked them, but that he expected to be short of cash.

'Do you think things will get better Father?' enquired Margaret as they walked towards Townhead.

He turned to look at her and was pleased with what he saw, and proud of her too for to his eye she had turned out very well. He saw a young woman with auburn tinted hair tied up at the back, a straight set of good shoulders, the creamy skin that often goes with redheads, no freckles, and a pair of pale blue eyes that gazed at the world with a level scrutiny, as if weighing it up. One eyebrow was slightly lower than the other, but the rest of her features were even and though not classically beautiful, she was certainly attractive to look at. Her other attributes were not so plainly set out, but she radiated a sense of being grounded and level-headed since there was a gravity to her bearing that said she could hardly be otherwise. Her extra years at home had given her the skills with which mothers wished to imbue their daughters, and which would be the envy of many. At a time when almost all of the daughters of working class people went into service, her accomplishments would set her among the better qualified young women embarking on such work. She could earn a wage, of that there was no doubt and she was in a way to improve her condition in life, for though like all boys and girls, she had left school at fourteen, she could read, write and do her arithmetic to an excellent level. She was pious, if not fanatical, loving, affectionate and was to his eye the best that a daughter could be to him.

'I think so. I can always get another job Margaret, but if it were not in Dearham we'd have to move. The vicar said that he's trying to do something and Mr Melrose is a man of his word. I want to hear what he says at the meeting on Friday before I take any decisions.'

Her face, though expressionless, hid a mind that was racing with an idea that he was about to say something of importance. Trained in housekeeping and management better than most, she knew that if the family income was going to go down to a main wage of ten shillings a week as he had told her, then changes were coming, and it was obvious what the biggest was going to be. Sensitive to the thought that he might be finding what she suspected to be a difficult subject to broach, it was Margaret who opened the conversation.

'Ten shillings a week is not a lot Father.'

'No, it is not, but we can get by with a few economies.'

'You, Mother, Thomas, Johnny - and me - on ten shillings a week, out of which three shillings rent must come. My two shillings don't help much.'

'Your money has been a great help Margaret.'

This question had a point on it. She knew what she had to say and in her direct way, she said it.

'But it's not enough for my keep. I must go out to service mustn't I?'

'I think you must.'

'It's as plain as a pikestaff that I have to. I am big enough to pay my own way and I'll be 19 soon.'

'You are a great help to your mother and her life is a lot easier with you there than it would be otherwise but I am in no doubt that you must seek a position and leave home.'

'Don't worry Father; I know it as well as you do. When you can ill afford it I'm another mouth to feed and you can quite well do without that. You've let me say it, but that's what you are thinking isn't it?'

John Adams looked at his daughter quizzically.

'Alright, I confess that I actually spoke to Mr Melrose last night and told him you'd be going. He said he would write you an excellent character.'

'It's not a problem to me Father and it's not a surprise; I've been expecting it. Most of the girls I was in school with are already in service and have been these last several years. The time was always going to come and I'm ready. I know I am. When shall it be?'

'The same as Omega it must be, Whitsun Fair, 12 May.'

'That's a month away. I've plenty of time to get ready. What does Mother think?'

'She agrees. She'll be coming with you as is her duty.'

This was true. When a daughter entered service it was her mother who went with her to the hiring fair. Assessing the look of, and conversing with potential employers was crucial in ensuring that daughters went to safe places, that the terms and conditions of employment were good, and that they got a fair start in their new lives.

'Now then lass, you get off to work and I'll see you later.'

Margaret headed off towards the vicarage where, washing breakfast dishes automatically, her mind fixed itself rapt onto the possibilities and the futures that were opening up to her and were now inevitable.

John Adams strode onto Main Street and past the impressive corniced seven windowed structure that was, according to the carvings above the windows, 'Maryport Co-operative Industrial Society Limited', and inscribed above the door 'Branch No 2.' A few doors further down he came to a nice little house with a sign outside saying 'Thorn Cottage' and knocked on the door. Footsteps came along the passageway and a man in his late 30s opened the door.

'Good morning, Mr Nixon. I think you've probably been expecting me but if you have time I need to talk with you.'

'Yes indeed Mr Adams, please come in. I have been expecting you to call. As you might imagine, I have had quite a few clients call on me this last few days and I'm thinking that there will be quite a few more. Come this way please.'

The house was larger than the little house down the Dib and had a small room at the front just big enough to hold a desk and chair, with two other chairs facing it. From the scullery out back came domestic noises.

'Sit down Mr Adams; this won't take long.'

John lifted an eyebrow as he looked at Lowry Nixon, but the insurance agent laughed pleasantly and hastened to reassure him.

'I'm a thorough man, Mr Adams, and I'm not one to be caught unprepared at times like these. I have a list of all my clients ready, how long they have contributed to their schemes, and how much payment they have qualified for. In your case I suspect that we are going to be in complete agreement.'

Pausing, he opened the left-hand drawer in his leather-topped desk and pulled out a file. Opening it, he began to leaf through, and extracted a piece of paper.

'Adams. There are advantages to having a name close to the beginning of the alphabet I think.'

John smiled in agreement.

'Now let me see. You have been a client of the Pearl Loan Company...' and here he absently caressed the little company sign on his desk, '...for over twenty years, which means that you have more than qualified for the maximum weekly payment in our unemployment fund. That is to say ten shillings a week.'

Here he leaned back and looked at John.

'Yes,' said the miner, 'That's what I thought.'

'You've been very prudent Mr Adams. There's many round here who have not done as well, and preferred to spend their money on drink. You on the other hand have paid up insurance for unemployment, sickness and pension. It's not riches, but it's enough to get by on, with care.'

'Well I do agree Mr Nixon that things will be very tight, but it is enough to get by on, given some adjustment of our circumstances.'

'The Pearl Loan Company prides itself on the regularity of its payments and in dealing squarely with its clients. All that need be done is to decide how you wish payment to be made. I can either drop it off to your house on my rounds each Tuesday, or if you prefer you may call here between nine o'clock and noon every Monday morning.'

John thought for a moment.

'You know Nancy well enough, so would it be possible for her to pick it up on Monday mornings?'

'I have no objection to that at all, and should be delighted to see her. It's always a pleasure to pass the time of day with Mrs Adams. She knows nearly as much as what is going on in this area as I do.'

The agent grinned appreciatively.

'Well she comes in to go to the Co-op every Monday morning anyway, so it seems that we have a mutual convenience. I take it that we start next Monday?'

'That is suitable Mr Adams and it will continue so for the next six months. I am sure that you will be in employment by that time.'

'I do hope so Mr Nixon. I'm not a man that likes to be idle when there's a wife and family to provide for. And I would not wish to leave them short on things for long.'

'No, Mr Adams, I am sure you would not. Our business is done I think...'

There came a knocking on the door.

'And unless I am mistaken that will be someone on exactly the same errand as you.'

'Then I'll wish you a good morning Mr Nixon, and thank you for your help.'

'A pleasure Mr Adams. Do give my regards to your wife.'

They went down the passage and the agent opened the door for John to leave. Outside the door was a man who should have been at work.

'Good morning Jasper, how are you?'

'Fair enough John, but I think I'm on the same errand as you.'

Jasper Johnson was the foreman at the brickworks attached to the Lonsdale pit.

'Are they shutting the brickworks too?'

'It seems like it because without the pit supplying it they'd have to buy in coal so we're all going to be laid off it seems. That's why I'm here. Good morning Mr Lowry.'

So saying, John strode away up the street and directed his steps to the door of a smaller shop above which was a sign, 'Thomas Ivison Grocer and Joiner.'

'Good morning to you John. How are you? I've not seen you for a while.'

'I'm fine thank you Tom, all things considered.'

The two men were perfectly relaxed in each other's company, as indeed they should be since they had been at school together.

'Yes, I know what you mean. I never thought things would come to this you know. They say there's a lot of good coal still down the Lonsdale. Closing it! It's like the end of an era.'

'Well they are right about the coal. There's a fortune still down there, but it's so splintered and fractured that getting it is becoming more difficult the deeper we go. Truth is that I don't think his Lordship had much option. I can't blame the man, because I have worked there all my life and I could see how it was going. Are you going to the meeting on Friday?'

'Wild horses John. It's my livelihood too you know. If a small shopkeeper loses the custom of 260 men and their families then it hits hard.'

'Have you heard about the brickworks?'

'No. What of it?'

'It's closing too. Without the coal there'll be no bricks fired.'

'Eh, dear oh dear,' said the shopkeeper shaking his head. 'I hope Mr Melrose has got something big up his sleeve.'

'You're not alone in that I think.'

'What can I do for you John?'

'I'd like a new mop please.'

The shopkeeper paused and looked at his friend.

'Margaret?'

'Yes.'

'It's about time John. A lass her age should be making her own way in't' world.'

'I know it, but she's been a great help. The time's ripe now, of course.'

'I fear you're right there. Here's t'mop. Seven pence please, John.'

John Adams paid the money, said his good-days and went off to see James Gibson the Market gardener at Haysborough Cottages. Gibson always went to the markets and fairs so John wanted to ask him for a ride to the fair for his wife and daughter so that they would arrive at the hirings fresh.

When Margaret returned home that evening John was sitting by the door in the evening sunlight and holding the mop.

'I've never seen you with a mop Father!' she said with a laugh.

'I'll admit that it's not a tool I'm used to,' smiled John, 'but I think it will prove useful in finding my lovely daughter a new life for herself.'

'I'll second that,' she said grinning. 'Don't feel bad about this Father. We all grow up you know and this was always going to happen. I'm looking forward to it now. I've got a month of sewing and putting usefuls together before I go. Anyway, I might not get a place. Too ugly or smelly.'

'Hey! My daughter's a bobby dazzler so less of that.'

'Most considerate of fathers.' She kissed him and went through the door to see her mother, but rounded over her shoulder as she passed,

'There's no bobbies round here to dazzle anyway…'

The next few days were passed idly by comparison with normal life for all was attendant upon whatever Mr Melrose might manage to do with Lord Lonsdale, Mr Walker, and Wood of Glasgow. Small groups of men hung about on the corners of the terraced rows of houses. Dearham was not a closely built village, but was scattered over quite a wide area and it was a place of clumps rather than of a settlement with a single nucleus. There was little for them to do and many felt that by staying at home they were getting under their wives' feet. Some went to a pub and drank, others watched the men who worked at the Dovenby go off to their morning shift with envy. Others began to organize communal events to help at the Welfare Institute in case things got really bad, but overall there was a curious sense of optimism because the Vicar had implied that something could be done. It is very hard for humans who have done something for many years, to habituate themselves to the thought that things have changed beyond all measure. They were in a strange limbo of being unemployed yet hopeful, even sure, that they would be employed again, and in Dearham, in the next few weeks. As to how this was to happen no-one was clear. It was a matter of faith, though in this village this was not strange at all. Miners work close to death and the next world, and the change from living to dead can happen very quickly in their line of work. Church attendance in Dearham was high, and if there was a divide in this community then it was not on grounds of class but sect. St Mungo's Church services were well attended, but a good half of the village were strongly Methodist and proselytizing, their most zealous itinerant preachers having earned a name across the north of England as 'The Dearham Stalwarts.' Foremost among these was John Tiffin who made boots and shoes at his shop in Main Street which is where John bought for his family. Many of the local people preferred clogs for their cheapness and durability, as indeed did the Adams family but John insisted that his family were well shod for church. It was a wonder that the cobbler had time for his trade, so zealous was he in religion, for he had been the driving force behind the building of a well-made Weslyan Methodist chapel which had been built in Main Street in 1883 when Margaret was eight.

The Vicar was a man of God and he had said that something might be done so all things waited on this. The meeting on Friday would decide the future of many families.

Friday 13 April 1894 was a day that passed more slowly than any other day than John and Nancy Adams could remember. The business of running the house went on as ever, for there were meals to be cooked, floors to be swept, beds to be made and a never-ending round of tasks to perform. John occupied himself with the mending of their chicken run which had partly rotted on one side and if left then would present Mr Tod with a free dinner.

The most optimistic person in the house was Margaret, who was actually quite excited as she worked out her notice at the Vicarage. A hiring fair was something of a lottery, but if she got the right position with the right family, then who knew where it might lead? When not working she sewed cloth into new aprons, she stitched sensible blouses and procured a roll of cheap but durable brown material suitable for scullery maid skirts, which she was cutting out for her workday clothes. Brown did not show the dirt, aprons rather than young girls' pinafores were for maids, and she would need a new black skirt in case she was asked to wait. And that was before making caps of which she felt she needed three, one for work, one for spare and one for best, for a maid should cover her hair. A new life beckoned and now it was imminent she was quite in a flutter about it.

The day did pass, however, and at about quarter past five John Adams took his hat and set out for the Boys' Board School up in the village. There was a school for girls too, and on the same site but the School Board had decided not to educate the local children in a mixed fashion. A high fence separated the sexes and four young but efficient schoolmistresses educated their charges in purdah, free from male interference. In the male enclosure four school masters of similar age, and all respectable married men with wives of their own took care of the boys. In this way the Board assured itself that they had done all they could towards setting a high moral tone in the differentiation of the sexes, and that they would not often have to replace their schoolmistresses. It was the convention of the day that if a lady school teacher married then she had to leave work. The Reverend Melrose approved of these arrangements, as indeed he might for he was prominent and vociferous on the School Board himself and it was much in the mould he preferred.

The Hall was packed, but John found a seat, nodding to acquaintances here and there, and joined in with the low muttering conversation which revolved round asking other people if they had heard anything. No one had.

Mr Melrose was already up on the stage sitting at a table and looking anxious, though he gave nothing away. With him were two other gentlemen, one of whom John knew by sight as Tom Cameron, the local representative of the Miners Federation. Leaving his hat on his seat he went to the stage and begged a couple of minutes with Mr Melrose, and looking at his watch the Vicar agreed. Quietly John explained that he wanted to ask a favour of him, and he listened gravely to what John had to say.

'I quite agree with you John, that is a serious matter. I shall do as you ask at the end of my sermon on Sunday, be assured.'

Leaving him with thanks, John returned to his seat, sure in the knowledge that what he wanted to be done, would be done.

At precisely six o'clock the Vicar got to his feet and began to say what he had to say.

'Gentlemen, thank you for coming to this meeting. Mr Cameron here needs no introduction I am sure and many of you know Alderman Pearson, who represents the district on the County Council.'

He paused to allow the recognition to sink in, as the good speaker he was.

'I am sure you all know that we have tried several times over the last few days to reach some form of agreement with the representatives of Wood and the royalty owners, but to no avail. This of course is nothing new, for I told you this on Monday and the intervening period has seen no change in that matter.'

A murmur of disappointment went round the room and the Vicar paused as a new look came over his face.

'Now as to what may be done, I must tell you that I made a proposal to Mr Ormiston that we be allowed to take over the mine and work it for the community.'

Now the murmur was of astonishment. Whoever had heard of such a thing?

'This may seem an odd thing to you but let me put it this way. What I proposed to the owners of the mine was that a Miners' co-operative be formed and that they who work in the mine should own it, work it, and share the profits. This is not so strange is it, for I know that many of you hold shares in the Maryport Co-operative and receive a dividend from those shares? There is not, after all, much difference between ordinary people owning shares in a shop, and owning shares in a mine.'

This was most persuasive in tone and now there was a note of excitement in the whispering.

'Unfortunately, the proposal was turned down flat by Mr Ormiston, but I have to tell you that it was for two good reasons. The first is that Mr Ormiston no longer owns the mine, because his bankers have taken it over owing to his insolvency.'

A gasp of dismay swept the room for the men knew that the mine had been short of cash, but they had not dreamed that the owner would find it necessary to go to bankruptcy. He was a man well liked so his misfortune met with sympathy.

'His bankers have investigated the commercial viability of the mine. Their mining engineers have prepared a report on it and their opinion is that the geology, which you all know is fractured, is too complicated to guarantee a yield on any investment. They cannot in all conscience recommend the investing of any more money in the Lonsdale Pit.'

A deep low groan of disappointment swept across the room, as it seemed that all hopes were to be dashed.

'However my friends, that is not the end of the matter; there is the second point to consider. The mining engineers referred me to the existence of the Crosshow Colliery. As you will recall, the Crosshow Colliery closed some years ago, but not because it was worked out, or because the geology was bad. It closed because the operators became insolvent. The engineers believe that there is much workable coal left in the Crosshow, that it may be more easily won than in the Lonsdale, and that it would be a very good investment for someone wishing to reopen it.'

Now the murmurs were over. There was downright excitement as conversations broke out all over the room.

Mr Melrose waited a couple of minutes before banging on the table with a smile and continuing,

'The engineers also informed me that between the Lonsdale pit and the Crosshow pit, there is a very large fault and it may be that the amount of water ingress to the Crosshow would not be as much as it has been in troubling the Lonsdale. If we pump out the Crosshow workings it should be possible to keep them dry. Lastly on this, they also ventured an opinion that the two yard band would be easy to locate in the Crosshow, and that a longwall would be possible that would be productive.'

Now the conversation was inspired. The two-yard band was that seam of rich steam coal that provided the wealth of the area. If they could tap it and share the profits then every man there would gain substantially.

'I see that my suggestion meets with some interest.'

This caused a laugh.

'Lord Lonsdale and Mr Walker say they would be delighted to receive royalties from the Crosshow if we can get it going. This thing may be done with capital and with the right men in charge; and with you of course. I shall now hand over to Alderman Pearson, who has some experience in the working of co-operatives, to speak to you, and then to Mr Cameron to give the Federation point of view.'

A ripple of applause swept round the room, then everyone listened intently to what the Alderman said about the organisation of a co-operative. It seemed like common sense and there were men in the area with ample experience of business and of running a Co-op. The more they listened, the more plausible the idea seemed. Mr Cameron of the Miners' Federation was bluntly in favour of the idea and said so. The Vicar then suggested a short break while people talked about the idea, so men drifted outside to smoke, to think, to chew things over. The atmosphere was feverish with optimism and hope. When they came back into the hall it was Melrose who spoke to them again.

'As you may gather, I have been taking some advice on this affair, and I propose the setting up of a limited liability co-operative with a working capital of £1,000 to start up the workings at Crosshow. I see that some of you are puzzled by that, so let me explain. What it means is that over the next few days I shall compile through invitation a list of people who are prepared to put money into a co-operative venture. You may put your savings into it if you wish, or any sum of money you please. If we get enough people pledging to do this, we shall raise the £1,000 and reopen Crosshow. If the venture fails then you will lose the money you have put in. However, if this failure does happen, then you as individuals will not be liable to pay any more. If the company were unlimited then you would be and you could be bankrupted as individuals, all your goods being sold, but that would be a very foolish arrangement and I do not consider myself to be a fool.'

He had their attention now, well and truly, for the risks had been laid out fairly and squarely. They could lose the money they put in. On the other hand they would not lose more, and they could gain greatly.

'So gentlemen, this venture is not without risk but it has much to recommend it, as I need not explain. Now,' and he gave a rueful smile, 'I am not a rich man, for what clergyman is? However, I am happy to subscribe the first £20 to this co-operative venture and have placed my name at the head of the list of subscribers.'

Hereupon he pulled out a piece of paper that he had prepared and waved it with a dramatic flourish. The effect was that he was cheered to the roof, men growing quite emotional and yelling hoarsely in enthusiasm. Waving both hands up and down in the universal motion for silence, Mr Melrose finally managed to get quiet.

'I am taking it that the feeling among you is in favour of this endeavour. Please indicate by a show of hands if you wish me to gather pledges to amass £1,000 of capital and to set about the realization of a co-operative scheme for the working of Crosshow Colliery.'

Every hand in the room went up.

'Very well gentlemen, I am taking pledges of any amount you feel able to venture as of this moment. I shall be in this hall every night for the next week except Sunday, so if you wish to go away and sleep on it, to think about it, to talk it over with your families, then please do. I shall be here at six o'clock promptly every evening. Next Friday 20 April at six o'clock I shall be here, but that will not be for pledges. That will be for a meeting to tell you what has happened, how much has been pledged, and what course we may follow from then. I look forward to seeing you there. Goodnight my friends.'

The cheer was, if anything, louder and the meeting dispersed with enthusiasm, but also with thoughtfulness. It was a splendid idea, a daring venture and downright manly in its risk. The gamble appealed to many of the men, but of course they had small savings and uncertain futures. They also had wives and children and to lose all could imperil their wellbeing. Home they went to ponder, to talk and to reflect, most of them with sobriety. In this, none was more sober as he went homewards, than John Adams.

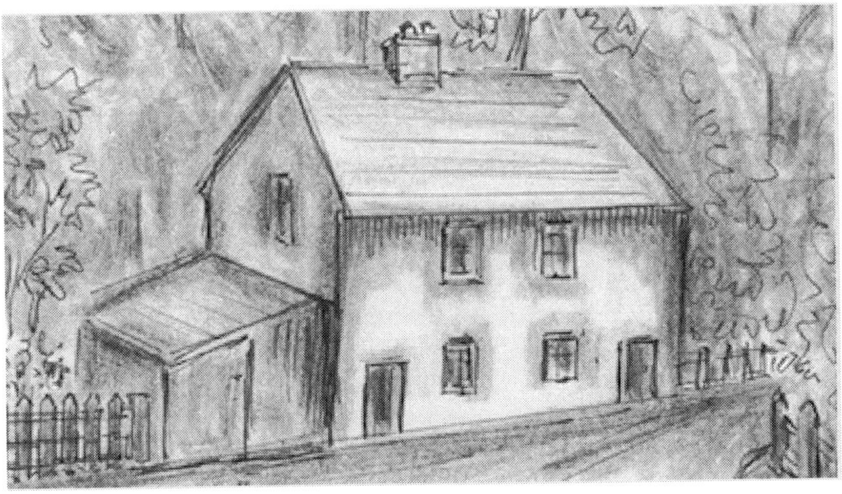

Chapter 4

Fate's Finger

The Adams's were pious in their religious beliefs and very attached to the Church of England, but no one could call them any kind of fanatics. They went to service once on the Sabbath, the children to Sunday school, and all said their prayers before they went to sleep at night. Each evening meal was accompanied by John saying grace, and they attended church on the great feasts like Easter and Christmas. This was a mild observance compared to many of their neighbours for Weslyan Methodism had undergone a great revival in the last few decades in Dearham and the surrounding area. John suspected that one of the reasons for the Reverend Melrose being placed in the living of Dearham was precisely because he was the sort of Vicar who could provide resistance to the onward march of the nonconformists. This was not to say that he was combative in any way, but from the first moment of his arrival he had thrown himself into local affairs with a whole-hearted approach that could be surpassed by none. He was on the local School Board, the Board of Guardians at the workhouse in Maryport and a dozen other local committees, in addition to all the work he did with the sick and poor and with his ministry. It was not surprising that during his time attendance at the ancient church in Dearham had increased substantially.

If Melrose's parishioners on the following Sunday had expected any revelations about how subscriptions for the proposed co-operative were progressing, then they were disappointed. He said nothing, but his sermon was less topical than it might have been. Many had expected a good talk about the Christian virtue of banding together to help each other; something uplifting about brotherhood and solidarity. The service went much as it always did, the proceedings differing from normal only in that there was a strange family in the front pew, just in front of the pulpit, possibly there by invitation. The gentleman who was head of the family was known to some of the congregation as Mr Fawcett, the President of Maryport Co-operative Industrial Society, who lived in Maryport itself. What he was doing in Dearham Church for Sunday service, no one knew but he was welcome for all that. He seemed much interested in the parable of the Good Samaritan and nodded several times during the telling of it.

When the Reverend Melrose had finished his sermon and prayers were over he addressed the pews saying, 'Children!' and beckoning. From all over the church children left their parents and gathered at the front, in what was obviously a rehearsed move, forming a choir in two ranks.

'I have, as you will notice, not placed a third hymn on the board for today's service. This is because I wish the children to sing a new hymn written this year by an American gentleman called Mr Theodore Baker, which they have been rehearsing in Sunday school. It asks a blessing on this congregation and this community, which I think is timely, though I was going to save it for Harvest until the events of the last week or so occurred. It is not in the hymnal, but I think you will agree that it is appropriate.'

The children waited for the organ cue and then commenced Baker's great hymn, the beautiful soaring melody pealing out from innocent voices:

'We gather together to ask the Lord's blessing;
He chastens and hastens His will to make known.
The wicked oppressing now cease from distressing.
Sing praises to His Name; He forgets not His own.

Beside us to guide us, our God with us joining,
Ordaining, maintaining His kingdom divine;
So from the beginning the fight we were winning;
Thou, Lord, were at our side, all glory be Thine!

We all do extol Thee, Thou Leader triumphant,
And pray that Thou still our Defender will be.

Let Thy congregation escape tribulation;
Thy Name be ever praised! O Lord, make us free!'

There were a few tears furtively wiped away, for many of them felt the need of intervention at this time. Unless something happened to help them soon, Dearham would become a ghost village; this congregation would break up and many would move away. Nonetheless, the new composition was welcomed and appreciated, though of course there was no clapping in church. When the choir had finished the Vicar spoke again.

'Before I give the blessing I just wish to emphasise what I was saying earlier in the parable of the Good Samaritan. That man helped a fellow in trouble. He did not stop to enquire what he was, but helped another human being in trouble. That is the Christian thing to do, for in the eyes of God we are all equal whatever we be, British, American, Black, White, or German.'

As he finished he looked round the congregation and his eyes looked directly for a moment into the eyes of Thomas Adams, who flushed and did not hold his gaze.

His thoughts though were thrown into deep confusion, wondering how on earth the vicar knew, finally settling on the idea that Mr Marshall, his teacher, must have told him. Or maybe it was just a coincidence? It never crossed his mind that his father might have had something to do with it. John Adams looked sideways at his wife with a smile, and in response to her unasked question, gave a little wink. Let it be recorded that Thomas never again gave vent to any prejudicial remarks concerning foreigners from that day on.

When service was finished the family strolled back down Church Street and the sun was high in the sky as it was about noon. As they turned to go towards Townhead a woman came down the Central Road towards the junction. She was in her early twenties and dressed in a mid grey jacket and skirt, her hair pinned up all the way round under a wide brimmed hat, and a most sophisticated air to her. The family turned towards the mill at the bottom of the hill and a well-known voice from behind said,

'Well don't you know me?'

Nancy turned and looked at the strange woman more closely and said, 'Omega! Why - what on earth?'

'Do you not know your own daughter now, Mother?' said Omega greeting her with a kiss.

'Well no, I have to say I didn't. What have you done to your hair? You look completely different.'

It was true. Omega had gone back to her employers' house the previous Sunday with her hair done in usual style, that is to say long, but gathered into a simple bun at the back. Now it was backcombed from the front and all the way round, being gathered all on the top of her head.

'It looks like a hair balloon. Oh. A hair balloon - I didn't mean to say that!'

Thomas danced round chanting, 'Ommy's a hair balloon, Ommy's a hair balloon.'

'Well I think it looks quite nice. What do you think Father?'

'Oh no. I'm staying out of this. Don't get me involved.'

Omega kissed her father and linked arms with Margaret and they all walked back to the Dib. It was her afternoon off, but she would be expected back in Maryport by six o'clock to recommence work, and she would have to walk, as she had done to get here. Margaret was not expected back at the vicarage until 6.00 pm, it being Sunday and a day of rest.

It was after Sunday dinner which was served at 3.00 pm that Margaret took Omega up to her room to talk. Alpha Nancy was there too for it was also her room, but at her age it did not matter.

'Well, you'll gather I'm going to find a place at the hiring fair, Ommy, and I'm a bit nervous about it. Can you tell me anything useful? What was it like?'

'Well. It was a bit strange to be standing there at first being looked at by a lot of strangers. But Mother will be there and that won't be so bad. You do get some odd people eying you up, but she's good at sorting them out.'

'Now what do you mean by odd?'

'Some of them are drunk Margaret. That's to be expected because it is fair time after all. I've seen a few fairs now since living in Maryport and there's an awful lot of drink. And there's the ones who leer and try to touch you in various places. But you won't be there that long. It's the ugly girls who are kept waiting longest and you aren't ugly, at least not very.'

Margaret slapped her not too gently and giggled, as did her sister.

'I wonder what that feels like? To be drunk?'

'Are you testing me?' Omega looked at her sister questioningly. 'Well if you are then the answer's no. I have not taken a drop, so I really cannot tell you.'

'Oh, but I didn't mean that, Ommy. I just wondered, that's all.'

'I forgive you even if you did. It's nice being Ommy again.'

'Whatever do you mean? It's your name isn't it?'

'No, I'm afraid it's not, at least not when I'm at work. Mr Furnival doesn't like Omega as a name for a maid. He thinks it's putting on the style and pretentious, so I have to answer to Jane.'

'Jane! That's a bit of cheek, taking away your name!'

'I think so too, but it's a job and a place so I put up with it and he is generally speaking, a good man if a bit strait-laced. I wonder what they'll call you?'

'Margaret. They'll call me Margaret.'

'I doubt they will. They'll call you Maggie, just wait and see. And it's no good taking on about it, because if you want to keep the place you'll do as they say. I can be Ommy for an afternoon a week and until I get married that will have to do.'

Margaret thought about continuing this line, but rejected it as fruitless, and something that she would sort for herself.

'Is there anything else I need to know or be careful about?'

Omega thought about this for almost a minute then said slowly, 'Yes. Young men.'

Margaret looked at her somewhat surprised.

'You mean followers?'

'No. You won't be allowed any of those. No I mean the young men in the house. Mr Furnival's got a son who's at university, but every so often he comes home, especially when he wants money.'

'So what's wrong with that? If his father is rich then he would do that.'

'Yes I know, but he keeps taking liberties, if you know what I mean.'

'No I don't.'

'Touching me where he shouldn't.'

'You mean brushing against you?'

'No Margaret, I mean touching. He grabs my behind if he's coming upstairs behind me and has caught me and kissed me a couple of times.'

'Now that's a liberty! Can you not complain?'

'Don't be daft! I'd lose my place in ten seconds flat. Besides. I don't want to complain.'

'Why ever not?'

'Well... he's very handsome. Just looking at him makes me go weak at the knees.'

Margaret stared at her for a minute then laughed. Then they both laughed.

'He might ask you to marry him!'

'The son of the solicitor marries the scullery maid!'

'He led me on.'

'Father will buy a shotgun!'

'I confess that the thought had crossed my mind, but seriously Margaret, his type don't marry maids. He'll want a lady.'

'You be careful Ommy. Don't lead him on.'

Omega sighed. 'I will try. I really will, but I am a creature of very small willpower. Don't worry about me. I can take care of myself.'

'I know you can.'

When Omega had gone home and Margaret lay in her bed her head buzzed with thoughts of hiring fairs, drunks, young men and hairstyles. Before she left, Omega had been persuaded to let her hair down out of the puffed up balloon shape that it was strictly pinned into, and had gone off with it tied back in her customary fashion. It was not after all, so she stated, a hairstyle for a maid.

The rest of the week passed in much the same manner as the previous one, except that Reverend Melrose was at the Board School every night taking pledges from men who would subscribe to the proposed co-operative. The effect on the men laid off was beginning to tell as it frayed nerves. Once Dearham was quiet during the day as the men were at work, but now it was common to hear raised voices as men got in the way or shouted at their wives in anger. In reality, it was a displacement of their own anger at themselves, impotent in the face of what they had no control over. All they could do was wait, and for men like these, used to making a living with hard graft and the sweat of their brows, it was difficult. Needless to say, the Board School Hall was filled to capacity at six o'clock on Friday when Melrose stood up to speak to the men assembled there.

'I will not beat about the bush gentlemen and I can tell you that I had hoped to raise £1,000 in pledges for our co-operative scheme, but in the last few days I have managed to raise only £275.'

A groan ran round the room for the game was surely up. The Vicar paused for a moment, his eye surveying the hall, then he went on,

'I am sure you know that this is as much a disappointment to me as it is to you; however to some extent I did expect it. Dearham is not a place where one may find £1,000 at the drop of a hat. I hear that you agree, to judge by the murmurs, so that being the problem, to wit the finding of £1,000, if it not be in Dearham, we must look elsewhere.'

Now he had their fullest attention and the silence was profound.

'Many of you will have noticed that I had the pleasure of entertaining Mr Fawcett, President of the Maryport Co-op in church last Sunday, and afterwards to dinner. We had a most interesting conversation and I am now at liberty to reveal to you what he said.'

Melrose had a most theatrical way with his pauses and the gift of keeping an audience in the palm of his hand, and now they hung on his every word.

'I brought up the possibility that the subscriptions may not prove sufficient for our purposes and briefly he told me that if that were the case then he had no doubt that the Co-operative Committee would be very pleased to receive a delegation from Dearham in order to ascertain what help they might be able to give.'

At this point he had to stop for loud murmuring broke out, and he held his hand up for quiet.

'Gentlemen, this is not a promise and not quite the parable of the Good Samaritan. The Committee of the Co-op is prepared to hear a case for them to intervene and indeed be our Samaritan.'

A voice from the crowd called out, 'You did the Samaritan on Sunday on purpose didn't you?' Rev. Melrose smiled, said nothing and an amused chuckle sounded briefly and generally.

'Now, as to what we do tonight, we must appoint a delegation. I am willing to be a member of it, but I think we need three men from among you whose legitimacy to speak for you can be attested by a show of hands. I would like you to think about this for ten minutes, then we shall name our delegation.'

After a few minutes of intense conversations and discussions several men put their names forward and the meeting showed by the raising of hands that they approved these people to act in their name. Melrose called the meeting to order and brought it to a close.

'Events may move quickly from this moment. The Co-op Committee is aware of the urgency of this situation and has convened an extraordinary meeting. If Mr Kirkbride, Mr Cottier and Mr Furness will stay behind for a short while, I think it would be well to decide what we are going to say. The meeting is at 2.00 pm tomorrow afternoon at the Co-operative Offices in Maryport. The delegation will leave by cart from my house at 1.00 pm. I do not think we need to gather again at this time, because your delegates can tell you what happens at that meeting. Whatever the Committee thinks, they cannot make a decision without hearing the voices of their members. That will not happen for a week or so, but let us hope that tomorrow goes how we would wish it to.'

The Committee that met in the impressive Co-operative Offices in Curzon Street was most sympathetic to the Dearham delegation, and keen to put them at their ease. This was very much a coal mining area and apart from the Vicar, the men from Dearham had no experience of dealing with men in suits who ran businesses from offices. They were remarkably nervous to start with, but after some prompting they set out their case for reopening the Crosshow Colliery in a direct and forthright fashion. Melrose had wished them to do this for themselves, as he did not wish to take the matter from them. He still hoped for a miners' co-operative and these men would have to lead it.

To their delight they found a ready audience, and Mr Fawcett had already explained to the committee what was happening to Dearham, the plight of which they were all too aware.

'It is a calamity, no doubt about that,' stated one of the Committee. 'If nothing is done, then it will see the heart and soul ripped out of that village, and that cannot be in anyone's interests.'

'I agree with you entirely,' said another member. 'We opened that store in Dearham five and a half years ago and in that time we have seen money come in to us to the tune of £48,573. Healthy profits there gentlemen. Healthy profits.'

A low growl of agreement made itself heard. Then Mr Fawcett spoke up,

'I also wish to point out that Dearham people have been very resolute in supporting the co-operative ideal, even before the opening of the Dearham store. I know for a fact that much money was spent over the counter in Maryport prior to the opening of the Dearham shop. The mining families there are some of our best customers. If we help them to maintain their employments we shall continue to receive their custom and a healthy profit I think.'

Another committee member thought that such enthusiastic Co-operators deserved the whole hearted backing of the society, for if they could not turn to them for help in hard times, who else could supply their need? Mr Fawcett then spoke up again,

'Gentlemen, I suggest that we ourselves are in a position to play the Good Samaritan,' and here he looked pointedly at Melrose, 'to a good and deserving community who particularly deserve well from us. Look after our customers and they will look after us. Now, we have our half yearly meeting open to all members coming up on 1 May. I propose that we put this matter to a vote there and call for a ballot of all our members in as short a time as may be possible. These people are in need of work, and we are in need of customers. It benefits none of us to delay.'

The motion being seconded and carried unanimously, the delegates from Dearham went home with high hopes and much elevated in their spirits. The word of what was happening spread like wildfire and if anything trade at the Dearham Co-operative store went up. Anyone who had anything they wished to buy went to the Co-op, so that the local shopkeepers suffered and had to grit their teeth. With any luck the customer drought they were experiencing would end before too long, but for the moment trade became slow. The snow-white aprons of the staff in the Co-op however, were never still, as Dearham commenced a love affair with co-operativism.

Sundry local residents were getting into trouble caused by the necessity of supplementing their diets. John Adams knew that Tom Hutchinson, the gamekeeper at Dovenby Hall, was a reasonable man and didn't grudge the taking of a few rabbits by men whose families were going through a bad patch. This was fair enough and very understandable. Game birds were a different matter and there were a few local youths who were adept at the trapping of his pheasants. Tom was aware of their tricks though and knew most of them. His position was greatly aided by there being a telephone at Dovenby Hall that was connected to the exchange at Maryport, and to the police station there. The suspicion that his runs were to be raided was enough for Tom to be allowed to use the phone and summon a policeman on a bicycle. Several young men had appeared in the Maryport Magistrate's Court in connection with having pheasants in their pockets and had been birched for their pains. The sight of Hutchinson, a policeman and a young man he knew trundling down the Row Brow heading for town was enough to make John warn his two boys not to get mixed up with any trouble.

'Does that include fish, Father?'

'Why do you ask that?'

'Well we could catch some.'

'Fishing in the River Ellen is private and forbidden Johnny. If you fished there, it would be stealing from the people who own the fishing rights and you'd be arrested.'

'No Father, I don't mean the river. I mean our beck.'

That brought John up short for a moment, because the Row Beck ran past his own back garden, and he had to think a minute.

'You know Johnny, that's not a bad idea. In fact I think I'll join you.'

Fishing was not a normal family pursuit so they had no hooks or tackle, but amazing things may be done, or so it seemed, with some bent pins, string and bacon rind. There was of course great excitement for each small fish they caught, and they could not tell dace from gudgeon or loach. Suffice to say that there were enough to flavour a vegetable stew and turn it into a fish stew, which was quite tasty and nourishing, though you had to be very careful with the bones. This became a useful, regular and welcome addition to the family diet.

Tuesday 1 May came quickly enough and the half yearly meeting of the Maryport Industrial Co-operative Society got under way in the afternoon, attended by the Dearham delegates. Mr Fawcett had enquired of a mining engineer with whom he was acquainted whether he could in short order prepare a report on the viability of the old Crosshow Colliery and he had undertaken to do so quickly. The meeting was attended by many members of the Co-operative Society and it quickly became apparent that the vast majority were in favour of the Dearham proposal. The returns from their Dearham store were substantial and if an investment could keep it so, then it was a good investment. Mr Melrose pointed out that this store had made a profit in the last six months of £684 12s 3d and all agreed that this was a handsome return. If it were not for the hard winter and the closure of the Lonsdale Pit then half yearly profits would normally be about £1,000 now. Indeed, over the five previous years the profits had been over £5,000 as their customer numbers had gone up, so the benefit of maintaining Dearham as a community prepared to shop at the Co-op was clear.

Mr William Robinson, a man much respected in the business community, pressed the point that it would be easy for the Co-op to invest £1,000 merely by forfeiting it from the dividends which were about to be paid out to their members, many of whom lived in Dearham. At the moment, if someone had £20 invested in the Co-operative then they would receive a dividend of two shillings and threepence in the pound. By reducing the dividend to one shilling and seven pence the members would have the £1,000 necessary to fund the Crosshow Colliery. Cheap at the price. This carried the day and the meeting was wholly in favour of the proposal.

However, there were two caveats. Firstly, they would have to see the report of the mining engineer who was about to survey the Crosshow Colliery. He was very familiar with it, for although he lived in Airdrie in Lanarkshire, he came from Dearham and Mr Heslop was known to many of the men present. Secondly of course, the members would have to decide and that could only be done when the report had been received. There were nearly 3,000 people who must be given a chance to vote on the matter. The subject was closed for now, but was placed as the main item on the agenda of a meeting scheduled for 9 June. On that day the committee would make a recommendation.

Depression, like a black cloud for some weeks now a feature of the air in Dearham, lifted and vanished. Optimism soared for the Co-op was going to save the village. Yes, there was another month of uncertainty to go through, but now there was hope, the possibility of employment and the probability of investment. A community that could have disintegrated now decided to hang on and await better things.

This was the atmosphere that surrounded Margaret Adams as the last few days of her girlhood ticked down. The Whitsun Fair was on 11 May and her life would enter a whole new phase. Fear, hope, pleasure, trepidation, thrill, nerves, exhilaration all bubbled through the channels of her mind at various times. As the day approached, she could hardly wait to get it over with. Fate's finger beckoned, and follow it she must.

Chapter 5

The Hiring Fair

    James Gibson, the market gardener, was up at five o'clock on the morning of Saturday 12 May loading his cart with boxes of his own produce. To call it by such a name was something of a misnomer for it was far more than a flat wagon on wheels. Inside it were display platforms or steps so that fruit and vegetables could be displayed in boxes on three levels; the side of the wagon folded up and could be let down to form a shelf with the bottom tier. Fresh cabbages, hessian sacks of his own potatoes, cauliflowers, carrots, turnips, parsnips, onions and so on were stacked ready for sale, and a pair of old scales for weighing out, were all contained in the central area. The whole equipage was pulled by one large horse called Gladstone, for James was a Tory by persuasion, and at the front was a seat for the driver should he choose to use the long reins. This morning, however, James was not in the seat, and instead he was leading the horse. Seated in state were Nancy and Margaret Adams in their Sunday best and, as the gardener said, they looked a rare bonnie sight. He would not wish them to arrive at Maryport tired and glowing from a walk, so he was only too happy to help them with a lift into town, especially considering that they had already walked nigh on two miles to reach him. Down the road they went, leaving at six o'clock sharp, and plodded at a slow but steady walk from Dearham down the long hill into town. It was an steady and gradual down, past a newish row of houses called Marsh Terrace and some rather more prosperous houses which Margaret thought must have been built by a man called Robinson, to judge by the name adorning their fronts.

    As they neared the environs of Maryport, heading for Fleming Square where the hirings would be, it became obvious that the town was very crowded. Margaret had been to hiring fairs before, but always later in the day when most servants had been hired and had drifted away from the gathering place. In addition to this of course the hiring fair was not just that. It was a full sized fair with all that went with it, including livestock auctions, wrestling, amusements and so on; Fleming Square was where Maryport's bustling market was held twice a week in a large cobbled open space surrounded by handsome Georgian houses. Stallholders were shouting their wares and the streets leading to it were crammed with people, not only from the town but from miles away, all over Northern England, for Maryport had a railway station to which special fair trains ran from Carlisle, Penrith, Barrow and Keswick with all stations along the way. The professional fair goers were doing a roaring trade, even at this early hour and it would get busier as the day went on. Already Margaret had observed two peepshows of different kinds. The former invited people to look through a hole at unusual objects gathered from all over the world, and the latter to look at strange animals and people. She knew one of the humans, who had quite a lot of fame in the local area; Mary Swinburne from Dearham was a little younger than her and had been in school at the same time as she had. She stood five feet eight and a half inches tall which was tall for a woman. Margaret herself was of average height at five feet one inch, so Mary towered over her; however, in addition to her height she weighed 20 stone and was known all over the North West as the Dearham giantess. She made no bones about letting strangers marvel at her physique nor of taking their money for the privilege of doing so. Certainly, it was far better and much more financially rewarding than the life of a scullery maid.

Some stalls were selling what looked like particularly indigestible cakes, which Nancy winced at. Others sold gimcrack toys, tough looking toffee and toffee apples, mosaic jewellery and parrots. The last drew a small and amused crowd because the birds could talk and indeed what made the crowd laugh was the profanity of these small birds that had evidently been well taught. Margaret was no shrinking violet and fancied a cage bird, but thought that she would not have one of these in her house. Her attention was particularly drawn to a couple of photographic booths where you could pose for your portrait against a classical or bucolic background and have your image taken for posterity. Of course, you must never smile, for if you did you looked like some sort of lunatic, but she would very much like to have her portrait taken with her siblings. Maybe one day she would. Some of the photographs on exhibition outside these booths were excellent, as good as or better than any painting and they could be had for a few pence; if she saved up then it might be possible one day. Scattered along the pavements were pedlars with trays or small displays selling wonderful things for a penny. A few small stalls sold cheap Brummagem trinkets, mostly in brass, but as Mother said, it was all very well to buy these shiny things, and a jackdaw might well love them for the glitter, but they all had to be polished. There was no point in wasting your money on something useless and making yourself more work in the process.

Then there were the more conventional vendors of produce, clothing, implements, old books and such like, but they were not the spectacular attraction. Caracoling down Crosby Street was a pair of white horses, their riders dressed in Spanish style, with placards fixed on either side of their rumps advertising Mr Newsome's Circus which was in a field just past the northern end of the fair. The horsemanship provided much interest to the spectators, and provoked a certain amount of awe and appreciation, for many of them knew horses and could admire the skill with which these were handled. Later in the day there would be other acts from the circus advertising their presence and in turn the strongman, the clowns, the elephants would all appear to lure an audience to the large marquee where the show took place. This was undoubtedly the single largest attraction in town.

There were others, in seeming unending number and they passed most of them, including the inevitable boxing ring where prizes were on offer for men who could beat the professionals. Looking at the tough pugs sitting waiting to be challenged

Margaret did not fancy any of their chances but there was never a shortage of challengers. Not far from them was a wrestling ring, but Cumbrian wrestling did not attract many professionals as retained employees. There were men who made a living by touring the contests, but they competed for prize money, not for a wage paid by the booth owner. Winning depended on whether you could 'stand' or 'fall' though there was rather more to it than that. Wrestling contests were held in 'Cumbrian,' 'Cornish,' 'Scottish backhold' and 'Greek' styles. There were also matches by weight, and these attracted many competitors for it was by far the most popular sport across the north of England. Business for the wrestling and boxing booths would pick up later in the day.

It was not too early for pickpockets to be out, so sensible people kept their money close to them and the Adams' ladies saw no incidents though fairs had a bad name for such thefts. Several public houses were advertising 'Dance' and had hired musicians for the day. Men and women could pay to enter and dance, with propriety of course, with perfect strangers who merely liked the look of each other. Although not considered 'respectable' these dances were very popular and a lot of drink was consumed here. Indeed, this was general all across the area of the fair. It might have been a Saturday and quite early in the morning, but old customs die hard in the North of England. For centuries, breakfast for many men was a draught of beer. In the case of respectable men or craftsmen this was 'small beer' which was a weak kind of ale, but many working men regarded beer as food. This was a Saturday and a fair day, a holiday, so already there were some rustics about the streets who were the worse for drink. Margaret noted that there were a lot of collier hands up from the harbour who seemed not to have slept the previous night and to have drunk a lot already. Coal boats out of Maryport to places like Douglas on the Isle of Man, Dublin, and Belfast attracted an aggressive breed of sailor and they had a name for casual violence, swearing and drinking hard. This was a tough town.

Eventually they reached a place just by the Market Hall in the centre of Fleming Square, where '19' was chalked on the ground and there stood a pedlar selling windmills and balloons, and he was very unwilling to move on. However, as James Gibson pointed out, this was his numbered pitch that he had paid for and he had a piece of paper to prove it; the pedlar left.

'Thank you, Mr Gibson. It was good of you to give us a lift and we are very grateful to you.'

'That's all right Mrs Adams; it was a pleasure. Just you be careful to see that bonny lass gets a good place. You'll need a lift back up that hill later, so just come back here when you're done and we'll arrange a time.'

Assuring him that she would, Nancy moved on with Margaret down the square towards the hiring area. They went past the small pens where horses, sheep and cattle were kept and threaded through the knot of country farmers paying attention to the gibbering auctioneer. Here, on both sides of the street were people, lined up roughly parallel and between them an aisle up which wandered other people looking at them. Each of the people lining the sides had some sort of emblem with them. Some of the women held mops, and others ladles to indicate that they were cooks. The men who held crooks were obviously shepherds, those with rakes were gardeners and most of the men had a wisp of straw pinned to their lapels to indicate that they were farm labourers. On a post at this end of the hiring area, and presumably on another at the other end was a notice advertising the fair going rate for servants by the half year:

'Men £10-£12
Half-waxed lads £6-£10
Boys £2 10s - £4
Women £4 - £6
Girls £3 - £4'

Nancy handed Margaret a mop with the abjuration,

'Now remember don't speak directly to any of them. You are 19 and not 21 when you can speak for yourself. Mother speaks

65

for you until then. Don't smile or you'll look like a flippertigibbet and don't fidget or they'll think you've got a screw loose.'

Margaret merely smiled and tried not to look anxious. Mother had said all this before, a dozen times. She held her mop, stood, and waited as people stared at her and moved on. Not wishing to look pushy she had not thought to choose a particular place so was right at the end of the line of prospective servants standing next to a horse, which though friendly, kept staling and making her nose wrinkle. He was a big, tall and friendly sort of horse who occasionally pushed his nose over the rail asking her to scratch him, which she did, for she liked horses, though she had little dealings with them. His owner was at a stall nearby drinking a mug of tea. Up and down the line of prospective servants she saw farmers stop occasionally in front of a man, for they seemed to be mostly labourers, and ask 'Are you for hire me lad?' It seemed to be a traditional question as its use was universal.

A woman stopped in front of her, plainly dressed and with an air of command to her, and spoke to Mother,

'What can she do?'

'She can cook, clean and keep house to a high standard enough to satisfy the most scrupulous of employers.'

'Is she a good girl?'

'She is most respectable, with no followers, does not drink, and attends church regularly. She has an excellent character signed by the Vicar of Dearham.'

'Has she been out to service previously then?'

'No Ma'am; she worked as a scullery maid on a day basis. She is seeking her first place.'

'Very well. How much?'

'£5 the half year.'

'Ha! For a young girl just out. You won't get that. Leastways not from me.'

'Nonetheless Ma'am, that is her fee and she is worth it.'

'Not to me. Good day to you.'

So saying, she moved on. There were to be several such conversations in the next couple of hours. The sun climbed high in the sky and the day wore on. Margaret had observed several girls get taken on, a lot of men and still the employers came to look up and down. She found that standing in one place was actually quite tiring.

Suddenly she felt a finger on her face turning it to the side, and there was a youngish man, plump in the face and prosperous looking, staring at her.

'Excuse me sir, but please do not touch my daughter in that way. It is not seemly I think.'

The man looked at Nancy with some sort of disdain and said, 'And who might you be?'

'I'm her mother as you might have gathered and I think you should not touch my daughter.'

Nancy was quite heated about it and he dropped his hand away.

'Well, you might be a little gentler with a prospective employer I think.'

'Perhaps I might be but she's not going with you, so you are not a prospective employer are you?'

'Oh and why is that might I ask?'

'Because she's not and that's that.'

He drew himself up and drawled, 'I am a respectable businessman and keep a good house. I would like a better reason than that.'

Several onlookers were most amused when Nancy replied.

'Because I know a wrong 'un when I see one, and you smell of perfume which I don't like. I think you're a lecher and what you're after is a bed-warmer not a servant. You're not getting my daughter, so there's an end to it.'

'Well I never!'

'And I'm pretty sure you did! So go and do it somewhere else.'

The man almost replied but hearing laughs he saw that he was becoming the centre of some attention and grew flustered. Then he turned pink, muttered something nasty under his breath and walked away.

Margaret said, 'Well you saw him off Mother.'

'There's manners in this game as well Margaret. They are not supposed to touch. That was the sort that would be touching you all the time and next thing you know you're in trouble, out of a job and with a child you never wanted in the first place. That's why I'm here, to stop men like that.'

Another man also got short shrift. He was obviously in from a hill farm and he stank of sheep, his clothes were dirty and his face was unshaven. Nancy judged that if he had a wife she was a sloven, his house was a dump and there was no advancement for her daughter in even thinking of such a place. Fiercely protective of her chick, she was not going to accept a place simply for the sake of the job. The next prospective employer, however, provided a situation that she could not do much about.

Along the aisle between the two lines of servants came about seven or eight sailors and they were very well oiled, almost unable to walk straight. However, they were at that stage of drunkenness where they could still think after a fashion and talk reasonably articulately. Generally speaking, there are three types of drunk. The first are harmless because they drink too much and then they go to sleep, often sliding under a table in a pub or eating-house. The second are also harmless, because they are the maudlin drunks who get sentimental, try to kiss the women in friendship, and swear eternal brotherhood with all the men. All the world is their friend. The last type can be nasty though. These are the aggressive drunks who want trouble. These are the drunks who beat their wives and children, who smash windows; they are the angry men who look for fights and hate the world. The sailors wandered along looking at the people for hire and they were led by a nasty drunk. He was amusing himself by making rude remarks to the women about their looks and their bodies. To the men he made similar remarks because he wanted to fight them, and most of them were peaceable farm hands who flinched from his gaze in fear and wished themselves elsewhere. He was confident that they would not retaliate and laughed beerily at them. At about five foot seven, he was two or three inches taller than the average man, and he was stocky, muscular and with an air of toughness to him that made people afraid. The clothes of this bravo and his mates were filthy and it was clear that they were the crew of a collier in Maryport Harbour. They were moving towards Margaret and Nancy and as they drew closer Margaret's apprehensions grew and she was afraid. She noticed that the big horse next to her in the pen was having his halter tied to the rail by the little man who was his owner. He looked at her and nodded, saying just one word 'trouble.' He was right.

The group of sailors came up the street towards her, their leader swaying from one side to the other offering insults freely. Margaret saw that there were no exceptions and soon it would be her turn. Sure enough he came level with her, and his attack on her was different in nature, for he did not insult her.

'My, my, what have we here? Hey boys this is a pretty one. Shall I hire her for a cabin girl?'

They laughed and cheered this suggestion, so he turned back to Margaret.

'Well my friends think that's a good idea. What do you think, my girl, will you come with us on a boat to Belfast and look after us all? We'd take turns of course. You might even like it!'

Nancy stepped forward raging, 'Leave her alone you dirty beast in the shape of a man. Have you no respect?'

'Ha! Not for you you old hag, get out of my way.'

He shoved Nancy backwards and she fell onto a pile of hay, which made the horse in the pen shy up on his rope. As his mates laughed and egged him on he came to Margaret and breathed sour beer over her. The smell of him was rank and he grabbed her as she struggled to get away.

'Come on now, don't be shy. Give me a kiss!'

'Go on girlie, give him a kiss.'

'Leave me alone. Get off me.'

Margaret tried to fend the drunkard off with her mop handle, but he grabbed it from her and threw it to the floor.

'Am I not good enough for you then? Shall I teach her some manners, lads?'

They guffawed and shouted that he should, so he attempted to kiss her again.

'You have no manners to teach me. Get off me you dirty drunk.'

'Dirty drunk! I think I will teach you some manners,' and he slapped her on the face hard as the people round her gasped. Her senses were confused as momentarily stunned she reeled. No one had ever hit her like that before, but a second blow never came.

She was not quite sure how it happened, but she watched in a fuzzy way as her attacker seemed to float yelling into the air in the arms of a giant.

Getting a grip on the world she blinked and saw that her assailant was helpless in the hands of an enormous personage in the costume of a Cumbrian wrestler. With no apparent effort he threw the drunk over the top of the pen where he landed hard against the rear legs of the tethered horse. Startled the horse immediately emptied his bowel and covered the bully in dung all over his upper body.

'If you've got any sense you'll stay there,' said the giant in a shrill voice, but the sailor snarled and drew a knife. Again in a high pitched voice the wrestler said, 'If you come at me like that in a most un-English way then I shall break the arm that holds that knife and knock you out.'

It did no good at all and the snarling drunk climbed out of the pen and launched himself at the giant, but he never reached him. With a neat sidestep the wrestler caught the knife arm and brought it down on his own bent knee. There was an audible crack and the sailor barely had time to start his scream before a tremendous forearm smash laid him out senseless on the cobbles.

There was no cheer because the sailor's companions appeared to have entered a state of sobriety and were inclined to seek vengeance. A couple of them drew knives and things began to look very nasty indeed. Then a second but bigger giant shouldered through the crowd. He looked at the men and asked them basso profundo,

'Are you picking on my boy and him only 12 years old? Shame on you.'

Then he grinned like an open coffin and stood beside his son. Margaret realized now her wits had come back that she knew her rescuer. John Tunstall, the Dearham Colossus, was only twelve years old, hence his unbroken voice, but he stood over six feet, weighed over twelve stone, and was the star of the Northern Counties Wrestling and Athletic Association. No one could stand

71

before him, and he had won belts all over the place; so had his father who now stood before him. It still looked bad though with seven sailors against two, though the sailors were now hesitating. Then she noticed some men she knew, attracted by the attention, and they ranked up with the wrestlers; they were joined by the little man who owned the horse in the pen, though he looked in his late 60s and could probably not be of that much help.

'Good morning Maggie,' said one of them, 'A bit of trouble here is there?'

'Yes, Mr Ostle. That man hit me.'

'Did he by God? Good job he's unconscious or I'd have done him myself.'

Dearham folk stick together and there were now a few unemployed miners round John Ostle.

'Knives! That's for cowards. Englishmen don't settle things that way. Foreigners do that. Put those knives away marras or you're going to be eating them.'

The odds had changed now and the sailors had gone quiet. They no longer wished to be in this situation and Mr Tunstall senior knew it.

'If you know what's good for you, pick that piece of offal up and get out of here. You'd better clean him up before seeing the doctor. And get sober. If you're seen in Maryport again there'll be trouble. Your pal hit a lass and we don't like that round here.'

The truth of this was apparent in Margaret's left cheek, pink from the blow.

'Are you hurt Margaret?'

'No, Mother. It was the flat of his hand and it stung. But how are you? You fell.'

'I'm fine. I fell onto straw and fell soft.'

'Mother, I don't think I'm going to get a place now. Lots of people saw that and they don't like trouble.'

'You didn't cause it pet. You'll get a place, never fear. I'll get some water from the horse trough and soak my hanky. If you hold it to your cheek the pink'll soon go.' Then she turned to the men who had seen the sailors off.

'Thank you, Mr Tunstall. I am - we are - so grateful. And thank you to you all.' Here she turned to the miners who grinned and muttered that it was nothing.

'Mrs Adams, I am sorry that you were subjected to it. It's a sore and sad thing that a lady cannot go about her business without being a victim to that sort of thing. Think no more on it. Now if you'll excuse me my son was on his way to a match and they will be waiting on us. It cannot be said that the Dearham Colossus was a no-show.'

So saying he and his son, the miners and the onlookers dispersed.

'Excuse me, ma'am.'

Nancy turned as the little man who owned the big horse came up to her. He was a twinkly man, small and wiry with white hair, bushy white mutton chop whiskers framing a clean shaved chin and mouth, and piercing blue eyes; moreover he seemed to be a nice man.

'Yes sir, you want to speak to me?'

'Yes ma'am, I think I'd like to offer your daughter a place. I've been here a fair bit during the day and I'm happy to meet your price of £5 for the half year. From what I've heard she can cook very well, sew, and clean. What else can she do?'

'Just about anything you care to name sir. She knits, darns, weaves, does laundry well, and would put most maids to shame in the care and handling of a household. She's been well trained sir, for I taught her myself and what I have not, the cook at Dearham Vicarage has.'

'I don't doubt that at all; it's Mrs Adams isn't it, from what I gather?'

'Yes sir, and you are?'

'My name's Barwise Little ma'am, and I would describe myself as a yeoman farmer and I breed horses and cattle up at

West End Farm at Edderside. I have a hundred odd acres there and we do well enough.'

'And you want a maid sir. May I ask what happened to your last maid?'

'We've never had a maid, because my wife is excellent with the household arts and has always been helped by my daughter. But I sent my daughter to finishing school in Switzerland a few years ago to learn how to be more of a lady, and if truth be told, to get her away from a certain gentleman in our locality. She's been back a couple of years, but got ideas about bettering herself. So she got a place in the Carlisle telephone exchange where she lives in. That means that my wife, who is no longer young, as indeed is the case with me as you may see, is managing the house by herself. It's been in my head to get a maid for a few weeks though I have been in two minds about it. She needs a hand you see, and what I saw here today settled it for me.'

'Settled it sir?'

'Yes, indeed. I liked the look of your lass anyway for she is well turned out and has pride in herself. And she's no shrinking violet either for when that - that 'man' slapped her she was resisting all she could and pulled herself together well afterwards. I note that she did not cry. And she tried to hit him with her mop handle. That's character and I like character so I offer her a place on her terms; £5 for the half year and all found. You'll find that we are respectable people if you ask around and you have a few days to do that. I'm well known round here, particularly at the auctioneers so feel free to ask them as to my bona fides. I shall not take it amiss, for a mother has to be sure that her daughter is going to a safe place.'

'Where would she be housed sir?'

'Not in the house, for we have not room. I have three sons besides the daughter so she would be housed in a pair of rooms above the dairy across the yard. She'd have what would be in effect her own little house for there is a bedroom and a small sitting room with a fire. For food she'd eat with us as family.

There's no servant's kitchen so we'll do it the old way and she'll eat below the salt.'

'That sounds very agreeable to me. What do you think Margaret?'

Margaret liked the twinkly little man. He radiated a feeling that he was good and that she would be in safe hands so she replied immediately,

'Yes Mother, I accept the place.'

'Good,' said Barwise Little, 'I am glad of that; I can tell my wife that Maggie the maid will be coming to live with us next market day.' Margaret once again winced inwardly, but if he was going to pay her and provide for her then he could call her Maggie if he wished.

'Now take this in earnest of our bargain,' and here he handed her a shilling and proffered his hand. She took the coin, and shook his hand, not too vigorously.

'I shall be attending the market here on Tuesday next so on the third day from now I shall meet you here with your bags at 3.00 pm which is when I head for home, and we shall go to Edderside from here. Does this meet with your approval?'

'Yes sir, it does. I shall be here.'

'I will see you then. Goodbye for now.'

So saying, he moved away and went about his business.

Margaret had a job. She had a place and she wondered what it would be like.

An older woman with a kindly face stopped her as she and Nancy turned towards home.

'You've done all right there my pet.'

'What do you mean?'

'I used to work at Edderside Hall for the Sharp family, just up the road from his farm. That's Barwise Little. He breeds champion horses and does very well. He's just won a £47 prize for his cattle too. A nice little place he has. And a lovely wife too. You'll be very happy there, I should think.'

That set the seal on Margaret's day. She had a place. It sounded like a good one and now she was looking forward to it. Thanking the woman, and glad in her heart, she set off with her mother on the two and a half mile walk home, carrying her mop with her.

Chapter 6

To Edderside

John Adams walked into Maryport with Margaret on the following Tuesday, wishing to meet the man who would be her employer, but also because it gave him something useful to do in carrying her bag. All of her clothes and possessions were in that bag and it was quite heavy. There was no sense in starting particularly early so they set off along the Ellenborough road shortly after 11 o'clock and were in town by just before 12.30. There was not much conversation between them, but the minds of both were whirring with emotion. It could not be otherwise. For John it was another milestone in his life because the second of his children was leaving home to enter the world of employment and adulthood; his second little girl was to make her own way. In Margaret's mind fountains of trepidation vied with optimism and showers of regret for what she was leaving behind; she was, as her mother might have said "a bundle of nerves". Her father knew well that her mind was in turmoil and as they entered the town he said, 'Let's go and have a stroll down the harbour eh, and see the sights? We've got some time to use.'

Grateful for the diversion, Margaret agreed and they turned from Curzon Street into Senhouse Street and soon arrived at their goal. Breasting the top of the rise and emerging from between the high terraces by the Golden Lion Hotel she caught her breath as the view opened up in front of her. Living where she did and with no omnibus service between Dearham and Maryport, her contact with the nearby town had been minimal in her lifetime and she had never seen the harbour area. She could hardly have picked a better time to do so for the day was beautiful, with bright sunshine, still a slight chill in the air, the year not being so advanced as to be warmer, and with visibility as clear as crystal for miles, without a trace of haze. The waters of the Solway Firth twinkled in the sun, a slight wind blew from the south, and in the far distance the hills of Dumfries and Galloway loomed out of the horizon.

'One day, one day, I shall go there,' she thought.

The harbour was busy, but she had expected that it would be and indeed the area was thronged with so much going on that she barely knew where to look. Coal boats were predominant with their low sturdy lines and smoking stacks. They were hybrid colliers; having a large sail at the front so they could economise on fuel by using the wind to augment their progress. There was noise over where the coal was stacked as it was delivered by chute straight into the thickly timbered holds waiting to receive it, then to be transported all over the world. Set apart from the coal boats by the thickness of a red stone quay were the local fishing boats where all was buzzing as well. The harbour area was grimy with dust and carbon deposits and there was a smell in the air of smoke blown on the wind from the chimneys, funnels and brickworks of Flimby pit. Up the river she could hear thumping and sawing and all sorts of clamour from men at work in Ritson's and Wood's shipyards. Ritson's, she knew, was famous in the area for launching ships sideways into the river, which was apparently an unusual thing to do. Maryport was important for so many reasons and she was glad to live in such a hard working and prosperous area.

She looked out over the harbour towards the pier and to the open sea. Her attention was caught by a large black ball that was rising almost imperceptibly up a mast sited at the landward end of the pier. As she watched, the ball reached the top of the mast and stayed there. 'Whatever is that for?' she asked her father who had pulled out his watch and was examining it.

'Ah now, that is a tide indicator Margaret; a very ingenious device that shows the level of the water in the harbour to any approaching boats. Some of them might run aground if there were not sufficient depth under that so it's rather vital to any vessel coming in.'

'That is rather important. I thought it was just something a bit odd, a sight to see.'

He paused a moment, sensing her nervousness at the approaching parting, so continued with diversionary small talk. 'Maryport Harbour gives you a sight to see just about every day. I remember being here in October 1879 early one morning shift. I'd been asked to help take a trainload of coal down to the harbour chutes. There was an earthquake while I was here, Margaret, and you were four years old.'

'I don't remember that.'

'Well at that age you wouldn't, but I do. That harbour was shaking and the water trembled so that every ship was rocking in it. I've never seen such a thing since and probably never will again.'

'I didn't think we got earthquakes in this part of the world.'

'Neither did I until then.' John Adams then pointed to a little bench overlooking the harbour.

'Have a seat Margaret, for we have a little while and there is a matter I would like to talk over with you that I have spoken with your mother about and that we are both of two minds.'

Margaret sat, wondering what this thing might be, but also feeling quite privileged, for her father was a man who habitually kept the running of domestic affairs in his own hands as befitting the head of the household. He divined her thoughts, 'You have a good head on you and a lot of common sense, so don't be surprised that I ask, because I know I'll get a straight answer.'

This was flattering and she felt honoured that her father was speaking to her in this way, stood on the cusp between childhood and adulthood. It made her feel rather more grownup and she almost felt herself grow in stature and significance as she gave him her full attention.

'I saw George Brown the other day. Did you know that he and his family have rented that field over Janet Bridge and up the brow on the way to town?'

Margaret nodded. The field was at Townhead and she passed it every time she went up into Dearham. George Brown had been a butty or shift overseer at the Lonsdale Pit, so was well acquainted with her father.

'Anyway, he told me that he was at the vicar's meeting with his brother and a few other Browns and they got to talking on the way home. They've got an idea to use the old shaft in that field and mine from there. The old men worked it back in the 1820s as a landsale pit and he thinks he can do the same. He's going to approach the royalty holders to see if they've got any objections, but since they'll only get money from it then there should not be any dissent. After all they won't lose anything.

'So what's he saying Father? That there's a job there for you?'

'Not in so many words, no. He said that they were going to ask a few good men to put some small amount of money in to start them off, and that they would work in the mine. It would be a co-operative venture so there would not be a wage, but a share of profits. He said if I was interested then I should come up and see him at Orchard House.'

'What's a Landsale Pit?'

'They sell the coal locally to householders so there's no tax on it. If you have a wet sale pit and sell overseas or transport by water, then it's taxed. Production is on a small scale and wages are generally low.'

'Are you going to do it?'

'I don't know lass and that's why I thought I would ask you. It helps to hear what other people think. I would not necessarily take advice, for I like to make up my own mind, but it is useful to toss your thoughts about a bit.'

Margaret considered this for a couple of minutes, staring hard over towards the iron foundry from whence came the loud thump of trip hammers working.

'I don't think you should,' she said definitely.

'Well that's forthright enough, as I expected. Can I hear your reasons?'

'Yes. I can see the temptation because it's two minutes down the road and you know George quite well. But it's risky isn't it?'

'What way is it risky?'

'Well there won't be a lot of money will there so it's all going to be small scale. And they'll cut corners. They won't be able to afford not to. But you've got Mother and two young sons and a daughter to support so you need a wage coming in. And the Co-operative Society is a better bet even though it's further to walk.'

John looked at her with a smile, 'Why is it a better bet then?'

'Because it will have the Co-op's money behind it, they will pay a proper rate and they will have enough cash so as not to cut corners. Small scale mining's got a name for accidents Father, so however tempting it might be, I'd rather have a dad than not, so I'd say stick with the Co-op.'

This time his look was fond, 'You just said more or less what I have been thinking Margaret, and for those reasons. The way things are going, I think George's venture will get under way in the next month or so, but the Co-op will not be up and running for a couple of months. I think perhaps I shall remain unemployed and wait on the Co-op.'

'Have you decided then?'

'Not entirely, but your mother was much of your opinion too, so I think it's likely that I shall follow your advice. Now, it's getting on. Shall we go and meet Mr Little?'

The conversation had steadied Margaret's nervousness and her resolve had returned; she knew that whatever happened in the matter of leaving home to take a place, she could and would cope with it, and indeed that she could cope with anything life threw at her. Accordingly they made their way to Fleming Square and to the appointed place where they found Barwise Little sitting on the seat of a little trap to which was attached the big horse that had been so friendly to Margaret. He nuzzled towards her as she approached and she stroked his velvet nose in return.

'Well, the horse is glad to see you Maggie and so am I. Three o clock sharp; that's nice and punctual and the best of starts. Good afternoon to you sir. I take it that you are her father.'

In response to Barwise's proffered hand John Adams squeezed it back, liking the smaller man on first sight. Something told him that his daughter was going to be in good hands and he approved of her first employer. He knew that she would not like 'Maggie,' but she had said nothing so he held his tongue.

'I thought this horse was for sale sir? I liked him but I never thought I'd see him again.'

'What? Richard for sale? No,' he said fondly and jumping down to scratch the horse's muzzle. I wouldn't sell Richard. We're friends aren't we old boy?'

So saying he patted the horse's neck fondly and Richard whinnied softly in return of the affection. He was such a small man to have such a large horse, but he seemed complete master of him.

Margaret could not resist a small laugh, 'Richard is a funny name for a horse.'

'Aye well, it is but I named him in honour of one of my ancestors.'

'How do you honour an ancestor by naming a horse after him, sir?'

'Ha-ha! Well, that's a direct question and it deserves a direct answer. One of my ancestors was an MP for Carlisle and he stood six foot four inches tall. They called him Great Barwise. Now this big horse of mine stands nineteen hands, the exact same height, so I called him after Richard Barwise. Richard takes me all over the place and he does all sorts of things round the farm so he's a hard worker and earns his hay. Don't you, you big soft ha'porth? He's a Clydesdale gelding and as good humoured and gentle as a lamb.'

John Adams was even more pleased. His daughter's employer liked his horse and was easy going. That she would treat her new boss with respect he knew, but Barwise's treatment of her met with his approval, so it was with no fear for her future that he kissed her goodbye. He knew that the distance to Edderside was six to seven miles so that would preclude her coming home on Sundays. Her half-day off would be spent in the locality of where she worked.

'My dear girl, work hard, be good and we'll see you in six months. Take care you write to us every fortnight.'

She kissed him, not without a few tears, and he handed her bag up into the trap. Mr Little climbed up beside her, jiggled the reins and said to the horse, 'Home Richard' and off they trotted. Turning round Margaret saw her father waving and she waved back until finally he was lost to sight behind a load of hay on a farm cart.

'We'll be home in an hour and you've plenty of time to get settled in,' said Barwise Little. 'My wife, Annie, is doing dinner tonight and you'll eat with us and the family, which will be the usual thing. You can start your actual work after dinner by dealing with the dishes. She'll like that. From then on you do as she says and we'll get on just fine.'

'Yes sir,' replied Margaret who was feeling rather hungry and glad there would be a dinner waiting.

'None of that if you please Maggie. I'm none of your sirs. That's for people who get ideas that is. You call me Mister, for that's what I answer to. Mr Little if you're so minded, but Mister to speak to; a lot of people do that.'

'And what am I to call Mrs Little, sir? Ma'am?'

Barwise Little grinned, then he laughed loud. It was, she found, a pleasant laugh, full of humour and fun.

'Hell's Bell's lass! Not on your nelly! She'd have a fit. No, you call her Missis. My boys and my own daughter call her Mam, but anyone else calls her Missis. That'll do nicely. Alright?'

'Yes, s... Mister.'

Richard trotted along at a smart pace along the road, which was not too crowded, although they had to overtake several market wagons on the way home. The road was smooth and ran between a high bank on their left side, which obscured their view of the sea, and a reddish stone wall on the right. Soon they passed an entrance with an impressive wrought iron gate with a lodge.

'See that Maggie? That's Netherhall, the home of the Senhouse family. Very powerful people, the Senhouses. They built this town you know.'

'Did they? They must be very rich!'

'As rich as Croesus Maggie. Money from slaves, sugar, coal, you name it.'

Margaret did not know who Croesus was, but decided not to say anything. Plainly he was someone very rich, but parading a lack of knowledge in front of her boss was not a good idea.

'It looks a very grand place.'

'Grand it is! I'm afraid we are not so grand, but we are comfortable I think you'll find.'

Coming to a fork in the road they turned left to take the coast road.

'Richard! Smartly now,' said Mr Little.

The horse picked up his pace to almost a canter for he knew he was on his way home. 'Some oats for you if we're back under the hour from now,' promised his master and he pricked his ears back. Margaret had to smile at his bribing of the horse as if he could understand. The road was long and straight, and the surface was good.

'This is a Roman road which is why it's as straight as this, so it means we'll not be too long getting home. There's the sea and that's Allonby Bay.'

To their right now were open fields with horses, cows and sheep, and to their left a sandy flat area leading down to the coast where the sea was a few feet below the land. Margaret breathed deeply of the salt air and looked out again towards Scotland over the choppy white-flecked waves that lapped the sometimes sandy, sometimes stony beach.

'You like the sea do you?'

'I do Mister, but I have not seen it much. I've always thought it would be nice to live in sight of it.'

'Well now you're going to. We are about a mile from it.'

That was a pleasing thought. Soon they passed through the pleasant old fishing village of Allonby itself and she looked at a large porticoed building, wondering what it was. Barwise Little read her thoughts.

'That was a seawater baths. You could go there and bathe for the sake of your health in heated seawater for your comfort. The Quakers built it years ago,' he snorted. 'Best to go down to the sea and go in for nothing if you ask me, but they get folk from all over the place staying at the Ship Inn just there and bathing in sea water. But not at the baths any more for it was not a success and is now a private house belonging to a retired officer. There's the reading room, that big red building. I go there occasionally myself to read the papers when I'm in the mood and they have some books they lend. Mostly I go to Mawbray Reading Room which I was instrumental in setting up. Now smell that!'

Margaret could hardly avoid smelling the air, which reeked of fish.

'Pongs a bit, doesn't it? That's Beeby's fish yard where they gut and salt herring. Make their own barrels too in the Co-operage there. I do like a salted herring, so I quite often get a little firkin in't winter. But spring, summer and autumn Missis gets fresh fish from the boats.' He chuckled. 'I know what you're thinking. It says Costins on the sign and so it is, but the Beebys owned it for years and I still call it that for I am stuck in my ways at my age.'

There were, in confirmation of Allonby's status in fishing circles, numerous boats dragged up onto the beach, and a perfect forest of herring nets drying in the breeze and strung out all along the green grass above the shore.

About a mile past Allonby the land was flat with pasture on both sides of the road, the grass on the left being unfenced down to the sea. Cattle grazed to their right behind fences and a narrow road went inland where was a fingerpost bearing the words Edderside and Tarns. Turning up this lane, Barwise Little told Margaret that they'd be home in under ten minutes, and the horse slowed down to a steady walk. The road rose almost imperceptibly as they journeyed towards some low hills ahead, but though she craned her neck, Margaret could see no sign of a house. Mr Little chuckled, 'Aye, you'll not see it until you're almost on it.'

Sure enough, the road turned left and then began to curl rightwards up a small hill and a roof came into view.

'That's us! Home.'

On the right as they entered the hamlet of Edderside was West End Farm, a long Cumbrian farmhouse with an outbuilding on the end of the house by the gate, and a barn on the other end. It looked solid and well kept. Richard trotted into a large yard on the landward side of the house and Margaret saw that there were outbuildings on the other side of the yard too.

'That's where you'll be living Maggie' said Mr Little, nodding to his left. There was a small two-storey building, the lower floor of which was obviously the dairy. External steps led up to a door and she wondered what she would find as she stepped down from the trap.

The farmhouse door opened as the inhabitants came out to view the new arrival. Foremost among them was the mistress of the house, from whom Margaret would be taking her instructions. As Anne Little approached her Margaret dropped a brief curtsey as she had been taught to.

'Well, I approve of that, and I suppose your mother taught you that you should do it, but we'll have none of that here. Just do as you're told and work hard and I need no bobbing to show me respect. I'm Mrs Little and you are Maggie so I am told. I'll be straight with you, I didn't want a maid at first, but I've grown into the idea. I hope I don't regret it.'

'I hope you won't Missis,' replied Margaret.

'I see he's told you what to call me. That's good. Now these ne'er do wells are my sons. This is Thomas, that's William and that's Joseph.'

'Master Thomas…'

'None of your Masters either if you please. There's one master here, so you'll call them by their given names, as everyone else does. You can call them by other things if they ever employ you. You'll find there's no side on us.'

Barwise interjected, 'Joe, take Richard to his stall and give him a feed of oats which I promised him if he made good time home.'

Joe, who was evidently well experienced with horses, led the big gelding away across the yard.

Mrs Little was short, slightly stocky, and had a happy rounded face under a lace cap. Like her husband she was elderly, and as Margaret later found she was 65 and Mister was 70. She wore a close fitting and stout bodice and a thick pleated skirt of stiff serge. Her manner was firm and there was no doubt as to who was the lady of the house. The sons had much of their father's look to them round the face, but their hair was different. William's was dark, parted in the middle and wavy, whilst on his face was a long and drooping moustache. He was about 27, had a shy air and was the sort of man she thought not at ease with women. Joseph's hair was paler than his brothers' and his moustache did not droop so much, though it was quite thick. He was the eldest son at 34, and his manner was confident and easy. Unmarried like William, he also lived at home, yet had hopes of finding a wife some day. Thomas she judged to be in his late 20s and he did not have much hair at all and though he did have quite a fierce moustache it was his eyes that stood out. Those of his brothers were brown, but Thomas had piercing blue eyes and a certain look to them which she had once seen described perfectly in what her father called 'a penny dreadful' as 'gunfighter eyes.' It was, she recalled, written by a Mr Buntline, a most unlikely name.

'Thomas, take Maggie's heavy bag to her room please and I'll follow and show her where she'll be living.'

Crossing the yard Mrs Little led Margaret to the short flight of stone steps that led up to an old wooden plank door, preceded by Thomas carrying the bag. He opened it and passed inside.

The room Margaret entered was tiny and in it was one item of furniture, which was a very old and well-worn armchair. It had a small open fireplace that was laid, and a candle lamp with a glass chimney. On the floor was a decent rag rug. On a shelf stood a kettle, a cup and an old battered metal teapot. There was also a chipped basin with a large ewer inside it. A small window faced out into the yard.

'That chair belonged to my father-in-law,' said Mrs Little. 'I think he got it at a farm sale in 1848 when he arrived here. Old, but still comfortable.'

Thomas had deposited the bag onto the chair.

'Now in here's where you sleep.'

Mrs Little led through a door into another small chamber in which there was a bed; high up in the wall was a small window. Though rather dark it appeared to be comfortable enough.

'My husband persuaded me to have a maid and I suppose he told you that I did not want a maid in the house?'

'He said it was too crowded Missis.'

'That's correct, but it's not all. I didn't want a maid under my feet all the time in the house. I'm used to having a house with family only it in, so it suits me to have my maid near, but not too near. My daughter's gone off to some fancy job in Carlisle so you'll be doing what she did round the house. You understand me?'

Margaret nodded. She understood very well indeed.

'Your workday starts at six o'clock every morning and it finishes when I tell you to be gone at night and that's usually after you've done the dishes, unless there's something else to do. So this is where you sit and sleep. You can get water from the pump in the dairy under here and there's a tin bath in the lean-to. I expect you to bath once a week and keep clean. Do you read?'

Margaret affirmed that she did indeed read. Then she looked at her bed which appeared comfortable enough and was made up, she was pleased to see, with sheets and pillow case and a patchwork counterpane. Beside it was an ancient chest of drawers and in the corner a small wardrobe into which she could put her few clothes.

'Good. I approve of that in a young person. Here's where you can do it after you've finished work. I suppose you find it a bit small?'

'No, Missis. At home I have to share a room. This is more than I've had and it looks very comfortable.'

'Well, I'm sure you'll soon make it homely. You can have a fire when you need, for I will not stint on warmth for anybody, and there's wood enough for all you might want in the woodshed along the yard. There's an extra blanket in the bottom drawer of the chest. We'll leave you now to unpack. Dinner is at eight o'clock every night and it never varies. Anyone who misses it goes hungry.'

So saying, Anne Little turned and went out through the door, Thomas in front holding out his hand to help his mother down the steps.

Margaret, left to survey her new abode, was well pleased. She had her own little house, and from what she knew, she was very fortunate. No other girl in service that she was aware of had this; Omega certainly did not. She lived in an attic room and was at the beck and call of her master at all hours. Mrs Little was an independent lady who was used to doing for herself and had no intention of letting go of the tiller. She liked to cook and keep house, for that was her role and if it were taken away then she would not like it. However, she was getting on a bit and needed some extra help; that was Margaret. If she were very lucky her workload would be lighter than it had been at home. She unpacked her clothes, set out a few things such as her hairbrush and her few ornaments and began to feel quite at home. Onto the mantelpiece went a small blue vase that her parents had given her on her sixteenth birthday, and a china cat in black and white that she had had since she was a little girl. Going into the bedroom and closing the door behind her, she found a mirror hanging on a piece of wire on a hook behind it. She placed her new alarm clock onto the bedside table, making sure that it was wound, and beside it a scallop shell that her father had picked up on Maryport fish quay; into this she was used to placing at night the tiny gold cross from around her neck that she had inherited from her grandmother.

Just before eight o'clock she went to the back door and knocked; it was opened by William.

'You needn't knock Maggie. You're the maid now and I had to come and answer the door. Maids come and go as they need, so don't knock.'

'Sorry Master William; it won't happen again.'

'You've been told I think. I am not Master William. Just William.'

'It doesn't seem right sir.'

'I'm not sir either. William it is. That's my name.'

'It seems disrespectful somehow.'

'Well it isn't. Respect isn't something you hang a name on like a coat on a peg. Now come into the kitchen.'

West End Farm was no great house. Dinner was served at a solid table in the middle of the red tiled floor. Mister sat at the head of the table and his wife on his right. Down the sides sat William and Joseph on one, and Thomas on the other. The empty place next to him was clearly for her, though the table was amply long for others if needed.

'Maggie - come and give me a hand to strain these vegetables. Now then, when you've done, put this dish on the table.'

For the next few minutes Margaret helped Mrs Little get the food ready, and she placed dishes in front of the seated men. Her duties, it appeared, would be rather like those she had done at home. The daughter of the house had gone to Carlisle to work, and she was taking her place in a practical sort of way. When the steaming dishes of vegetables and another of roast potatoes were on the table, a huge joint of beef had to be taken and put in front of Mister who sharpened a knife on a steel, then cut it thickly before placing it on plates and handing them along. This was a prosperous Cumbrian breeding farm and they did not stint on the food they had earned. Margaret found herself looking at as much meat as she would normally expect to eat in a week and wondered how she could get through it.

Each person at the table loaded what they wished onto their plates and then looked at Mister. Margaret bowed her head, looking slantwise at Mister, but he just nodded and at the nod everyone picked up their knives and forks and began to eat. They did not say grace! That was her first surprise, for although they did go to church on Sundays, the Littles did not make much of religion. It discomfited her somewhat, so before eating she said a little mental grace to herself, and that satisfied her need. Having said that, the rest of the meal was in the same old Cumbrian style as in her own home. There was no conversation and the exchanges between the diners were limited to requests for the salt or the mustard please. There was a loaf of bread on the table and the men had pint glasses of ale to hand. Mrs Little and Margaret had glasses of water.

Just as she had cleaned her plate and found that the others had finished before her, she discovered that something else was different to home. Mrs Little had her up to the range and instructed her to take a pan of hot white sauce and pour it into a jug for the table. Out of the oven she produced a huge jam roly-poly which she divided into dishes. Margaret almost felt despair that she would not be able to eat any more, but somehow she managed to cram it down on top of what she had already consumed. Pudding was not eaten in the Adams' household, nor that of anyone else she knew. The meal itself sufficed. She would have to have a tactful word with Mrs Little, for although her intentions were of the best, if things continued this way, Margaret would get very fat.

At the end of the meal Mister Little gave his instructions for the morning.

'Joe – there's them two colts need breaking, so that's what you're to start in the morning. Tom and Bill in the dairy as usual when Agnes gets in, and get those churns out as soon as you can. Breakfast is when the milk's out. Right. Off you go.'

So saying the master of the house rose and went with his wife into the parlour, there to sit with a bright paraffin light and read his book, she to darn and sew. The three young men rose up and each went their own ways. Thomas in particular took the trap and harnessed his own horse to it, going off somewhere on his own. Before he left, William handed Margaret a candle lanthorn.

'It's dark crossing that yard Maggie. This is for your use so hang onto it.'

That was thoughtful of him she felt, for though it was plain he was shy, he was evidently kindly with it. There was enough light in the kitchen to see what she was doing, and once all was tidied, dishes washed and dried and put away she looked round to see what else was needful. The kitchen was well appointed, but looking in a wall cupboard she found a broom and swept the tile floor clean of mud and bits. The door opened and Mrs Little looked in and nodded.

'Good lass. You'll do well, but that's enough. Go to your room now. It's an early enough start. Goodnight.'

Wishing her mistress goodnight, Margaret went over to her little apartment and found it cold. Lighting the fire as she had been given permission to, she soon warmed it up and by the light of her candle she decided to read for a while. By her bed were a few books she had brought with her and had read before, but that was no bar to reading them again. Picking out 'What Katy Did,' she read until she was tired enough and her brain, suffused with the events of the day, allowed her to go to bed and sleep.

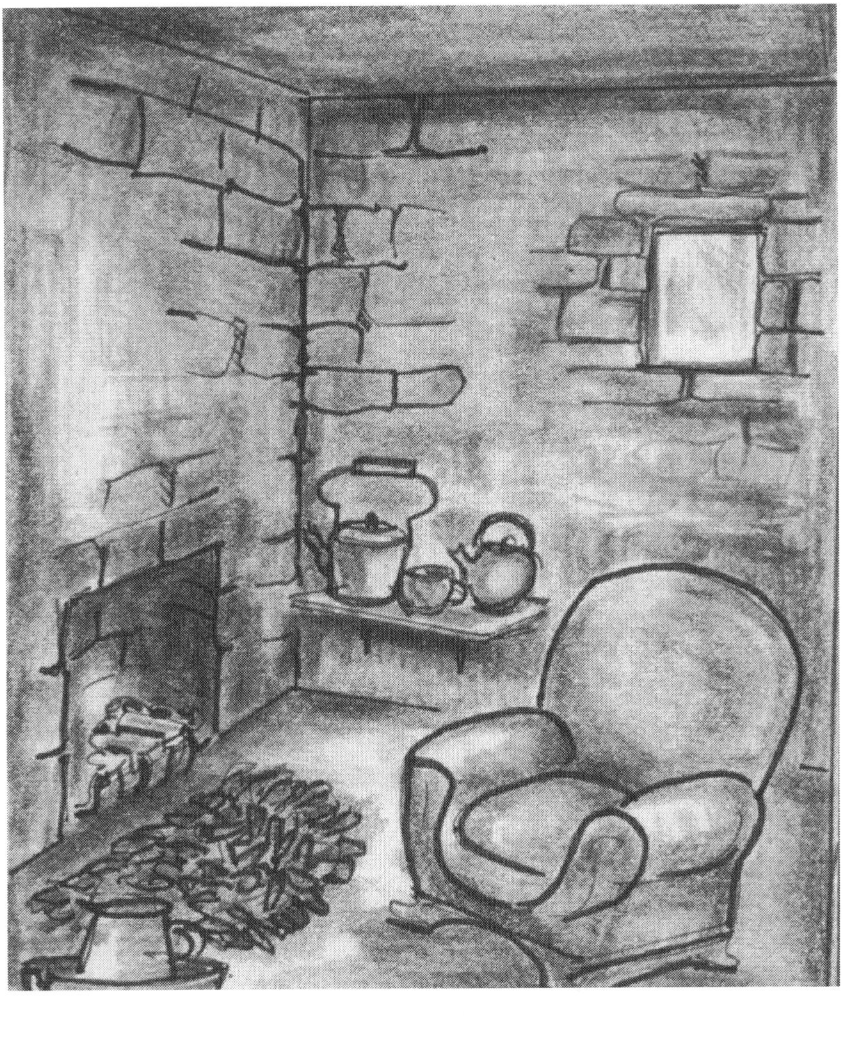

Chapter 7

A Maid of all Work

Although Margaret slept very soundly, her awakening was somewhat rude, and it happened well before her alarm. The cheap double bell alarm in its tin case had a very loud tick, but it had not kept her awake and she trusted it to get her up at the right time. Her father had given it to her just before she left home and cautioned her that she should not expect to keep her employment if she did not keep time well. Since Missis had told her that she started work at six she had set it for 5.30 am, thinking that this was ample time to get herself awake, have a wash and get across the yard to commence her duties in the house. There was a clashing downstairs as of metal banging and a man and a woman were talking cheerily; it was evident that sleep was done with. It was still dark outside and she reached across to find her matches, lit a candle and looked at her clock to find that it was only 4.30 am. Loud mooing sounds told her that the yard was full of cows. Dressing quickly she took her ewer and went downstairs into the dairy in search of water from the pump. Entering this room, where a paraffin lamp now burned brightly, she found Thomas talking with a young woman of about her own age whom she did not know. Seeing her, he looked momentarily surprised, then exclaimed in self-annoyance,

'Of course! I'm sorry Maggie. I forgot that you were upstairs. We've wakened you early.'

Not wishing to offend one of her employer's sons she replied with a lie, 'It doesn't matter sir. I was awake anyway.'

It did not fool him for one minute, though he smiled at her subterfuge.

'Of course it does. You don't start work till six. I should have remembered, and now I've robbed you of some sleep. Well it won't happen again.'

'I'm the new maid sir, and maids do what they're told to do. I'm not unhappy to be up with the lark.'

'I think you're a bit before the lark and anyway, maid or not it's as well for them that employ maids to be considerate of their employees; is it not Aggie?'

The question was directed at the young woman he had been talking to and her reply was affirmative.

'I agree with you Tom. Servants look after masters better if masters look after servants.'

'Well said! Now Maggie, this is Aggie!' and here he laughed at the alliteration. 'Perhaps I had better introduce you properly. Maggie, this is Agnes Shilling, our milkmaid. She lives just up in the village.'

Margaret did as she had been taught for polite introductions and bobbed slightly, 'I'm pleased to meet you Miss Shilling.'

'Ooooh!' was the response to this, and with a broad smile Aggie bobbed back. 'Pleased to meet you Miss......' and tailed off.

'Adams,' said Margaret.

'Miss Adams,' went on Aggie. Then she laughed again and the laugh was rounded, pleasant and full. Margaret decided she liked Aggie.

'Quite seriously Maggie, we do not need to be in here at this time,' said Thomas. 'We only come in here because the new churns and the buckets are in here, but they don't have to be. There's plenty of room in the small barn next door.'

'But isn't this where they should be kept, sir? This is the dairy.'

'Well it is and it isn't if you see what I mean. A few years back when we used to sell our own milk locally this was the place, but now it is not used as much as it was. Not since Mr Carrick opened the big dairy in Aspatria and sends it all south. We get a lot more money than we used to and less trouble selling it round the streets.'

Margaret could see that there was a lot to be learned here, but did not question Thomas, as she felt it was not her place to do so. He was having none of that though and felt the need to explain.

'Agnes uses this as a dairy later on when she takes some of the milk and makes our own cheese and cream and butter, but most of it gets taken away in churns which we put outside. The dray comes from Cumberland Dairies at about nine o'clock in the morning and takes it away, but they leave fresh clean churns to be filled for the evening milking which they collect tonight, and so on you see?'

Margaret nodded and asked, 'What are the buckets for sir?' feeling very daring.

'We milk into them and pour into the churns. They do not go to the dairy and we clean them here. This is where we live Maggie, but it's where we work too. It's a family business. William and I handle cattle and Aggie helps us get the milk.'

'And we'd better get on with it Tom, or Mister will not be happy.'

'That is true, and so we shall. And Maggie, you hear what Aggie called me? That's what you call me. Everyone round here calls me Tom and you were told that yesterday.'

'Yes...Tom,' she managed to drag out.

This amused him no end and he told her, 'That was hard was it not? But you'll get used to it.'

Outside William appeared, 'What's keeping you two? First three's ready!'

'Aye aye – we're coming,' and all three left the dairy heading for the three cows tethered in the byre munching away at hay in front of them.

Left to herself Margaret went back upstairs with her water and finished her ablutions. When she was done, she went over to the back door of the farmhouse and let herself in. There was no one about so she decided to make herself useful anyway. The fire in the range glowed weakly so she raked it out and put the ashes into an ash can standing to the side of it; she would have to discover where to empty it later. When she had put coal onto it she lifted the lid of the inbuilt boiler to find that it was less than half full so she went over to the large square sink and turned the tap to find a weak flow of water with which she filled a jug and topped up the boiler.

'Well I see you believe in keeping yourself busy,' came a voice from the door, and turning she saw Mrs Little standing there in a nightdress and cap.

'Yes Missis, I don't like doing nothing when there's stuff to be done.'

'Well that's very good. Maybe you and I shall get on. I suppose you were woken by the milking?'

Margaret agreed that she had been, and went on to describe her conversation with Tom. His mother nodded and said, 'Yes. A tired out maid is little use to me. And a maid in here before six is something that I do not wish to see. Now don't misread me because I'm not cross, but I heard you downstairs you see.'

Margaret was mortified that on her first morning she had woken up her mistress.

'Oh poppycock girl! I'm only too pleased to see that you're not an idle baggage, but in future mark this. My husband is still snoring in bed where I would be and normally till six o'clock. We're getting on a bit and like our sleep. Joe's still fast asleep and he won't be up till six either, because he's the horse man along with his father. Tom and Bill get up at four because they have to get the cows from the inbye and ready for 4.30. It's all timed you see. Very efficient.'

Margaret nodded. She did not really see how it was so efficient, but understood the routine. In future she would not enter the house until six o'clock.

'Now put that kettle on and make us some tea, for I am parched.'

The next hour passed without work, because Missis did not want Margaret to do anything in the house and disturb the slumbers of her husband and eldest son. Instead she told Margaret a lot about West End Farm, or as she called it 'the family business,' of which she was inordinately proud. The farm consisted of 107 acres of pastoral land, some of it good and some of it marshy. Twenty-four acres of this were for 24 cows. Fifteen acres of it were for ten Clydesdale mares and three of it were for Richard the gelding and two ponies used for transport. The rest was corn and hay. In addition to this was a fairly large garden in by the house containing a number of fruit trees. Margaret was beginning to get the notion that everything here was being run on rather scientific lines and asked if it were so.

'Scientific? Oh yes I should think so. Barwise is great friends with Henry Thompson.'

Here she looked at Margaret's face with a querying look but drew only a blank.

'Good grief girl! He's famous. Well he's our vet for a start and tends to all the beasts if they get ill, but he's one of the Dauntless Three.'

Again seeing no recognition in Margaret's eyes she ploughed on.

'Him and Mr John Twentyman and William Norman set up the Agricultural Co-op and the Agricultural College in Aspatria. The boys all went there. Round here it's all about improving agriculture, getting the most from your land and farming properly. You'll see farming round here that you won't see anywhere else.'

Margaret had to admit that she had not seen much of any farming at all, to which the older woman humphed and told her that she would be seeing a lot of it from now on. The rest of the hour was spent impressing the maid with Mr Thompson's virtues and how he had persuaded Barwise to salt some of his pasture to kill pests and all the other good work he did for the council and the fire brigade, and how he came from Allonby. The last explained her pride in the local vet for Mrs Little herself, as she averred, was born in Allonby and justly regarded the vet as an ornament and a decoration to her birthplace.

Just after six o'clock Mister and Joe came down blearily wanting tea, which Margaret supplied, and then could set about her duties. The first of these involved the emptying of the chamber pots which were set under each bed. The toilet was an earth closet across the yard so the use of pots at night was universal. The pots had to be emptied onto a midden in the corner of the yard, which apparently was occasionally sold as fertilizer to arable farms through the local co-operative society if not used on their own fields. Then they had to be sluiced out and cleaned at the yard pump. This was supplied by the same well that fed the dairy. There was, as she found, a second innovation made possible by the same society, which was to buy the latest farm equipment and machinery and sell it to its members at good prices. The invention that made life easier in this case was a pump in a lean-to adjoining the end of the house, which had a large wheel with a handle that you turned. This was now part of Margaret's duties because it pumped water up from the well into a header tank that supplied the house. From now on, if the tap ran feebly it would be her fault.

With the two remaining men now out attending to horse matters Margaret's job was to assist Missis in the preliminaries for the family breakfast which would happen when the churns were out, and then to commence cleaning various rooms. This was not an activity to be taken lightly. Like all decent housewives and maids of their time Missis and Margaret were quite aware of and in dread of 'germs' and had been since Mr Pasteur and Mr Lister had published their work some years before. Each room had to be dusted and swept, and the furniture had to be moved when the floor was washed with hot water and borax. The beds would be stripped and the mattress removed; the framework of the bed would then also be washed down with the same mixture. Then all must be put back. This process happened in each room once a week in rotation. Rugs would be taken off and beaten outside, which was heavy and strenuous work, whilst carpets received a different treatment. Margaret discovered another benefit of scientific education soon after arriving, when she was instructed to clean the carpet in the parlour. For several days she had been religiously saving all the tealeaves from all the teapots, putting them into a sieve and swilling them through at the pump. The parlour carpet was big and heavy and only came up once a year for the spring cleaning. But it had to be cleaned at least twice a week. Margaret, like the well trained maid she was, went round the room spreading damp tea leaves all across the surface and was just about to commence work rolling them over the whole carpet with a brush when Missis came in.

'Good Heavens girl! You've been taught very old fashioned haven't you? Well it was a good way to do it when I was your age, but we can do better than that.'

So saying she disappeared, returning a few seconds later with a carpet sweeper; Margaret had seen pictures of them in magazines, but it could not have been afforded in her own house. With a silent blessing for Mr Melville Bissell, she moved the cleaner backwards and forwards over the room and soon the carpet was dust free, tea-leaf free and spotless.

Apart from the rolling and endless programme of room cleaning, she helped prepare meals, did the washing up, which Missis detested, dusted generally, swept floors and anything else she was asked to do including Monday laundry and ironing. Missis soon discovered that she was good with a needle and handed her a pile of socks and clothes needing attention.

'My eyes are not as good as they were, but if you've a mind to sit in that corner of an evening after dinner by the range and do a bit of sewing, then you needn't leave the house until you want to.'

The kitchen being comfortable, warm and bright Margaret did not mind at all, so gained admission to the house outside normal working hours.

Mealtimes were not onerous as Missis insisted on doing most of the cooking. It was obviously an important part of her identity and raison d'etre to do this, but as she explained to Margaret very forcefully, 'I employed a maid, not a cook. I'm the cook in this kitchen.' There was an obvious delineation of power in this room and Margaret began to miss exercising her own culinary skills, though Missis did make very good food. Her Yorkshire puddings were a dream, and though Margaret did not ordinarily like tripe, the way Missis fried it with onions and sage was, it had to be admitted, very tasty.

One afternoon Margaret was told to go and get some butter from the dairy and wait if it wasn't ready. She crossed the yard to where Aggie was at work. The dairy maid was pink in the face, cranking away at the handle of a butter churn, and it was obvious that there was no butter to be had yet.

She wants the butter? Well I only finished milking a short while back, so it'll be a while, but I'm done churning.'

Pulling a bung out of the churn she drained out the buttermilk into a jug and put it to one side with a cloth over it.

'She'll want that for cooking.'

Heaving the churn up onto the surface by the sink she upturned it onto the cold marble slab where the contents sat in a wet oozing pile on a large square of cloth. The sink was full of fresh pumped water. Aggie sprinkled some salt over the mass from a metal measure that she had on the side, and took a couple of wooden paddles and cut and mixed the salt into the butter. Satisfied with the mix, as Margaret watched in fascination, she gathered up the corners of the cloth and squeezed the fatty mixture over the sink. Then she dipped the whole into the clean water, still squeezing and in answer to Margaret's questioning look she explained, 'It cools it down and makes it go solid.'

She tipped out the now solid butter onto the bare slab and took her paddles again.

'These are called Scotch hands. They're made of elm and they're good for this work.'

So saying, she patted the butter, slapping it vigorously into a slab, which took a few minutes until it was done to her satisfaction.

'We used to make a lot more of this and Mister would sell it to a shop man in Maryport, but this is just for use in the house and round here. Mister gets me to sell it for a few pennies, but he gets most of his money from Cumberland Dairies now. There now, take that over for Missis.'

So saying she handed a plate with a large pat of butter on it to Margaret.

'Here. Have a taste.' Margaret did so.

'Not too salty?'

'Just right I would say. Very nice indeed.'

The dairy maid's eyes shone; she appreciated having her craft praised. Then she thought a moment.

'I'll tell you what Maggie, afternoon milking starts at three. If you like, you can ask Missis if you can come over and I'll show you how to milk. You never know, it might come in handy some time.'

As Margaret walked across the yard, Tom and Bill appeared outside the gate herding the cows back in for second milking, so she did ask Missis, who decided that it was a good idea.

'After all, if Aggie ever gets ill it might come in handy. Alright Maggie, half an hour and milk the first cow. Then I want you back here to black the range.'

Aggie was already in her byre when Margaret came in where the first of her cows was tethered. Tom and Bill were already hard at work, but the milkmaid said, 'I thought she might let you. You've seen what they're doing. Do you think you can do it?'

Margaret thought that should could so she sat on the little milking stool, placed her hand round the teat on the cow's heavy udder and pulled. Nothing happened except that Aggie smiled. Margaret pulled again, and this time Aggie chuckled. With determination Margaret pulled harder and the cow lowed in protest, at which Aggie roared with laughter.

'Eh you townies! I don't know. Here, get up and I'll show you how.'

Margaret, feeling slightly humiliated rose up and noticed that Tom was looking at her through the slats into the next byre. His eyes were twinkling with amusement and she noticed that they were just like his father's. She went pink and felt four inches tall; observing this he composed his features into a poker face and looked away, studiously attending to his own cow.

'Now watch. First of all you have to wash it down with warm water which I've already done. Then stroke the udder. If you ever watch a calf go for milk they nuzzle and stroke first, and this brings the milk down. That's what we call it. She's got to be relaxed or nothing comes.'

Ever willing to learn Margaret watched with attention.

'Now you take the teat between thumb and forefinger and clamp it between them. It doesn't hurt them at all, then just squeeze. See? Now you try.'

A squirt of milk shot out of the teat and into the bucket. Sitting at the cow again Margaret did as she was told, clamped and squeezed and a jet of milk resulted to her great delight. She had learned a new skill.

'Now just keep doing it,' said Aggie. 'You soon get into a rhythm. Use both hands on different teats.'

After a few minutes Margaret's hands were beginning to ache and Aggie took over.

'It takes about half an hour to do the full milk, but when you first start you do get achy hands. You get used to it after a while. Anyway you know how to do it now.'

Tom was looking at her again, but this time she did not mind. She had learned how to do it, so she looked back without any abashment and simply smiled, to which he responded, 'Well done,' and got on with his work.

For most days, although her duties varied, the routine of the farm did not. Tom and Bill were up by four each morning to bring the cows in for morning milking. Twenty-four cows had to be milked by three people between 4.20 am and some time between 8.30 am and 9.00 am. Each cow took about thirty minutes and with turn around time they were lucky if they finished and had the churns out on the platform by the gate by nine. The dray from Aspatria would pass on its round, collect the churns and leave fresh at about 9.30.

Afternoon milking started at three and the process was complete by about 7.30 to start again in the morning. There was then time to clean things up in time for dinner at eight o'clock. Milking regulated the running of the farm and provided much of its income from the sale of an average of ten gallons that each cow provided per milking. In this way West End Farm provided the butter, milk, cream and curds for the industrial towns of Northern England, courtesy of Mr Thomas Carrick and his Cumberland Dairy Company, or more directly through Mr Stephenson, his manager in Aspatria.

Breakfast was eaten by the family when the morning milking was done. Mister and Missis always had bacon, eggs from their own hens, and bread, with tea. Their sons preferred porridge, and though Missis insisted on cooking her own bacon and eggs, porridge was delegated to Margaret and pronounced good. She herself had a small bowl of porridge, determined that her waistband would not expand because of the huge evening meals.

Lunch was not a meal in the Little household. The men all went off with a 'bait box' just as her father did to work. In the tin box the diet never varied. There was a hunk of bread and butter, a chunk of cheese and an apple. Each man carried a white enamel tea billy filled with cold sweet tea and they ate wherever they were.

The evening meal was always substantial and Margaret had to sit at the bottom of the table and eat with the family. This also was not unusual for Barwise Little was much in the mould of the old Cumbrian Statesman farmer and in his establishment master and servant took their meals together. It was not long before she got accustomed to being with this family, for they were friendly and used her as an employee, not a mere skivvy. She may work for them, but she always felt that she was respected, as indeed they seemed to respect all people. It was two months after her arrival that an event occurred which was to change her life forever, though at the time she did not realize it.

Between the morning and afternoon milkings was a period of five to six hours where the men got on with the other work of the farm, and there was a lot of it. They were never idle and she thought them a hard working lot and was happy to work well for them in return. It is surely easier to graft for people with a strong work ethic than for sloths. The day was warm and the windows were open to let out the heat, but of course the kitchen range had to be kept going. Without it there would be no cooking. Margaret raked out the grate and found that the ash bucket was full. Seeing that she must, she heaved it up in her left hand and set out towards the ash heap behind one of the byres to dump it where it would be most useful. Occasionally the men would take ash to fill in and firm up field entrances that had grown muddy from use; it could also be mixed with the night soil for fertilizer if desired. She had just tipped the bucket when her ear registered a noise round the corner in a small holding pen. Her curiosity roused she put the bucket down, walked round the corner and for a moment wished she had not.

A cow was lying on its side on the floor panting and in some distress. Tom was lying on the floor behind it pulling hard on two ropes, sweating and getting nowhere by the look of it. With a slight fascination she saw that two small hooves were protruding out of the cow's rear end. He looked up at her, urgent and peremptory.

'Don't just stand there! Grab this rope and pull like blazes.'

There was no time to think about it. She kneeled down, took the rope in both hands and pulled.

'It's stuck and there's no time to get the vet. I think it's a breech birth, but it's got to come out. It'll be born dead though. Now heave!'

Obeying the command she heaved and slipped over, finding herself lying side by side with Tom, yet never loosing her hold, and pulling with might and main. If she thought about it she might have felt sick, but it had all happened so quickly.

Suddenly the calf came out and it came fast in a flood of water, slime and blood. It lay for a moment, then its eyes opened.

'It's alive!' she said.

'It is that,' and Tom wiped the muzzle of the new born calf with a wisp of straw. 'Now just hold on Gertie.'

So saying he reached his arm into the birth canal and felt about before pulling a mass of what looked like bloody jelly onto the floor.

'Afterbirth. It's got to come out. Dogs'll have it.' As he spoke one of the farmyard dogs did come along, grabbed the mess and ran off with it.

Gertie the cow looked round at her new born calf and shakily got to her feet, her ordeal over. She nuzzled it and began to lick it as Tom asked Margaret,

'Have you ever done that before?'

'No. I haven't.'

'Never been at a birth?'

'I was there when my youngest sister was born.'

'Well you've learned something today. Are you alright?'

'I am now. I felt a bit sick at first, but I'm fine thank you.'

'Well it's not strictly in your duties is it Maggie, but you did well. Thank you for your help,' and he held out his reeking hand covered in dung, slime and blood. For a moment she hesitated, then realized that her own hand was exactly the same and shook his as his eyes wrinkled in appreciation. He had, she realised, very nice eyes. They had done this thing together and new life had come into the world because of it and they sealed their experience with blood. Somewhere a small spark glowed.

'I'll tell Mister about it and he'll be pleased.'

Because of this Margaret was pleased, and she had reason. She was not just a maid, but had contributed substantially to the work of the farm. A calf was valuable property and she had helped to save this one. Her status had advanced in the household, but as yet she did not realize quite how much.

Chapter 8

A Co-operative Colliery

Time lay heavy over Dearham in the summer of 1894 and for John Adams as much as anyone else. He and Bill Gannon were now counting their pennies and filling time until the decision would be made about the Cross How pit. The proximity of his house to the workings at Townhead however were to prove most useful, as he passed the site of the reopened colliery every time he went to Dearham. Because of this, he had a fortunate meeting outside the gate of Townhead with Jack Brown who accosted him one morning,

'John Adams! I haven't seen you in a while. How are you?'

John having made the requisite response, his eyes glanced over to what was happening on site where he could see a new horse gin had been built and was waiting to be put into place by the numerous Browns who were putting their savings into this venture. Above the shaft of the old mine he could see a stout set of three sheer legs with a large pulley and a thick rope disappearing downwards. Over the other side of the site was a partly renovated wooden shed, from which came the sound of a small steam engine.

'Aye, as you can see we're doing it the old way but the pump's good. We had it second hand from Lowca Engineering. They were glad enough to sell it to us from Dearham Pit instead of carting it all the way past Workington. They had trouble with water back in the '20's so we just used their old pump shaft over there. The sump was deep enough I can tell you!'

John nodded in understanding that the old workings would of course have been flooded out. He observed the steady flow of water out of the pipe that led from the shed down towards the Row Beck.

'Now then John, I can understand that you wouldn't want to come in with a small pit for a regular job, but there's some work if you're interested? It'll be a few days, maybe ten, and I'd pay you well because I know you're a good underground man.'

'I thought your family were going to do all the work to start with.'

'Most of it yes, but getting the pit going again will be quicker if we pay for some extra help at the outset. We've got a few pounds in reserve, but we need to start earning and we cannot cut coal yet. The place is dangerous, John. Most of the wood's rotting from the damp and we need to replace it. You've a good eye I think.'

John had to agree that he did. At the age of 44 he had been working underground for 30 years and knew his way round.

'Post and lid?'

'That's right John. No need for footblocks either for it's firm underfoot. You'll have to notch the timber yourself.'

'It would be quicker work with a marra.'

'You have someone in mind?'

'Bill Gannon.'

'He's a good man. Five bob a day each?'

'Six and you have two men.'

The two men shook on their deal then Jack continued,

'The shaft is 70 feet and we are working at that level on the metal band seam. There's enough room for six stents. There's a slope down to the crow seam but we'll not be working that yet. So we'll need the help with the first level. After that, when we get to make a profit we can take on some permanent men. Start tomorrow?'

John's homeward walk was happy, for he and Bill at least had some work to help tide them over. It was not a full-time employment, but at least he would not be kicking his heels doing nothing. A man had to feel useful, especially at the age of 44 when he still felt at the height of his powers. The work would be hard and strenuous, but he had been used to that all his life.

For the next ten days he and Bill turned up at the pit every morning to join the Browns in their work to bring it into production. They were a most engaged and industrious family of uncles, nephews, brothers and sons all working beyond normal hours to build sheds, ramps, placing the gin, manning the hoist and bringing into being a working colliery where had once only been an abandoned shaft. As John and Bill set to work by the light of Davy lamps, other Browns were laying a timber roadway for the trucks, placing spruce rails into the heart of the workings and using a gauge carefully to keep them exactly a bogey's length apart. The spruce was unwaxed, and would rot in two to three years, but they knew that capital costs were a consideration, and once the mine started to pay its way they could be replaced. Each prop that John and Bill used had to be heaved along the main tunnel which was four feet high and about the same wide, from the foot of the shaft where it had been let down on a roped platform from the sheer legs on the surface. Once the gin was finished it would be simpler, but there would be a couple of days to pass before that happened. Eventually trucks and heavy loads could be placed in a proper cage and a strong horse walking round the gin would be able to raise and lower larger quantities. Then, instead of heaving timbers they would be able to roll it through on a truck.

When the timbers reached where they were needed, Bill Gannon attacked them with a hatchet that had been honed as sharp as an adze, whilst John took a collier's pick to prepare a small hole to sit them in. By the time John had finished his post holes, one on each side of the tunnel, Bill had cut a semi circular nock in the top of each post. Then they took a heavy semi-circular timber and placed the flat of it on the roof, lugging the end of the props round under it to hold it in place. Then John used the flat side of his pick to hammer it home until the roof timber was firmly wedged in against the props on both sides. The next set would be done three feet further and so on until the tunnel was adjudged to be safe.

In such labour the days dragged no more, and the month turned to June before they were done. By 8 June their casual work was finished and the Browns needed them no more. The first coal was trundled out along the wooden rails and the first truck was hoisted up on the gin. With a production of thirty tons a day the Brown family reckoned to sell it locally and each morning their wagons trundled off laden with coal sacks to customers they had secured in outlying villages, in Maryport and in Cockermouth. John was content and glad of the work, so when he was paid off he took his money with a smile and wished them luck. He hoped that they would do well, but he also hoped that tomorrow would bring better news for his own future and that of his family.

When he awoke next morning his day started with an unusual event, for the postman delivered a letter from Margaret as he sat having his tea at breakfast. There is a certain pleasure in opening personal letters, and especially from one of your children, but this was no missive to be read quietly, as a round of inquisitive eyes circling the table told him. With a smile at his family he took the letter from the halfpenny stamped envelope, opened the folded paper and began to read aloud,

'Dear Father and Mother, Thomas and Johnny and Alpha,
I hope this finds you all well and in the pink as ever. I just thought I would send you a few lines to let you know how I am and that I am happy and well. It is a good place here because although the work is long hours, it's very like what I used to do at home, only more of it. Mr Little is as nice as you thought he was Mother, and is kind to me though he is very firm with his sons. I have not met his daughter Annie yet, as she works away from home, but Mrs Little is also very welcoming and glad of the help, though she does not let me cook.'

'Doesn't let her cook! Well they don't know what they're missing.'

John looked at his wife patiently, then continued reading.

'I am in the house most of the day for six days a week, but my favourite day is Sunday. After breakfast the family all go the church at Holme St Cuthbert though they don't call it that. Everyone round here calls it 'Rowks' but I don't know why. Tom

thinks it might be something to do with rooks. We all get onto a large cart with seats on it, and Richard the big horse pulls us while Tom drives. I think Richard knows the way there and back though.'

'Who's Tom?' asked Thomas.

'Someone who there's too many of!' retorted his mother, 'Common as muck are Thomases. Now do be quiet or too many Thomases will confuse me.'

'You will be pleased to know that it's a church rather like at home, only not as old, so I am able to take communion and say my prayers just as I ever did. The Vicar is Mr Bardsley and he preaches well, and is almost as interesting as Mr Melrose. After church we come back to the farm for bread and cheese and tea, then I am free to do as I wish until six in the evening when I must return to my duties. I wish it was not such a fiddle to get home and back in the time allowed, but we are four miles from Aspatria and by the time I got home it would be about time to go back again, so what I like to do is go to the sea and walk along the beach if the weather is nice. There's a path across from the farm to Allonby that is only a couple of miles, though I have to be a bit careful. It crosses some marshes and there's two plank bridges over streams which can be slippery. Tom told me that on one of them the owner of Edderside Hall just up the road had a fall a few years ago and died of it. That is a bit worrying I can tell you because I am never sure if I believe in ghosts or not, but I always try to get back while it's light. When the way is too muddy I prefer the road though it's a bit longer.'

'Hm, I remember reading about that,' said John, 'The poor man fell off the bridge into water and mud and was there all night hanging on until they found him.'

'Oh do go on Father,' said Johnny.

'Agnes is the milkmaid here and she and I go together for she also is free on Sundays. Last Sunday we went there and it was a fine and lovely day with a lot to be seen. It's quite a fashionable place there Mother and you should see it for the ladies as they are

all silks and shawls, flounces, ribbons, laces and such hats as you never saw. You cannot just walk along the beach when you reach the village because it is divided into areas for ladies and gentlemen and they have bathing machines for both. Agnes told me that this is necessary for some of the older gentlemen still bathe in the old way and that stretch of beach is patrolled by a man warning folk away.'

John and Nancy looked at each other with slightly raised eyebrows. Neither of them had bathed in the sea, but the old way of bathing meant stark naked, and though it was dying out in favour of bathing costumes for both sexes, they were not sure that they approved.

'The ladies however are most respectable and wear a costume called 'The Allonby' which is quite becoming I think, though I do not expect I shall be sea-bathing. There are many Quakers here who live in the village or visit the Meeting House, and some of them built a very large reading room which is open on Sundays because they take the religious papers. I go in there to read the Christian Herald just like at home Father! It's quite interesting as well because the Keeper's son, Mr Kitchen, has a collection of animals which he has stuffed in there and some are very curious. Sometimes Agnes and I have an ice cream if it is very hot, though I know what you are thinking Father. These are not served in penny licks, which I agree are very unhygienic, but come in a small pastry cup served by a man who has a little trolley by the iron bridge in Allonby. He says that he makes all his ice cream himself and keeps it cool with a large block of ice which he said he bought at Silloth and which comes all the way from Norway! We also like to look in the window of Mr Heskett's shop where he does display some very nice shoes, but we cannot afford them. Mr Bookless's drapers shop interests me too, because he sells very lightweight dress material which is not too expensive and I think I shall get some for next summer. Mr Bookless is quite a sportsman and knows Tom well.'

'This Tom is mentioned a few times.'

'Well, he must be an interesting man. Shall I continue?'

The family indicated that he should.

'When it is not nice weather on Sunday afternoons I simply stay in my room and read. They have a small selection of books at the reading room in Allonby and I am able to borrow from there as it is open on Sundays. At this time I am reading 'Three Men in a Boat' by a Mr Jerome K Jerome, an odd name, though the book is quite amusing. Mrs Little has said that I may stay on here when my half-year is done as I am quite satisfactory, in her own words. I am glad of that because it saves me having to do another hiring fair, but it means that I shall not be able to come home until after Christmas, for she will need me here. She says that she will be able to spare me to come home briefly after Christmas as her daughter is visiting. I shall look forward to seeing you then, and hope that Ommie is home at the same time as me. Your loving daughter, Margaret sends all of you a kiss.'

'She's happy and she's got herself a good place. That's what counts and though it would have been nice to see her at this table on Christmas Day, she's well looked after. If she is content then so must we be.'

There were a few glum looks from Thomas, Johnny and Alpha that they would not be seeing very much of their big sister at Christmas, but they understood that she had entered the great and mysterious adult world of 'work' and there was no help for it.

'So,' said John, rubbing his hands, 'We shall make the best of things and especially of today. I have high hopes of today my children, so pray for what your father's thoughts are fixed on at the meeting this afternoon in Maryport. It's open to the public so I am going to attend.'

His most sanguine expectations were realized for the meeting of the Maryport Co-operative Industrial Society was populated with rather enthusiastic people whose imaginations had evidently been fired by the possibilities offered by the proposed colliery. They agreed that the Committee would make a recommendation to members and that a ballot would be held on the matter. John watched the face of Mr Melrose across the room and saw gladness, though it seemed tempered somewhat. The reason for this soon became apparent. The recommendation was proposed and carried, that the society should invest £1,000 in the Crosshow venture, that is £200 in shares and £800 as a loan. It would not however be a wholly co-operative scheme but a limited company. The Committee had been in contact with and had attended the County Coal Committee that consisted of representatives from other co-operative Societies across Cumberland, but they had not managed to secure any offers of help from them. This meant that any more capital would have to be raised by the issue of shares, and that depended very much on whether or not people would buy them. There was something of a hush in the room as Mr Heslop rose to speak. The mining engineer was well-known to many of them and respected as a man well grounded in his profession.

'As you know, I was asked to conduct a study into the viability of the Crosshow pit and you've listened to the committee give their support to it. They have of course read my report in some detail and it is available for any member to see who wishes to peruse it at their leisure. However, I will set out my findings very briefly to you now, so that you may see the reason behind their recommendation.'

He paused and the atmosphere in the room grew expectant.

'The Crosshow colliery was abandoned some years ago as the previous owners ran out of capital at a time when there was a slump in the price of coal on the market. This was largely due to an increase in competition from American mines. I need hardly mention that demand for coal has increased in recent years, and particularly for good quality steam coal that commands a higher price than almost any other type. I have examined the workings as far as I was able to and have consulted with records and known geological surveys, and I have come to the conclusion that the Crosshow mine is likely to prove productive and could yield 75,000 tons per annum.'

There was no doubt that he had their attention now as the hush deepened.

'Now I expect that many if not most of you will be wondering how that translates into hard cash…'

Nods and murmurs of agreement heralded his continuing.

'I think it reasonable to expect a profit of four pence a ton. That is a median figure and it could rise or fall, but on a conservative calculation I think that realistic; I see some of you nod. That would bring in £1,250; if we subtract say £350 for depreciation costs which are unavoidable then we are left with £900 a year, which is a considerable amount of money.'

Again he paused for the note of sound round the room was not as excited as before.

'I see that some of you are disappointed and I can understand that. You must understand that we cannot expect to employ all 260 men from the Lonsdale Pit at once, indeed if ever. The output may increase and that would enable the owners to employ more men, but until we know the geology better, then we cannot determine how big the workforce will be. I emphasise again that my figures are conservative, but if you find it more encouraging I do believe that if all goes well, the mine should employ perhaps eighty men by next year, and over a hundred the year after that. The scale of the endeavour will depend much on how much we can persuade people to invest and what we find in the geology. Failing financial help from other societies, we must find sufficient funds from elsewhere if we are to make a success of this business.'

Once again the air in the room had turned interested, for if he was offering not a whole cake, it was at least a cake.

'There is also the question of the brickworks which I have recommended be part of the same arrangement. It is my understanding, and my examination of the clay bears it out, that the bricks produced are exceptionally good and that there is always a demand for them. The works should yield £400 a year and that is a venture most definitely to be recommended.'

A voice came from the floor asking the very pertinent question, 'But there's virtually no profit there. By the time you've paid the wages there's probably nothing left. What's in it for the Co-op?'

Mr Melrose immediately rose and asked if he could be permitted to answer the question, which the Chairman allowed.

'The answer to that question may be found in two words, namely 'customers' and 'gratitude.' The whole principle of co-operativism is that we are stronger together, that by joint endeavours we improve the lot of all. This is firmly rooted in Christian teachings, but in this case it pays off in hard profit. I think I can safely speak for the community of which I am a member, that if the Co-operative does this wonderful thing, engaging dozens of men in gainful employment, then they will know where to buy their goods. You will not find us wanting when it comes to spending what is earned, and the Co-op's gain will come from a solid, grateful and loyal customer base. That must be assured profit.'

'Hear hear!' sounded from several places in the room and a ripple of applause broke out. A period of open discussion broke out but the tenor of it was in no doubt. The Maryport Co-operative Industrial Society would support its customers in their new venture, and the customers would in turn support the Co-op. When the discussion was finished, the Chairman expounded what was hoped to be achieved in the absence of the hoped for investment from the other Co-ops.

'Our investment is but a start to this idea. Under our auspices and drawing on the considerable business acumen within our own ranks, we propose the formation of a Limited Liability Company that will raise a capital sum of £8,000 in accumulated preference shares of £1 each. These will not necessarily pay shareholders annually, but release an accumulated dividend of 6% when possible, which is a handsome return I think you'll agree. An additional bonus for investors is that we do not think we shall have to call on them to pay more than 17 shillings and 6 pence in the pound to buy their shares. I propose that we vote by show of hands now as to whether or not we put this to the members of the society in a ballot.'

The motion was carried with no dissenters at all, and over the next few days 2,900 ballot papers were sent out to members of the society and the proposals set out on a double-sided sheet of paper enclosed with them. Votes could be placed into sealed boxes at the society's five shops in Maryport, Cockermouth, Flimby, Dearham and Crosby. When, after two weeks, the voting closed and the ayes and noes were counted, it was found that 398 members were against the proposal and 673 were in favour out of the 1,071 who had voted. In the meantime, a second engineer, the aptly named Mr Drain, had been commissioned to prepare a fuller report on the proposed mine so that the prospectus to potential investors could be accurate. His findings were even more sanguine than those of Mr Heslop. He identified six seams of coal that could be worked within the pit which could provide three and a half million tons of coal to be won. The return he set was bigger too, based on eight pence a ton and 50,000 tons per annum and an overall clear profit of £1,666. This would of course support a larger workforce, and he agreed with Mr Heslop that the brick works would also give a handsome profit.

Events now moved very quickly and in the latter days of June the Committee set up a Board of Directors to run the new company. One of the new directors was a particularly fortunate choice as Mr William Hine was a partners in Hine Brothers, a shipping company operating out of Maryport and whose steamers would provide a ready market for Dearham coal. There was one ex-miner on the Board, Mr John Kirkbride, but that was it for mining expertise, though they were a group very experienced in business and the law.

Not unnaturally, the Board wished to get work going in the colliery as soon as possible, so at the beginning of July a process began in which John Adams and his fellow hewers played little part. A gang of engineers led by Robert Steel, the newly appointed manager, descended on the site of the old Crosshow colliery and set about the rigging of new winding gear, cage, and an array of sheds and offices, whilst platelayers began to renovate the rails that joined the colliery yards to the mainline railway. There being no need as yet to sink a new shaft, and the bottom being at only twenty fathoms, the work went apace. This was assisted greatly by the sides of the shaft being found to be firm and sound. At this level was the yard band of good steam coal and although the 'old men' had worked much of it out, there was enough to commence work, and by late August the first hewers and their marras were being taken on and descending to work in a new rigged cage. There were not too many of them to start with because the lower levels were inundated and it become apparent very quickly that two things were needful, the first being new pumps. The second was that the existing shaft was not wide enough for the amount of production envisaged, so a new one would have to be sunk further along the workings. It was even more important that the mine become productive.

John Adams, Bill Gannon and many other men from the old Lonsdale Pit now found themselves back at their accustomed work, and many of them suffered from it. They had been laid off for several months without their usual daily strenuous activity and it paid them back with stiff and sore muscles, a couple of bad backs and a lot of puffing. John and Bill's having kept their bodies at work in the Townhead allowed them to work on a full shift and hew as much as they were able. Their being paid on a good rate once again allowed them to take their own efficient pace and each shift they could turn out about six tons of good coal. The Browns with ten underground workers were shifting about thirty tons a day so the coal from the Crosshow was competitive.

Life down the Dib resumed its normal pace and money was no longer short. Dearham in the late summer of 1894 began to assume a more cheerful aspect as families who had been thinking of moving on decided to stay put since it was known there would be more jobs in the village soon. Many men were able to make ends meet more easily by travelling round a wide area of country and working as casual labourers on the harvest, which was a good one. By far the most popular man in the village, even though half the population was Methodist, was the Vicar. His habit of holding a service each year for the Cumbrian Cyclists Association, once thought of as rather an eccentricity, was now viewed with affectionate indulgence. Reverend Melrose welcomed several dozen of them as they flooded into the village on all sizes and shapes of machines, and they gathered outside the perimeter of the settlement where they were met by the Church of England brass band. The villagers turned out to see them and gawp at the penny-farthings, the ancient bone-shakers and tricycles that trundled along Church Street and were propped up along the churchyard wall. It was quite stirring to see them wobbling along following the band marching through playing good Christian airs like 'Onward Christian Soldiers' and 'Fight the Good Fight' for the Reverend was a muscular Christian who believed in the virtues of hard work and sport. Himself a keen cyclist who was often seen with his wife and children trundling off for a ride in the lanes out towards the mountains, he had no objection at all to packing his church with *velocipedistes* in strange garb. The band played the cyclists into the church with hymns from Ancient and Modern and they filled up the pews along with the normal congregation whilst many cyclists took up places in the choir. Mr Melrose preached a very good sermon on physical recreation in relation to spiritual life and a most rousing version of 'All Glory Laud and Honour to thee Redeemer King' ended the service. As the congregation filed out of the Church after the service it became evident that many in the village had decided to join the celebrations as a mark of thanks, for a large throng stood in the churchyard, and as the Vicar came to the door his appearance was greeted with applause and a most enthusiastic singing of 'For he's a jolly good fellow,' which he deprecated in vain, for when it was over they gave him three cheers and a tiger. He stood vaguely blushing as they made the welkin ring with 'Huzzah, Huzzah, Huzzah' then the roar of the 'Tiger' almost blew his hat off. He was then invited to sit in a chair which four stalwart miners took on their shoulders and carried him in state down to the Mission Hall just outside the gates where he and his wife had laid on tea and biscuits for the band and the cyclists. Thus the village assured their Vicar of their goodwill, across their denominations and cemented him in their affections. It was well deserved for what had been done in terms of industry and saving dozens of livelihoods, was little short of heroic.

The year wore on and the weather grew colder, but work at the Crosshow colliery continued and fresh planning forged ahead. The Board of Directors saw no merit in delay and had decided that very early in the New Year they would sink a new and wider shaft to open up a more direct access to the unworked parts of the seams in the old mine. It was now urgent that they do this for they had to spend capital on new and more powerful pumps which, even though second hand, had cost them £450. Though the payment of a dividend to shareholders in the following year could be delayed, it would be far better if the coal output could be increased quickly. They fixed the day for the cutting of the first sod of the new shaft at Tuesday 15 January 1895 and to her great delight they asked the Vicar's wife to cut it and name the colliery. Mrs Melrose accepted the honour with much alacrity and pleasure.

To John Adams walking home towards the end of the year, life felt satisfactory. He had work, assured income and his family was provided for, but it was most annoying in a man of his years to have to chase his hat that was blown off his head as he walked down towards Janet Bridge. The wind was getting up, and though he caught his hat, as he returned down the Dib it was getting stronger. That night, 23 December, was, to his mind no way to begin the celebration of Christmas. Within the hour he was glad that his house was down in a dip because a mighty roaring sound commenced, heralding the arrival of one of the worst storms in living memory. Slates and tiles flew off roofs across the village and people stayed indoors as the fury of nature raged around them. In Maryport, exposed to the sea, an old man was blown into the harbour and drowned and another would have shared his fate if bystanders had not pulled him out. The houses next to the sea were flooded and in one of the streets a large sea trout was picked up and taken home for dinner, though it may be imagined that it did not enjoy the experience. A dozen boats were damaged, whilst every boat in the Elizabeth Dock broke their moorings and banged about so much that the fishing fleet suffered enormous damage. One collier was smashed to pieces and two others rendered unseaworthy, whilst all up and down the coast were visitations of death, damage and disaster. Hunkered down in their cosy cottage John, Nancy and their children along with Bill Gannon thought themselves lucky and played cards and dominoes on the kitchen table. As he went to bed that night John said his prayers as usual and then special ones for his daughters, not so far away, that they would be sensible enough to stay in, that they would be safe and that the angry rage outside would pass over leaving them unscathed.

Chapter 9

A Change of Attitude

Margaret was busy at this time, cosy and snug in the kitchen at West End Farm and cooking to her heart's content alongside Mrs Little, whose prohibitions on anyone else displaying culinary prowess in her kitchen had evaporated, but only in favour of Margaret, because she was special. The wind blew fiercely, but the farm was sheltered from most of the blast by the mound that partially hid it from the west. She and Missis had forged a new relationship that she could not have foreseen when she first arrived at Edderside. This circumstance had come about because of a series of events in late October. To be precise it had commenced on 21 October in Church where Missis had taken herself to sit next to a particular friend of hers called Mrs Longcake. They did not see each other too often and chatted before and after the service. The rest of the family were in a pew across the aisle so were well away from Mrs Longcake's snuffles, for it seemed that she had a heavy cold. A few days later Missis and Margaret were engaged in the bottling of fruit with a wide range of screw-top Kilner jars spread across the top of the table. Margaret's particular job was to use a heavy pair of cast iron sugar nips to snip chunks off a large fourteen pound sugar loaf. These chunks had then to be placed into a mortar and pounded down until fine enough to meet Missis' satisfaction. Missis also found it useful for Margaret to remove the stones from small mountains of greengages and plums from the trees in the garden. It was a relief that they had not had the picking of these for Mister had decided to take on a sixteen year old lad from the village as an extra farmhand, and one of Nick Osborn's first tasks was to strip the trees, which he did by climbing round them like a small monkey with a bag over his shoulders. There were literally buckets of fruits to be treated and they had started the previous day when the washing had been finished. Large kettles of fruit had been boiled in the copper with sugar and water until nearly tender then left to stand. The stones had to be blanched separately, then today the fruit had to be boiled and the stones added for ten minutes. At the end of this the stones and scum had to be skimmed off the top and discarded. The fruit could then be ladled into one pound jars and syrup poured after it. When cold, the glass lids were pressed down to the exclusion of air and there was a jar of preserved fruit to last the year. The Little household would use it all and it was stored in an outbuilding in a very sound cupboard, for they all loved sweet things. They especially liked jam, but Missis did not make it as it was very heavy on the use of sugar and therefore expensive. She bottled all the fruit she could get her hands on, including blackberries and was more than happy to send Nick out 'blackiting' round the hedges of the field.

The various processes involved were long and laborious and they were nowhere near finished when Missis straightened up with a low moan and passed her hand across her forehead.

'What's up Missis?' asked Margaret with some anxiety because such a display in the older woman was unknown to her.

'Oh I do feel strange Maggie. I feel awful,' came the reply in a weak voice. 'I've got pains in my legs and I feel sick and my head hurts.'

'Oh no!' thought Margaret, 'I know what this is.'

'Shall I fetch Mister?'

Receiving an affirmative response Margaret hurried out to a barn where Mister was sawing at a piece of timber and told him Missis was ill. Within seconds of seeing his wife he was at the door bawling, 'Tom get on that nag of yours and get Dr Coulthard. Never mind the trap; ride him, he's fast enough.'

A few minutes later Tom had saddled the farm pony whom he called Marra, and was on his way out of the yard on his way to Aspatria at a smart trot. Margaret thought he looked rather dashing as he turned right to go through the hamlet. William and Joseph also appeared, but Mister told them to get their mother up to bed then get back to the milking because there was nothing more they could do and work still had to be finished. Tom returned about an hour and a half later leading the doctor in his two-wheeled gig who examined his patient thoroughly. When he had finished he came downstairs and spoke to Mister as Margaret looked on.

'Well Mr Little, she's got acute pain in back and loins, she's dizzy and feels like vomiting so she'll need a basin by the bed. She's also got a frontal headache, pain in the eyes and she's starting to shiver. To my mind there is no doubt that she's got the 'flu.''

Mister looked dismayed, but the doctor cut across him.

'Now look, I don't think you have too much to worry about, though your wife is not a young woman. We've had a lot of trouble with 'flu' this last few years as you know, but there's not so much of it about this year and I'm happy to say that the strain is mild. I don't think that we are looking at a serious illness and Mrs Little should be well again in a couple of weeks.'

'Is there any medicine I can buy Doctor?'

'I'm afraid not. But there are certain things that must be done if you've got any space to do it. She must be separated from the rest of the household and if she spits then it must be into disinfectant. Keep her well away from other people and give her bed rest and warmth with lots of hot drinks when she can take them. There's some would advise two grains of quinine every morning to lessen the effects, but to my mind it has little or no effect, so as your doctor I do not advise it unless you want to throw money away. All I have to charge you is five shillings for the visit, the diagnosis and the advice; repeat visits will be four shillings, but there's nothing more I can do, so I advise you to save your money because I think she will recover well.'

Thanking the doctor and paying him out of pocket Mister returned thoughtfully to the kitchen and looked at Margaret.

'Can you cope with this lass?'

'I think I can Mister. In fact, I know I can but I do have a suggestion. You need to separate Missis from the family or you're all going to get it.'

'Aye that's true enough and it would not be good for business if we did.'

'Do you think Missis would agree to sleeping in my bed?'

'What you mean sleep over the yard?'

'Yes. It's warm and comfortable in there and I can look after her.'

'Where would you sleep?'

'On a shakey-down on the floor in my little sitting room. That way I could look after her at night.'

'But you might catch it too!'

'Well that's true Mister, but I'm not scared of 'flu.' I've had it before and I once had a little sister Nancy who died of it in 1889. The doctor said this is milder than that and I helped my mother nurse my brothers and other sisters through it.'

Mister thought about this for a moment then said slowly, 'It sounds like a good idea, though I would not have asked it.'

'It is a good idea Mister, though the drawback is that I'd fall behind with my cleaning work.'

'Pshaw! I don't care a whit about that Maggie. No, lass, if you are prepared to do it then I think you are a ministering angel. Now what do you need?'

'Well first of all you'd better talk to Missis, though my advice would be to stay clear of her at the moment.'

A few minutes later, Missis having seen the sense of the suggestion, Margaret sped across to her small lodgings and prepared them to receive a patient. Within the hour she was helping Missis, wrapped heavily in a large quilt, across the yard, up the steps and into her own bed. There she gave her a hot cup of cocoa, placed a stone bottle full of hot water in the bed, 'To make you sweat,' and brought a scuttle of coal from the main house to augment the logs she usually burned in her own fireplace. Missis was soon asleep and Margaret saw that it was safe to leave her.

Back in the kitchen she finished the bottling of the fruit that had been started and then looked at the buckets of fruit in buckets.

'Nick!' The boy came across the yard and she told him to take the buckets across to the dairy where he was to cover them with sacking. The fruit had not been stoned so it would keep like that for a while. Then she set to again, because the family would be coming in from work and would need dinner. Time was short and they would have to take what she could make quickly. When she had done and dinner was in the oven, she went back to sit with Missis who was slumbering away quite peacefully for the moment, but was running a very high fever.

At eight o'clock the men sat round the table and Margaret set in front of them a huge metal tray, its contents steaming from the oven.

'Tattiepot!' exclaimed Mister.

'I'm sorry Mister. I know you like meat and two veg, but I had to do something quick that I could just put in the oven and leave. I didn't want to be running back and forth doing basting and roasting vegetables.'

'Don't apologise, lass. I love a good tattiepot, but Missis is not fond of it. Mind you, the smell of that one I think she might change her mind.'

Margaret smiled, 'That's as may be, but by your leave I shall take a plate first and feed her.'

'Isn't she asleep?'

'Yes but I'll wake her to eat. She has to keep her strength up.'

'Well take yours with you so you'll get it hot.'

'Right Mister, I will. There's a tapioca pudding in that pan with the lid, and for those that want it, there's fresh fruit preserves in that dish.'

Seeing the family fed, Margaret took her meal and a plate for Missis over the yard, woke her patient and coaxed her to eat,

127

though she was very unwilling and complained of feeling sick. That night she did not get much sleep because Missis was coughing a lot, spitting into a disinfectant bowl and when she blew her nose it bled which caused her alarm. She also complained of pain in her midriff so Margaret kept a hot kettle beside the fire to replenish the stone bottle, the heat seeming to comfort her. Eventually she drifted off to sleep so Margaret managed to get some rest.

Over the next few days she was rushed off her feet, but she coped in her usual level-headed way. She was helped by the fact that Missis generally went shopping just once a week in Aspatria and patronized delivery services who were well used to her custom. Thus, the baker called every day with six loaves, as this was eaten at every meal and the butcher called every other day, selling fresh meat to be kept in a marble slabbed cupboard. Twice a week a fish seller came from Allonby, and fruit and vegetables were largely, though not entirely, supplied from the farm garden. Missis did not bother growing potatoes though, because the area was dotted with arable farms and Mister simply bought a few sacks of potatoes when they were needed, from his neighbours. There were items of course that had to come from shops in Allonby, Mawbray or Aspatria such as cocoa powder, good flour, chocolate, cigarettes and tobacco, and for this Missis took one of her boys to the Co-operative. She drove herself and the accompanying son was for carrying heavy things or for company. Fortunately her stores were well stocked and Margaret did not need to go shopping. There was one thing that made her spirits soar, however, for she was mistress of the kitchen now and there was none to gainsay her. High up on a shelf was a copy of Mrs Beeton's *Book of Household Management*, which did not seem to have had much use. Reaching up high she took it down and opened it up, her eye brightening as she read; here was food for a serious mind. Mister's remarks had more or less implied that he did not mind a change of diet in the present circumstances so she decided to experiment a little. She knew that he was fond of salt fish, which Missis made for him occasionally, boiled with potatoes and beans so she made a mild beginning and served it the following night with egg sauce. Steaks stuffed with forcemeat, haricot mutton, particularly fine Irish stew and pork pies in her own pastry followed in this order. It was food that was English enough for their taste, different to their usual plain fare, and delicious enough to make them want more. It was notable that the quantity on their plates was sufficient and the consumption of bread fell, until she served a wonderful fluffy bread pudding, lightly spiced and laced with currants, soused with custard. It was apparent to them all that they had a good cook within their midst whose talents they had not been using.

Missis evidently felt this too for she much appreciated what she was being fed, and when she was not in the kitchen Margaret spent all her time either upstairs or downstairs at the dairy. Anne Little was worried about all the fruit that had been picked and thought it would spoil before it could be bottled, but Margaret handled that problem by bottling it in the dairy, stoking up the fire under the mostly disused copper to provide the heat she needed. All Missis had to do if she wanted something was bang on the floor with a stick that Margaret gave her, and she would be at the door, wiping her hands on her apron, making tea, plying a chamber pot and helping her mistress to perform all the intimate actions necessary for cleanliness as she lay in bed. Once a day she took a flannel, a bucket of warm water and sponged the older woman down to make her feel fresh after another day of fever and sweating. She asked William, Joe and Tom to find reading matter and they scoured the neighbourhood farms to borrow books and magazines that Margaret could read to the sick woman. They came to see their mother, but were not allowed past the bedroom door; Mister would come and sit on the step just outside the door and talk to her in the evening when work was done, reading to her from his paper, but was not allowed in. The days went by and the house grew dusty, though the men did not seem to mind. It was plain that when Missis was recovered there would have to be some catching up to do.

Six days after her virtual collapse Missis was sitting up in bed and obviously on the mend though she felt weak and debilitated. She was also feeling very sorry for herself and was inclined to be weepy, but Margaret was having none of it.

'No, Missis. You mustn't get up yet. I know that 'flu' can take ten days to clear and you still might spread it to the rest of the family.'

'Well you haven't got it, so why should they?'

'I don't know why I haven't got it. Maybe its because I've had it before, but it doesn't mean they won't. If they get it then this place will shut down, so you really must just rest where you are for a bit longer.'

The moaning and grumbling continued for a few minutes and then finally she wailed,

'But I'm bored out of my mind!'

'Well you've got books, a magazine and a cup of tea right there by the bed. Some people would give their eye-teeth to be comfortable like you are when they're ill. Now please pull yourself together, because I can't be doing with folk feeling sorry for themselves.'

There was stunned silence and Missis looked at her with complete surprise.

'I never thought a maid would talk to me like that.'

'Well I'm sorry, but I work for a strong woman who knows her own mind, not some wet week who spends her time moaning.'

Again there was silence and a strange light entered Missis' eyes.

'Barwise was right about you. He said you had character.' She paused for a long half minute and it was evident that the gears in her head whirred. 'Alright. I suppose I needed that. Now I'm going to read one of these books. You can be about your work.'

It was actually too late in the day to start cleaning rooms and just a little too early to commence preparations for dinner, but

Margaret wanted out of the sick bay, as she now thought of her apartment. She went down the stairs wondering if she would find herself sacked without a character after talking to Missis like that, and she noticed that Aggie was still in the dairy and making fresh butter.

'I thought you'd have gone home by now, but I'm glad you haven't.'

'Oh I was just going to finish this and be off. Need someone to talk to do you?'

Margaret told her briefly what had happened and what she feared might be the result.

'I shouldn't worry about that if I were you. Missis is a good sort and you were right. She said she needed it so I reckon you did right. You'll have to wait and see. Anyway, the men will not wish to see you go will they?'

'Why do you say that?'

'Well from what I hear they've been fed champion this last week or so and you know what they say about men and their stomachs!'

'Oh I don't think cooking ever won any man's heart, not really.'

'You might be surprised Margaret. I read in the paper a couple of years back that there's almost a million women in this country more than there are men. You know what that means.'

'Well not quite....'

'Oh you are slow sometimes. That means there's almost a million women in Britain that will never find a husband. I hear there's a lot of women going to Canada and Australia where there's a shortage of women, so that they never become old maids.'

'Yes but what's all that got to do with cooking.'

'If a woman's a good cook then it's another string to her bow isn't it? And you're not bad looking. Maybe even one of the lads here might look at you.'

Margaret snorted. 'A serving girl! Anyway now that you bring it up, why are none of them married? Three great healthy men and none of them have ever married.'

'I used to think that too, but I can see why and it's not so hard if you think about it. They're tied to the routine of this farm and hardly get any time off. They don't meet many women except local ones and most of them are married. There's one of them I wouldn't say no to.'

Margaret giggled at the unexpected confidence.

'Which one?'

'Well Joe of course!'

'What? But he's nigh on 20 years older than you.'

'Fifteen! I don't care about that. He's a manly man and he smells nice. He's also fit and strong. You should see him throwing sheaves about when they bring the hay in. He takes his shirt off and he has muscles galore. There's a few lasses round here wouldn't say no.'

'Are you doing anything about it?'

'I've made a few encouraging noises, but he's not really attuned into it. I think I shall try harder soon, because I'm fed up living at home.'

Margaret's mind whirled that the bubbly Agnes was enamoured of the taciturn Joe; it was very illuminating.

'What about William?'

'Oh William,' said the dairymaid with a slight smile, 'He's not a ladies man Maggie. You can forget that. He's very shy around girls and I have the idea that he'll never marry. I'll grant you he's nice to look at, but he is so awkward and just does not want a girl. Born to stay a bachelor I think.'

'What about Tom? I don't get that feeling about him and he's 30. Why is he not married?'

'Have you noticed what Tom does after dinner every other night?'

'Well, yes. He goes off in the trap with Marra.'

'Have you ever heard him come back?'

'No, I'm always asleep.'

'He comes back after eleven and nearer twelve from Mawbray.'

'What is he doing in Mawbray at that time of night?'

'Wasting his money on beer, singing, telling jokes and having a good time with a bunch of his friends down there. He likes a drink does Tom, and it's a good job Marra knows his way home, because Tom sleeps in the wagon and wakes when Marra drives into the barn.'

'But what's that to do with not being married?'

'It's to do with why he started drinking. At first he drank to forget, but now he just likes to drink.'

'What was he trying to forget?'

'You might well ask. There was a girl called Dolly Jefferson who lived up near Silloth. Well, I don't mind telling you that when Tom was twenty he was head over heels in love with her. He wanted to marry her and offer his all to her. She gave him the impression that she returned his feelings.'

Here Agnes sighed in a rather exaggerated way and Margaret thought that she had been reading too many stories, but enjoyed it as a parody.

'Why did they not marry then?'

'Now this may seem funny to you, but I don't think it is. She led him right to it and he got down on his knee and she turned him down. Tom was losing his hair then and that baggage told him straight to his face that she could never ever marry a bald man for she had a horror of them. She did not know how any girl could. I'd like to slap her stupid face for that, so I stay clear of her.'

'But that's only one girl. Did he not find others?'

'I think he carried a torch for a while, even when she went and married a sailor up in Silloth, but she damaged him.'

'What do you mean damaged?'

'Well he's as bald as a coot and he's got the idea into his head that no self-respecting girl would look at him. I'm very fond of

Tom and I'd like to tell him different, but it's hardly my place is it? Nasty cow!'

Margaret liked Tom and now she felt sorry for him. From what she had seen he was a very good and decent man and she felt that he had deserved better from one of her sex. Men, she thought, were so fragile that they could be hurt by a shallow flippertigibbet with feathers for brains. Still, it was not her business.

She did not receive notice for talking back to Missis and in fact the invalid was soon back on her feet and in her kitchen. However, her attitude had changed and Margaret, so it seemed, could do no wrong. Her family had reported very favourably on the food that they had been eating, so Mrs Beeton did not go back on the high shelf, but stayed down on a shelf near the sink. They began to cook together, looking for innovative recipes and dishes to try, and enjoying the joint experimentation. Soused pigs cheeks did not meet with universal approval, though pig's trotter did. Joseph was set to shoot some rabbits which were hung, then served stewed with bacon and herbs. Variety came into meals that had once been tasty though routine, and the process was enjoyed by everyone. Margaret's status had gone up several notches and Missis was now very willing to tell anyone who would listen that Maggie was a good lass - a good lass - a repeated phrase that became a habit.

The new found confidence in her maid allowed Missis to leave Margaret alone to get on with tasks in the afternoon whilst she formed a habit of visiting her sister more often. Missis' sister was Phoebe Sharp who lived in Edderside Hall, which was about 300 yards down the road. Despite the proximity Missis did not walk but always took the trap because, as she told Margaret she did not wish to get muck on her skirt to visit Mrs Sharp. Margaret was much amused by Missis always referring to her sister in this way but she found that Mrs Sharp always called her 'Mrs Little' back. Despite the apparent formality Phoebe Roper and Ann Roper, now in their married state and very fond of each other, were much upon their dignity as to their status. The advent of a maid upon whom Missis could rely meant that they could take tea with each other more often than before.

Having had sickness in the house it was of course necessary to make sure that the routine cleaning of the rooms with borax was continued as soon as possible so these duties recommenced. Margaret was in Tom's room one day, having just completed the cleaning when she noticed the pictures. She had seen them often enough, but had never looked at them closely; that she did so now might have told her, had she realized that it was because she was more interested in Tom than she had been, but they caught her attention and she was looking at them when he came in the door.

'Oh Maggie. I didn't know you were in here.'

'I've just finished Tom and was just looking at your pictures. I'll be on my way now.'

'I don't mind you looking at them. Here, let me show you. That's me at school, second from the right. Silly hats we had and a daft way to pose really.'

'Why were you kneeling like that? It looks rather uncomfortable.'

'Well the teacher told us to, but I do look a bit strangled by my jacket, don't I?'

Margaret laughed and agreed that he did rather.

'That was in Aspatria. Now these I did the year I left.'

'A thatched cottage dated 1880. It's very good.'

'This was a static exercise in class.'

He showed her some drawings of gothic arches, old pumps, a steam whistle and a sketch of the agricultural college at Aspatria.

'These are really very good. Do you still do your art?'

'No not at all. I have no time for it.'

'Well it's a shame I think. It looks to me as if you should be an artist.'

'I'm a farmer. I probably always will be.'

'Maybe Tom, maybe but we can't tell can we?'

There was something nice about Tom. That he was a good son she knew. She felt for him that his love had been turned away brutally, and she had seen in him a gentle artist that he hid very well from people outside. Maybe one day he'd get over Dolly Jefferson and meet a nice girl instead.

Tom now looked thoughtful and after a small hesitation asked her, 'Do you have any plans for Sunday afternoon?'

'I have made none. Why?'

'Well it strikes me that it might be a good idea if you learned to drive a pony and trap, you know, so you could go errands if Missis wanted you to.'

'Oh! Well that sounds a good idea, but a bit scary.'

'Ha, there's nothing to it. Alright. That's settled then. I'll tell my Mam, and we'll get it done. Marra's an easy horse to get used to so it'll be him. We'll go up the coast to Silloth, I'll show you how, and you can probably do most of the driving. How's that?'

With a certain trepidation Margaret agreed. It was something that she had never thought to do, but a skill she would not mind learning. Sunday afternoon was something to look forward to. The day before, however, was to provide something of interest all of its own. It was just after one o'clock and Margaret had almost finished her bread and butter, when there was a knock on the kitchen door from someone in the yard.

'Oh get that will you Maggie? Probably the fish man.'

It was not the fish man. When Margaret opened the door she was confronted by an apparition that had stepped back from the door and stood poised and ready with a fiddle under his chin. To describe him as tatty would have been an understatement; from his baggy grey trousers over stout and lumpy clogs, to his voluminous and greasy jacket, marked with the remnants of ancient meals, he was the perfect tramp. An old and well-stuffed Gladstone bag, very dirty and scuffed hung on a stout cord round his neck. His beard was long, grey and knotted, while the visible face was brown and wrinkled with beetling brows, long iron coloured hair and an old brimmed hat surmounting the whole. It was rather fitting that her impression was that he smelled slightly as she imagined a fox would, for bright and very blue eyes smiled at her as he began to play '*John Peel*' and jigged up and down as he played and sang. Margaret did not know quite what to make of him, but Missis pushed past her.

'It's Jimmy Dyer. I have not seen you for a long time; well let's hear you play.'

Then she jigged up and down in obvious enjoyment of the music and as Margaret realized that this was no threat or intruder, she smiled and did the same. Live music was something she enjoyed but did not hear very often. Missis and she joined in the last chorus;

'For the sound of his horn brought me from my bed
And the cry of his hounds which he oftimes led,
For Peel's view halloo would awaken the dead,
Or a fox from his lair in the morning.'

When the minstrel had finished he swept his hat from his head and bowed low.

'Madam I give you good day. It is a pleasure to behold your face again and that of your lovely daughter.'

'This isn't my daughter, Jimmy. Maggie works for me, but give us *The Horn of the Hunter* and you shall have your bait.'

The Cumberland Bard did not immediately play, but looked at Margaret and broke into verse.

'Margaret are you grieving?
Over Edderside unleaving
Leaves like the thing of man, you
With your fresh thoughts care for, can you?
Ah! As the heart grows older
It will come to such sights colder
Bye and bye, nor spare a sigh

Though worlds of wanwood leafmeal lie.
And yet you will weep, know why
Now no matter, child, the name;
Sorrow's springs are the same.
Nor mouth had, no nor mind expressed
What heart heard of, ghost guessed;
It is the blight man was born for,
It is Margaret you mourn for.'

Not unnaturally, Margaret was somewhat taken aback by this and asked worriedly, 'Why whatever do you mean? What does he mean Missis? I'm not grieving for anything.'

'Never mind his nonsense Maggie. It's just his way. He likes to bamboozle people, don't you, you old trickster? Did you write that one?'

'Ah now, there you have me Missis. I have to confess that I did not. It was a man called Hopkins who I think as good a wordsmith as myself. However, if it's verses you have a mind to I can sell you plenty of my own.'

Here he opened the large bag round his neck which was stuffed with hundreds of scraps of paper bearing his own rhymes.

'Not today thank you, but I have a mind to hear my tune if you will.'

'Gracious lady, your wish is my command. Faint I am with hunger and in need of sustenance.'

'Better get on with it then I think!'

He nodded and poised his fiddle as the men came out of the side buildings in the yard with Aggie from the dairy, and he played *The Horn of the Hunter* in which all joined,

'For forty long years have we known him,
Cumberland yeomen of old.
And twice forty years shall have perished
Ere the fame of his deeds shall grow cold.
No broadcloth of scarlet adorned him

No buckskin as white as the snow
Of plain Skiddaw gray was his garment.
And he wore it for work, not for show.'
Etc.

'By, it's a long time since I sang that last and I enjoyed it. Well done Jimmy, and here's for your trouble.'

Mister fished in his pocket and brought out sixpence that was graciously accepted.

'I'd like to hear more but it's a working day. So back to your work you lot. Give the man some bait Missis and good day to you, Mr Dyer.'

'Let me have your can, Jimmy.'

Obediently the wandering minstrel fished in a capacious pocket and pulled out a large enamel container such as her own men folk used and she took it into the kitchen. A couple of minutes later she returned with half a loaf, a large chunk of cheese and the can.

'Don't tell Mister, she said softly.'

'Missis, you have a kind heart, and a man should never tell a tale when he's given good ale. I wish you all joy, and I'll be on my way.'

So saying, he departed leaving Margaret staring at his back as he went off down the road to find a nice patch of grass on which to have his bait. Missis evidently had a soft spot for the needy.

'Don't just stand there Maggie. Back to work. I've known Jimmy Dyer these last thirty years or more. Normally he wanders around the Carlisle area, but he comes round this way two or three times a year and he'll always get some snap from me as long as he can liven my day with a tune. He's a natural, one of God's good creatures and I don't grudge him a crumb.'

Margaret was liking this woman more and more, and glad that she worked here, having as she thought, fallen on her feet. And tomorrow she was going to drive a pony and trap. Certainly life at West End Farm was proving to have a certain variety.

That evening, as she sat in her little room above the dairy, she was knitting by the light of her candle, a task she did not need much illumination for as she was well practised at it. The wool was soft and grey, purchased in Dearham before she left home in May. Ever a practical girl, she knew that she wished to make her father a present for Christmas, and his scarf was slowly growing under her moving hands. Her Christmas gift list was not exhaustive. For her mother she wanted to buy some lace handkerchieves; Omega would have a hand-sewn sachet filled with dried lavender that she intended to buy at a small shop in Mawbray; Tom, who read a lot, would have a bookmarker that she was embroidering. For Johnny she intended to buy a wind-up toy that she had no doubt he would love, and for Alpha there would be red ribbons for her hair and dress. Aggie, for whom she was developing an increasing fondness, would also have a coloured ribbon for her blonde locks. There would be some home-made fudge and apples for all to share, but those would be sorted out just before Christmas.

To a knock on her door, that made her start a little, she said, 'Come in,' and stood up. It was Mister, who entered and stood a moment before speaking.

I've come to give you your wages, Maggie, it being the half-year in about a week since you joined us. I'm doing this now because I'd need a week or so to replace you if you had decided not to stay on. Martinmas hiring is coming up at Aspatria, you see.'

Momentarily, she was taken aback by the implication. Then replied, not without a certain anxiety, 'Would you like me to stay on, Mister?'

'Would I like you to stay on? Would I like you to stay on?' He moved forward and took her hand.

'Lass, I'm that pleased with the bargain that I made last May in getting you here, that I cannot tell you. Not only are you a good help to Missis, but you nursed her through her illness and coped with everything in your stride. I know quality when I see it. Of course I want you to stay on. Will you?'

He peered at her rather anxiously, and his habitual twinkle was absent, replaced by a worry obviously felt deeply.

'Of course I will, Mister. I really like it here. I could not wish for a better place.'

'I'm glad of that. It's settled then. Now to the matter of your wages. I have been to the bank and obtained five pounds in crowns and half-crowns. I hope you don't mind, but there's many shops do not like to have to change large coins and I thought you would find it more convenient than five sovereigns.'

'I would, Mister. I was wondering about that, and I prefer smaller amounts. It's a lot easier.'

'That's what I thought. There you are then. You can count it if you like.'

She smiled and replied, 'I trust you, Mister. Thank you.'

'And thank you, Lass. I'm glad you're staying, right glad.'

With that, he stuck out his hand and she took it and they shook solemnly. Then he turned and went out of the door.

'Good night, Maggie.'

'Good night, Mister.'

When he was gone, she did count the money. Laid out in piles of coins on the table in front of her it looked an enormous amount, riches indeed. She had money to spend that she had earned. It made her feel independent, good in herself, and somehow empowered. She had more money than she had ever had in her life and was staying where she would earn more; she must send some of it home. True, it was a maid's wages and objectively she knew it was not a fortune, but that did not detract one iota from her satisfaction and pleasure. The thought crept into her mind that she must obtain a lockable box to put her money in. It was perhaps understandable that she smiled and gave herself a little hug. Life at West End Farm was good and getting better.

Chapter 10

Margaret Learns to Drive

The following day was bright and sunny though a little chill. This was not so unusual, as it was late November by now and the countryside was damp with leaves falling russet and gold all over the roads and hedges. By the time the family came back from Rowks and church the day had warmed up rather. It did not take long to have lunch that, on a Sunday, included cold cuts and pickles.

It was not too long before Tom brought up the subject of their ride.

'Now then Maggie, if I'm to show you how to do this thing we'd best be off. I still have to get back to evening milking.'

'What thing is this Tom? It's Maggie's afternoon off.'

'I know, Mam, but you remember I offered to show her how to drive the trap.'

'Oh yes, that's a good idea I thought. If she's any good at it she can drive me to Aspatria on Wednesday when I go to the shops.'

Outside in the yard Tom led the big grey pony, Marra, out of the stable and Margaret saw that he already had leather harness on him,

'I did him just before lunch to save time. It doesn't take long.'

As he spoke he backed Marra between the shafts of a large trap, a thing which the horse was very inclined to do, and he laughed,

'Aye Marra likes a bit of a run and he knows he's going out, don't you boy?' So saying, he rubbed the horse's nose affectionately. Tom was kind to animals, and Margaret thought that was a nice thing.

'You won't have to do this ever I think, but these are his traces and that's the breast collar. I attach the shaft on this side with these breeching straps both sides, and at these saddle tugs.'

As he talked he tightened straps and explained, but Margaret knew she would never remember it all.

'This is the backstrap and that's the crupper. See the reins run up through the forked neck piece to the throatlatch there and the bit there…'

He looked at her and saw a mazed look in her eyes, and grinned,

'Alright. I'll shut up with that, but you might learn it in the long run. All you need to know right now is that the reins are not caught anywhere and they are free so you can let him know what you want him to do. Now hop up onto the seat and I'll drive us down to the coast road and along a bit.'

So saying, he touched his whip to Marra's rear, 'Walk on,' and they walked out of the yard and turned left.

'You'll notice that I'm on the right, because the brake's on this side. It's not a lot of use when you're going along, but when you're stopped he would not be able to start off very easily. I also hold the reins very loosely because they are connected to his mouth and there's no need to pull hard on them. His mouth is very delicate and I have no wish to hurt my horses. There is a bit of slack on these reins and I don't want to get tangled in them, so I usually sit on them.'

As the road straightened up he touched Marra again, 'Step up!' and the walk increased to a trot. 'Now he's doing about eight miles an hour, or maybe ten and that's fast enough for what we want to do.'

Down the road they went and as they approached the junction with the coast road Tom pulled on both reins gently and said, 'Slow,' and Marra slowed down to round the corner heading north. Then he stopped.

'Right Maggie, change sides now because this is where you drive. Sit on the slack as I did; now take the reins, gently now.

The hard work is sitting like this all the time for it strains your back a bit to be sat upright, but that's how you guide the horse. Mind you the road is long and straight. If you want him to turn then you give a gentle pull on the side you want him to go. I'll do the commands for now and you can do them later. Are you ready?'

On Margaret's hesitant, 'Yes,' which might have been between gritted teeth, he touched Marra's rear again and told him to walk. She found herself holding the reins as Marra walked along at a steady three miles an hour.

'He's a good boy, but I know he wants to go faster. He's also got sense and eyes so if at any point you want to go faster then we can give it a go.'

'Not just yet, thank you,' said Margaret, for whom the horse was going quite fast enough.

Tom smiled and leaned back as the trap went steadily towards Silloth. Other traffic came towards them, but Margaret had been warned that the trap was wider than the horse and she should keep well to the left; she hardly needed to because Marra seemed to know what distance to keep.

'I've never been to Silloth.'

'Have you not? Well I think you'll like it. A very pleasant place. Now remember, if you need to turn him the softest of pulls will do it.'

Margaret's confidence was growing as Marra walked steadily towards Silloth.

'Shall I make him go faster?'

'If you feel happy about it then do. I can tell he wants to. He's not impatient, but he does like a trot when he's out. But a trot is enough.'

'How do we make him trot?'

'Just touch him on the rear end with the whip and say, 'Trot'. He knows what it means.'

'I saw his ears twitch when you said it.'

'Yes, but you need to touch and say it loud.'

Margaret touched Marra's bottom with the end of the whip and said, 'Trot,' and he quickened his pace to a brisk pace.

'Oh! How fast are we going now?'

'About ten miles an hour now. He does like to shift a bit. We'll be in Silloth soon.'

It really was quite exhilarating, though she did not have to do much, as Marra plainly knew his way. The air was clear and not as cold as it had been in the morning; at this pace it cut through her shawl and made her shiver.

'I should have thought of that. Hang on.'

Tom had noticed. He reached down behind his seat and pulled out an old plaid blanket.

'Mam uses this when she drives out and it's cold.'

Then he reached round and gently put the rug round her shoulders and she immediately felt the benefit of it. He smelled, as did all the men she knew, of sweat and tobacco, but his particular odour was faint, that of a clean man, and intermingled with it were strong notes of horse, leather and equine liniment. The road was flat and very straight; on her left was the Solway Firth and over the water, getting nearer were the hills in Southern Scotland, a far off place that she wished to visit.

'One day I'm going there.' She nodded at the distant humps.

'Why there particularly?'

'Because I can see them, yet I've never been. I know that curiosity killed the cat, but I simply have to see what it's like over there. It's a small ambition. A dream if you like.'

'Well then you must do it! Not today though. We have to be back for milking.'

At that she smiled. All hung on the milking.

'What a long beach it is! I never realized how much of it there was.'

'Well that's why people come to Silloth from all over. Very fashionable is Silloth for taking the waters. They get folk from Scotland and all over the north and there's all sorts there. I'm surprised you've never been up here. It's not that far.'

145

'My dad's a coalminer, Tom. We can't afford holidays, or travel.'

He flushed a little, 'I'm sorry Maggie. I forgot....'

'You forgot that I'm a servant? Well I am. There's plenty of people can't afford to go away. That's just the way things are. I'm here to learn how to drive a horse.'

She saw that he was looking a little uncomfortable and softened a little. 'I'm not your equal Tom, but thank you for thinking of me that way. I appreciate it, but I have a place to keep.'

'We're not so different in our stations in life I think.'

'That's as may be. But I am a maid in your parents' house.'

'That doesn't stop us being friends.'

'Yes it does. It doesn't stop us being friendly, but you can't be friends with your servants Tom. You might end up having to dismiss them. It's not a good basis for friendship.'

He looked at her thoughtfully, then said, 'Well that's how it shall be then.'

'Fair enough Master. Now shall we get to Silloth?'

'Don't call me Master! You know that.' He grinned. 'Silloth it is.'

The rough sea grassland, on either side of the road was replaced by cultivated fields, and it was apparent that they were approaching a settlement of some size.

'Is this Silloth?'

He laughed at her excited tone.

'No this is Blitterlees. Soon now though.'

Just a few minutes later the iron rims of the wheels began to clatter over granite cobblestones as they bowled along past handsome villas towards the town ahead where a pointed spire marked the probable centre. As they did so, Marra seemed to know to slow down. Tom appeared quite relaxed and was content to loll back in his seat pointing out the sights to be seen.

'Now this is Criffel Street and that's Christ Church and this nice green park on the left is Silloth Green. Finest turf in the world they say.'

'It's a funny thing - it reminds me a bit of Maryport, but I couldn't say why.'

'Oh, that's not so funny. They are both planned towns; both started as a little village and they were deliberately built as modern towns for different purposes. Maryport was for the exporting of coal.'

'And this one?'

'Now then. This one's a bit different. Mainly it was built as a seaside town for Carlisle and other places so people could get to the beach by the railway. But it was also built as a port. They've got a nice little harbour here and you can get boats to Liverpool, Ireland, the Isle of Man and across to Scotland. There's even one that calls down the coast to Maryport. It's quite a successful place this.'

It looked prosperous. Even at this time of year, large hotels, had no shortage of guests apparently. On this sunny afternoon in late November there were plenty of fashionably dressed people promenading up and down. On the pavement boards advertised various attractions that were on offer with dances, pierrots on the pier and Christy minstrels. There were little shops selling cheap and gaudy goods, toffee apples and seaside rock. The trees bordering the park were not very big and it was obviously quite new. Margaret pulled gently on both of Marra's reins and he came to a stop, waiting further developments.

'They mounded the park when it was made in the '60s partly to shelter the town from the sea breezes. If you look up there you can see the Pagoda. Lovely views from up there and a promenade.'

Margaret saw bed of shrubs and other places where flowers would be in season. This was especially so along the edge of Criffel Street where oval beds promised a riot of colour and which she resolved that she must see when the summer came. Her eyes twinkled with amusement as a clown came long the street leading a donkey on which was a dwarf, also dressed as a clown. Behind them came another clown holding a banner advertising a variety show on the pier that evening at 7.30 pm. She would be getting dinner ready at West End Farm.

'There's salt water baths there in the Green, or if you've got the inclination and the money, you can change there and be taken to the sea by carriage if you please, milady.'

That made her laugh. It was hard to keep a line between her and Tom. She decided that he was a bit like a friendly puppy and hard to say no to.

'Over there they've got lawn tennis grounds and a big putting green. No expense spared to get people here you see.'

Just then a mighty muffled explosion shook the air in the distance.

'Whatever is that?'

'Ha! That's the Battery out at Blitterlees Bank. They test guns out there. Seems a bit odd to have it next to a seaside resort, but they've been doing it a few years now. It doesn't seem to put the visitors off.'

'Should we not be getting back now Tom?'

'Yes I think so. Just touch Marra, for there's nothing coming either way and the street's wide enough for him. Now a gentle pull on the right rein and tell him to walk.'

Margaret turned the pony and felt that she was really quite in charge of him. She drove him all the way back to Edderside with no problems at all and as they turned into the yard she felt that she could hardly wait to do it again. Missis came to the door and called out, 'How did she do?'

'Very well I thought. She drove most of the way there and all the way back with no bother.'

'Well I'm glad of it. In that case she can drive me to Aspatria and back on Wednesday. There's no point in taking one of you from your work when I've a big strong lass to help me.'

So that was her motive in agreeing that Tom should teach her how to drive the trap. Well it suited Margaret, for driving to Aspatria and back would be a welcome break from her routine which had eased a little bit of late. To her great surprise, shortly after Missis had recovered from 'flu', Margaret had gone her morning round to empty the chamber pots and found them all done, except that of Mister and Missis. At first she wondered why this might be so, but when it happened three mornings in succession she could no longer contain herself and asked Missis why.

'I told them to empty their own pots. They get up earlier than you do and they've got hands, so I saw no reason at all why those great gowks should not empty their own mess. You've got better things to do. But you'll keep doing ours, because we've also got better things to do.'

If Margaret had heard what Missis had actually said to her sons she might have been gratified for she had asserted that Margaret was far too good a lass to be doing with their doings and they were quite capable of emptying and washing their own pots out. If they didn't want to do it, then as far as she was concerned they could go out in the yard at three in the morning if they had a mind to, but that lass was an angel, an angel, and not made for waiting on them hand and foot. She was there to help Missis and that was it. However, Margaret never knew this until long afterwards and none of the sons mentioned it, just did as their mother said.

It was on Wednesday that Missis decided that they would go to Aspatria. She waited until the milk was out then told Tom to put Marra in the trap. Full of trepidation Margaret again took the reins, but Marra was Maggie-proof, and Missis was an experienced driver anyway. Aspatria was only four and a half miles anyway. The lane through Edderside was deserted and they saw no other traffic until they turned down the larger road that ran through Westnewton to Aspatria. It was a good straight road and

Marra trotted into town in fine style. Missis quite clearly approved of another younger woman doing the driving.

'When I go to the shops with one of my lads I always drive. If I didn't they might get it into their heads that I couldn't do it. It's been my care to show them that women are capable human beings and I hope that's rubbed off on them. I wouldn't want them look down on us.'

'Us' was a female solidarity thing that Margaret recognized and smiled at. They were running into town past terraced rows of houses and Margaret felt quite at home as it reminded her of parts of Dearham. As with her own village, this was a settlement grouped round, and based on, coal mining. Passing down King Street and past St Kentigern's church, they came to the main shopping area.

'Keep going through Maggie. We're for the Co-op first.'

Margaret slowed Marra down to a walk as they proceeded southwards. This place was busy and her eye was taken by a group of soldiers swaggering along the pavement on her right which was raised three feet above the level of the road, and banked with stone at this point just outside Allan's furniture store.

'Oho lads! There's a bonny lass. Will you walk out with me Miss?'

'Margaret shook her head, smiled and set her face to the front whilst Missis glowered, 'You watch your manners young man; I'll thank you not to accost my maid in the street. She's a very respectable girl.'

He made a moue at her, and his friends laughed at his being turned down, but he said no more.

'He's right. You are a bonny lass, but you should be able to go down the street without that. There's a Border Regiment place here and they get them from all over.'

'Well I haven't broken any cameras, but they meant no harm Missis.'

150

'Aye pet, I know. But there's a time and place. Broken any cameras!' This made her laugh.

Missis had called her pet. Margaret didn't say anything, but though her attitude to Missis had been changing, this was a great leap. She did not think that Missis realized what she had said. Maybe she had momentarily slipped and confused her with her daughter. It was best, she decided, not to say anything about it. They came at last to the handsome sandstone and balustraded building that housed the Aspatria Co-operative Wholesale Society's shop. The windows were full of the promise of teas, coffee, new sultanas, currants, polishes, cake flour, cocoas, new season's fruits from all over the Empire and pots of jam. Missis tied Marra up by his reins to a ring in the side wall of the building and they both entered the shop. Upon the instant she was attended by a young man in a white apron to serve her every want. Into Missis's bag went much of suet, currants, raisins, sultanas, flour, spices, Birds Custard powder, a couple of jars of toothpaste and some potted meat spreads. She did not pay when she had finished, but put it all on her account, and was helped out of the shop with the bag and back onto the trap. Margaret noticed that the Co-op had a clothing department for ladies right next door, which was full of hats and blouses and ready-made skirts, but Missis evidently was not of a mind to peer at these.

'Now then, I like to spread my patronage of these shops about a bit. If I spent all my money in one place then some of them might go out of business, so just go up to Oglanby's store and wait outside while I get some chocolate. Barwise does like a bit now and then after dinner.'

After the chocolate purchase, it was to Askew's where tobacco was bought for the menfolk, pipe for Mister and Joseph, rolling tobacco for William and Tom. None of them smoked very much and it seemed to be an activity mostly reserved for after dinner in the evening, though Tom had rolled and smoked one on the way to Silloth on Sunday. This really was a busy little place, with the wives and daughters of coalminers just like her and her mother scurrying here and there about their business. The men themselves were either at work in Brayton Domain Pit, just to the south of the village, or at home asleep, off shift, so there were few to be seen though a few ancients in flat caps hung round the corners.

'Now there's an interesting place Maggie. That's the Agricultural College where we sent our lads. You wouldn't think it to look at them, but they did Latin, French and all sorts of stuff there. All of them passed their exams too.'

Margaret looked at the impressive battlemented building and thought it must be a grand thing to be educated to such a level.

'Do they have girls there?'

'Bless you girl! There's no hope of that I think, at least not in my lifetime. No. It's for the sons of farmers and no women allowed. It's supposed to improve the standards of agriculture and I think that it does. Barwise knows the men who founded it you know.'

Missis waited for Margaret to be impressed so she looked suitably attentive.

'Mr William Norman, Mr John Twentyman, and Mr Henry Thompson. It was all their idea and they got help from Sir Wilfrid Lawson out at Brayton Hall.'

'The MP!'

'Oh yes. That's why Barwise uses machines and the latest techniques. Those are men you listen to. Now pull Marra over to the side and stop.'

Margaret did so as she was not inclined to dispute the way with what was coming down the road. Four Clydesdales, every bit as big as Richard, were coming down towards her harnessed, one ahead of the other, pulling the most enormous tree on a huge wagon.

'Is there enough room?' she asked nervously.
Missis looked at the road and the wagon, 'Yes. There's about three feet to spare. Don't worry Marra will stand as they go past.'

Actually, with a more nervous horse it might have been touch and go because as the lead Clydesdale came up to Margaret's pony he swung his huge head over and had a good sniff at Marra's head, which he did not like, rearing his own head up and flattening his ears back. The lead drayman had been concentrating on his second horse, but now pulled the leader's head away and told him to 'Get on!' Then he looked at Missis and said, 'Sorry Missis,' which made Margaret giggle. He touched his hat and moved on past. The huge tree trundled heavily on its way down the road towards the sawmill. Greatly daring Margaret said, 'He knew who you were…'

Missis looked at her for a moment then laughed.

'Yes, he did didn't he. Everybody knows who Missis is.'

This thought evidently tickled her and for the next few minutes she chuckled to herself occasionally and every so often she looked at Margaret as if sizing her up, but her maid did not know quite what for. Margaret drove home under the older woman's supervision and there was no doubt at all that she was becoming quite proficient at handling the horse, or at least allowing Marra to do his job. As they drove, Missis went into a reverie which lasted about ten minutes, then she told Margaret that she had something to say and that she should listen, and then she should write home. Having got the shopping in and handed the pony over to Nick for stabling, she did as she was instructed and went over to her rooms to write a letter home.

'Dear Father and Mother,

I hope this finds you well and that all at home are in the best of health. I am writing to tell you that I am able to come home for a few days in the near future. Mrs Little is very pleased with me here and she has told me that her daughter Annie is coming home for Christmas on 24 December. I may have told you that she works and lives at the telephone exchange in Carlisle.

Mrs Little wants me here in the run up to Christmas and on Christmas Day, as there is a great deal to do, but she says that after that her daughter can help her. If it is agreeable to you then

I am allowed to come home to Dearham on Boxing Day morning and return to my place on 30 December. This is a lot longer than I expected and I have to say that I do not know why this kindness is being given, except that I nursed Mrs Little when she was ill and she seems to like me. Certainly, I like her as I think her good and kind, but Father, you know what you say. Never look a gift horse in the mouth, so if you are able to allow it, I should very much like to come and visit.

Mrs Little says that it's no more than eight or nine miles and that it's an awful shame if a girl can't see her parents over the Christmas feast for a decent amount of time. She knows that she would not like it if she could not see her own daughter about her. She will tell one of her sons to drive me over on Boxing Day morning and pick me up to go back on the afternoon of 30 December after church, that being Sunday.

If you and Mother are agreeable to this, please write and let me know. I am, as ever, your loving daughter, Margaret'

This important missive was handed to the postwoman from Mawbray at the gate of West End Farm the very next morning. Margaret was entirely excited by the approach of Christmas. She would be at the farm for Christmas itself which would undoubtedly be far different and more opulent to anything she had ever experienced at home, but then she would see her family for several days, and that she had not expected. She wanted to hug herself for happiness and indeed she had surprised her mistress beyond all measure by hugging her in thanking her after she made the suggestion.

'Well I never did! What a way to treat the mistress of the house.'

But she smiled as she said it, and her eyes sparkled with the success of her gesture to her maid. Missis had conferred happiness and that made her happy. Margaret had also asked if she minded her using the dairy to make some home made fudge from her own ingredients to take home for her siblings, but Missis would not hear of it.

'The dairy! The dairy! I should think not. The proper place for cooking is on the range in the kitchen. You cook it in there my lass. The dairy indeed! When would you like to do it?'

'Well I was planning to make it a few days before Christmas.'

'Fudge is best when it's fresh. How about making it after dinner on Christmas Day, when the dishes have been done?'

Margaret thought that was a very good idea and it was agreed.

Christmas was coming; it was going to be good.

Chapter 11

A Christmas Tree

Margaret was very busy in the late afternoon of 2 December, for it was, as in every house, 'Stir-up Sunday' when by tradition, the Christmas Pudding was made. Missis had put all the ingredients out in the bowls, many of which had come from the Aspatria Co-op, but Margaret had the hard part to do. Every single one of a half pound of raisins had to be cut in half and the little stones removed. Because she had quicker hands, it was she who sliced the candied peel very thinly, then she who grated the bread crusts to make three quarters of a pound of breadcrumbs. However, she was the apprentice to Missis's sorcerer and the casting and weighing of the materials for the magic was all hers. Margaret's young arm was deputized to stir the mixture hard and for several minutes until Missis was satisfied with the mix, with one silver threepenny piece added, scrubbed and shone for the purpose; then it was the lady of the house who pressed the mixture into a copper mould, tied a muslin bag round it and told Margaret to boil it for exactly five hours and thirty minutes. If she did it five minutes more or less then Missis would know and she'd have her guts for garters. Margaret smiled at this for she knew by now that the older woman's bark was far worse than her bite. Such an amount of boiling would make a lot of steam so she had prepared the copper already in the dairy and set her alarm clock.

The coming feast was the subject of much conversation at the table that evening when the meal was over. Mr Little was holding forth on how he thought Christmas should be done.

'You know what I think William. I've told you enough times. I was born in 1824 and all the Christmases we had when I was a nipper had none of this nonsense. It all came in when our Queen married that German fellow.'

'Yes Dad, I know, but Prince Albert brought a lot of things in that people do at Christmas now, and a tree is a tradition.'

'Not in this house it isn't. It never was. My father would never have one in here any more than I have. He used to say that it was all very well for the Germans, but as far as he was concerned, the place for a tree was in the forest.'

'Well you're happy enough with the paper chains. And you send cards.'

'The paper chains are nice, I'll give you that, but red and green only. That's fitting with the holly and the ivy and I only do the cards because your mother makes me. I think it's a damn fool idea. I cannot see the point of it. And trees are dangerous.'

'Only if people are stupid dad. If you use your common sense there's no danger to them at all. There's no denying that they look very nice and festive.'

'I'll give you that, but I'll tell you something. I will never pay for a tree to be brought into this house.'

This was evidently Mister's trump card, for he slapped his hand on the table as if that were the end of the matter.

'I'll pay for a tree myself if you'll allow it in the house.'

A small flash of annoyance crossed Mister's face.

'Well, what do you others think of this idea?'

If he expected the Christmas tree suggestion to be rejected, he had misjudged his audience, because his wife and his two other sons were very much in favour of it. Margaret of course was not asked. Having sought opinion Mister, now gave in with a bad grace.

'If you want to waste your money like a fool then go ahead, but don't burn my house down!'

So it was settled that West End Farm would, after so many years, be adorned by a tree over Christmas, though in all other ways it would remain as Mister liked it. Margaret retired to her own rooms after dinner and dishes, leaving the family to their privacy, but every so often trotted downstairs to the dairy to stoke the copper and check the water level in the pan. She timed the boiling exactly then removed the bag containing the now cooked Christmas pudding, and carried it over to the kitchen where she hung it on a hook with a pan under it to catch any liquid that dripped from it. On Christmas Day it would be boiled again a further two hours then served with a flourish. Missis spent time every few days dosing with brandy a large Christmas cake that she had baked at the end of September and kept in a big tin on a high shelf.

The interval between Advent and Christmas Day passed slowly. Rain was a common feature of these days and the countryside grew dank and weeping as water dripped from branches and fences everywhere, and leaves rotted in the ditches and gutters. The farmyard soon grew a skin of mud, cow dung and clods that Nick was required to sweep out of the gate once a day and this effluvia formed a stream of muck down the hill and into the pond over the road which had a scum floating on the top of it.

Missis, particular about her floors, provided Margaret with a pair of wooden pattens that she had to use when crossing the yard and take off at the door. On the Saturday two days before Christmas Day Mister harnessed Richard to the big cart and set off with Missis, William and Joseph for Aspatria and visited the brewery for a large barrel of beer. Then they went to the aerated water factory where they bought a crate for William who was not so fond of alcohol as the rest of the family. William's errand was particular when he went to the Market Hall where just outside was a stall selling Christmas trees and paid two shillings and sixpence for a three foot high specimen which he carried back to the cart in triumph. He also paid a visit to Pattinson's chemists and came out with a spicy smelling paper bag that he put into his pocket. There were a few sideways looks from Mister as the tree came into the house, to be stuck upright in a half barrel of earth, but Missis was short with him, 'Don't be such a scrooge, Barwise. You said he could if he paid for it and he has.'

'Bah. Humbug!' said the master of the house, and headed out to the barn. It was not yet time for the evening milking and Margaret found herself conscripted into the decorating of the tree

158

that was placed in a corner of the parlour where the family sat when they were altogether. The base was wrapped in coloured paper, then various things were hung round the branches of the tree. William set about hanging coloured ribbons and candies wrapped in paper that he had obtained in town. Margaret's particular job was to take popcorn and string pieces onto a thread with a large needle.

'These are really for children you know William.'

'Yes Maggie, I know that, but this is the first time we've ever been allowed a tree. When I was little I always wanted to have a tree with popcorn on it, so now I'm going to.'

Joseph, the elder brother, took the position that might have been expected of him and asserted it to be a lot of stuff and nonsense, but William was smiling and quite clearly enjoying every minute of decorating his tree. Big brother could object all he liked. He winked at Margaret, 'Take no notice of him. He'll like it when it's done, but he won't say so.'

'Hmmph,' grunted Joseph as he went out the door into the yard.

Margaret smiled back, for she liked William. He was a terribly nice man, but she sensed in him that he was not a particularly happy one. He seemed out of place on a farm and maybe he did not even wish to be there. With many, if not most men, there was a tension of being 'other' and they enjoyed the company of women precisely because they were women. William did not emanate any such message, rather he broadcast an air of neutrality and reserve that set him apart from people. She knew what Agnes meant when she said that he was not the marrying kind.

Outside the wind had begun to get rather fierce and it was not long before a gale was blowing. The sheltered position of the farm took away much of its fury, but it was not too long before a howling in the distance signified that a storm of some enormous strength was raging across the countryside. Margaret hoped that her family would be safe, and decided that she would add prayers for ships at sea to her usual bedtime conversation with God. She was safe and warm inside and would not go outside unless she had to.

She thought the tree did look rather nice with its ribbons, and paper streamers, hung with sweets and stuck round with blobs of cotton wool for snow. William's piece de resistance was when he produced a bag of coloured candles with wire loops and carefully twisted them onto branches that stuck out furthest from the centre, so as to minimize the risk of setting fire to those above. The effect was completed when he took from the paper bag he had in his pocket sticks of cinnamon then tied them in small bunches and hung them from the beams not far from the fire. A spicy Christmassy odour began to suffuse the room.

The door opened and Tom came in, took in the scene and commenced to sing and they joined in,

> '*Deck the hall with boughs of holly,*
> *Fa la la lala, la la la la!*
> *'Tis the season to be jolly*
> *Fa la la lala, la la la la!*
> *Don we now our gay apparel*
> *Fa la la lala, la la la la!*
> *Sing we now a Christmas carol*
> *Fa la la lala, la la la la!*'

'That's all very well,' said William, 'But where's the holly?'
'It's just outside the door on the cart.'
'Oh, I'll get it Tom,' said Margaret.
Tom caught her by the arm as she tried to go past him.
'No Maggie, you can't do that. Do they not tell you anything in Dearham?'
'Well I know that lots of people have holly and ivy in the house but we never have. There's no holly near us and we never have really done much decorating at Christmas time.'

'Why Maggie, it's tradition! Holly has to be carried into the house by a man. It's bad luck for a woman to do it.'

'Why ever is that?'

'I really have not the foggiest idea, but it is the case, so now I shall fetch it in. Anyway that wind's too strong for you. You'd be blown away.'

The wind was indeed raging but he went outside and returned in a minute carrying an armful of holly, its red berries glinting with moisture, for he had cut it fresh from a hedge across the field from the house. The next armful was ivy, which was easier to find, and as he went off to put Marra in his stall, William and Margaret continued their efforts and placed the branches and boughs in strategic places round the house. Margaret twisted some of the holly sprigs and ivy into a wreath, which was hung on the door-knocker. The last touch was to decorate the parlour itself with red and green streamers that went from side to side and along the picture rails, immeasurably brightening the room with its heavy dark furniture. Plaiting some of the paper Margaret finished the room off by placing a crown round the top of the old Grandfather clock that ticked away the time in the corner of the parlour. It had a nice painted picture of a lady reclining on a bench at the top of it and the name 'Js. Telford, Maryport' inscribed on the face that was set about with Roman numerals. On the side of it was a hook from which there hung a belt that had not been used for many years. Missis told her that when the boys were young, if they were naughty their father used to strap them with it on the bottom. The first step towards this had been that they had to go and fetch the belt, which added to the force of the punishment. Margaret left the parlour to William who was engaged in putting presents under the tree; this was a matter that did not concern her. She knew that it was not her place to give presents to the family, and she must not expect anything from the family on Christmas Day. There was, for good and valued servants, the possibility of a box on Boxing Day, but that was another matter. That night a great storm blew across the land, though at West End Farm sheltered in its little nook, they slept soundly.

The next day, after church Margaret walked down into Allonby where there were a few small shops that she wished to visit. The overnight storm had blown itself out but the signs of it were plain to see where some of the fishing boats had been driven far up the beach and some of the seafront houses had signs of damage to windows and slates. She was going home on Wednesday and there were some items she needed to purchase, so she was glad that the shops at least were open. Storms were not going to close down the English shopkeeper. By the time she returned it was late afternoon and getting dark and cold; the storm had evidently blown in a change and winter was arriving. Turning into the gate she walked towards the steps up to her chambers, and saw that the door of the dairy was part open, and that there were two people inside. It was Joseph and Agnes and they were kissing, apparently so oblivious to the outside world that they did not notice her. Hurriedly she moved out of line of sight and up her own stairs, smiling and trying not to laugh. Agnes had made her move, but what would Mister and Missis say if they knew about it? The elder son and heir kissing the milkmaid! Well good for her, and it least it brought some interest into the dairy.

Tom and William went off with a large two-man saw on the morning of Christmas Eve and they came back with the most enormous log which they dragged into the yard then carried into the parlour. It was obviously not green wood and Margaret surmised that it had been cut from a dead tree on a neighbouring farm, for the Yule log has to be given, not bought. It sat on the bricks of the fireplace waiting to be lifted into place on the fire when the time came, but that would not be until evening. At the same time two large candles of coloured wax were placed on either side of the mantelpiece but not lit. Missis was nowhere to be seen, having gone off in the trap upon an errand of her own with a large covered basket on the seat beside her.

Then there was Annie Eleanor. She breezed into the kitchen fresh from the train, for Mister had picked her up from Aspatria station, and was plainly very pleased to have his daughter back for a while. A small and neat person with warm brown eyes and chestnut hair pinned back and up into a bun, Annie exuded a professional air. This was probably because she was a telephone girl and at this time such an occupation for a young woman offered a touch of glamour and independence. Few such opportunities presented themselves for young women, the pattern of whose lives was mostly set round domestic service, then marriage, but women were held to be better at telephone work than men, so it had become a feminine profession. Her face was handsome rather than pretty, and though small she presented a robust air.

'So you're the famous Maggie that my mother has been writing about.'

Margaret's cheeks flushed a little.

'I hope there's nothing bad there Miss.'

'Quite the reverse I think.' Here Annie smiled, 'I'm glad she's got someone who's up to the job of taking my place.'

'Oh I'm not taking your place Miss. I'm just the maid, and I could never take your place.'

'Ha-ha! Don't worry Maggie. I'm not jealous of you. Quite the reverse. You are my liberator and I should thank you.'

'Liberator, Miss?'

'Yes. You set me free. All the jobs that you do, I used to do. I was stuck in this place and getting more grumpy by the minute. I wanted out of this farm Maggie, and to set myself up independently and do things. Now I do, so I owe you a debt. You see now?'

'Yes Miss.'

'Oh do stop calling me Miss. My name's Annie.'

At this, she stuck out her hand and Margaret stared at it.

'Oh stop it Annie. You're embarrassing her. She doesn't know what to do.'

'What do you mean Tom?'

'I mean that Maggie is a maid in this house and she likes to keep the line in place.'

Margaret looked at him rather nonplussed, but his face was completely straight.

'I see,' said Annie. 'Well you're not my maid, so here goes.' She grabbed Margaret's hand and pumped it up and down, then she kissed her on the cheek. 'And that's for nursing my Mam when she was sick. I think you're a brick. Now can we get a cup of tea round here because it's been a long way from Carlisle and I'm parched.'

At eight o'clock the family came in for their evening meal, but on this particular evening there was a departure from routine. Instead of sitting to the table they gathered in the parlour, and Tom and Joseph lifted the yule log into place on the fire. There it must burn all through Christmas and not be relit, for to do so was considered bad luck. They hoped it was big enough to last the full twelve days. Missis, as the lady of the house, lit the Yule candles on the mantelpiece, then William, with a flourish, took a taper and lit it at the fireplace. As all watched with bated breath he lit the candles on the Christmas tree, and as he lit the last one he burst into singing with a good high tenor,

> *'We wish you a Merry Christmas*
> *We wish you a Merry Christmas*
> *We wish you a Merry Christmas*
> *And a Happy New Year.'*

He was joined quickly by his family and Margaret too as Annie nudged her to sing,

> *'Good tidings we bring,*
> *To you and your kin,*
> *We wish you a Merry Christmas*
> *And a Happy New Year.'*

The tree looked wonderful, the dark green of the branches set off by the flickering and colourful candles, and William sang again,

'Oh Christmas Tree, bright Christmas tree,
How gaily decked your branches.
The coloured candle's lovely light,
Is shed around for our delight.
Oh Christmas tree, bright Christmas tree,
How gaily decked your branches.'

'Yes yes, that's all very well' said his father, 'But now I want my dinner.'

'It looks well though, doesn't it Dad?'

'Aye it does. I'll give you that, but now food.'

The family trouped through into the kitchen and took their usual places round the big wooden table. At 8.25 pm dinner was served, and Mister adhering to his traditional ways, it was frumenty which Missis had shown Margaret how to prepare the day before and set in a bowl to wait the day. The recipe was one that Missis favoured, though she knew that there were others. Margaret had never had it before and watched carefully as Missis parboiled grains of wheat in a pan, which she then strained and then reboiled in milk. She then flavoured it with cinnamon sticks and hard boiled eggs chopped up, but she explained, 'Mister likes a savoury frumenty, but there are many that prefer it sweet with fruit and sugar.'

Margaret was allowed to place a huge steaming bowl of this on the table with a big spoon for the diners to help themselves, but the achievement was Missis's as all knew. It was eaten with venison, a huge joint of which was carved very expertly by Mister at the top of the table and he doled out liberal slices all round. At each person's elbow was a half pint pewter tankard for posset. This drink was again a traditional recipe of Missis's devising. Fresh milk had been boiled and then mixed with good ale from the

Aspatria brewery. This had curdled the milk and the liquid was then flavoured with cinnamon and nutmeg and a bit of sugar. Margaret had tasted it and found it delicious, so to her delight she found that she too was expected to drink this. She worried at first that it had alcohol in it, but she had taken no pledge of abstinence, though her father had done many years before. Here she was confronting something new, and she decided she would like to try it. Had she known that the heat of the milk had removed most of the alcohol she might have been less excited about it. William, she noticed, had a glass of bubbling water, but he was the only one who did.

It was fortunate that Margaret's habit was to place a large cauldron of water on the side of the range before she sat down to her evening meal. This meant that when dinner was over and the family retired to their rooms or the parlour, she could attend to the dishes very quickly, which gave her more time before she went to bed.

Afterwards it was never clear who noticed the danger first, she or Mister, for he suddenly dropped his knife and fork and shouted, 'By God!' just as Margaret leaped up. Missis and Annie screamed, but Margaret made for the pan straightaway and was through the door into the parlour before most of the family was on their feet, the men now yelling in alarm. It would be accurate to say that the Christmas tree was on fire, but not fully ablaze. Another few seconds and it would have been a conflagration, but Margaret, with great presence of mind, took an instantaneous decision to knock it onto the flagstones of the floor and pour water over it. Within seconds the fire was out and she was stamping out the last sparks with her shoe. Missis was wailing in the doorway and Annie had her face in her hands.

'I'll just get a mop and bucket Mister.'

'You'll just get a mop and bucket! On my life you will not! You've just saved my house from burning down and everything in it. Sit down lass. William!'

'Yes Dad.' Poor William shuffled forward. 'I'm sorry. I should have put the candles out when we went through.'

'That's no odds to me. That's the first and last tree in this house. Do you understand me boy?'

'Yes Dad.' A more crestfallen man could hardly have been found.

'Now you get a mop and bucket and clear this up for it is your mess. I'm taking this lass back to finish her dinner.'

'But Mister…'

'None of that! I am master here and I know how to be grateful. Sit down and finish your dinner Maggie.'

'It's alright Maggie. Dad's right. I was careless and you don't have to clear this up.'

William set about rescuing what he could of the sweets and tree hangings, then wiped up the mess with a mop from the kitchen.

Hesitatingly Margaret resumed her place as did the family and continued with their meal as William carried the wet tree out into the yard. After the excitement and her automatic intervention, reaction was setting in and she felt a little shaky. Missis suddenly burst into tears, and the moment she did so, Annie and Margaret did the same.

The men looked shaken, and amid all this female upset Mister strode to the sideboard and poured three thimble glasses of brandy and set them in front of his wife, his daughter and his maid. As an afterthought he poured a glass each for himself and his sons as well.

'Now drink that down and you'll feel better.' Then he turned to Margaret.

'It was a good day I took you on. That was quick thinking Maggie. Tell me now, why did you knock the tree on the floor before using the water?'

'Well the flames were heading for the ceiling Mister, and then there were the presents.'

'The presents?'

167

'Yes. The presents were all under the tree. If I poured water over them they'd all have been spoiled, so it was better to knock it flat then pour away from the presents.'

'Clever as well. That was good thinking.' He gestured round the table. 'Good thinking. Brains and beauty.'

A male voice whispered almost inaudibly, 'Hear, hear.'

Mister continued, 'You've saved my house and possessions and who knows - maybe more. Well I shall see you right on it my girl, as you shall see. Now dry your tears and finish your food.'

The rest of the meal continued as usual in silence except that they were eventually joined by William returning from the yard, who looked at Margaret and winked to show all was well.

'It's just beginning to snow out there.'

'Oh!' They all went to the door and the window to watch thick snowflakes drifting across the surface outside.

'If I'm any judge of it, that is going to settle,' said Mister. 'It was hard last winter and I think it'll be hard again this one.'

'White Christmas though. I like a white Christmas personally.'

'It's pretty Joe, I'll not deny it, but at my age I feel the cold. Now close the door and let's stay warm,' this from Missis, who shivered and wrapped her shawl more closely about her shoulders.

'It's a funny thing,' mused Mister, 'When my dad was alive he kept the cows and horses out all winter. His view was that they were beasts and that was where they belonged. Since the agricultural college opened I've thought differently and I'm happy that they're all in the barn and we've enough feed to see us through.'

'Well it made sense, didn't it?' asked Tom. 'They stay healthier, don't lose weight and they carry on producing milk in good quantity and quality. Yields have gone up.'

'Oh aye, it's true enough. I suppose it's common sense when you think about it. Now let's finish our food for this meal has been interrupted enough.'

At the end of dinner the family trouped through into the parlour and Margaret, as usual, washed the dishes, dried them, and put them all away. She swept the floor, washed the table and the surfaces, and her duties were done for the day. As she moved towards her pattens prior to crossing the yard, a hand tugged at her elbow and turning, she saw Mister.

'Nay lass. Thou'lt not be alone on Christmas Eve. That would not be right. You shall come and pass the time with us.'

So saying, he led her firmly by the arm into the parlour and announced, 'Look what I caught in the kitchen.' Then he sat her down in a chair near the fire where the Yule log burned brightly as the family cheered. Margaret smiled, for it was as plain as day that she was welcome here. Resolving that she would not outstay her welcome she settled down to enjoy the warmth and the company of her employers. There was sherry, and nuts and mince pies later, and ghost stories. Margaret did love a ghost story, and she heard of the headless lady of Hutton Hall, the rocking pulpit of Lowther, the Lorton Spectre, the Newtown Bogle and the Crackenthorpe ghost, which sent delicious shivers down her spine. Eventually, it was her turn and she had to admit that she knew no true ghost stories, but she knew a tale. With some small encouragement she commenced,

'The story goes that in Dearham when my father was a young man there was a Temperance Society hall in the village where young people could go to dances. It was all very respectable you understand, because it was organized by the minister and of course there was no alcohol….'

'Shame, shame!'

'Do be quiet Thomas!'

'Yes Dad.'

With a glance at the offender, Margaret continued,

'They would serve tea, lemonade and cake and all behaviour was as it should be. There was a young man there by the name of Turnbull, but he was a rough and was given to drinking, though he did not at these dances. He was enamoured (Margaret liked that word, for she had read it in a romance) of a young woman from the Row Beck end of the village. She did not like him however, and was herself in love with a man called Adam Brown, who in turn liked her. So when Turnbull asked her for a dance she turned him down repeatedly.'

'Repeatedly?' said Mister, 'If he was any sort of gentleman he would not have repeated the request. A real man should take no for an answer.'

'Yes sir. I agree. Turnbull would have liked to have fought Mr Brown, but he was bigger, stronger, did Cumbrian wrestling, and he feared him. Therefore, he decided to get his own back on the girl in some way. The next dance was in October and late in the month so the evenings were getting dark. There were six girls from Row Beck who used to meet outside the Ship Hotel and walk together up into Dearham to go to the dance. The dance went ahead, but there were none of the Row Beck girls there, not a single one, and Mr Brown had no-one to dance with. Not surprisingly he found his lady-love the following day and asked why none of the Row Beck girls had attended the dance.'

'Why Adam? We were coming to the dance and were heading up the hill past the old Townhead pit when a figure appeared in the ground of the old mine. It was all clothed in white from head to foot, clanking chains and moaning. Every girl in our group, including me screamed like billy-oh and ran back home. Hattie Holroyd got into such hysterics they had to put her to bed. There's a ghost at the old mine.'

Now this was a good story. The Littles looked at each other; their maid could tell a tale.

'Although some people kept watch for a few nights after that, there was not any sign of a ghost, but at the next dance there were no girls. The same thing had happened again. It was then that Mr Brown had a word with two of his friends and this is what he said,' here Margaret essayed a masculine voice, to the amusement of her listeners. 'It seems that our ghost likes dance nights and only dance nights. I propose that we keep watch from behind the wall on the other side of the road on the night of the next dance. I'll persuade the girls to come to the dance as usual, but not tell them why.' It took some persuading I can tell you, but as Christmas approached, so did the dance, and on the night in question Mr Brown and his two friends were in position behind the wall as the group of girls headed down from Row Beck and up past Townhead. As they passed the low fence of the old colliery a white moaning figure appeared and clanking chains were heard. Immediately the girls screamed in fear and took to their heels. Mr Brown said afterwards that a cold chill went down his spine, but as the girls disappeared down the road, he heard the white figure laughing. Then he said, 'If that's a ghost, then I'm a Dutchman's uncle,' so the three of them bounded over the wall and went after the ghost. He saw them coming and ran for it, but he tripped over his sheet, for such it was, and they caught him. It was Turnbull. That was the end of the Townhead Ghost and the girls could go to the dance again.'

A small ripple of applause went round the room.

'Well,' said Missis. 'Is that it? Did he get away with it? Did they do nothing.'

'Yes Missis, they did. They say he could not get out of his bed for a week. The local constable heard of it, but he would not act on it because his view was that Turnbull had got what he deserved.'

'Quite right too!' said Mister. 'I'd have given him a welting such as would have put him in bed for two weeks.'

'He's not joking you know Maggie,' said Missis. 'Barwise was a Cumbrian wrestler in his youth. He stood at Grasmere Sports one year and was undefeated. That was in the papers. Thomas does it too.' This last bit was said with pride.

In festive mood and seasonal ghost stories, the evening passed and it was 11.30 before Margaret decided that she was for bed. Without prompting, Tom crossed the yard with her, holding an extra lanthorn for the snow was now falling thickly and was already about an inch deep. As she turned at her door to say goodnight, he kissed her on the cheek.

'Thank you Maggie, that was quite a thing you did tonight. And Merry Christmas.'

She closed her door as he returned across the yard and thought of that kiss. His moustache had tickled her face, and she found that she liked it.

Chapter 12

Christmas Day 1894

Farms do not stop for Christmas, for cows have to be milked and fed, horses have to be attended to and work must go on. There was nearly two inches of snow covering the countryside when Margaret left her room at 5.55 on Christmas morning. Agnes was already hard at work milking in the yellow lamp-light, but she stopped when Margaret came up to her.

'Merry Christmas!' they both said at the same time, then laughed. Margaret handed her a small package and Agnes said, 'Well, you shouldn't have you know, but I did too,' handing her a package from her pinafore pocket with an accompanying kiss.

'I love Christmas presents!' declared the dairymaid.

'So do I,' said Margaret with excitement.

'Well are you going to open it then?' asked Aggie?

In answer, Margaret opened her little parcel as the other girl did likewise. Inside was a cloth bag for keeping small objects or coins in, beautifully sewn by Aggie and embroidered with exquisite little flowers. She could keep her money in it for now. Agnes was delighted with her ribbon and said,

'I'm going to keep this for best and I'm certainly not wearing it for milking.'

So saying she tucked the package of ribbon into her pinafore pocket.

'You may look to see this in church later for I shall be wearing it. Now I'd better get on and so had you.'

A kiss parted them and sealed their relationship as not only friends, but friends who gave each other Christmas presents.

As Margaret crossed the yard to go to her work, she hoped that the snow would not get any deeper, however seasonal and pretty it looked. Her anticipation of seeing her own family the next day made her pray that the farm would not be snowed in, but she need not have feared. The weather had been so mild in the past few weeks that primroses and daisies had been blooming all round; the dusting of snow for Christmas was a foreshadowing of winter, but the full grip of it was not yet come. When the morning milking was over, Agnes was given the rest of the day off until afternoon milking, which pleased her very well, and the family sat down to a Christmas breakfast of scrambled eggs, toast and smoked salmon. The latter had been procured from Costin's smokery in Allonby, who usually cured herring for kippers, but specialized in this traditional Christmas dish for a short time each year. Margaret had never had it before and thought it quite delicious. After this, the family prepared to go to church, with much of laughter and 'Merry Christmas' being shouted at Margaret and indeed anyone and everyone. The bells from the church could be heard across the fields pealing out for Christmas morning and the snow across the land lent a high electricity to the winter air that filled all with hope and energy. It was one of those mornings when it felt good to be alive. Tom brought Richard into the yard, and the big horse was obviously pleased to be getting some exercise when he was backed between the shafts of the large cart with seats. Mister sat up front beside Tom who had the reins. Behind them sat Joe and William, their mother snuggled in between them and on the back, facing the road sat Margaret and Annie. It was very cold and both of them had warm rugs wrapped round their knees. The family could have very easily walked to church as it was less than one and a half miles, but Mister and Missis were not as young as they had been and preferred to ride. Annie had already managed to glean something of Margaret's life during the previous evening, but the maid had not learned much in return. It is perhaps a very basic part of human nature that people like little so much as talking about themselves. There is nothing quite so interesting and it is a tendency that it is well to beware of unless one wishes to be a bore. Margaret knew this proclivity very well, so was not averse to talking, asking Annie, as an opening remark, why she had called her a 'liberator' on the previous evening. Then it struck her that perhaps Annie might not wish to talk about this in a conveyance loaded with her parents and brothers. However, Miss Little was having none of that and laughed as she realized that Margaret had suddenly become diffident.

'Oh never mind them! They all know very well why I left. I'm not cut out for life on a farm. I never was and I always wanted to do something more exciting. It's all very well for those that want to put up with it, but I wanted a bit more interest in what I did with my life.'

'Too good for the likes of us then,' said Joe and it was more of a statement than a question.

'You know better than that Joe. You like farming and one day this farm will be yours. But I have no inclination for it. Neither do William and Tom if truth be told.'

'Leave me out of this,' said William. 'I don't know where you get your ideas from.'

Tom's face if she could have seen it, was solid and expressionless; he said nothing.

'I've got a mind William, and I can read people. You'd rather be doing something else for a living. I can see that as plain as your face.'

'Well, he's needed on the farm and he's a farmer. How would we live without the lads working hard here?'

This demand by Mister was not answered by Annie, who merely pursed her lips at him and turned away; none of the young men responded, for Mister was in charge and arguing with him did not pay.

'He had ideas for me you know Maggie,' continued Annie. 'That's why he sent me to finishing school in Switzerland for six months. He wanted me to be a lady and marry a gentleman. But I had other thoughts.'

'Waste of good money,' came from the front seat.

'It wasn't a waste at all. It showed me some of the world and what I could do. That's why I joined the telephone company. It's new and it's modern Maggie, and most of all it's not marriage, or

175

farming. I can make a living, earn my own money, spend it on what I like, and do what I want with my life.'

'What's it like being a telephone operator?' asked Margaret, thus unbolting the door to Annie's oratory and giving her permission to wax lyrical.

'I love it. It's a responsible job and I love that too. In the Carlisle exchange we have a few hundred subscribers, but we have lines that go all over the country, so there's all sorts of people depend on us to put their business calls through. But you don't half have to keep alert. You can get several calls come through at once and you have to be able to deal with it all, Argus would not be happy otherwise.'

'Who's Argus?'

'That's what we call her though she is our supervisor officially; she sees everything. We sit in rows at our desks and in front of us there are boards with lots of holes in them. We have to plug lines in the right ones to make connections and we're trained to do that.'

Margaret did not understand the reference to Argus, the one hundred eyed giant of Greek mythology at all, but went straight on to ask a further question,

'Don't all the bells drive you mad?'

Annie laughed.

'There's no bells Maggie. If a subscriber rings us up, a small metal disc falls down with their number on it and it's almost silent. That's why you've got to pay attention. I've got a little earphone that fits over my head, and in front of my chin there's a mouthpiece that hangs down. I'm plugged into the board in front of me so I can hear people and talk to them.'

'But what do you say to them?'

'Usually its, 'What number do you require please?' When they tell me, I ask them to wait a moment and then I connect them.'

'How do you do that?'

'Well in front of me on the board are hundreds of jack holes and each one of them is a particular telephone. On my desk are hundreds of plugs on connecting cords and I have to put the right plugs into the right jack hole to connect them so they can talk. When they are finished a little metal disc drops to let me know. Then there's annunciator drops, cams and ringing buttons.'

'That all sounds very technical.'

'You mean you don't understand what they are?'

'Yes.'

'I know Maggie. I was baffling you with science, but it was more for the benefit of my brothers, who never seem able to accept that their little sister knows things they don't.'

Here she threw an affectionate glance over her shoulder at her brothers.

'Where do you live?'

'We have to live in dormitories above the exchange.'

'That sounds like going to a boarding school.'

'It is actually a bit like that; at least it was like my school in Switzerland... now here we are at church, so I'll tell you more later.'

They were indeed at St Cuthbert's and in good time for there was room to tie Richard up alongside the other horses, though more were coming up the lane. There was a throng of people arriving, so there followed more shouts of 'Merry Christmas' and much smiling and shaking of hands. Friends and neighbours were gathering, farming folk, wedded to the soil and their way of life; they had much in common and some of it was in ties of blood and marriage. The church was full of people in their Sunday best, and the bells were still pealing. They had not only come to worship, but to belt out some carols at the tops of their voices and the vicar did not disappoint them. Hark the Herald Angels, Oh Come All Ye Faithful, and Good King Wenceslas were up on the hymn board and they did them full justice, singing out with gusto. The church was not decorated though, the vicar not approving of such heathen practices, but he preached a fine sermon on the brotherhood of man in Christ that set many heads to nodding and murmurs of approval to be heard. The Vicar could be relied on to say the right things at the right time and that was much to be valued. Margaret's attention was taken by a man across the aisle from them who was devastatingly good looking, and whose head kept on turning to look across. At first she thought he was looking at her, but it soon became clear that he was not; it was Annie who was the focus of his attention. This was something of which Annie was obviously intent on taking no notice, for though her face was slightly pink, she kept her eyes studiously facing forward and evinced no signs of recognition at all.

Agnes was there also in her best Sunday dress of white and lace, with a pleasing blue sash and a straw hat with a flat brim, trimmed with the ribbon that Margaret had given her that morning. Margaret had seen her wear that sash before and had asked where the ribbon had come from in order to match it. Agnes turned round in her pew, saw Margaret and winked an eye of cornflower blue, which caused her to smile.

After the service the congregation filed out, each of them shaking hands with the Vicar, and wishing him a Merry Christmas. A small crowd of people gathered in the churchyard and were inclined to chat, give season's greetings and offer nips from hip flasks, but Annie walked straight out clutching the arm of her father. At twenty-five Annie was beautiful, far and above the ordinary girl in the locality. She was also very fashionably dressed in a dark plum coat with matching bonnet and looked, as might be said 'a picture.' It may have been expected that such a person would be the centre of some male attention, and so it was. The man from the church was standing by the path and as she approached him he took his flat cap off his head and said, 'Good morning Miss Little. I am glad to see you again.'

'Good morning Mr Metcalfe,' was the somewhat frosty reply, and she moved away from him holding Mister's arm as if it were a lifejacket. The wretched Metcalfe was evidently unwilling to let this be the end of the conversation and moved to follow her, but Joseph stepped in his way.

'Look John. You know how things stand. I must ask you to leave my sister be.'

'Joe, you know that things have changed.'

'I know they have. You've prospered since you made your offer and can well support a wife and family, but you asked and were refused.'

'May a man not try again?'

'Aye he may that, but as you well know Annie has no wish to be a farmer's wife. She told you that when she said no. I think you should respect it.'

'But what's wrong with being a farmer's wife when the farm is prospering and he loves her well?'

'Nothing at all, John. There's many a lass would be thankful of your offer, but not Annie. She's made it quite clear that she has other fish to fry. She's not for you; now please leave her alone. I have no hard feelings for you and wish you a Merry Christmas.'

At this he held out his hand, but it was ignored.

John Metcalfe walked away, his pain full on his face for all the world to see. Joseph shook his head, grimaced slightly and joined his family on the cart.

'He should learn that no means no,' said Missis.

'Ah the man's lovesick,' said Joseph, 'but he'll have to get over it.'

Margaret regarded Annie with some curiosity, wondering if there would be more of this relationship that she knew nothing of, but Annie's face was pink, somewhat inclined to tears and determined to put on a gaiety that she obviously did not feel.

'Now then, you were wanting to know how we live in the dormitory.'

Sensing Annie's need to talk of other things, Margaret encouraged her, resolving that she would get what she really wanted to know from Agnes later.

'It is a dormitory, just like in school and we have a cupboard and a small bedside table to keep our things in. It's all good fun actually; there are ten girls in my room and ten in the next and we get up to all sorts of things. We are allowed out when we are not on duty, but we must be back by ten o'clock at night or we would face dismissal.'

'Where do you cook your food though?'

'We don't. There's a canteen where we eat and the food is good and not expensive so mostly we eat there.'

'Are there any followers allowed?'

'Oh lor no Maggie! Anyone bringing a man into the digs would be out on their ear. Not that there's much time for that sort of thing. We start at eight and finish at eight with twenty minutes break in the morning and twenty in the afternoon and a rotated lunchtime. Mind you it pays well.'

Annie knew that ears would be pricking up in the front of the carriage, so she whispered in Margaret's ear.

'How much?'

Annie put her finger to her lips and whispered.

'Shhhh. Little pigs have big ears.'

Margaret's mind whirled. Annie was earning nearly £2 a week and that was more than her father did. This slip of a girl was getting very good money. It had to be borne in mind that she had more education than Margaret, was very well spoken and had been to finishing school, but all the same she must be putting a lot more money away than Margaret could.

'It is long hours Maggie, I will say that, but I get a lot of my Sundays off and many Saturdays. Businesses aren't open you see so they don't need so many of us on the boards. I can earn even more in the not too distant future as well.'

Somewhat dazzled by this, Margaret asked her how she would manage that.

'If you man the boards at night you get a little room to yourself and do your sleeping during the day. Someone has to answer the phones if a subscriber wishes to make a call overnight, so the girls who do that get paid more. You have to be well qualified though and I've only been there a few months. Next year I shall put my name forward. Now here we are home.'

It was clear to Margaret that Annie was 'coining it' and thought that she was doing well. However, when she thought about it, the matter of how much time she had to do things was a serious issue. If Annie worked until eight in the evening, then ate a meal, there was not much left of the day, especially for someone who had to be back on duty at eight the next morning. Then the weekends could be cut into by a rota; and Annie did the same thing day in and day out without variety. Annie might be earning good money and liking her job, but she had not been there very long and Margaret could not help wondering how long it would be before she got bored with it. There were very few careers open to women, and such a repetitive one might be, in the long run, very wearing on the soul. No matter; this was serious stuff and now it was Christmas, a time to enjoy and be merry. She would be as festive as she was allowed to be and resolved that she would enjoy every minute.

A few minutes elapsed after the return to the farm while people changed from their church clothes then Missis, Annie and Margaret set about the Christmas dinner. A huge joint of beef had been put cooking in the oven when they left and was nearing perfection when Missis gave it a basting. Parboiled potatoes were set to roast. Vegetables had been prepared beforehand, and the mix for a great Yorkshire pudding was soon poured into a hot sizzling tray. Before long a feast was ready as parsnips, carrots, cabbage, roast potatoes, peas, beans and, as a concession to modern times, forcemeat stuffing, were piled onto the table, small mountains of food that Margaret thought they surely could never eat. The stuffing was from Mrs Beeton and was a joint effort between Missis and Margaret who had worked the mincer for it. A bottle of wine was set between Mister and Missis, Tom and Joseph preferred beer, William had water and Margaret saw a glass by her place and wondered what she was to drink. This was very quickly answered when Mister filled it with red wine.

'You saved my house from a fire last night and now I'll drink your health in good claret. A Merry Christmas to you my lass.'

So saying he raised his glass as did everyone else, and, not knowing what else to do, she did the same, returned his greeting, and took a sip. She immediately knew that she would have to be careful, for it made her feel heady within a few seconds. Then there were crackers which she had also never had before. Between her seat and that of Tom was a cracker that seemed to belong to her, but he held his out towards her first.

'Come on Maggie. Pull the biggest part and it's good luck for you.'

Smiling she reached over and pulled the cracker; she got the largest part, and a small metal ring fell out with a red glass stone to it, along with a red paper hat.

'Not much use to me that,' So saying Tom picked up the ring and put it on her little finger. Margaret looked at it with some confusion, not knowing what to make of this, but then she looked at Tom who was quite deliberately looking away and joining in the general conversation, the giving of a ring having little consequence to him. He pulled a cracker with his mother, and Margaret settled on William. When they had all put on their silly hats with much laughter and teasing about appearance, Mister carved the joint and dinner commenced.

When it was over the family retreated into the parlour. There was a little time left before the afternoon milking and Margaret knew what they would be doing. Presents would be given and they would play games for a while. Many families preferred to exchange their presents on Christmas Eve as the Magi had done, but the fashion was coming in of using Christmas Day instead, as indeed her own family did. She would have no part in that, nor did she expect to. She was the maid and family should be with family at Christmas. She did feel a little upset that she was not with her own, and for the first time since leaving home she missed them keenly. However, her steely streak retorted to her brain that she should stop being daft for she would see them on the following day. There were many dishes to be washed and dried, pans and roasting tins, but this was all grist to her mill and in an hour or so she was done. In the parlour there was conversation, laughter and evidently the family were having Christmas fun, so it was a good time to make the fudge as Missis had suggested. She drew out of a cupboard the ingredients that she had bought and within a short time the kitchen smelled of caramel. This brought Missis out to have a look and she approved heartily, telling Margaret that it was as good as what she used to make the boys when they were little, but they were not to have any of it. They had eaten quite enough and would have more later.

'But we'll make sure Maggie; take it over to your room to cool so they don't get their greedy hands on it. I know what they're like.'

For the moment they had had quite enough to eat, and they would be hard put to get out of their seats for the milking, but it had to be done.

'I was wondering, Missis, if I could buy a few apples from the store to take home tomorrow please?'

'Yes, well I think we can sort that out in the morning before you go; there's plenty of apples in there. Now then, there's little to do for later so I will not be needing you until eight so why don't you go and have some time off?'

Margaret knew well that the evening meal at 8.00 pm was different to any other. The family was so stuffed that they would not wish a full meal. There would be mince pies, Christmas pudding and crackers with rum butter for any who wanted them, but no great repast. The mince pies were of a wide provenance for it was tradition that each one had to come from a different household, and each wife in the neighbourhood had her own recipe. Margaret had minced the beef very fine indeed for Missis's pies, of which she was very proud.

183

'Mrs Ostle thinks she's got the best round here, but I don't think they're a patch on mine. They are good though, I'll give her that.'

Missis had taken Marra and the trap out on her own and round a circuit of the neighbouring farms, swapping pies with the various ladies of the house.

'Will there be wassailers from the village Missis?'

'No, that doesn't happen here. We stick to the old ways. Twelfth Night is the proper time for Wassail and if any come here before then they know fine they will not get anything.'

Christmas Day in the late afternoon was quite a restful time for Margaret as she was able to finish knitting her father's scarf, and read for an hour or so. Then she filled a little cardboard box with the presents she was taking home. At eight o'clock she was on hand to help with the pudding, which had to be removed from its boiling pan and hung to drain, but the collation for the family was to be placed on a small table in the parlour. This was very informal. She was quite terrified when Mister came out and took a small bottle of brandy from his pocket and poured it over the pudding, then set light to it. Of course, she had heard of this but never seen it, so she stared in fascination at the blue flame as it flickered over the surface and crisped the holly sprig on the top. Mister chuckled at her discomfiture.

'Quite safe Maggie. You won't catch me burning the house down.'

He carried the flaming plate and its load into the parlour to clapping and cheering, followed by Margaret holding a great jug of brandy sauce.

She expected to eat her portion of pies and some sort of small snack in the kitchen, but as she turned to go he looked at her and said,

'Nay. It's Christmas and I've told you, you'll pass it with us and you are welcome Maggie, very welcome. Now just sit over there and we'll have some pies.'

And so it was; she sat by the fire where the Yule log sizzled, and was plied with two mince pies, and thought them delicious for Missis had made many more than the traditional twelve. There was joking and laughing and talk of the farm and local matters, through which she kept quiet, but enjoyed, munching on spoonfuls of pudding with a sauce she had never tasted before. Missis had given her a steaming glass of punch that did much to combat the winter weather outside, then Mister motioned her over to the table, 'Come and get some more pudding Maggie.'

Obediently she moved towards the table, but he intercepted her half way, one hand in his pocket and said,

'Maggie. It's Christmas and in front of my wife and on her instructions, I'm going to give you a kiss.'

Wondering greatly at this proceeding Margaret offered her cheek and received a chaste peck.

'Merry Christmas Maggie. Now look up.'

As Margaret looked up Mister reached up to above her head where a sprig of mistletoe hung and plucked a berry off it.

'There now. I have to give you a gift and here it is.'

So saying he reached into his pocket and gave her something wrapped in blue tissue paper,'

'Well go on then. Open it.'

She did so and was overwhelmed to find a golden guinea nestling in it.

'Oh Mister. What's this for? It's too much.'

'I'll be the judge of that. You put a fire out last night. I told you Barwise Little knows how to be grateful. Now you see I do.'

A small round of applause greeted this little ceremony and the formalities were over. Now it was time for games and Margaret enjoyed this better than anything she could remember. There was no awkwardness for conversation was not necessary. The games did all the talking.

They played *How, What, Where, When* and had to guess what object was written on a piece of paper by the person being questioned. Then they played charades about books. Posset was eaten, nuts were cracked and Tom began to roast chestnuts on the shovel in the fire. The posset had been made by Mister, who apparently prided himself on it. Into a big pan he poured fresh milk and heated it to boil. Then he had curdled it by pouring a quantity of sweet wine into the pan and adding various spices, notably nutmeg and cinnamon. It smelled lovely, but it caused Margaret some confusion because it came in a pewter tankard with a spoon in it; she had never had it and did not know what to do until she watched the others eat it like soup. To her surprise there was a coin at the bottom of her tankard and she fished it out as Missis noticed what she had.

'Aha Maggie. You've got the shilling. That means good luck to you all of next year. Spend it on something good.'

It was when they played *Ha, Hee, Hoe* that Margaret realized that she loved this family. It was such a silly game, but provoked so much laughing that all solemnity, all decorum and all thoughts that she was the maid and they her employers just vanished, as did her reserve. Undoubtedly the punch was having an effect, but she found it very hard to hold a pose when they essayed a game of *Sculptor*, which made Mister bellow with joy, and when finally they played smile, she could not win a game for she kept dissolving into giggles. This was most un-maid like and no doubt she would regret it, but she was having the time of her life. She felt no sense of betrayal at all when finally she was escorted over the yard by Tom with a lanthorn after eleven o'clock and sat for a few minutes thinking it was the best Christmas she had ever had even when she was at home. Then she caught sight of the ring from the cracker that Tom had placed on her little finger. Taking it off she saw that it was pliable metal with a gap so that it could be stretched over other fingers. Widening it slightly, she put it onto the ring finger of her left hand, almost without thinking and wondered what it would be like to wear it all the time, to be married. The thought lingered, for in her world married women had status, for unless they were bluestockings, or followed a secretarial career, or like Annie, became telephonists, to be married was, for many, the summit of ambition.

Then she remembered who gave her the ring. She took it off and put it into the blue vase on the mantlepiece.

'Silly Margaret!' she told herself off, and took herself to bed with a steely determination that she would not endanger her place by foolish dreams. Such thoughts belonged in those newspaper stories of empty-headed girls that Mother did not like her reading. Tomorrow she would be seeing her own family and that would put her feet back on the ground.

There was something to look forward to.

Chapter 13

A Seasonal Adventure

To Margaret's surprise, the baker's boy appeared at the gate early on Boxing Day morning with a bag of very fresh muffins. His appearance was not unusual for most of the shops had been open on Christmas Day too, but the muffins were an addition to the usual bread order and she had not expected them. Missis was somewhat amused by her obvious surprise and quickly explained that it was the family tradition to have muffins, bacon, eggs and mushrooms for Boxing Day breakfast. Despite the quantities of food consumed during the previous day, the appetites of the family had not diminished and when the churns were put out they came in and very swiftly cleared all in front of them.

Annie was there as well, but she was something of an exception to the others round the table for she picked at her food and ate slowly.

'Maggie. Annie will not be going to church today. Would you mind staying with her please to keep her company whilst we are there?'

Margaret was taken aback by the request, because the idea of missing church on Sunday morning was completely alien to her, but this was her employer asking, so quickly she responded that she would not mind. So it was that shortly afterwards she watched the family trot off down the road to Boxing Morning service behind Richard as he pulled the wagon down the lane. Annie was sitting at the table and Margaret looked at her wondering if she was ill. Her face did look rather puffy and her eyes were pink round the edges, so it was possible that she was unwell. However, it was not her business to pry. She set herself about her tasks and washed the dishes. Annie looked at her with watery eyes and suddenly let out a sob and buried her face in her hands. Margaret was instantly at her side, all protocols forgotten, for here was a woman in need of comfort, so she put her arms round her and just held her.

'Oh Maggie I feel so miserable I don't know what to do.'

'What is the matter?' asked Margaret though she thought she knew fine what the answer would be.

'It's nothing really. I know it isn't, but I can't help it. I feel so torn in two.'

'Is it that Mr Metcalfe?'

'Yes it is, of course. But you knew that.' Here she peered at Margaret with tears running down her cheeks. 'But it's so silly. I feel so stupid.'

'Well you're not stupid and not silly either. Why do you think that you are? Do you love him?'

Annie almost wailed, 'Yes I do! I have done ever since we were in the village school and we were small.'

'And would you want to marry him?'

This caused a very timid 'Yes...' but it was overshadowed by a loud 'No!'

'Yes and no.' She looked at Annie and said, 'Well that's logical.'

At least that drew a watery smile.

'I do love him Maggie, and I would marry him, but I don't want to. Does that make sense?'

'Of course not, but I know exactly how that feels. It's head and heart isn't it? Your heart wants one thing and your head wants another.'

'Yes. And that's my problem. I have a good job and I've escaped; I'm earning good money and saving and I have my independence.'

Here Annie burst into tears again.

'But I saw him at the church yesterday and he looked so miserable. Oh I don't know what to do!'

This was the classic dilemma faced by the vast majority of the human race at some time in their lives and possibly more than once. Annie did not wish to be a farmer's wife; at 25 she was still too young in her eyes to settle down and she wished to have a career of her own away from Edderside. In such a manner do we hesitate and hang on to what we have, desperate to stave off the next phase of life in case it is a mistake. In front of Annie were two roads and one was well trodden. If she took it then she would have a man who worshipped her, a home, children, status, and live in the community in which she was brought up. The trouble is that the road less trodden looked green and alluring and could lead to who knew what exciting possibilities. Like the shining bauble or the fairy on top of the Christmas tree, out of reach of a child, it glittered with all the promise of achieving ultimate desire. Most of us chase that all our lives and never win it, that holy grail, for we do not actually know what it is. In Annie's case if she envisaged marriage at all then it was probably with a knight in glittering armour on a white horse who would sweep her off her feet and carry her off to everlasting marital bliss. The trouble was that he does not exist and he never has. To be sure, there are knights and shining armour and white horses, but the bliss part probably would not fit in with any human nature. John Metcalfe was a farmer, not as educated as she was, and content to stay on his farm providing for himself and his family. That was not good enough for Annie's ambition, which was aspirational and hungry.

Margaret, a wise head on young shoulders, knew much of this and responded very briefly,

'You will do whatever you want to do, for better or for worse. But whatever you decide, it has to be your decision. I can't tell you what to do, or your Mam or Dad or brothers. But there's one thing I do know and that is that you don't have to decide now. It takes time to think things like this through, so you just take all the time you need.'

'He might marry someone else though. What would I do then?'

'Well if he does, then he does. It means that he will have decided to move on and the decision will be made for you. He'd have no difficulty doing that for he's a very good looking man and well set up, but somehow I don't think he will. Not in a hurry anyway. You have time to think, so my advice is not to do anything in a hurry.'

Margaret continued to hold Annie for some minutes, but the tears had subsided. Eventually the older girl sat up and moved out of Margaret's arms and looked at her with a weak smile.

'You know for a maid you're not bad. Not what I was expecting at all. Actually Maggie, I was right. You're a brick.'

Margaret laughed, 'I never am what people expect. I can't help it though, I'm just me.'

'I feel a bit better. You are right. I don't have to decide now. I want my job and my career; the rest can wait. I'll worry about it when I have to, but not now. John Metcalfe must be content with what he wishes and I will be content with what I have.'

She did not sound very convincing; indeed there was a brittle edge to her voice as if her statement was borne not out of resolution, but determination. The road less travelled would be explored a bit further; somewhere down the way and behind a tree the white knight smiled and gave a soft laugh.

When the family came back from church Annie was, on the surface at least, quite composed and in control of her emotions, which caused Missis to shine an approving look in Margaret's direction. After soup and bread, it was time for Margaret to leave, and William was elected to drive her to Dearham, which caused in her a vague disappointment for she had been thinking it would be Tom. She placed her box of presents behind her seat on the trap as William got Marra ready to leave, but as they were about to set off the whole family appeared at the door of the house. It was Missis who spoke.

'It's Boxing Day Maggie. Do you know why it's called that?'

Margaret did know, but did not wish to appear to be dropping any hints, so she replied, 'I'm not sure Missis.'

'Well we are. It's called that because it's the day when maids and servants who have been satisfactory are given boxes by their employers for Christmas. You have been more than satisfactory so we have a box for you. Don't open it now, but there you are. Merry Christmas pet, and although I hope you enjoy seeing your family I want you back here for I shall miss you. And here's another box which you can open but I would not do so now. It's full of apples with a Merry Christmas to your family.'

'Hear hear!' came from Mister and his sons, and Margaret received kisses from Missis and Annie; then such was the esteem in which she was held that they waved her out of the gate and round the bend. The snow on the road was quite thin and in no way impeded Marra's progress. The air was cold and crisp, but the sun shone and Margaret had a rug round her knees and another round her shoulders. William was wrapped up in a good thick greatcoat with scarf, flat hat pulled well down. Margaret liked William and so she did not hesitate to initiate a conversation about what Annie had said the previous day.

'William, may I ask you something?'

'Aye if you like. I might not answer though.'

The last was said with a grin.

'Annie said on the way to church yesterday something about you not particularly wanting to work on a farm. Is that true?'

He looked at her, but was not smiling; rather a wistful look had come over his face and his reply was slow, as if drawn out of him.

'I would have to say that the answer to that is yes, though I'd rather you did not mention it to my Mam and Dad. They would not like it. I'd rather work it out on my own.'

'Why do you not like the farm William? It seems a nice enough place to me.'

He drew a deep sigh, 'Yes, I know Maggie and in many ways it is. It's like an old coat you put on. I do my work and Dad pays me a good share of profits. I live well enough, but that's an end to it.'

'An end to it?'

'Yes. It puts food in my mouth and money in my pocket and makes me bored out of my mind. Look at me Maggie.'

This last was spat out with some degree of passion and she looked at him curiously.

'I'm 27 years old, and the plan of my life is laid out as plain as day. I get up every day. I milk cows. I put churns out. I milk again. In the summer this is varied by cutting hay. I'm bored Maggie. I want to do something else for my living.'

'Why don't you then?'

'I have tried talking to Dad, Mister, about it, but he says the same thing every time. The farm is a family business and it provides for all of us. I am needed and the family would suffer if I left. It's emotional blackmail. Dad holds the whole thing together and if he were not there then we'd all go our separate ways.'

'All of you?'

'Oh yes, there's no doubt of that. Joe wants to farm; he's a son of the soil all the way through is Joe. Tom would farm as well, but he would not do cows. He'd like to set up on his own breeding horses in a small way, and you know about Annie.'

'But what about you? What would you do?'

'Ah now there's the question.' His eyes grew distant.

'I don't want much Maggie, but as you are aware none of us left school at fourteen. Dad paid for us to go to the agricultural college and it kind of broadened my horizons you know. It made me see that there's more to life than farming.'

He laughed.

'Actually that's quite ironic that an agricultural college would give me that message. What do I want to do? Well I'll tell you. The college used to take us to places to look at some of the new practices they were encouraging in the area. We'd get on a wagon and go and look at new machines or equipment that the Co-operative was lending out to members. Only one day we went to see a model farm over at the Brayton Hall estate where they were having some buildings put up. One of them was a Dutch Barn I remember, but there were others. Anyway, there was a man there working for the agent that showed us round and he was sitting at a desk writing. I looked over his shoulder and saw that he was setting down columns of figures, so I asked him what he was doing. He told me that this was his work and he was a quantity surveyor.'

'Is that like someone who surveys for houses or buildings?'

'Just a bit Maggie. A quantity surveyor works with the cost and the quality as well as the amount of material that is needed for any building project. Anything to do with buying the right amount of say bricks or cement, finding the best price and checking the quality of what is bought and the work done on site; that's what a quantity surveyor does and that's what I'd really like to do. I've always had a head for figures and I'd love the chance to give it a go.'

'Have you done anything about it, William?'

'Yes, I have actually. There's a chap called Smythe that I knew at the college. He went on to do the exams to be a quantity surveyor, but that's not the only way to get into the trade. He says he'd be willing to take me on as an apprentice, even at my age, for he knows I am good with figures. He has an office up Bothel way and too much work, or so he says.'

'So why don't you?'

'I'm a coward Maggie. Life to me is full of peril and shadows. Mister says I must stay on the farm where I am needed, so I stay. I may rebel one day, but somehow I doubt it. The way things are going I shall be on the farm till I drop dead. Anyway, enough of that – let us talk of pleasanter things.'

It being clear that he had had quite enough revelation for now, they did indeed talk of more frivolous things and it was only about an hour and a half after they had set off that Marra was pulled up and told to stop at the top of the Dib. Someone, probably her father, had scraped the snow from the surface, so it was a few seconds work to run down the slope with her bag and into the arms of her mother who appeared at the door as she reached the bottom. William followed on carrying her boxes and was invited in for a cup of tea where pleasantries were exchanged. Margaret was the centre of a small storm of excitement where Thomas, Johnny and Alpha whirled and jumped around her in glee that big sister was home. From her father a paternal kiss and hug, whilst William got a handshake and thanks for delivering the daughter home safe. The afternoon was advancing and he did not wish to be out after dark, or for Marra to stand long in the cold, so within a few minutes of drinking his hot tea, he was on his way back to Edderside.

Nancy surveyed her daughter.

'You look well. They feed you enough I see.'

'Yes Mother, I think they feed me too much sometimes.'

'Well you're blooming on it. I'm so glad to see you I can't say. That was a nice young man, very personable.'

'Oh Mother, you can stop that right now. William is very nice, but he's not the marrying kind if I am not mistaken. You'll not be marrying me off yet I think. Anyway he's the Master's son and I'm the maid.'

'Hmmph!' snorted Nancy. 'You're a maid and he's a man. I wouldn't think your being a servant would stand in his way.'

'William is more like…a monk Mother. I don't mean in a religious way, but I just don't think he's interested in girls or marriage. Now I have some gifts to give out.'

Reaching into her present box she produced a tin into which she had packed the fudge she had made the day before, and which was received with great enthusiasm. Next came her offerings to her siblings. Johnny was thrilled with his wind up train all in green, red and black, and was soon running it round the floor making 'Choo-choo' noises. Thomas was undoubtedly pleased with his bookmark.

'You made this yourself didn't you?' he enquired.

'Yes I did. Do you like it?'

'I do. It's very nicely done. That's why I thought you did it because it's so neat. Thank you and Merry Christmas.'

Alpha had her red hair ribbon which Margaret tied into a bow that sat on top of her head whilst she looked into the mirror. The little girl was pleased with it, especially when her mother told her that it made her look very pretty. Then she sang to her,

*'My mother bids me bind my hair
With bands of rosy hue
Tie up my sleeves with ribbons rare
And lace my bodice blue.'*

Father sitting beside the fire with a scarf of soft grey wool wrapped round his neck looked rather comical and his eyes smiled with thanks as he kissed her and put it carefully to one side.

'I shall have to keep that for best I think. No taking that one to work.'

Mother was very pleased with her lace edged handkerchiefs declaring them to be so soft and elegant and ladylike that she would only use them to flourish about in church.

'This is for Ommy, Mother. It's a little lavender bag that I think she will like.'

'I think she will. I see that Mr and Mrs Little have given you a box Margaret. Have you opened it yet?'

'No I haven't. Shall I do it now?'

There was no doubt that she should do so. It was a plain box sealed with brown sticky paper and with string tied firmly round it that required scissors to deal with. Lifting the lid, the first thing Margaret saw was a length of cloth wrapped in tissue paper. It was light, and a pale oyster colour. It quite took her breath away.

'Well that is gorgeous and just the thing for a best dress,' said Nancy. 'It's silk poplin I think, and Irish if I'm a judge. Your mistress must really think a lot of you after nursing her and running the house. I could not say it's too expensive but it's just right as a mark of appreciation. You'll be cutting and sewing for a while in the next few months I think.'

Under the cloth was more tissue paper which, when removed, revealed a box of chocolates, a tin of humbugs and a packet of silk thread just the colour necessary for sewing the material given.

'That's very handsome of them,' said John Adams. 'The most Omega gets in her box is left-over food and I think that's more usual than not with servants' boxes. You've fallen on your feet with your place my girl.'

'I think I have,' said Margaret with a smile. 'Now boys and Alpha you may eat the humbugs as I am not fond of them, but the chocolates remain under my control.'

Now it was time for Margaret to open her gifts. From her parents she received with pleasure a pair of warm red mittens knitted by her mother, that could not have been better timed for the weather outside. Johnny gave her a picture of the house that he had drawn to remind her of home, whilst Thomas presented her with a notebook of paper that he had folded and stitched together himself. Alpha very shyly gave her a nice Keswick pencil to go with the notebook. Margaret was delighted and everyone got a hug and a kiss.

'And what is in this box?' asked Mother.

'I asked Missis if I could buy a few apples, but she gave me a box full to bring with me for everyone.'

'You make sure that you thank her from all of us then – and I will write a note for you to take back with you. They look quite delicious and as if they will keep a while.'

'We have a lad called Nick who works at the farm. Missis set him to picking apples and wrapping them in paper to store in a loft. There are loads of them for we have six trees.'

'There are some cookers here too. It's very kind of her. Very kind. I'm glad you are being looked after so well.'

'I will tell her that. She'll be happy to hear it. Now is there much news?' asked Margaret.

It was her mother who replied, 'You mean of the village? Not much really. The Co-op's doing well as you might expect. People are that grateful that they've saved all those jobs that some are shopping nowhere else.'

'Having a bad effect on others though,' said John Adams. 'Serginson says he won't be able to stay in business if they carry on like this.'

He paused to try to think of other items.

'The Vicar's got himself a new bicycle to go out and about on. I don't think I'd care to try it though. It's one of those penny-farthing things and it looks very dangerous. I should think if you fell off it you'd break your neck. Oh, and Bill Gannon's away south to Barrow on the train for a few days to stay with his sister and her family over Christmas.'

Margaret thought it was just as well that he was not there for although she was not expected to give the lodger a present, she did feel slightly guilty that she had not thought of it.

'Now you sit down Margaret,' said Nancy, 'and tell us all about what you do and what it's like.'

There was so much to tell. Boxing Day evening was spent in tales of West End Farm, of its inhabitants, what they said, did and owned. As Margaret talked they ate her fudge with much appreciation. Margaret described her job, and Agnes and Allonby and the horse and so on, until her family felt that they knew it almost as well as she. Over the next few days she settled back down into the routine of the house, which she found was much like being at work. Here she helped her mother and the only difference was that the provision in Edderside was more munificent, as befits a prosperous farm, whereas down the Dib the food was as would be found in a collier's house; that is to say sufficient but not luxurious. Father did say that he was looking forward to earning some extra money in the new year for the new shaft was going to be sunk so that Crosshow colliery could extract more coal. He and Bill Gannon had volunteered to work on the shaft sides, making it good as the men with the pneumatic drills did their work. For as long as it took he would earn seven shillings a day then go back to working a stent when the shaft was done. Mining was hard and dangerous work, but it was regular pay and kept a roof over their heads, clothes on their backs and food on the table.

The Temperance Society was having a festive entertainment for the season and John Adams decided that the whole family should attend on the Wednesday evening. They braved the cold and dark and took lanthorns up into Dearham where the hall was rapidly filling with people wanting to view what was an ever-popular form of entertainment, a magic lanthorn show. Margaret, feeling that discretion was the better part of valour, did not reveal to her father that since leaving home she had partaken of the demon drink and quite enjoyed it, but could not help a sneaky little feeling of guilt and the thought that she should not be there. However, she comforted herself in the inner voice that reminded her that she had never taken the pledge, even though Father and Mother had.

The magic lanthorn was an impressive looking piece of apparatus that had been hired from a large photographic shop in Maryport. Inside it was a paraffin burner with quite a bright flame generating quite a lot of heat that came out through slitted vents in the top of the casing. Protruding from the case were no fewer than three sets of lenses, each of which could take a slide that could be pushed into place one after the other. The lanthorn was manned by a young man from the shop who was skilled in the use of it, as he had to be; Margaret knew that such projectors could catch fire and set places alight and she noted a bucket of water standing by, just in case. The narrator for the evening was a local showman called Mr Cope, and a very impressive figure he was, looking like some villain from a melodrama with a twisted and well-waxed moustache. However, his voice was wonderful, so well projected that even at the back of the hall every syllable of what he said was clear as a bell. Most of the stories were short and some of them were very funny.

The first set of slides was about 'the bashful man' but he was not so much bashful as completely inept and clumsy. His attempts to speak to the girl he loved but could only stutter to had most of the room in stitches, as the showman rendered him so well to match the image projected onto the screen. He was in the library and accidently destroyed a valuable book whilst all the time trying to put it back from where he had taken it. Then he lost a bar of soap and could not find it and his lady-love's father trod on it and slipped down the stairs. Finally, when he had made such an exhibition of himself he poured a glass of brandy, drank too much and fell over in a pantomime tableau being staged for Christmas. The coloured round pictures of the scenes from the story left no need to imagine and they were so comic that everyone, Margaret included, was hooting and helpless with laughter. Aesop's fables were next and the morality of them drew interest and nodding, but no laughter. The best part of the evening was the tale of the elephant and the tailor. There was a tailor sitting at his bench by the window and an elephant looked in. The look on the tailor's face was hilarious, but the elephant's was a picture. In the next slide the nasty tailor pricked a needle into the elephant's trunk to make him go away, and this occasioned some booing and nasty remarks for his cruelty. But the rest of it was pure genius, for though you knew what was going to happen, it was the anticipation of it that caused the uproar. First the elephant was seen filling his trunk at the horse trough in the street, which caused someone in the crowd to exclaim 'Oh aye, I know what's going to happen!'

'So do we all; haud thee lollicker!'

Then the elephant tiptoed to the window, which sight was so funny that some of the older ladies laughed themselves purple in the face. But when the elephant stuck his trunk through the window and shot a full load of water straight at the hapless tailor, the whole place just dissolved and was helpless for a good five minutes. Margaret felt that she had never laughed so much in her life.

This was the high spot of her home visit, though mostly she just enjoyed being back with her parents and siblings for a few days, the only exception being Omega who could not get away until 30 December. However, on 28 and 29 December the weather, which had been merely cold, turned bitterly arctic in nature, which curtailed many things round the village as people did not wish to go out. Saturday 29 was a day that would long stay in Margaret's memory, because the heavens opened and it snowed as if all the snow in the world was falling and would never cease. Winter had arrived with a vengeance and would not relax its grip for the next four months; seven inches of snow lay on the ground when they woke on Sunday morning, and the beck had frozen solid and they had to hack chunks of ice to thaw for drinking. They did not know it, but not far to the south and east, Lake Windermere had frozen over with ice 18 inches thick, an event remembered ever afterwards as the 'Big Freeze.' John Adams had been back at work since the day after Boxing Day and Bill Gannon had returned from Barrow, but their Sunday morning was partly spent digging to clear a path up the Dib to the road and sprinkled the whole with cinders. However, as head of the family he decided that he was not prepared to take his wife and younger children to church; the snow alone was not the main factor in his decision, but the biting chill of the wind. Instead he decreed that they would have family prayers round the table, and they would sing hymns and he would tell a sermon just as if they were in church. God would understand.

'I think Margaret that you must not expect your sister today. I hope and I pray that she has enough sense to stay in her room.'

The same thought had occurred to Margaret, who, although she would have loved to have seen Omega, did not want her walking from Maryport like an arctic explorer.

'Well, if she does not come Father, I think I will leave her present here for her if you don't mind giving it to her for me please.'

'I will do that Margaret,' replied her father. 'I also doubt that you'll be going anywhere in this. The snow will clog up any cart wheels because it's very clingy.'

201

Margaret considered this was very likely and thought that she may well be staying at home a little longer than she had planned. However, she decided not to take the business for granted and packed her bag just in case someone should come to get her.

A small question that had sat at the back of her mind for as long as she could remember was resolved on this day, because she went up to Saul Serginson's shop to buy some aniseed balls for her father, since he was fond of them. As she stood while Serginson weighed out the sweets she asked her question.

'Mr Serginson; why does your bell have a number 5 on it?'

Serginson laughed and said, 'Well fancy you noticing that Maggie. No-one has ever asked me that before.'

'I've wondered about that since I was a little girl, but never dared to ask.'

'Am I really that fierce? The answer's simple enough. It's one of a set of twelve Maggie; handbells that are played in sequence and each with a different note. There's some people form groups and use them to play as a band; there's even contests between them like there are for brass bands or choirs. It's been going on for hundreds of years.'

'Did you ever do that then?'

'Bless you, no. I have a set and I use the 5 bell on the counter because I find it a particularly pleasing note. No. The reason I have a set is because when I was young I used to live in a town far to the south of here where I practised the ancient art of campanology.'

Seeing her puzzled look, he continued, 'Bell ringing Maggie. Church bells. I used to ring the bells in a great cathedral, but it was not always convenient for us to practise on the big bells. The sequences we used to play the bells with are called changes, and we used to use hand-bells to practise the changes. I still have the rest in a cupboard.'

'Do you not ring the bells here?'

'No.' There was an almost amused note to his voice. 'St Mungo's has a small set of light bells and nothing like what I used to use. It would be like using a rowing boat if you used to be an officer on a man of war. Anyway I'm too busy for all that; as you know I'm open all hours.'

Margaret left the shop with a small smile on her face; it was strange what little secrets were to be found in ordinary people, but at least the puzzle of 5 was solved.

Father doing the prayers turned out to be rather good and made her think that he should turn Methodist and become a preacher, a suggestion that he laughed at later.

He began with the third collect for grace and said it as clearly and with so much expression as Mr Melrose the vicar did,

'Teach us good Lord to serve thee as thou deservest
To give and not to count the cost,
To fight and not to heed the wounds.
To toil and not to seek for rest
To labour and not to ask for any reward save that of knowing
that we do thy will.'

When this was finished they sang *Fight the Good Fight* very rousingly except that they heard clapping from through the wall as the neighbours applauded their efforts.

When this was done Father preached a sermon by telling them the tale of silly Rebecca. This was a girl who had thin patches on the soles of her shoes and knew very well that she would need to buy some soon. She had been saving her money for new shoes and went with her mother to town to go to the cobblers there, but it was market day as they arrived in town. Thomas interrupted briefly to ask if it was Maryport, but his father assured him that it probably was and went on. Silly Rebecca was almost at the cobblers when she saw a cheapjack pedlar and on his cloth, spread out on the pavement was a beautiful blue-lidded vase. It had deep colour, lustre and would look wonderful in her room with flowers in it; or, because it had a lid, she could keep herbs or sweets in it. She wanted it so badly and the desire to possess it grew in her so much that it diverted her away from anything else. She told her mother that she wanted the vase more than anything else in the world, but her mother told her that she had come to town to buy shoes. Rebecca looked at the vase, then at the cobbler's window close by and said to her mother that she could not make up her mind to get the vase or the shoes. Mother would have to tell her what to do; however her mother refused and said that life was full of decisions that had to be made. Rebecca would have to learn to make her own choices. Torn this way and that, Rebecca decided that the vase was far more important than shoes that after all, had not quite worn through yet. She paid the pedlar for the beautiful vase, he wrapped it in a sheet of paper and she and her mother began the walk home. When they reached the edge of town she could wait no longer and unwrapped the vase and took off the lid. Oh horror! The vase was not blue at all but a plain cheap glass vase filled with a foul smelling blue liquid. Desperately she poured out the liquid to see if any of the glass was blue, but it was not, being little more than a glorified jam jar. Her mother looked on with a grim face, but accompanied her back to where she had made her purchase, only to find that the cheapjack had gone. That winter she had holes in her shoes and wet feet so how she did cry, though her mother gave her no sympathy at all.

'Now tell me what we learn from this story Thomas.'

'All that glisters is not gold Father. It's the same story as we get in Sunday school.'

'Well done. Now Johnny. Any other moral here?'

'That if you choose, then it's your own fault, nobody else's.'

'Quite right. Margaret?'

'Choose shoes, every time!'

This quip brought a smile, but a rebuke too.

'We are in church my dear. Alpha - what does this story tell you?'

The little girl puckered up her face and thought very hard then said,

'The pedlar was a nasty man.'

'Indeed he was my child and we should never trust nasty men should we?'

The end of the service was heralded by *'He who would valiant be'* which the neighbours joined in with through the wall, and the Lords Prayer.

They had just finished when there was a knock on the door. It was Tom Little who had come to collect Margaret and transport her back to West End Farm.

When he had shaken hands with Father and Mother, and said hello to Thomas Adams, Johnny and Alpha, he accepted a cup of tea by the fire.

'I need this Mr Adams, I can tell you. It's cold out there. I must not stay too long for though the horse has a rug on, I think he'd like to get going again.'

'I cannot understand how you got here through such thick snow. Your wheels must get stuck and clogged up.'

Tom grinned and replied, 'There's no wheels Mr Adams. None at all. I came on the farm sledge. Our Annie's gone back to Carlisle on the train yesterday and my mother says she cannot do without Maggie any longer, so I must go and get her.'

A short while after, it was time to go. There was much kissing and hugging and everyone went up the Dib to see Marra, who was indeed hitched to a farm sled with two runners and two seats at the front.

'We used to use this a few years ago when the beasts were kept out in the winter. That was before we built the barn to improve their health, and feed had to be taken out to the fields. We've still got it and it's rather useful in weather like this, as I found last winter. Now then Maggie, my Mam sent these to put round you.'

Tom produced the two woollen blankets that Margaret wrapped round her shoulders over her coat, and over her knees, but he handed over something wide and dark. It was an oilskin sheet.

205

'That'll keep the wind off you, for it's the wind that makes you cold.'

'What about you?'

'Well by your leave I have my own rug, but the sheet is big enough to go over both of us, so will you share?'

This was said with a pleading smile, but of course she would. It would not do to have Tom freeze. She had expected William to come and get her, but she was glad it was Tom who was more lively and somehow more spiced with the force of life and masculinity.

Soon they were off, Margaret turning in her seat to wave to the family at the top of the Dib as they went easily down Row Brow, but slowly for Tom did not wish Marra to slip as he went down.

'It's very easy along the coast road because it's flat. I swear that Marra finds this sled easier than the trap. I doubt he'll shed a shoe in it either. He did the other day and I had to take him round to the smithy at Mawbray to get it seen to. You can have his old shoe for luck if you want. It's hanging in the barn.'

'I'd like that please. I'll put it on the mantelpiece.'

'Remember to have it upright like a U or the luck will run out.'

'I will.'

Beneath the oilskin Margaret felt warm for she had a good thick skirt on and two petticoats as well as a coat, mittens, woolly hat and the wool rug. She was also very conscious that Tom generated a fair bit of heat, for she could feel the warmth of his leg to the side of her. The air was so cold though. She'd be glad to get back home. The thought of that made her pause and smile; she had thought of West End Farm as home and in a way it was, for she had, in her mind, two homes. One was home home, where Mother and Father were, but now she had work home and she liked that one too.

'Did you enjoy your stay?'

'I did, but I'm sorry that I did not see my eldest sister. She was supposed to come home this afternoon, but I suppose she could not do it in the snow.'

'Well, that's not surprising really. There's a lot of it.'

Indeed there was. Skimming along the road behind Marra who seemed very snug in his blanket, Margaret looked over a countryside covered in a thick coat of snow fully seven inches deep, but where the wind had drifted it, to about five feet. It looked very picturesque, but hardly a soul was out.

'Where does your sister work?'

'In Maryport.'

Tom turned to look at her.

'Well we're going through Maryport. What street?'

'Wood Street.'

'That's easy enough. I'll take a run up Wood Street then, instead of turning at the junction. You might see her.'

He would not be dissuaded and as they came to Curzon Street they did not turn for Edderside, but carried straight on.

'She won't be out this weather Tom and I can't go knocking at the door.'

'You won't have to. Notice any other traffic?'

She had not; the road had a thick layer of snow and a few wagon wheels had compacted tracks, but they had seen no-one else. On the other hand, the sight of a horse drawn sled was such an unusual sight that they drew interest, indeed stares from the people that they had seen who were brave enough to be out. As Marra trotted up Wood Street Tom reached down and began to turn a handle on the side of the driver's seat. It was a rather loud rotary bell, and curtains began to twitch as residents came to see what the noise was. Margaret looked up at the top windows where she knew would be servant quarters and took her hat off which though it exposed her ears to the frost, meant that she could be more easily recognised.

'Do you know which number?'

'I don't Tom. But aren't you worried we'll get arrested for disturbing the peace or something?'

'For ringing a bell? I'm warning people that I'm coming; that's what the bell is for. I won't be arrested for that.'

They slow trotted up Wood Street until they reached the High Street where, there being no traffic, Tom turned Marra round and then proceeded back down the same route. Halfway down, outside a large porticoed house set back from the pavement a familiar figure stood by the roadside. Margaret jumped down to give her a hug,

'Ommie! I haven't seen you in ages. How are you?'

After sisterly kissing and introductions were made Omega told Margaret,

'I'd love to ask you in, but I can't. It's not allowed under any circumstances even on my afternoon off.'

'I know that Ommie, so we won't keep you long. It's too cold for that and you'll freeze.'

It was true for Omega was shivering. Having seen Margaret on the sled she had dashed downstairs and outside without a coat.

'I have no doubt at all that Mr Furnival is looking out of his window right now and I will get a telling off for making an exhibition of myself in the street, so I can't stay. But there's things I want to say, so I'll write you a letter soon. And even better news is that in mid April they are starting a horse omnibus from Maryport to Allonby for people who wish to visit the beach. We could meet there.'

Mr Furnival was indeed looking out of his window, and as a respectable solicitor, clearly did not wish his maid to make a scene in the street outside.

'I just wanted to see you and give you a hug. I didn't know I was going to see you or I would have brought your present. Father has it for you next time you go home.'

'I wasn't expecting to see you either, but I'm glad you did come. I brought your present down when I saw it was you on the sled outside, but now you should go and let this nice young man take you home. Open it when you get there.'

Here she handed over a slim package with a kiss and 'Merry Christmas' which Margaret returned. Then she looked at Tom, saying nothing but with a considering look. He was a nice young man; well at 30 he certainly was not old. She did not care that he was bald, but in his hat that could not be seen and he looked like a boy, certainly younger than his years. With the fierce moustache and the rather piercing eyes, he looked very male and rather formidable if you did not know him.

Leaving Omega with kisses, to go and placate her employer, she and Tom took the sled back up the street and turned out towards Allonby.

Their talk was fairly everyday and innocuous; in fact it was curtailed by cold as Marra trotted with apparent ease through the snow, pulling the sled without great effort. They fairly flew along the winter countryside, but they were no more than halfway to Edderside when Margaret felt herself getting colder and colder. Her toes seemed to be freezing and she was sure that she could not feel the end of her nose. The thought crossed her mind that if the journey continued like this then she was going to freeze solid. She'd end up like one of those people she had read of in Russia who went out in the snow and were later found frozen into blocks of ice. She turned to look at Tom just as the wind blew a thick flurry of snow in off the sea and her eyes were streaming with tears caused by the cold.

'Are you all right Maggie? What are you crying for? Is it because you've left your family?'

Really men were so dense sometimes, was her thought when he said this, but it at least made her smile though the muscles of her half frozen face ached as they forced themselves into a grin which she immediately wished she had not, because her lower lip cracked slightly.

'I'm not crying for upset Tom. I'm freezing and the cold's making my eyes water. I never thought it would be so cold. If I don't get warm somehow soon, I think I shall faint from it. How far is it to go?'

'It must be about three miles I think. I'm quite warm myself.'

How typical it is of the male half of the human race, when faced with a woman stating a problem, to straight away compare it with their own; it did not help her situation. Tom was evidently considering the problem though and then he brought Marra to a halt.

'Right Maggie,' he said, unfolding his blankets. 'Snuggle up close to me. Think of it as a friendly act, for I am warm enough and there's no reason not to share it is there?'

Needs must when the devil drives and his suggestion made a lot of sense so she moved across to sit next to him.

'If you want the full benefit of it, put your arms round me, so they will warm up as well. You don't need to use them so I'll wrap the blankets round you and cover your head with them with the oilskin over the whole.'

Such an invitation from a man was, in ordinary circumstances not be thought of, but Tom she knew to be an honest and decent man who was trying to help, so she accepted his offer. Soon they were progressing along towards Allonby again and she was a lot warmer. Was it, she wondered, that men were hotter than women? He really was warm, and under his rugs and the oilskin with a Tom sized hot water bottle she grew quite snug. Not for the first time, she decided that she liked the wholesome smell of him; that he was acting like a gentleman in her predicament recommended him to her even more.

Could she have seen Tom's face she might have been slightly more concerned, for a myriad of emotions were flashing in and out of his eyes. Occasionally, he looked down to where her head rested against his shoulder, her hat visible above the oilskin. To a casual observer his expression would have been quite riveting, for he was trying to seem unconcerned, but failing signally. He liked Margaret with her arms round him and that was for sure, though the situation was far from romantic, and if she liked his smell, he liked hers just as much. Tom was no shrinking violet in his approach to life, and he had had women's arms round him before, but of course there are arms, then there are arms. Margaret was a very attractive young woman, accomplished in the household arts practised by all the women around. He was not a man of iron, and though he was probably wrong to do so, this was the day he always remembered as being the one when he first really noticed Margaret. In fact, he had noticed her before, but had kept his acknowledgement of it suppressed. He had read too many stories of maids and masters with the trouble they could get into.

Soon they arrived below West End Farm where he slowed down and reminded her that they had better not be seen in this attitude by the family, or the wrong construction might be put upon it. By now nicely warm she wrapped her rugs round herself alone and shortly afterwards the sled turned into the farmyard. She was welcomed enthusiastically. Someone had lit a fire in her rooms, so they were cosy; here she opened her sister's present and found it to be a lovely decorated tortoiseshell comb, perfect for pinning her hair up behind for special occasions like church. It was, she thought, in very good taste, but much that Omega did was in good taste and she really should have been born a lady, not a maid. Soon she was back at her place by Missis' side preparing liver, bacon and onions for the evening meal at eight o'clock sharp. She looked round the warm kitchen with its wooden table, bread ready for the hungry men just finishing the milking, and sighed.

It was good to be home; even when, that night, she dreamed of Tom, his moustache, and Marra the talking horse who told them to behave or people would talk.

Chapter 14

Dolly and Folly

The postman called at West End Farm in the late afternoon of 5 January 1895 and left an envelope containing news that caused Margaret a lot of surprise, making her shake her head in disbelief. Omega had promised to write her a letter when she had seen her just before the New Year, but evidently her situation had changed somewhat since the hasty interview in the snow by the sled. Her sister had given no indication that anything untoward had occurred up until then, and indeed if it had it would be hard to think that she could have suppressed it. Since that meeting events had occurred in which Margaret thought Omega had been very unwise, for if news of what she had done got out then she would be what novelists referred to as 'a ruined woman.'

'*Dear Margaret,*

I hope this finds you as well as you looked when I last saw you, though not as cold. I still have not managed to get home because of the snow, so do not have your gift yet. When I saw you I promised to write you a letter, so here it is, but it is not the one that I thought I would be writing. That letter would have been quite ordinary, but since last Saturday things have changed so much that I can hardly believe it. I have to tell someone or I shall burst, but please do not tell anyone else and especially not Father or Mother, for they would be very angry I know. The only person I can confide in is you, dear Margaret, so please be my confessor and don't be cross.

I believe that I have told you before that Mr Furnival has a son who is at university where he is studying law. The intention is that he shall follow his father into the practice. He came home for Christmas of course, and since then he has spent much of his time indoors, for he has no close friends in the neighbourhood. He has been behaving much as I have described in the past, touching me on the stairs and thinking it a joke, but I said nothing because I did not wish to lose my place. When I have been called on to wait on him his eyes followed me everywhere, so I took to bolting my door at night in case he should get any ideas. It's not that I found him repulsive, for I do not, it's just that I know it would never work and I had no intention of travelling that well-trodden road that you read about in the Daily Mail where servant girls get ruined.

On Sunday Mr Furnival was out in the afternoon and I was coming down the backstairs when Edward, that's his son, was coming up. He was not supposed to, for as you know, back stairs are for servants. However, he said that he was looking for me, so I asked what I could do for him. He said that I was a nice looking girl and very pretty; that he'd had his eye on me for absolute ages and he'd come to find me because he was going to jolly well give me a kiss. I know that I should have said no Margaret, but as I told you before, the look of him turns my brain to mush and makes me go weak at the knees. He has nice dark hair, blue eyes and a thin moustache and is so well made that I like to look at him, for he is a proper man. So I said he could and leaned forward thinking he would kiss my cheek. Well, that was not what he had in mind and next thing I knew he had me in a clinch and was kissing my mouth. I need not go into details I am sure, but he then took me up to my room and we did things there that we should not have. When it was over he was most attentive and affectionate and swore that he would marry me and would have no other. He said I must not tell his father, but that he was in his last year of study and would set up practice in his own right soon, and that I should be his wife. Just think of it Margaret! I am going to be a solicitor's wife.

I know I should not have done it and I am sure that the Church would not approve of it, but I simply cannot feel guilty at all about it. In the next few months Edward will find the time to tell his father and we shall be married I expect during this summer. I am so excited that I can hardly sleep and I had to tell

you. Please understand dear Margaret; I do want you to be glad, because I just know everything is going to be wonderful.
Your loving sister, Ommie X'

Margaret was very troubled by this missive. She thought that Omega had been very unwise to allow things to go as she had described, and hoped that the confidence was not one that she would repeat elsewhere. Omega would become an object of rebuke in her own community and for miles around if word got out; she would be labelled as a loose woman and called all sorts of names. On the other hand, if all was as she had said then there would be no doubt that she had advanced her station in life beyond all expectations. She just hoped that Omega loved Edward and that he did the same. She would hate to think that her sister had been so easily taken advantage of, but if all was as she said then she looked forward to a wedding later in the year. Privately, and in the recesses of her own mind, she did not think much of Mr Edward Furnival for taking advantage of a serving maid in such a manner, but on the other hand if he did it out of true love then all would come well. She wrote Omega a reply designed to be comforting, as if what she had told was the most natural thing in the world. It was a newsy letter and one full of the implication that it was not for her to judge what Omega had done, that she had her sister's love and that she hoped all would turn out as Ommie wished. She also thanked Omega for the gift of the comb which was really pretty and very practical.

On her own mind was the matter of Tom, because she had really begun to notice Tom. Before the ride home on the sled she had liked him, but the trouble was that now she liked him even more. She would find herself in a daydream occasionally, where she was holding him under the blankets to keep from the cold, and she would remember his warmth and his odour. This was something that stern Margaret could hold in check, reminding herself of her position and that it was not the place of a serving maid to even be thinking such things, but it did not make them go away. To add to the trouble a sort of tension now existed between her and Tom. She had caught him several times looking at her, and was pretty sure that he looked at her a lot more times when she did not see him. Quite how to describe that look she was not entirely sure, but she had seen it on the faces of men before, and had learned to be wary of it; if any word fitted that expression it was 'hungry' and it suited Tom's look very well. He would have to be handled with care, she decided.

After dinner that evening the family were sitting round the kitchen table prior to dispersing to their various activities, and Margaret was in the parlour placing some coal for Mister and Missis to come through to, when music began outside the front door. This door was hardly ever used as most people came in through the kitchen; outside it was a small area between the house and the lawn with a wall, and a path led from there to the road through a small wooden gate.

'It's the Waits!' cried Mister. Seeing Margaret's puzzled look he continued, 'Waits lass. We don't get them every year. They come round sometimes with the Wassailers and play their music for people to sing to. You must not forget that this was Christmas Day on the old calendar and things change slowly in these parts. Let's go out and greet them. Joseph pour the wassail and bring the bowl. It's a bit heavy for't lass.'

Margaret did not think it was too heavy for her at all, but Joseph was undoubtedly a strong man and would find it easy, so she let him. The wassail was mostly ale that Mister had warmed on the stove, but then he had poured an entire bottle of sherry into it and added some cinnamon sticks. She brought up the rear with a tray of cheap glass tumblers as Mister threw open the front door with Merry Christmas and Happy New Years being shouted all around.

Three men stood there, one with a drum and another with a trumpet, whilst the third had a flute; they jigged up and down as they played; a crowd of men and women with children from the village sang,

*'God rest ye merry, gentlemen
Let nothing you dismay
Remember Christ our Saviour
Was born on Christmas Day
To save us all from Satan's po'er
When we were gone astray
O tidings of comfort and joy,
Comfort and joy.
O Tidings of comfort and joy!'*

It looked very seasonal as they stood in the snow, some with lanthorns, others with tarred rag wrapped round as flaming torches, and others with an end of candle in a jam jar, hung from a piece of string on a stick.

'That's well sung,' cried Mister, 'now let us have of your wassail and you shall have of ours.'

Two milkmaids came forward, one of whom was Agnes, and between them they carried a large milkpail full of another wassail mix. Whatever was in it smelled nice and spicy. Each member of the household was given a cup of this and had to drink it shouting 'Wassail!'

Margaret felt a presence behind her and found that Tom was there and he handed her a cup of the mixture from the pail.

'I feel silly shouting Wassail. What does it mean?'

'I'm told that it means good health in the old English tongue Maggie, so I recommend you just do it.'

She looked around at the expectant eyes watching her and suddenly felt quite shy. She did not, as Mister had done, throw the whole cup back in one go, but sipped it in a much more restrained manner and said rather diffidently 'Wassail' upon which, like all the others, she got a cheer.

'Now then you Waits must earn your fee. Drink some of this house's wassail then play us another tune.'

'What shall it be Mister?'

'I'd like '*I saw three ships,*' so strike up and blow hard.'

This was sung with enthusiasm, and at the end of it the whole party drank from the farm wassail until it was all gone.

Then Mister felt in his fob pocket and said, 'Now where's your boxes? Bring them forward.'

The Waits' box was first and into it he put three shillings and then into the wassail box he also put three shillings; this was generous, but it only happened once a year and he had a reputation for open-handedness which he had to keep up. Now once again there were cries of Happy New Year, and the wassailers began to move on to the next farm.

'I'm going with them' said Tom on impulse. 'I like a good sing now and then and the opportunity should not be passed up.'

William announced that he would join him, and to their surprise Joseph, who usually showed no enthusiasm for this sort of thing, said he would accompany them.

Missis looked at Margaret, 'You're a young woman Maggie. Why don't you go with them?'

"May I?'

'Of course girl! You've finished for the night. Go and enjoy yourself.'

So it was that after a hasty visit to her room to get her coat, hat, scarf and gloves, Margaret set off a wassailing with the crowd of people from Edderside and the surrounding farms. It was dark and chilly, but the Little men all had lanthorns with them and they could see well enough, but she found herself struggling a little bit on the icy road, for her shoes were not up to the job. Ahead of her was Joseph and he seemed to have thrown caution to the wind for he was a different man; he was walking along without a care in the world with Agnes hanging on his arm chatting away without cease and he back to her; she would not have thought to see such a thing. If Mister and Missis heard of it she wondered what they would say? It was then than she fell on the ice and hit her knee, and oh it did hurt.

Tom was there immediately with his lanthorn; everyone else had moved on and she had not thought he was behind her. She had pulled her skirt up to see her knee, but could not in the dark until he appeared.

'It's not cut Maggie, but I think you'll have a bruise on it tomorrow. Are you all right to go on?'

Tom had seen her bare knee.

'I know what you're thinking, but I've seen a girl's leg before so don't fret on it. I'm not going to jump on you.'

It was a good job it was dark as she felt her face go red. 'I've torn my stocking.' Tom had seen more of her than he should have done, and whilst she felt a strange thrill at the idea there was a part of her that wished he had not. Then she reproached herself for being a prude. After all, neither of them had done anything deliberate.

'Let me help you up now and I think you'd better hang on to my arm. It's very icy here, I'm not going to fall over and Mam would not be happy if you were out of action, would she?'

She had to admit that he had a point, so for the rest of the promenade she hung onto his arm and it was a good job that she did. Tom was as steady as a rock, because he was wearing his very sturdy hobnail boots. It was cold and crisp, and the earth was really as the carol said, hard as iron, water like a stone. At each stop they sang enthusiastically and Tom drank some of the wassail, at which he seemed to be quite merry. It was obvious that he was very fond of a drink and Margaret hoped that he would be steady enough to get them home.

Eventually the wassailers finished their circuit and came back round to Edderside, and people began to peel away to go back to their various homes. They knew that the contents of the box would be split up fairly by the masters of the wassail and that many present would receive a seasonal contribution in the morning; but it would not be wise to divide it up in the dark and cold. Tom was really quite boisterous and she wondered if he was tipsy. He certainly was, as she found without doubt when they walked up the slope towards the farm. He leaned over and kissed the top of her head. Then he turned her round as she tried not to fall over on the ice.

'Now then Maggie I'm going to give you a kiss,' he declared as he pressed his lips against hers; however, she pushed him back in great anger and made her feelings very clear.

'No, you are not Tom. You stink of alcohol, you haven't asked me if I want to be kissed and you are forgetting who we are.'

'But I thought you liked me.' This was not a wail, but rather plaintive.

'I do like you, but not at the moment. You're drunk and you just tried to force me to kiss you.'

'I'm sorry Maggie. I'm really sorry Maggie. Lemme make it up to you.' Here he tried to shake her hand but she was not having that either.

'Now you're a maudlin drunk. Father told me there are three types of drunk, angry, gormless and maudlin and that's what you are, maudlin. Go to bed Tom and sleep it off.'

They were just outside the gate of the farmyard, so Margaret walked in through and up to her own room where she slid the bolt firmly across. Tom, looking rather like a stricken spaniel, went through the back door into the kitchen where his mother had not yet gone to bed. She heard her voice raised at him and thought that if she clipped his ears then he probably deserved it. If a man was going to drink, then he should be able to control himself and not let it take him over. With that virtuous thought she drifted to sleep.

In vino veritas is an old and hackneyed phrase, but it is often true. Tom had tried to force her to kiss him, which raised the spectre in her mind that she might have to seek a new job. Omega's experiences with Edward Furnival made her wary of anything in her own situation that might lead to a similar situation. Tom was the son of her employer and though she liked him, he was a man with prospects and money whereas she was a penniless maid. Well, not quite penniless, because she now had money from her earnings. It would not do, and however much she liked him or he her, there would have to be a line drawn between them. If there was no line then she would have to be at the next hiring fair in May. Men were beasts, so her mother had told her often, and they did beastly things in which they could not control themselves. If Tom was going to do things like that, then she would control the situation if he could not.

The next morning she woke at five o'clock and lay for a while in the warmth of her bed thinking about what had happened, but eventually lit a candle and dressed herself. She could hear Agnes bustling about and knew that the milking was going on, but there were a few minutes to go before she would have to present herself in the kitchen. She heard feet on the steps outside and then there was a gentle knock on the door; when she opened it, it was Tom.

'I'm sorry Maggie, I'm really sorry. I don't know what came over me.'

'I do Tom. It was the drink. Why did you drink so much?'

'I don't know. I just like the taste of it I think, and I had too much.'

'I know you had too much; you did not behave like a gentleman.'

He winced, 'I know. And I've come to say I'm sorry. I should not have done it and I make no excuses for my disgusting behaviour.'

He really did look quite appealing she thought, like a little boy being told off, but he was still who he was, so she was not going to labour the point.

'I accept your apology Tom, and would be very glad if it did not happen again.'

'It won't. Anyway there's something else I want to say.'

This was in almost a whisper and obviously made with effort.

'What is it Tom?'

After some more hesitation, 'Look Maggie, what I did last night was wrong, and it was the drink, but it was not all the drink.'

'What do you mean?'

'Ah, this is hard. I mean that the drink let something loose which I've been thinking a while now. I'm not going to hide it.'

By now Margaret was divining what he was going to say, and intervened very quickly,

'I think you'd better say no more, Tom. I'm the maid in your parent's house and you are my employer's son.'

'Did you see Joseph last night? Hanging on to Agnes. If he doesn't care about walking out with the milkmaid I don't see why I should care about walking out with the housemaid.'

'That's different.'

'How's it different? You're both maids.'

222

'Agnes is a milkmaid. Every farm round here needs milkmaids and will until they invent a machine to milk cows.'

Tom laughed, 'They already have Maggie, but they're not very good. Let me be clear about this. I like you. I find that I like you a lot and I would like to walk out with you. Will you Maggie? Do you like me enough to walk out with me?'

'I cannot walk out with you Tom. If your parents found out that you wanted that then I would probably lose my place here and I don't want that. It's a good place and I'd like to keep it. Can't you walk out with another girl?'

'You're the first girl I've met for years that I wanted to. Please say you'll walk out to Allonby with me on Sunday.'

'I will not.' Now Margaret was backed into a corner and had to defend her position. 'You're a nice man Tom, but I am a paid servant in this house. There is a line between us which neither of us must cross, so I will not walk out with you. In fact, if you insist on pushing this then you will force me to do what I don't want to.'

'And what is that?'

'I should have to give my notice and go to seek another place at Whitsun hiring. Is that what you want?'

'No. That's not what I want.'

'Then you must leave me to my work, Mr Little, and don't mention this again.'

'Mr Little! Are we not friends now?'

'We were never friends Tom. We are friendly, but I'm the maid. Remember? You can't be friends with the maid. Think of all the newspaper stories where there's been a scandal because the son of the house did something regrettable with the maid. Well that's me. I'm the maid. Your parents would no doubt wish you to marry across or up, but with me you'd be marrying down. I have nothing but my wage and the clothes I wear.'

'I don't care about that.'

'You may not. They probably do. Now are you going to let me keep my job and say not another word about this, or must I give notice?'

He was really sulky this time, 'I'll not ask you again.'

'And I won't mention last night again to anyone.'

He nodded, made a strange twisted expression with his mouth, and left. Margaret simply sat on her bed and felt as if she'd been put through the mangle.

The year wore on and the cold grip of the winter held until mid March when all melted and the fields became sodden. The buds began to show and the grass in the fields, laid down under the weight of cold began to perk up whilst birds flitted to and fro chirruping for the new life to come. The weather was not nice enough to go out on Sundays so Margaret spent much of her time reading, a fact which Missis took notice of.

'You know Maggie, if you want to read some good books you should try the Mawbray Library for a change. Barwise is a subscriber and I'm sure that if you asked, it would cost you nothing.'

Mister was a trustee of the Longcake Charity which had been set up many years before by a bequest of one of the Longcakes, an ancient and well respected farming family in the Solway Plain. He had left a sum of money for the improvement of religion and education in the area. In 1890 Mister had been instrumental in funding and equipping a library in a two roomed cottage in Mawbray which subscribers could join for quarterly, half-yearly or annual fees, and for which visitors could pay a one off fee. Since Mister, Tom, Joe and William all subscribed, Margaret had no difficulty in gaining permission to use the library on Sunday afternoons and as a favoured servant she paid nothing. The reading room downstairs in the cottage had eight chairs and a table, was heated by a coal fire and lit by an oil lamp; this became her oasis where she went for a change of scenery and to get away from her workplace. Most of the books there were religious, though not all, and they could be borrowed and taken back to the farm for a period, and that was very useful to her.

Since arriving at the farm Margaret had made it her business to make friends with some of the horses that she met. Of course, she had seen horses many times, for this was the age of the horse, but she had never had close acquaintance with any. The first horse that she had made any real relationship with was Richard, the large Clydesdale gelding who had met her on the very day that she had been hired. Marra, of course, she was fond of because she had learned to drive him; he was so tractable and accommodating, so genial an animal that she took to him greatly. The smell of horses she found pleasant, and she loved to stroke their velvety noses, look into their intelligent eyes and talk to them. Occasionally, she gave them a small treat in the shape of an apple or a carrot from the garden, but her special favourite was Dolly, one of the Clydesdale mares. It was perhaps because Dolly was so very female and was having a foal that she took to her so well. Dolly had been pregnant all the time that Margaret had been at West End Farm and was in the special care of Joseph, for under Mister he was the man who dealt more with horses than cattle. Margaret was very curious as to how Dolly had managed to get with foal because there were no stallions on the farm, both Marra and Richard being gelded. In her naïveté she had asked Joseph at the end of last summer where Dolly's husband was, which made him roar with laughter.

'Bless you girl, but that's the best laugh I've had for months. Husband! That's a good'un.'

Margaret, somewhat pink replied, 'Well I didn't mean it like that. I know horses don't get married.'

This had the effect of pouring petrol onto flames as Joseph roared even louder, 'Hosses in't church! Standing in front of the parson! Oh my poor sides!'

He was a kind man though in his very bucolic way, and seeing her confusion he relented.

'We don't have stallions on the farm. They can be very vicious and especially when there's mares about. It's best to keep them apart. We pay a man to bring a stallion along when we want to breed ours.'

'You pay him?'

'Oh yes. There's a lot of money in it Maggie. If you've got a stallion you can make a decent living off it. All you have to do is bring him along and turn him into a field with mares and nature does the rest. You get paid forty, eighty, even a hundred guineas just to rent him for a season. If a farmer can't afford that then you get about £5 just to put him into a field for a while with a mare.'

'That's a lot of money.'

'Yes it is, but the owner of the mares stands to make more. You'll sell a good horse for £50 and upwards, maybe £100 or more. These big draught horses will fetch more if the market's good.'

'When will she have her foal?'

'She's due to give birth sometime round mid March next year so you'll see her foal. Horses are pregnant for 11-12 months'

'I'd like to see it born.'

'Would you now? That's not a usual thing for most people. Why do you want to do that?'

'I'm curious. I have helped at babies being born before, even with my own little sister, but I've never seen a horse being born. I'd just like to see it.'

'All right Maggie. I'm not one to stand in the way of that. If it's possible, when the foal is due. I shall take care to let you know.'

The time had now come around and Margaret knew that Joseph had separated Dolly from the other horses and put her into a stall of her own, with much straw on the floor. She had asked him how he knew that Dolly's time was almost come and he had answered her a bit evasively saying that there were signs, but that she was restless. When pressed on this he said that she was showing what he called 'nesting' behaviour, had gone off her feed and was also dripping milk. That was as far as he would go.

The afternoon of Sunday 10 March was wet and windy so Margaret, on her afternoon off, was resting in her own room and reading Jane Eyre which was engrossing her, so closely did she identify with Jane. Joseph, in some hurry, came to her door and told her to get her skates on if she wanted to see Dolly give birth. Of course she did so she followed him quickly down the stairs, across the yard and into the birthing stall where Dolly was in labour.

'How do you know it's time?'

He looked at her blearily, having been up since the small hours of the morning, roused from the mattress he was sleeping on upstairs in the stable.

'I've been doing this since I was a nipper. It's time. Just wait.'

Dolly was circling round her stall scuffling at the straw and sniffing at it.

'She's been in labour for a few hours and the waters broke nearly two hours ago.'

'Why didn't you fetch me then?'

'Nay it takes that until the final phase. She's nearly there. Just watch.'

Suddenly Dolly lay down, slightly on her side and began to snort and breathe in a way that indicated exertion. Joseph climbed into the stall and cleared the straw away from her rear end and lifted her tail.

'Eh go on lass,' he said soothingly to the horse. 'Just push it a bit and let's see.'

Dolly evidently could not understand this but pricked her ears back and snorted a little more.

'There we are. See Maggie.'

Margaret craned her neck forward and saw two little hooves poking out of Dolly's rear encased in a bluish bag which Joseph pulled apart with his fingers, then took some sacking 'to give me grip', and began to pull gently at the hooves. As he did so Dolly began a series of repetitive grunts and was obviously pushing.

'Atta girl. Keep doing that,' said Joseph pulling more. Now the whole front legs were in view at which point the foal seemed to get stuck. Margaret held her breath as Joseph pulled again and Dolly grunted and grunted making choking noises until, all of a sudden the foal's head came out. With one more pull the rest of its body emerged with a last rush of blood and fluid, and it lay still on the floor wrapped in the birth sac. Quickly Joseph removed this, disentangled the back legs and the entire foal was lying there, shiny and wet with very skinny ribs. Then he massaged its mouth and head until the foal took a breath. Still joined to its mother by an umbilical cord, it began to move its legs round on the floor and to lift its head.

'It's a colt.' In amused response to her questioning look he continued, 'It's a boy.' Then he laughed, but so did she, taking pleasure in the moment as he did. Dolly hung her head down, exhausted for the moment.

'What happens to the cord? Do you cut it?'

'No. There's some do, but I don't. It can be twisted off, but just wait. You'll see.'

As Margaret watched Dolly revived enough in a few minutes to turn herself round to look at her foal, and as she did so, the cord simply broke.

'Will that not harm them?'

'No not at all. It's just nature's way. I'll give them both a wash there with clean water later, but they'll be fine.'

'He's lovely. Can I come and touch him?'

'Yes you can, she won't mind.'

Dolly was nuzzling and licking at her new son.

'It's for all the world as if she's kissing him.'

'Aye, maybe she is.' Then Joseph looked thoughtful while Margaret stroked the newborn's head, absolutely charmed with him.

'He's beautiful. What will his name be?'

'I hadn't given any thought to it really. Would you like to give him a name?'

'Me?'

'Why not?'

'I'll have to think a while. You are looking very thoughtful Joseph. Is something the matter.'

'I didn't bother hiding from you on twelfth night. You saw me and Aggie before Christmas in the dairy didn't you?'

'Yes I did.'

'Yes I thought you did. I saw someone through the door very briefly, then I heard your feet go upstairs. But you didn't say anything to anybody. Not even to Aggie and she's your friend. Why is that?'

'Because it was not my business Joseph. It's your business and Aggie's business. I have no business telling anyone else about it.'

Joseph thought about that for a moment, 'You know how to keep a still tongue in your head. If you didn't I daresay there'd have been trouble. Mind you there will be trouble soon enough, but I like to choose my own time. I appreciate what you've done, or rather what you haven't.'

Then he thought for a moment longer and stuck out his hand. 'My name's Joe, Maggie. Please don't be calling me Joseph again.'

She took it with a smile, for a barrier had been broken most comprehensively. Names are important and Margaret's was to her, but although Joe had broken a barrier, she could not; she was still the servant so to him she must remain Maggie.

'Because you've got a close mouth I don't mind telling you that Aggie and I intend to marry in due course.'

Maggie gasped.

'We have told no-one yet because we decided not to do it until next year when she's twenty-one. That'll give me time to tell Dad and Mam. I've no doubt that there will be words, because Dad had ambitions for us, but I'm through with waiting round for Dad's project.'

'His project?'

'Oh yes. You'll not know, I think. My great granddad John Little was a squire and lord of the manor back at the beginning of this age. Lord of the Manor of Bromfield and Blencogo, which is not far from here. We are rooted in the soil Maggie. As you know we are also related to the Barwise family, who have been important round here for centuries. Dad always thought we'd better ourselves, which is partly why he paid for us all to go to the college and for Annie to go to finishing school in Switzerland. He'll have a blue fit when I tell him, but I'm 34 and I know my own mind. He needs me here as much as I need him and the farm, so he'll have to like it or lump it.'

'I'm glad Joe. She's lovely.'

'She is, and she thinks the world of you. I can see why. She'll be over in the dairy now I think. You can go and tell her I told you. I told her I might. By the way, what did you want to call this foal?'

'Oh, it came into my head as we were talking. I'd call him Folly.'

'Folly! Well maybe you'll tell me some day why, but Folly it shall be.'

Leaving Joe to his weary wait for the afterbirth to pass, she heard him laughing softly and repeating 'Folly' as he stroked the foal's head.

Agnes was in the dairy and Margaret, seeing that she was alone, quickly imparted to her that her secret was out.

'Oh good, I'm glad of that Maggie. I really wanted to talk to you about it, but I could not say anything. Did you guess?'

Margaret quickly advised her that she had hardly guessed, since she had seen her kissing Joe.

'Do you love him, Aggie?'

'Oh yes. Yes I do. I'd marry him tomorrow but for the difference in our position. It's not unknown for milkmaids to marry farmers round here, but Mr Little is a great one for status. He'd think Joe was marrying beneath him.'

'Joe doesn't seem to think so.'

'No he doesn't, and that's another reason for me to love him, apart from the fact that he's big and kind and strong and good looking and loves me.'

'Well, I think you're too good for him and he's lucky to get you.'

Later, in her room Margaret tried vainly to put her attention back into Jane Eyre, but was having difficulty concentrating after such an eventful afternoon. It was just getting dark when there was a shout from the gate as the postwoman called 'Post!' She was very late today. There was only one delivery on Sunday and she usually came about lunchtime, if she came at all; it seemed to happen when she felt like it.

'It's for you Miss Adams,' and she handed her a letter with Omega's writing on it, and cycled away down the lane.

Some letters bring hope, some bring bad news. This one brought disaster for Omega. She had missed her time of month in January, but knew that this could happen occasionally to many women. However, In February this had occurred again along with other signs that had made her certain that she was with child. Omega was the eldest Adams sister and had seen her own mother pregnant several times so she knew the signs. Margaret knew that if she said that she was expecting a baby, then it was so. Omega had written to Edward Furnival at university and he had written back stating that he knew nothing about what she was writing. If she was with child then she must have been doing something that his father would undoubtedly disapprove of and that she should make arrangements to deal with the situation she had found herself in. There was no doubt in his mind that when it became apparent then she would receive her notice. He advised her to go home to her parents and throw herself on their mercy, but that he felt sorry for her so enclosed a £5 note to help her in her time of trouble. He did not know what was in her mind to accuse the son of her employer who had given her such a good place to work in and such considerate treatment, of being the father of her child, but he denied it utterly. She should be careful with such accusations or she might find herself in court, charged with the very grave offence of slander. Omega needed help and advice. She was at her wits end and did not know what to do. She had to see Margaret as soon as possible.

Margaret now had a friend who could help her and who she felt she could trust. She walked quickly to the stables and the look on her face prompted Joe to ask, 'What's up lass?'

'Joe, I need to get to Maryport and back next Sunday afternoon. My sister's in trouble.'

He looked grave. 'I'll get you there Maggie. I've a few friends there I have not seen for a while, so I'll pay them a visit while you do your business. Is there anything I can do?'

'No Joe, there isn't. But getting me there and back is the best help of all. Please don't tell anyone though.'

'My mouth is as closed as your own.'

Leaving him, Margaret wrote a letter to Omega telling her that she would meet her at two o'clock outside the Furnival house in Wood Street next Sunday, the first time she could get off. This she handed to the postwoman when she came to the door early the next day. The week that followed was a normal working one, but she felt that it could not go quickly enough as time's wings seemed made of lead.

Chapter 15

Troublesome Times

John Adams might have been forgiven for thinking that his week would be a normal working one and indeed Monday 18 March was exactly that. It all changed on Tuesday when what may have been just another humdrum day at work took on entirely another character during the late afternoon.

He and Bill Gannon were back working at their stent, which was a twenty yard stretch on a hundred yard long wall along the yard band seam. Although this was the richest steam coal, in the area, the face they were working on was little more than three feet high. John was undercutting, while Bill was loading a tub; the putter would be on his way back from the cage with an empty one and there was no hurry. It was hard and hot work and John spent most of his time lying on his side. Occasionally Bill placed small props to hold up the overhang to stop it falling before they wanted it to. Both men had, as was the habit of all at the face, stripped off their clothes and left them at the shaft bottom. A very old pair of trousers, cut down above the knee served for decency, but many did not even bother with that, being content to protect their nether regions with what many would recognise as a sort of loincloth. By the dim light of their Davy lamps Bill peered at the coalface.

'Judd and Jenkin's ready to go John.'

This was a colloquial reference to the overhanging coal, which John had been working to undercut.

'On its own or with help?'

'Oh I reckon the wedges will do it.'

They began to place the long chisels and wedges preparatory to an attempt to bring down the overhang without using shots, when all hell broke loose. From a couple of stents down the face came hoarse shouts full of fear and a rushing sound. Water!

'Get out, get out!' someone screamed and a flood of water came down the face as John and Bill grabbed their lamps, holding them up for fear they should be in the dark and they followed the men in the next stent and stood up in the maingate and simply ran as fast as they could do in the dust and dark, to shaft bottom. The cage was down and miraculously all the men from their face were there. Water was following them down the tunnel, but strangely, after the initial rush the inundation had slackened in force. However, a mine being flooded is no place to dawdle and the pit evacuated very quickly. It might have been funny to a casual observer at the pithead to see a large group of men standing round either naked or semi-naked. Many were black from head to foot with coal dust, and they bore a vague resemblance to a convention of imps freshly released from Hell for a day's outing. All they lacked were the pitchforks, but even those would have been discarded in the rush to get out of Crosshow Colliery that day. The reality of it was less funny to the men involved, because whatever the temperature was down the mine, it was still March up on the surface and it was cold.

Word swiftly spread through the village that there had been a flood at the mine, and the road soon filled with women rushing to see if their sons and husbands were hurt so no-one was inclined to laugh. The nakedness of the miners was soon clothed with the shawls of the helpers and the roll was called. Miraculously, it was found that everyone was present; there had been no casualties at all. It was not too long before shivering men were taken off home to wash and to be properly clothed, thankful that their loss was not in terms of life, but their clothes and bait boxes, which had been left behind in the scramble to get out.

To Robert Steel, the colliery manager, the problem was not of telling families that their breadwinner was dead in the mine, for which he thanked God, but he had a colliery that appeared to be flooding. The pumps were sending a lot of water, much more than usual, down towards the river, but he had to know if they were holding their own. He decided to descend the shaft on the maintenance ladder set into the side, and had the cage lifted clear to allow him access. A very experienced mine engineer, he was under no illusions that what he was doing was not perilous and he had a rope tied under his arms so that he might be pulled clear if caught by rising water. A team of men stood by to heave away if he shouted for a pull, and with a Davy lamp slung to his wrist he very gingerly began the climb down. The shaft was only sixty feet deep, so not many minutes had elapsed before he shouted that they could pull the rope up. He was at the bottom and they could send down the cage. It transpired that the tunnel was dry, though he could hear the sound of water rushing further down in the dark. Before too long he was joined by the under manager, one of the buttys or foremen, and his doggy or under-foreman. Walking cautiously, prepared to run back if necessary, they advanced down the maingate towards the sound of the water. Halfway to the face they came to where an adit sloped gently down towards one of the lower levels and at this point they found a stream disappearing down into the depths of the mine.

'Why that's not much more water than you'd find in a beck,' said the butty.

'I agree,' said Mr Steel, 'but where's it coming from?'

They were able to walk ankle high through black water all the way to the face, but did not choose to get down on all fours and go along it.

'We are very close to the surface here,' said Mr Steel. 'It might be that we have breached a watercourse, but not a very big one to judge by this flow. I think we should go and have a look at the Barley Beck gentlemen.'

Back on the surface, he led them slightly to the west of the colliery precincts and down a little slope into the small valley containing the Barley Beck. There he found a gaggle of small boys who were most disconcerted that the stream had disappeared and their expedition to catch tiddlers after school had terminated very quickly. They were staring into a black hole that had appeared in the stream bed, into which the water of the beck was tumbling.

'If I were at the coal face now I could probably stand down there and wave up at you. It can't be more than fifteen feet down, but we should be more than that below the stream bed.'

'We would be, sir,' said the butty, 'but that's a swimming hole where children jump in during the summer. It's a sort of pothole deeper than the rest of the stream; that would be why the initial inundation made it appear worse than it is.'

'Ha! And we happen to have mined straight into it. Well it's not too much harm done except to some peoples' dignity, and we shall use it to our advantage.'

'How might we do that, sir?'

'Starting tomorrow morning we shall divert this little stream away from the hole by digging a culvert round it and resuming its proper course further down stream.'

'And what shall we use to fill the hole in sir?'

'We won't. Providence has been good enough to send us another airshaft. We shall have some of our rippers make that hole regular then we shall line it, set a ladder in it and it will help our ventilation. I'm afraid the children will have to find somewhere else to swim in the summer.'

There was a thankful feeling over the village as the word spread that the problem was minor and could be overcome very quickly. Not only was their employment safe, but no-one had been hurt or had died. Men had been killed too recently in the immediate area, one from a powder explosion and another from a misfired shot, whilst yet another had died in a roof fall, so an inundation like this one was benign in comparison. It would not take a team of skilled miners very long in the next few days to dig a culvert, line it with stone slabs and divert the stream. Production at the face would be resumed very quickly, and in fact, because other faces were being worked lower down, it hardly dented production at all. John Adams, once the adrenaline had worn off and the excitement was over, was simply thankful to be alive. As a miner, he knew what it was like to deal with sudden emergency, to cope with it, and to rise above it. A religious man, his prayers after the inundation were quite fervent and he resolved that on Sunday his thanks would be magnified in church as he would, this week, double his offering. This was a fortunate circumstance for Omega, because it was on this very Sunday, when John was in this thankful frame of mind, that Margaret went with Joseph to meet her sister in Maryport.

'Your sister's in trouble isn't she?' said Joe as they trotted towards the meeting with Omega on Sunday.

'Yes Joe, I'm afraid she is. That's what I told you.'

'No. I mean she's in trouble; that kind of trouble.'

'However do you know that?'

'Oh, it wasn't me. It was Agnes. She told me that she was certain.'

'But how would she know? I have not even mentioned it to her except that Omega has a problem.'

Joe laughed, 'She's a woman. That's how she knows. Is anything else necessary? Nay, don't look so worried. I'll say nothing, but Aggie thinks I should hang about, because you might want to go to Dearham.'

'I suppose that is possible. It's very kind of you Joe. Where will you wait?'

'Oh, there's plenty of places to get a pint and a cigar. I'll show you where and you can come and get me if you need me. It'll be The Golden Lion.'

'I know where that is. Thank you Joe.'

Omega was waiting outside Mr Furnival's house and looking very anxious, but Margaret made her climb up onto the trap and ride between her and Joe. There were seats down by the harbour and the day was fine, with many people in their Sunday best passing the time of day by promenading. It would be easier to have a private talk in the open air than in the confines of a saloon bar or tearoom. Strangely enough, the only unoccupied bench that they found was that which Margaret and her father sat on the day she went to Edderside for the first time, or rather it became unoccupied as the couple who were on it decided to leave just as she and Omega got down off the trap. Joe headed into The Golden Lion, tying Marra to some railings outside, and Margaret settled down with as bland an expression as she could summon, to hear what Omega had to say.

She was, on the face of it, quite composed. Margaret listened to her as she went through what had happened in more or less the same way as she had done in the letter. When she had finished she gave a bitter little smile and fished about in her handbag.

'He sent me another one two days ago. Have a read of it.'

'Dear Jane.'

'He knows my name well enough. He chooses to use my servant name.'

'Dear Jane. I know that you will not wish to make any trouble for me but I thought that I would write and let you know that I am engaged to be married and have been since last month. She is a very jolly girl and is the daughter of a prominent barrister. It will be quite a help for me in my career to make such a marriage as I am shortly to qualify and have no doubt that numerous advantageous offers of work will come my way as a result of this match. My father knows about this and he is wholly delighted since he has heard of my fiancee's father and thinks well of the engagement.

Now I know Jane that you would not wish to make any trouble for me, or my chosen wife so I would ask you to stop making your false allegations concerning me being the father of your child. I have no doubt at all that the young man with whom you have evidently been consorting will be very glad to make you an honest woman so I suggest you ask him what he intends to do about it. I enclose another £5 to help you a little because it is quite clear that you cannot remain in my father's service, the situation being quite impossible. When I next come home, with my intended, I expect to find that he has a new maid.

If I find that you are still working in my father's house by next month I shall assume that you do not intend to leave, and since it makes it quite impossible for me to bring my fiancée to see him with someone in the house making false allegations against me, I shall ask him to dismiss you and tell him that you have lied. If you leave now you will get a good character from him and I shall continue, occasionally, to send you small sums of money to help. Yours &c E. Furnival'

'Well he's got a brass nerve, I'll give him that! First he tries to buy you off with another £5 and the promise of more to come, denies he's the father and threatens you. What a scoundrel. Who is this young man he's talking about Ommie?'

This was the time for Omega to burst into tears, but she did not. She did not indeed seem upset, but a strange calm possessed her as if the vulnerability in her had been overtaken by a clean cold anger.

'There is no young man Margaret. That's another one of his fictions. The only man I have ever been with is Edward Furnival and although I was crying my eyes out over this some days ago, now they are dry. I might cry later, but right now I just want to do something nasty to him with a pair of scissors.'

'Well I might just help you do it. So apart from crying about it, what are you thinking of doing?'

'I don't know. All I know is that I'm being sick in the mornings and my skirts are getting tight in the middle. It won't be very long before Mr Furnival sees it and then there'll be trouble. I'll have to leave. He's very big on respectability is Mr Furnival.'

'But if you leave like that he won't give you a character. You won't be able to get another place.'

'How many times do you think I have turned that over in my mind Margaret? I lie awake thinking about it. I just wish there was some magic button I could press and turn back the clock so it never happened. But I can't. I'm going to have a child in six months and you know what the worst of it is? It's his. He's not a man that one. He's a pig and I wish the poor cow he's engaged to joy of him. He'll not make her happy, not his type. He's a skirt chaser and she'll never be sure who he's been with last. I'm well rid of him.'

'But Ommie, what do you think is going to happen?'

'Gallowbarrow I suppose. Off to Cockermouth probably. I'm not the first stupid fool who's believed a handsome face and ended up there.'

Margaret caught her breath. Her sister was speaking dispassionately about going into the workhouse as if it was the most natural thing for her to do.

'You can't go there. It's just slavery and how do you get out?'

'I know that!' Now Omega's self control broke and she burst into tears.

'What else can I do Margaret? It's not as if I have a whole lot of choice now is it? It seems quite a clear one to me. I can either go into the workhouse or I can jump in the harbour. Shall I do that?'

Here she jumped to her feet as if she were going to carry out her threat.

'Do you know how many bodies they fish out of that harbour; bodies of girls like me and in my condition? I live here Margaret and I hear things from people who've seen. They fished three babies out of the harbour last month. Babies. Unwanted children who've been thrown into the river to drown and they floated down here and fetched up on a mud bank. Is that my choice? Is it?'

'Here she flung herself back into her seat and covered her face sobbing as passers by looked at her curiously. Margaret put her arms round her and for a few minutes rocked her back and forwards while she thought fast and furiously.

'You see Margaret, I don't have too many choices do I? I'd rather not jump in the river, so the workhouse it will have to be.'

The hopelessness of Omega's situation might well have overwhelmed Margaret save for her greatest strength, which was the steely determination at her core. She may bend, but she did not break and this now worked to help her sister. Condensed at the back of her mind was that there was a third way and it involved Edward Furnival being made to pay in some way and taking responsibility. He had made it perfectly apparent that he was not going to pay and had no intention of taking responsibility, so it had to be made to happen some other way. It was also a certainty to her that Omega could not be left like this. Something had to happen, and it had to happen today; it was not enough to simply come to Maryport and make comforting noises when someone had mentioned jumping into the river. No, this was a grownup problem and it needed a grownup solution. It was then that her father took his place in her thinking. In all of her world she knew no-one more grounded, sensible or grownup than John Adams.

'You must tell Father.'

'I can't. I just can't. I thought of it, but it's just not possible. I'm afraid to.'

'Why? He's Father. He'll be cross, but you're still his daughter. He's a very wise man our father. He'll know what to do, and if he doesn't then Mother will.'

'You want me to go to Father and tell him I'm expecting a baby; to stand in front of him all on my own and tell him that. I'm a coward Margaret. I'm not strong enough to do something like that.' Here there was a fresh flood of tears.

'Well I am. We're going to Dearham right now and you are going to tell him with me standing right by you. And if you don't then I will, because I'm not leaving it like this Ommie. Something has to happen right now and if you won't make it then I will.'

'You'd do that?'

'Yes I would. You're my sister whatever happens and the only way any good is going to come out of this is if you tell Father.'

'Really?'

'Yes, really. So come one. We're going.'

Omega did not question how they were to get to Dearham but with Margaret's arm round her they crossed the road to where

Marra was tied up and Joe, who had seen them through the window came out to speak to them.

'Dearham?'

'Yes please Joe.'

He turned the trap, flicked Marra's rear and set him off.

'I've an apple in my pocket Marra. You get there in twenty minutes and it's all yours.'

Was it Margaret's imagination or did the horse pick up his pace significantly? But she chased the thought away as ridiculous. Soon they stood at the top of the Dib and Margaret went down to her father's door.

'Margaret! I was not expecting you. Your mother's out visiting and the children are playing down the beck. I'll get them; they'll be glad to see you.'

'No, please Father. I'm glad you are alone because I, we need to talk to you alone. It would be better if Mother was here, but we need you Father. We need your help.'

'We?'

'I've got Omega outside in a trap with Joe Little.'

'Well what's she doing outside? Fetch her in, and Joe. I'd like to meet him.'

'I won't fetch Joe in now, and he knows that. I'll just get Ommie.'

Within two minutes Omega was sitting at the kitchen table, her faced marked with tears and her eyes red, while Margaret sat beside her, an arm round her shoulders.

'Well girls, I don't know what to make of this. Who's going to tell me what's going on?'

Omega took a deep breath and began to speak, and as she did so, the tears began to fall again.

'Father, the fact is that I fell for a man who said he'd marry me, and now I'm expecting his baby and he denies that it is his. He says it must be someone else's and that he's engaged to someone else.'

John Adams' face gave no indication of what he was thinking, though a look into his eyes would have revealed that there was turmoil within. Of course it was not unheard of for girls to get pregnant out of wedlock, but there was such a social stigma attached to it by 'respectable' people that to have it happen to one of his daughters was a profound shock. Omega continued her story in a halting way, punctuated occasionally by Margaret clarifying some points. Eventually, she produced the two letters from Edward Furnival and read them to him as his brows lowered in annoyance, though still he said nothing. Finally, she came to the end of her sorry tale and said, 'So I don't know what to do, Father. I really don't know what to do and I'm so sorry, so sorry to have brought this on you and Mother. I don't know what to do.'

He sat for a moment, his face once more expressionless; then he rose to his feet.

'You will stay here Omega, and you also Margaret. I'm going for a walk up the brow to have a think. We'll talk when I get back.'

With that he took his hat and went out the door. Through the window they saw him stop and shake hands with Joe, then he turned right to walk out towards the countryside. Omega was still crying and was by now shaking with the fear of what might happen next.

'What's he going to do Margaret? What happens now?'

'I don't know Ommie, but it's a good sign. He didn't explode did he? He always likes to go for a walk when he's thinking things over. We'll have to wait and see.'

It was twenty minutes before their father returned and he had Nancy with him. She was looking rather worried, but immediately went to Omega to hug her.

'Margaret, get that bible over there and read out aloud, Matthew 7 verses one to three.'

'Yes Father,' said Margaret, wondering, for she did not know her bible well enough to know what this portended. Opening the heavy book to the correct page, she began to read and as she read, her heart pounded and her spirits rose, for her father was a religious man, as she knew, and his decision had been made.

'Judge not, that ye be not judged. For with what judgment ye judge, ye shall be judged, and with what measure ye mete, it shall be measured to you again. And why beholdest thou the mote that is in thy brother's eye, but considerest not the beam that is in thine own eye?'

'It is not my place to judge you Omega. You are my first born, and my love for you is never in doubt. My duty as your father is to see that right is done to you and it shall be. This young man may not be willing to do what he should, but he shall not walk away from this thing without consequence. Does your employer know what has befallen you in his house?'

'No Father, he has threatened to tell Mr Furnival so that he will dismiss me, but he has not done so yet.'

'That is a good thing, for I shall tell him of his son's villainy in the morning. You shall accompany me to pack up your things and collect what is due, but after that you shall not stay in that place again. You have been most despicably used in his house and I'll not have you there any longer.'

'But the disgrace Father. I'm a ruined woman and people will point the finger and talk about you and Mother if I'm in your house.'

'Omega Adams! Since when did I ever care about what people think? Let them waggle their fingers and gossip all they like. They that have no sin shall cast the first stone! Your child will be born in this house and it shall be Adams, be in no doubt of it. That's our first grandchild you have there, and though its father may be a scoundrel, no blame attaches to the innocent through that. I shall not be hiding what is going on and nor will anyone else in this family. It is part of nature, a new life is on the way, a new member of our family and we shall rejoice in it. If any think badly of it, then so much the worse for them, but I care not a jot.'

'Mother? Do you think this as well?'

'I do my dear. Your father and I spoke of it as we came back down the brow. This is life Omega, life, and that is what it is all about. You carry a new life and we should rejoice in that I think, though you should have been more careful.'

'I know that, Mother. Oh believe me, I know it well.'

Here she found more tears, which set her mother crying too, and as it is an infectious thing, Margaret started as well. A great weight lifted out of Margaret's mind; she had known her father would find a way through this matter.

'But how shall I make a living. I can't expect you and Mother to keep me? I won't even be able to get a character from Mr Furnival.'

John Adams smiled thinly, 'You shall get a character and more my dear, believe me you shall. Now Margaret, it is late in the afternoon. Perhaps we should give that stalwart young man up there a cup of tea and you should be on your way?'

Joe would not take a cup of tea because he too thought it was high time they were getting back. As John Adams had indicated quite clearly that he did not intend to hide Omega's situation or regard it as any sort of disgrace, she had no difficulty in relating all that had happened to Joe as they drove back along the coast towards Allonby. When she had finished he whistled and said, 'Well she's not been very wise your sister. It's not exactly the approved way of doing things but there's many that do. You'll not hear any condemnations from me Maggie or among farming folk round here; many weddings on Solway Plain have been made that way. I have to say that when I marry all will be above board and there will be no thought of children until I have a ring on her finger, but there's many that do not bother with that. She set her cap high though. A solicitor!'

'I don't think she set her cap at him Joe. It was him that made the running and she gave in.'

245

'I see your point, but she should not have given in really. However, people are people and they do what they do. I'll cast no stones. May I speak of this to Aggie?'

'You may, and so will I, but I'd rather no-one else. Your Mam and Dad employ me and I don't want them thinking badly of me by association. I'm not that kind of girl, but some people are so narrow minded and tar a family with the same brush.'

'None of us would think that for a moment Maggie. We all know what you are and my Mam thinks very highly of you.'

That was nice to hear, even though she already knew it. They turned into the farmyard just after six which was when Margaret was due to resume her duties, so their busy afternoon had not put out her work time. However, she did feel exhausted both mentally and physically and would far rather have gone to lie down somewhere, though it could not be. As Joe and Margaret brought the trap to a halt she saw Tom look at them out of the barn and to her surprise his face was like thunder. Whatever was the matter with him? Ah well, she would find out about that later; time to peel vegetables.

Chapter 16

A Gentlemen's Agreement

John Adams waited in the kitchen of Mr Furnival's house at 9.30 am on the next morning. It was a Monday and the solicitor had gone to his office in Curzon Street so he had told Omega to go up to her room and pack her bag. The only person present was Cook who informed Omega that Mr Furnival was not very happy at her absconding yesterday, because the fires had not been lit and Cook had to serve his evening meal. Though he was a widower, he dressed for dinner every evening and sat at table to eat; a maid was a proper functionary to serve his meal and his *amour propre* was quite put out by being waited on by his cook. John Adams said nothing to this, determined to keep his counsel, for his silence was a potent weapon that he fully intended to use. After a few minutes Omega came downstairs with her bag, which he took; he then left her at an eating-house in Senhouse Street with a cup of tea and a teacake.

'I don't think I'll be very long Omega. Just wait here until I return.'

A few minutes later he presented himself at the door of Mr E Furnival Snr, Solicitor at Law, proclaimed as such by a fine brass plaque, and requested an interview on a matter of urgent business with Mr Furnival from the clerk at the front desk. Soon he was sitting in front of his desk as the solicitor sized up his potential client, seeing a well set man in his mid forties with a certain gravitas to him, but unmistakably a working man.

'And what may I help you with today Mr Adams?'

'Something rather urgent, sir. I am the father of your maid.'

'My maid! Then perhaps you can tell me why she has absconded? I have not seen her since yesterday. That's not very good Mr Adams, not very good at all. It's breach of contract.'

John was not a man to be intimidated by this, so he continued, 'I would not allow her back into your house after what I learned yesterday Mr Furnival. She is not safe there.'

'What do you mean that she's not safe in my house. What are you implying Adams?'

'I have a handle to my name Mr Furnival, same as you do. My daughter is not safe in your house, so I have removed her from it, and she will not be returning. You will have to find a new maid, but I shall make it my duty to warn her.'

Mr Furnival looked as if he were about to explode, for he did not like someone of lower class talking to him like this, but his professional manner kicked in and he said with great self control, 'Very well Mr Adams, pray tell me on what basis you say that your daughter is not safe in my house. Permit me to observe however that it is a scandalous thing to say and I resent it considerably.'

John Adams looked at him levelly and replied, 'Whatever resentment you may feel Mr Furnival is as a pale shadow of what I feel, I do assure you. My daughter is with child sir, and the event took place under your roof.'

'Whatever do you mean to imply?' The solicitor's face had gone red and he looked fit to explode. 'Do you mean that your daughter has had a follower? That some strange man has come into my house that I knew nothing about, and has put your daughter with child? If Jane has been so outrageous in her behaviour, I shall dismiss her now and without a character!'

'Her name is not Jane. It's Omega. No sir, that is not what I mean.'

'What? Are you implying that I... I.'

'No Mr Furnival, I am not saying that either. The culprit in this case is your son, who took disgraceful advantage of my girl in your house over the New Year. He has abused his position as the son of her employer, made promises of marriage that he had no intention of keeping, and as a result my poor daughter is expecting his child.'

'My Edward! That's absurd. He would never lower...' Here Furnival stopped and caught his breath.

'Lower himself to make love to a scullery maid? Yes Mr Furnival. That's what he said. In fact, I have two letters from him in which he says more or less just that.'

'Well, there you are. Your daughter's a liar. She's got herself into trouble and is now trying to force my son into an unsuitable marriage. Well it won't do Mr Adams. He is engaged to make a very advantageous match.'

'Yes Mr Furnival. I know that too.'

'Then why are you here. I should call for a constable and have you ejected.'

'I would not recommend that.'

'Oh, and why not?'

'Because I know well that Omega is a good and moral girl who has been brought up to be God-fearing, regular in church and honest. In the farming community in these parts an event like this would be taken as a matter of course, but not in the village where I live; this predicament has the power to ruin her life. She tells me that your son is the father of her child, so he is the father of her child. I do not doubt it for a moment. And Mr Furnival, my daughter would take a bible oath on it, so I feel no compunction to keep silent on this matter. I trust that you take my meaning?'

Furnival's mind raced in a fever of horror. If this allegation was bruited around town then people, would talk. His reputation would be damaged and rumours might reach the eminent barrister who might call off his daughter's engagement. He might lose clients and people would snigger behind his back.

'This is blackmail.'

'No sir, it is not. I merely want what is right for my daughter.'

'But my son can't marry your daughter man! It's impossible. You are a...'

'Miner, sir. I am a miner. I work hard and I earn what I can. And I know as well as you that she cannot marry your son. It is not possible in our society as she is far beneath him. But even if it were possible I would not wish it. My opinion of your son is not high and I would wish her with a better man. You'll have to swallow that Mr Furnival, but he has behaved disgracefully.'

Furnival was momentarily flummoxed. 'Well what do you want?'

'It's very simple sir. I do not place any blame on you for your son's actions, but my daughter faces the workhouse or living at home with myself and my wife. To do that she need a competency.'

'Then you do want money!'

'I do not want a penny Mr Furnival. But my daughter will not be able to work. With a sufficient competency she will not have to. She can live until the child is of age and she can find herself another place.'

'Another place?'

'Yes. Omega has been brought up in the knowledge that you have to work for a living. She will find herself a place and she will do so because you will write her a very good character. She has, after all, been a good maid.'

'I'll give you that. She has. But why would I write her a good character?'

'For the same reason that you'll give her a competency. Still tongues are very useful in a town like this.'

The solicitor swallowed.

'One thing more, Mr Furnival. There is the question of the child. It will have to be cared for, clothed and fed.'

'Would that not be part of the competency Mr Adams?'

'That would be for Omega. Let us be frank about this. We are speaking as two grandfathers, Mr Furnival. This will be my first grandchild, and unless your son has been in the same situation before, then it will also be yours. Your grandchild must be cared for and have an allowance until he or she is able to start employment. I cannot provide that on my earnings, so your son must.'

250

The thought that he was going to be a grandfather was a new one to the solicitor and he paused for a moment, taken somewhat aback, but then he retorted,

'My son denies all this. What is there to stop me snapping my fingers at you and telling you to go to the devil?'

'Nothing at all. But I give you my solemn word that it shall be all round town by next weekend, and I shall also tell Mr Melrose, who christened Omega and has watched her grow and attend his Sunday School.'

To Furnival, social death beckoned, gossip, a ceasing of invitations, and tittle tattle. Mr Melrose was known to him as a force in the community.

'What do you want me to do?'

'I am a reasonable man sir. I suggest that you write to your son and ask his opinion.'

'But he'll deny it. Of course he will.'

'Indeed he would. However, if you write to him and tell him that you actually know what he's done, leave him in no doubt that you hold him to be the father, then I fancy that you would come by the truth.'

Furnival thought for a minute and then said, 'Very well. I shall write to him now. I would expect a reply by Thursday at the latest. Then I shall send for you and if you are lying....'

'Then you may send for that constable. I'm on late shift so may attend you most of the day. I have no grudge against you Mr Furnival, but you are a man of law. I ask only justice in this.'

The telegram arrived at eleven o'clock on Thursday morning. This caused quite a stir on Row Brow for the inhabitants were not used to the giving or receiving of such messages. It merely said, 'Come. Furnival.'

'Any reply?' said the boy, but there being none, he swung back onto his bicycle and was on the road back to Maryport, followed a few minutes later by John, walking a steady pace back to see the grandfather of his daughter's child.

When he entered the solicitor's office, he was shown straight through. Mr Furnival was subdued and came straight to the point.

'You were right Mr Adams. I told him that I knew beyond doubt what he had done, and he simply caved in. My son has behaved disgracefully, and under my roof too. I cannot apologise enough.'

'It was hardly you at fault sir. I do not blame you, but now that you have seen the truth of what I said I should like to know what he and yourself propose to do about it.'

For the next few minutes the two men discussed a settlement, and at the end of it they signed a document of which John was given a carbon copy, along with a letter in an envelope. Finally he got up to leave.

'You're a fair man Mr Furnival. You may rely on our silence. I just wish that we had never had to do this.'

Furnival looked older and more drawn than he had seemed earlier in the week.

'So do I, Mr Adams. So do I.' He paused, then went on. 'I'm not very proud of my son to be frank. He's behaved like a lecher and a cad. I'm glad that his poor mother is not alive to see it.'

Here he held out his hand with almost a pleading hopeful look in his eye, and after a moment John Adams took it.

'It wasn't you sir and I don't blame you. This is as right as you can make it so thank you for that. I'll send word when the child is born. Now I'll say good day to you.'

As he opened the door he turned, as Furnival said,

'Mary. Her name was Mary.'

John nodded and left.

Back at the house down the Dib he put the document and the letter down in front of Omega; she picked them up and looked at them. There was a cheque attached to the first.

'One hundred pounds! And the baby to have £3 a month until of employable age. Father, how did you do it?'

'He's a fair man Omega, though I know you thought him a stern master. Now you don't have to work, or go to the workhouse.' Here he grinned, 'Not that I was ever going to allow that. Now give me a kiss and read that.'

She opened the envelope and read;

'To whom it may concern. I hereby make known that Omega Adams, lately employed as a domestic servant in my house, is of good character, accomplished in her tasks, and industrious in the carrying out of her duties. She is honest, may be relied upon to keep house to the highest standards, and displays great intelligence in fulfilment of her instructions. I recommend her to your notice without reservation. Signed; E Furnival Snr, Solicitor at Law'

In the book of life, Omega's page had turned; this one was bright, full of colour and showed a clear way ahead. Now she could look forward and feel a pleasure at it.

Chapter 17

Brotherly Strife

Wounds left unattended may soon turn septic; boils left unlanced may burst and turn to bad ways. It is also so with human feelings, because once a wrong thought has taken root in a healthy brain, it may become a canker worm that eats and eats away at otherwise good thinking, and niggles at three o'clock in the morning, keeping the sufferer awake. Tom Little had a problem. There was now no question in his mind that he had fallen in love with his parents' serving maid. He was not to be blamed in this, for though it was undoubtedly a cliché and one that he had read of and heard of many times, Margaret was quite a package. Tom thought her beautiful, but he also saw her accomplishments, her qualities, her grace, and her humanity; the whole was underpinned by such a bed-rock of grounded common sense that he knew how rare she was, and how much he might treasure her. The difficulty was compounded by the undoubted fact that he had promised her that he would not ask her to walk out with him again. Any sort of advance, any courtship, any move towards this would precipitate her giving notice, and indeed he understood why, in fleeing from a man who had broken his promise. She did not return his feelings, and would not or could not, by virtue of her position. In the meantime, caught utterly between boldness and prudence, all he could do was keep silent; but as he did so, in the chit-chat and the burley of everyday life, her every move was becoming more of a torment to him. Like Tantalus, tied to a tree, he could neither reach the fruit he craved, nor slake the thirst of his desire, because his lips could never have what they sought.

It is not so surprising then, that the day Joseph returned from Dearham with Margaret came as a solid shock to Tom. Joe was the least communicative of the brothers and in his stolid and laconic appearance most people saw what they wished to see, a man who kept himself to himself and said very little. Margaret knew a different Joe, since she knew Aggie and Joe had opened up to her because she had not betrayed what she had seen in the dairy. Seeing Margaret coming back in the trap with Joe, having spent her afternoon off with him, hit Tom like a billet of wood across the head. He knew of course that Joseph had been walking out with Agnes, unknown to their parents, but that made the situation with Margaret worse. Joe was a good-looking man and he had a full head of hair which irked Tom as he saw it an advantage with women. That Joe was prepared to walk out with two women struck him as outrageous greed. They were brothers; surely he must know how Tom felt?

Of course, Joe was completely unaware of this and had no knowledge that every smile he gave Margaret, every request to pass the gravy, was watched by eyes that wrote into his actions things that were the polar opposite of what he intended. Love, being a sickness, had infected Tom with a feverish green jealousy. The family noticed a change of behaviour in him because once fairly cheerful, even garrulous after dinner and around the farm, he began to emulate Joe's former reticence; his elder brother on the other hand was full of the joys of spring and in good humour all the time. No-one pried because in west Cumbrian etiquette, it would not be seemly, but sooner or later whatever was bothering Tom would come out. Weeks went by and the routine of living went on at West End Farm; nothing occurred to dissolve the pressure building up in Tom's head, and nothing to change his perception of what he thought he had seen. On the surface all was normal, but under the smooth exterior of his skin great forces were shaping and bending the courses of his mind into unwonted channels. The months turned through April, May and into June of 1895. The explosion finally came one evening just before dinner one night; the milking was finished and Joseph had just returned from Aspatria in the trap with a few sacks of oats, which he was putting into Dolly's feed to help her with milk.

'Give me a hand with these will you please Tom?'

'Do it yourself.'

'What's got into you? Are you not going to give me a hand with these sacks?'

'No. I've done my work for the day. I don't need yours an' all.'

'Well, if you feel that way I'll do it myself right enough.'

Joe was puzzled, but heaved the sacks into the stable block, and as he deposited the last one, he turned towards the door and there was Tom glowering at him.

'What's got into you our Tom? You look like you'd lost £5 and found 6d.'

'I'm not your Tom. I'm my own man.'

'I never said otherwise,' said Joe easily. 'What's this all about Tom?'

Tom's eyes blazed as he rapped out, 'You've got a brass face you have. You think I don't know about Agnes and Margaret? Do they know? I think it's disgraceful what you're doing. Deplorable!'

'Eh? What have I been doing?'

'Don't come that innocent with me! I know fine you've been walking out with both of them. I've seen you. Do they know eh? You're playing round with two lasses at the same time and that's not right.'

'I have not!'

'I saw you, you damned liar. Walking arm in arm with Agnes on twelfth night and then that Sunday you took Margaret out in't trap, God knows where.'

Joe saw a great light.

'Oh, you think I've been doing that do you? Well I haven't, you see?'

'I've got eyes and I know what I saw.'

'Tom, I am not walking out with two girls. I'll tell you that free and for nowt, but I can't say more.'

Indeed he could not. The only person who knew how Joe felt about Agnes was Margaret because she had seen them kissing. Tom had not, and Joe did not wish him to know until he was ready to inform the family on his terms. He had no way of knowing how Tom felt about Margaret, but looking at his brother's face and behaviour he knew he was upset about something. Joe was a good man, but he could never be accused of being imaginative or intuitive; it did not occur to him for a moment that Tom was acting in this strange manner because of Margaret, but he was exasperated by the heat of his language.

'It's a hard word, liar. I'm not a liar Tom and I think you should take it back. There's nothing underhand going on, and there's bits of it that aren't your business, so just take it back and we'll forget this little scene.'

'I'll take it back when I'm good and ready and not before. Not my business he says, when my brother is playing fast and loose with two good lasses and both employed on this farm. Absolute disgrace.'

So saying Tom jumped up on the trap and turned Marra to go out of the gate.

'Where are you going?'

'None of your damned business.'

'But dinner's almost ready.'

'Bugger dinner.'

So saying Tom drove off down the lane towards Allonby, leaving Joseph to scratch his head, then to go into the dairy where Agnes was finalising her clearing away before going home. There he related to her what had just happened, but Agnes was intuitive and knew the ways of men with a sure instinct, so her mind immediately made the link that Tom was jealous over Margaret.

'It sounds to me Joe, as if he's jealous of you, but not because of me. I see a lot of Tom because we work together but he's never so much as looked at me the way you do.'

'You think he's fallen for Maggie?'

'It sounds like it to me.'

'Are you going to tell her?'

'I don't think so, not yet. You can push people into things you know Joe, that they might not do otherwise. If it needs telling then I'll tell her, but at the moment Maggie's quite happy and it's not our business is it?'

It was much talked about after dinner that Tom was not there and although his missing a family meal without notice was not thought a good thing, there was a feeling that his time was his own at his age. This liberal approach was dispelled completely just before midnight when William and Joe had to be called from their beds as the trap turned into the yard driven not by Tom, but by John Spark who lived the other side of the village. Tom Little was in the passenger seat held in place by a loop of rope round his waist and he was most incoherently drunk and soaking wet. As the light of a lanthorn fell on his face they could see that it was bruised and he was developing a very prominent black eye. Margaret, disturbed as she was reading in bed, opened a window quietly and was a silent spectator.

'What on earth has happened to him Mr Spark?'

'Well he's drunk a lot in a short time Mr Little, but as you can see he got himself into a fight.'

'Who was he fighting with and why?'

'I don't want to disparage the young man sir, but he was looking for a scrap and he started it. He'd already had a few and there were these two sailors who were minding their own business and he heard their accents.'

'Their accents?'

'Yes. They had Northern Irish accents sir and young Tom went over to them very unsteady on his feet and told them Gladstone had been right. They were Orangemen you see, Mr Little, and they didn't like what he said. I have to say that I didn't either. I don't think the Irish having their own home rule parliament in Dublin is a good thing. They are right in Belfast, home rule would be Rome rule…'

'That's by the by. How did the fight start?'

'He offered them out sir. He told them he was a Cumbrian, and a wrestler and as good as any two of them and told them to come outside.'

'And then what happened?'

'Well they went and the three of them stood on the grass over the road and people stood round. He swung at one of them and missed, then he went for the other who, fetched him one crack that laid him out; he fell down the bank into the stream and they hauled him out. I have to say that he did ask for it. That's the full extent of his injuries Mr Little; they were decent men and they didn't kick him or beat him when he was down, just went on their way.'

'Where was Constable Johnstone when this was going on?'

'Oh, he was in the pub sir having a pint, and saw the whole thing. There'll be no action over it sir. The constable says that the offended parties acted most properly and acquitted themselves well; Tom has had enough punishment and he is content.'

'Ah well. Thank you Mr Spark for bringing him home. I'm obliged to you.'

To say that Tom was in the doghouse would be something of an understatement when morning came. He was unable to get out of bed and slumbered on way past the time for rising.

Friday 19 April 1895 dawned and shone brightly on Margaret's 20th birthday and she opened an envelope postmarked Dearham, that had arrived the day before. In it was a card inscribed to their lovely daughter from her mother and father, and also signed by Thomas, Johnny and Alpha in a little girl scrawl. She set it on her mantelpiece and dressed herself. She had just finished when Missis ran up the steps and knocked at her door.

'Maggie, Aggie tells me that you can milk. I'll do the breakfast, but that great gowp Tom can't get up. I want you to help with the milking this morning.'

Thus, Margaret found herself clamping and squeezing, using her fresh found skills to advantage, doing what Tom would normally have done. In the next stall was Agnes, doing the same, and evidently the events with Tom had changed her thinking from the day before. She had wished Margaret many happy returns of the day and had also given her a card with a small package. In it was a handkerchief embroidered with Agnes's skilled hand with a letter 'M' and the recipient, appreciating the skill in it, was charmed and thanked her profusely. Agnes then told Margaret what he had said and done with Joseph and described what had happened in the Ship Inn the previous evening, just as Joseph had told her when she arrived at work that morning.

'He was angry Maggie, and he was looking for a fight. I think it's you. I really do.'

'You think what is me, Aggie?'

'I think that Tom has strong feelings for you.'

Though Margaret shook it off and told Agnes that she should not be so daft, a seed had been planted. She had no doubt of her own mind; she liked Tom a lot and thought him most attractive to her. In any other circumstances, if he were not the son of her employer then she would willingly walk out with him. He was good looking, smelled nice, dressed well when not working and had, from his conversation, ideas about life that she found very congenial to her nature. He was of course above her station, but not too far and he had prospects; a woman could do a lot worse, but it was not to be. She absolutely refused to entertain the idea of letting herself fall in love with him.

That evening the Littles did not disperse after their evening meal, but sat round the table whilst Margaret attended to the washing up, trying not to make too much clatter. Tom was there with a very black eye, but his misdemeanours of the night before were not mentioned. Mister had waited until Tom had finally woken up and eaten breakfast, then he had required his presence in his office. Behind the door, for the space of an hour there had been a raised voice and it was not Tom's. The family name, the good reputation of the farm, his father's honour, laughing stocks, the neighbours, the area for miles around, the police, the evils of being a sot and the upset to his poor mother had all been dwelled upon at some length as well as the waste of time having to put the maid to milking instead of helping Mother in the house. Tom emerged subdued and shame faced, but as with the beatings he had received when a child, his punishment was over and would not be referred to again. The subject of conversation round the family table after dinner that night was not a usual one, but concerned a paragraph in a letter from Annie Eleanor. It appeared that she had become a suffragist in her thinking and had been reading some literature from a Mrs Millicent Garrett Fawcett, who wanted women to have the vote. The general tenor of her thinking was that there were many problems attendant on women that were not sufficiently addressed by an all male parliament. Good thinking and intelligent women sitting in the Commons next to male MPs would be a better representation of the nation than an assembly where they were absent.

'I do not agree with votes for women in our nation's parliament,' declared Mister.
'They have quite enough already, why since 1888 single women can vote in local and municipal elections and can become councillors and Mayoresses in their own right. That's enough in my opinion.'

Missis thought this too and echoed her husband's thinking, 'I just don't think that voting is a very feminine thing to do. It's much more fitting for the men to do it and for women to preserve their femaleness and strength to do what they do best. Making a home and looking after the children.'

'Hear hear!' said Mister banging the table with the flat of his hand. 'I always say that it's like the making of water. Men do it standing up and women do it sitting down. Different spheres!'

Although this caused his sons to laugh, Missis was not amused.

'Barwise, that is too vulgar, far too vulgar. I'll thank you not to speak of such things at my table.'

'I'm sorry my dear,' said Mister with an abashed look, 'but you take my meaning. There are things that are proper to the male and things that are proper to the female. They already have the vote locally and that's enough. They should not have a say in the running of the country as they are not fierce or brave enough.

Women do not fight for the nation so should not expect to vote. Besides which, can you imagine a woman minister? Good grief, if we had a woman Foreign Secretary negotiating treaties with foreign nations, she might burst into tears over crucial parts, and then where would we be? No, a virile and strong nation needs good strong men in charge. What do you say Joseph?'

Joseph, back in taciturn mode without his Agnes, just made a big broad smile and avowed that for all the life of him he didn't care one way or another. If lasses had the vote or not, it wouldn't bother him. William on the other hand made a severely logical and economical case.

'I think you have to ask yourself who has the vote. There's about seven million men have it and they have it because they have a business or own property or use property worth £10 a year. Now the thing is that there's a lot of women fulfil that qualification too. If that's the rational basis for having a vote then women should have the vote. There's no logical case to deny it. You've also got to bear in mind that there are many women who pay taxes. I remind you that the Americans went to war with us and won their independence using the slogan of no taxation without representation.'

'I take your point William,' said Mister, 'However it does not undermine my prime consideration that women are creatures of emotion and incapable of running the country. Let's ask a young woman what she thinks of all this. Maggie. What do you think of votes for women then?'

Margaret was caught between a desire to say what she thought, and the knowledge that what she said was in direct opposition to what her employer had already said; she had no wish to take part in this discussion in which she was nowhere near an equal. Masters with uppity maids might decide to find themselves someone else.

'I don't think it's my place to comment Mister.'

'Oh, I've put you on the spot haven't I Maggie? Come on, speak your mind.'

Margaret thought quickly, 'I think I'll be like Jesus advised me to in Sunday School Mister.'

'Jesus? What's he got to do with votes for women?' Mister looked round with a smile of baffled amusement.

'He told us to render unto Caesar that which belongs to Caesar Mister.'

'How does that apply in this case then Maggie?'

'That I will do what the law of the land tells me to do. If the law of the land allows me to vote then I will vote. If it does not, then I shall not.'

Mister laughed, 'I might have to swallow my words here Maggie. It's quite plain to me that whatever else, you're a born diplomat. Sir Wilfred Lawson himself could hardly have said better. Well done my girl. Well said.'

'Well I think there's no question about it,' said Tom. 'Women should have the vote and I am in no doubt of it.'

'And why so?' said his father.

'Because I've met women smarter than me, more intelligent than me and just as capable of stringing a logical thought together as well as me. The idea that lunatics and convicts should have the vote while clever women should not is just daft. There's women doctors now who have no vote, and there's men round here I think as thick as two short planks who do have the vote. Where's the logic in that?'

'True. You have a point there, but there's still the emotions.'

'Emotions? Come now Dad, I'm not particularly proud of what I did last night, but I can hardly say that I was in control of my emotions. I can't say I've ever seen a woman go out and deliberately spoil for a fight. It seems to me that if we had a few women in the government there might be a few less wars.'

No-one replied to this.

'Then there's William's point about taxes. We're always told that there is a property qualification for voting and it's because of that that women got the local vote in '88. What is the point of

263

giving property-owning women the vote locally but not nationally? It just doesn't stand up to common sense.'

His father was not convinced.

'Well, it seems to me that men do a pretty good job of looking after women's issues in Parliament. Look at the Married Women's Property Act and the Marriage Act.'

'Those redressed evil things Dad. If there had been women in Parliament the right to beat your wife would have been repealed decades ago. That it survived as a legal practice until recently was scandalous. So was the idea that a woman's property all belongs to her husband the moment he marries her; that was just legalised robbery and a charter for forced marriages. Then there's other women's problems about which nothing has been done.'

Tom had evidently thought much about these matters and as she listened Margaret looked at him and saw a rare man; he actually cared about women enough to think things through and not dismiss them.

'There's many more women in this country than there are men. I think a lot of the reason why women aren't given the vote is because some men are afraid they'll take over. Our parliament does not even begin to look anything like representative of the nation and it never will until we get some women in there. I think they'd be as good in government as men and some of them even better. One of the greatest rulers we ever had was Elizabeth 1 and then there's our own Queen. She does a champion job as I trust you'd all agree.'

There was general assent. Of course Victoria did a good job; it would be unthinkable to say otherwise.

'I've seen children crying outside pubs for food because Father's inside drinking away the weekly wage that should feed, house and clothe his family. It's his right because he's a man. If a man runs away from his wife and children he is under no obligation to provide for them and abandoned women are forced into degradation because of this. Children starve and homes go neglected. If a wife runs away to escape his cruelty then the children are his by right because he is a man. The family house and property are his, not a shared asset. A man is master in his own house, but woman remains a chattel in so many ways. It's unjust and cannot stand. I would not be surprised to see a war of women against men in the future.'

'A war of women against men! I never did!' exclaimed his mother, whilst the table laughed good-naturedly.

Tom flushed, 'I'm ranting aren't I?'

Margaret thought he had been impressive actually, but his family agreed that he had been ranting rather; in a good humour they all repaired into the parlour to sit and talk more. That was how Margaret left them when she finished her duties shortly after nine o'clock and crossed the yard and up the stairs. It being June, the sky was still light and the pleasant green heavy smells of the evening in the countryside were beginning to suffuse the air so she left the door open to enjoy it. Looking at her mantelpiece, she saw a thin layer of dust on it and chided herself for allowing it to become that way, so took a duster out of a drawer. She lifted the little vase and something in it tinkled; it was the cracker ring that Tom had given her at Christmas which she had forgotten about, so she tipped the vase up and it fell into her hand. For a moment she looked at it, then her self-control gave way to an impulse. She slipped the ring onto her wedding finger and held it out, looking at it as the red glass sparkled in the light of the evening sun through the window.

'Oh Tom. Tom, you silly man. I'd walk out with you gladly if things were different.'

He had been without sound not on purpose, but because he had crossed the yard in his slippers; without her hearing him, he was standing in the doorway now looking utterly thunderstruck. Margaret felt her face go crimson and her mind turned to a useless pulp; what to say? What to say? She hastily removed the ring and put it back into the vase.

He crossed the room in two strides, took her hands and said, 'I came over here to apologise for making extra work for you. You shouldn't have had to do the milking this morning. I'm sorry, but I am so glad I came over Maggie. So glad I can't tell you.'

She still did not know what to say, because she had so completely betrayed herself.

'You can't say I broke my promise; I kept it until you said what you did. You didn't know I was there.'

This was not a question, but a statement. He smiled then winced with pain.

'Your poor eye.' Margaret put her hand up to touch it gently, then recollected herself and did not complete the move.

'It'll heal. It was my own stupid fault. I thought you were walking out with Joe and I went looking for a fight.'

'Joe? No I'm not walking out with Joe. What a thing to think. He's quite stuck on....'

'Agnes? Yes I know that now. I've done him an injustice, the dog. I shall have to be nice to him. I really do want to walk out with you; I have done for ages.'

She could hardly deny any longer that she shared his wish.

'There's a midsummer dance tomorrow on the green outside the Lowther Arms. Will you come and dance with me?'

'But there's work until after dinner.'

'That footpath just over the road goes straight to Mawbray and it's only about a mile across the fields. We can slip away after dinner when you're done. It'll go on till late. You are your own boss when you're finished for the night. We can walk across the fields there and back. With a lanthorn we'll be all right.'

'But your Mam and Dad...'

'They don't have to know. Come on Maggie. Say yes.'

She had not had time to think; not had time to remind herself; not had time to be cautious. Caught up in his enthusiasm she heard herself agreeing to go to the dance, to sneak away unseen and dance with the son of her employer in front of all eyes. They would know about it in the end she was sure, but she loved to dance and had not done so for such a long time.

'I'll be a sight for sure with this eye and ugly as sin. There's a few people will be pulling my leg, but I've been going there for years and it'll all be good humoured. You'll enjoy it.'

'You're not ugly Tom. And I think I'll enjoy it too. But I do want to keep my job.'

'We'll talk about that anon. I'm just set on enjoying the moment right now.'

'You'd best get back Tom; they'll be missing you.'

'Aye I know. I will; we'd better keep it secret to protect your position. I'll be off then.'

Turning to go, he saw the two cards from her parents and from Agnes on the mantelpiece.

'It's your birthday?'

'Yes it is.'

Then I wish you many happy returns of the day Maggie. You should have said.'

'Employers do not usually celebrate their maid's birthdays Tom.'

'Hmpph. True. Goodnight then.' And with that he left.

Her universe had shifted; she was going to a dance with Tom, though her sensible self told her that she had not actually agreed to 'walk out' with him. It had all happened in such a short space of time. She needed to think, and lay awake a long time, but for the moment her brain, frozen, did not know what to make of what had happened. Her happiness stood like an edifice of spun sugar, and she dared not touch it in case it fell.

Chapter 18

A Midsummer Dance

The morning brought regret and anticipation mingled in approximately equal proportion, for her intellect told her that she should not be going out to dance with Tom; the situation was inequitable. She was the maid in Tom's house, waited on him at table, cleaned his bedroom, washed his clothes and was there to serve his domestic needs. A servant should not walk out with the master and no good could come of it. On the other hand, she thought him very good looking, was flattered by his attention and was attracted to him, despite the divisions of class, as a woman is to a man. However, the die was cast, and though she dreaded what was to happen, she also looked forward to it. She'd be able to dance and perhaps enjoy herself away from work, and a nice man, for he was a nice man, would be paying her attentions. Since it was going to happen anyway, she decided to make the most of it and to display herself to advantage. For summer wear she had a skirt in a dove coloured material and a gingham blouse with a high neck and leg of mutton sleeves, both of which were fairly light and cool. To top it was a rather absurd straw hat that sat on top of her hair, kept in place by two pins, surrounded by a striped ribbon and surmounted by a spray of artificial flowers of her own making. This is what she was wearing when Tom, carrying a lanthorn, came up the steps to her door shortly after nine o'clock, but under all she was wearing her boots, because crossing fields in the dark was not an activity for light footwear.

'Maggie, I'm going to go out now and down the path, so just wait a few minutes if you please and meet me just where the path begins. We won't be seen out together from there.'

She did as he asked and soon they were crossing the first field, heading up the shallow rise, on the other side of which was Mawbray. Tom was in a high good mood with many smiles, but though he offered his arm over the ruts, she did not take it as the ground underfoot was dry and firm. It would not do to make too many concessions if she was to recover any sort of balance out of this business. Conversation was awkward, as well it might be, for to her mind there was an impenetrable wall between them that she could not climb; it struck her as strange that he could not see it. If he did, then it made little difference to him as he appeared to be sublimely unaware of any difficulty. Maggie was going to a dance with him was all that he cared about and he just chattered away about nothing in particular, making it clear that he was as happy as a sand-boy. About halfway to Mawbray the track took a small jink to the right by the headland of a field, then carried on as a well-marked track alongside Mawbray Beck. She stopped by a hayrick and turned to him.

'Look Tom, I've had time to think and I've done wrong; I really should not be doing this. What I said to you still holds good.'

'No it doesn't. You said you'd walk out with me.'

'Actually I didn't. I said I'd like to walk out with you if things were different. They aren't.'

'They're very different. I know now that you want to walk out with me.'

'That's as may be, but that's only one thing. I said if things were different, but they're not. I'm still Maggie the maid. What would your parents say if they knew I was here with you?'

'I'm not sure that I care a lot about that.'

'Yes, I thought you might not, but I do. There'll be people at this dance that know us. They'll have seen me in church or they've called at the farm. They'll know I'm your maid. What will they say?'

'Now you have me there. I actually do not care a fig for what they think. If they say anything to my parents then I'll cross that bridge, but as to what they think, they may do as they please.'

'But I can't take that attitude Tom. This is my job. I might get the sack.'

"Oh, I think that's highly unlikely. Maggie the maid is a gem as far as Mam is concerned.'

'That might not last if she's seen dancing with her son!'

'Look are you saying that you'd rather not go? Is that it?'

He looked rather like a small child that had been promised a sweet, puts it up to his mouth, then has it taken away. Margaret was not so inhuman as she wished to be. She had said she would go to the dance with him and so she would. Besides, she wanted to and a strong side of her said that if Missis or Mister heard about it, then so be it. A compromise was called for.

'No Tom. I said I'd go to the dance with you and I will go. I want to and I'm going to enjoy the dance and your company, though it puts my position in danger and I know that. I'll run that risk as a one-off, but I never said that I would walk out with you regularly, so this is it. I'm not doing it again, but as I am here, I intend to have a good time.'

Momentarily a shadow of disappointment passed over his face, but he recollected himself and replied to her.

'Well if that's the case, then so will I, as if it may never happen again. This will be the only time we walk out if that is what you insist upon. It would charm me if the woman who will be the prettiest at the dance would do me the honour of taking my arm whilst we take time out of reality and enjoy the moment.'

That made her laugh. Margaret had never seen herself as pretty, though many men saw her so. She would be flattered to be deemed handsome, but Tom evidently thought her more than that, an idea that she enjoyed. They continued along the beck and music became audible as they got closer to Mawbray.

At the Lowther Arms were people she had seen in church and she recognised Mr Brough, Mr and Mrs Armstrong and Thomas Hamilton, though doubtless there were others.

Some of them greeted Tom and he responded with a grin and a handshake in most cases, and the expression that he knew that they knew how to keep their mouths shut. One farmer winked broadly at him and told him that as far as Barwise was concerned, the word was 'mum'. Tom had banked on his being known and since he was on universal good terms with his neighbours, they knew that he would resent any gossip on their part.

'That's a grand eye you have there Tom. I heard that he put you down in one.'

'He did that. A hell of a crack. Mind you, I asked for it.'

'So I heard. Not planning on doing owt like that tonight I hope?'

'No, Billy. No call for that tonight. Just dancing is what I'm here for.'

'Good, good.'

Tom got himself a pint of beer, but had resolved that it was going to be his only one. When it was done he had decided to have recourse to a large bowl of spiced and minted fruit punch that had been mixed for ladies to sip to cool themselves down. This was to be Margaret's drink for the evening, which suited her, as although she had drunk alcohol with the family at Christmas, it was not something she was wedded to as a regular pursuit.

The musicians, who had been taking a break for beer, soon struck up a new tune and it was a waltz by Strauss. Evidently they had catholic tastes as most of what they did was country dances, but this was just the start that Tom had wanted. The dancing took place on the road itself and on the green to the left of the pub and Margaret found herself floating in Tom's arms in the first waltz she had taken part in since leaving school. All the girls had been taught dance steps in school, though strangely the boys were not; the last person she had waltzed with was Elizabeth Greenup. Dancing with a man, with Tom, was nicer she decided, and she found that she wanted to do more. She was completely unconscious of the impression she was making on the watchers, who looked at her graceful sweeping movements with a certain envy and respect. Nor did she hear John Hodgson tell Tom that he had the bonniest lass at the dance, which was probably just as well, as Tom replied that he knew it well. Some things are best not heard.

Billy Hetherington had a wicked sense of humour and was noted for practical jokes. When soldiering in the army one of his friends was a practical joker just like himself. But unfortunately he had died of a fever whilst serving in the Calcutta station. His comrades, to whom he had given so many merry laughs, were sorry that he was gone and decided to give him as good a military style send off as they possibly could. Billy was one of the pall-bearers and as they carried the coffin down the steps of the church on their way to the graveside he decided to try a little trick that he'd heard was played a few years before at another army funeral. He rapped on the coffin side and imitated the voice of the dead man without moving his lips.

'Oh, for God's sake boys, let me out. I'm suffocating hot in here. Please let me out.'

Not unnaturally, this caused great consternation among the bystanders and the coffin was set down in great haste, and the lid was removed. There, lying peacefully and as dead as ever, was the corpse of Billy's friend. The humour of the army is always dark and this was accounted a great joke by the people present and it caused belly laughs throughout the Indian Army when the tale was related in other areas. Such was the calibre of the man who now decided that the party needed livening up; since the men were drinking and most of the women were not, it seemed logical to him that the best thing to do would be to give the women a drink. Since they would probably refuse if offered he decided to give it to them anyway. He had lately returned to Maryport from a trip across to Belfast to sell some cattle, and in his pocket was a bottle of potheen. The flavour of potheen is described in many ways, but this is because there are many types. Billy's potheen was a clear spirit, burned like fire as it went down, had no peculiar odour, and would, if diluted into fruit punch, not betray its presence if used judiciously. Accordingly, he contrived to tip half the bottle into the punch bowl just after it had been filled up, and mixed it round with the ladle. Consequently, the dancing got very merry indeed and men found their partners dancing less elegantly, laughing in sometimes abandoned ways, and becoming more affectionate in clinging on to them as they whirled round. Sir Roger de Coverley, the Gay Gordons, a Strathspey reel, all went well with much squealing and shouting and Margaret was having the time of her life when it came to Strip the Willow.

Tom was becoming more and more attractive to her with each passing minute and she could not believe that she had never noticed how very handsome he was. It is true that she was quite flushed and giddy, but she put that down to tiredness and the dancing. She had not, after all, been drinking, and had stayed with the punch all the time. There was no harm in that. It was very noble of Tom to also drink only punch she thought, because she did not wish him to be as drunk as he was when he tried to kiss her at Christmas. Thinking of this, she would not mind at this particular moment if he did kiss her, but he had not. That struck her as extraordinarily remiss of him and the more she thought of it, the more absurd it was that he did not. So she kissed him. Not unnaturally he laughed, grinned very broadly and kissed her back. Looking round other people were doing the same which was odd because ordinarily they would not dream of doing things like that in public. What on earth had got into people? Oh, never mind. Time for the last dance before home, so better to make the most of it. By the time she had finished the Cumberland Square Eight, had galloped, and starred and swung and circled, she felt so giddy that she thought she was going to fall over, so laughing like a loon she finished her punch and told Tom solemnly that it was the bestest night of dancing that she'd ever had, which was true as she had utterly abandoned her habitual reserve. Tom cadged a light for the lanthorn, and laughing tipsily they both set off down the dark lane back along Mawbray Beck, heading for home.

Where the lane ran out and turned to footpath they only had two downhill fields to cross to get home but Margaret discovered in herself a need to sit down, so she subsided beside the hayrick and Tom collapsed beside her.

'Oh, I don't know. I must have danced too much. My head is spinning.'

'Me too,' said Tom. 'I feel like I've had six pints, but I only had one and then punch.'

'Ah never mind. I'll be fine in a minute. You can kiss me again if you like. It's rather nice.'

Kisses are often not the end of the matter and in this case they were not. With sober reflection things would probably have been otherwise, though at the time they seemed the most natural and enjoyable actions in the whole world. Neither of them could have been deemed so tipsy as to not know what they were doing; in fact they both knew exactly what they were doing, but their inhibitions had completely gone. The society they lived in had strict rules that what they did in the hayrick were reserved for those who were married, with severe penalties of ostracism and social denigration for those who transgressed. This was true at least in theory if not in practice. All that mattered was the moment and the discovery of appetites that simply had to be taken care of. Margaret did not even notice that in all the fumbling and frantic shifts of position, her hat had fallen off into the rick. Afterwards their maudlin fondness did not end, but they clung to each other all the way to the farm gate where Margaret and Tom, with loud noises of 'Shhhh!' parted, she to her room and he to the house. That much propriety prevailed.

In the morning it was a very good job that Margaret had set her alarm before she had gone to the dance. The thunderous bell woke her at 5.30 am and she dragged herself out of bed, her head thick and pounding, then she remembered. She had gone down the same road as Omega and surely someone must have put something in her drink. Her ears burned in shame at what she now saw as the wantonness of her behaviour, because she remembered quite clearly that she had kissed Tom and started the whole thing off. What if she found herself with child? What would Father say? Her thinking was so muzzy that she could not decide what to do, but took herself down to the dairy which was thankfully empty and pumped water to wash herself. Tom evidently had more of a head for whatever it was they had drunk because he was at work, but he looked pasty and gave her a sheepish smile, though he could not speak, Aggie, William and Nick being present. Thank goodness it was her afternoon off. She'd be able to rest and maybe have a little sleep to help this headache go away. Missis noticed that she was 'a bit off colour' and hoped that she was not 'sickening for something,' but no sign was given that she thought anything untoward. At church, in a clean mob cap as she could not find her hat, Margaret noticed a few smiles from people who had been at the dance, but most of them looked rather the worse for wear too, particularly the girls. After the service George Holliday stopped Tom for a word.

'Are you feeling a bit under the weather Tom?'

'A bit, considering that I only had one pint the whole night. Not much for me, but I feel as if I'd had a lot more.'

'Did you drink anything else?'

'Nothing but punch. Why?'

'I thought so. Word's going round that it was tampered with.'

'In what way?'

'Some people think that something strong was put into it. All the lasses who drank it were acting as if they'd been hitting the beer all night.'

'I did notice that. Anybody suspected of this?'

'Nobody at the moment. Mind you, we may never find out.'

Nor did they. Billy Hetherington, a known practical joker, never saw fit to confess what he had done, thinking no harm of it, so the prime agent of Margaret's loss of virginity got clear away with it.

Human thinking often takes place at an unconscious level. Throughout the morning Margaret's recovering brain had whirred into overdrive on the implications of what she and Tom had done. She had enjoyed it; but in the cold light of day she was ashamed because she had acted like a beast and done beastly things. That was all very well for married people, but she was not married. After lunch her time was her own and she deliberately put on her boots and set off for a walk back down the route of the previous night in search of her hat, which she thought she must have dropped.

The situation was impossible, so her thoughts ran; having had such an intimate thing happen with Tom she could not possibly stay at West End Farm as it was simply not an appropriate relationship between master and servant. Every time she saw him she would feel shame at what she had done and know herself for a libertine. She would leave as soon as she was able and of course she would get a good reference. Tears came into her eyes at the thought of leaving, but she would think up an excuse and knew that she could carry it through. There were other ways of getting places and a good excuse might be that she wanted to work in a bigger establishment like Brayton Hall where there were many servants. She would go to the reading room at Allonby and look at the situations vacant columns; failing that she would wait to give notice until September and attend the hiring fair again.

Tom stepped out in front of her when she arrived at the hayrick, and he was holding her hat.

'I thought your hat must be here so I came to get it for you. I'm sorry Maggie, I didn't know what I was rightly doing last night. I didn't want it to be that way.'

'I'm sorry too Tom. It wasn't all you, you know. I was there as well.'

'They think that someone put something into the punch and it made everyone go a bit wild.'

'Just a bit!'

'Well, yes. More than a bit.'

'I've decided to leave Tom. It can't continue like this after last night.'

'But I don't want you to leave. I'm in love with you.'

'You're the master's son and I'm the scullery maid.'

'I don't give a damn about that.'

'But I do, and that's why I have to go. It's not proper and it's not right.'

He took her hands, 'I have something else in mind. Could you love me?'

'I don't love you, I like you a lot though.'

'That's not what I asked. I asked could you love me do you think?'

'I think that I could. Yes. I think if I got to know you, it would be hard not to. But at the moment I don't. I need time to get to know you.'

'That's what I thought too Maggie, and that's what engagements are for.'

'What do you mean?'

'I mean Maggie Adams that you get to know someone through a long engagement and if you don't like them then you can break the engagement off.'

'That's true, but we're not engaged,' said Maggie, bursting into tears.

'What are you crying for?'

'I'm a woman Tom. That's enough.'

He smiled, 'There is truth in this.' Then he went down on one knee. 'Maggie, I'm in love with you and I have hopes that you will feel the same of me; will you marry me please?'

'No, Tom, I won't.'

'He looked astonished, 'May I ask why not?'

'You may. You just asked Maggie to marry you. My name's Margaret.'

For a moment he looked puzzled, then his face cleared.

'Margaret, will you marry me please?'

'Yes please, Tom. I will.'

After he had kissed her for the first time as a sober man, she asked him, 'What on earth are Mister and Missis going to say?'

'It's not that relevant to me Magg… Margaret. I've got a bit put away and if there's any nonsense we'll away and set up on our own. I'm damn near 30 years old and I'm not going to tiptoe round Mam and Dad. Let's go and tell them.'

'Wait. Should we not wait?'

'What on earth for? Life's too short.'

'I'm only 20. I can't marry without permission.'

Tom thought for a moment, 'Then I will ask permission.'

'You don't think it best to wait until I'm 21?'

'Nearly a whole year? I don't think so. It's June now and I would think that six months is enough to get to know each other better. What do you say to a Christmas wedding?'

'I reserve the right to break it off though Tom, if I think we are not suited enough.'

'That's understood, but I think we are now.'

'Well, I think we might be, so if we get to the wedding day and I have not broken it off, you'll know I agree with you.'

They strolled back to West End Farm arm in arm and in through the door to the kitchen. Mister and Missis were in the parlour when Tom walked in and told them he had something to say.

'I have just asked Margaret to be my wife. We are engaged to be married and I intend to ask her father for permission to marry her in the New Year.'

Mister said, 'Who?'

'Margaret. This is Margaret. I've just asked her to marry me and she's said yes.'

Missis jumped out of her seat, and to Margaret's great surprise put her arms round her and kissed her solidly on the cheek. 'Well done lass. I'm that pleased I could do a jig. It's about time.' Looking at her husband she said, 'Now then Barwise you daft old devil, it's no good your taking on about it. It's done and there's nothing you can do about it. And if you tried to I'd throw the frying pan at you.'

Mister smiled, 'No, no. I'm older and wiser than I was. You're right; it is about time. I'm 71 and time's cracking on. Time my boys were married and don't think I'd want a better lass for a daughter-in-law.'

'You don't mind?' asked Tom with some incredulity.

'I do not. I've grown to like this one a lot. She's bonny and bright and brings gladness to the house. She'll do you proud. The first of my sons to marry! Here, shake my hand. Now I've got some fine old whisky for us to toast the bride.'

'And sherry too, Barwise. Bring that out too!'

It is not too surprising that Mister and Missis set aside all thought of class and social station when presented with a fait accompli such as this. Farmers are closer to the soil and nature than most human beings, and the ebb and flow of the seasons made it natural for them not to resist the changing of the generations. They had four children, but as yet no grand children;

it was high time that something gave way, and now that it had, they welcomed it.

Tom soon found his brothers to come and join in the celebrations and Joe was so taken aback that he almost went to fetch Agnes to confess his own engagement. On a brief reflection however he decided not to. This day was for Margaret and Tom and he would not spoil it. He and Agnes had decided to wait, and they would do so; but he was grateful to his brother for he had cleared away any obstacles like an elephant ploughing through scrub.

'So you don't like being called Maggie?' asked Missis.

'Well, I was christened Margaret. That's who I am and what my family call me.'

'Right, well from now on you're Margaret. Why on earth did you not say so when you first came?'

'It wasn't my place to Missis.'

Missis looked at her and laughed.

Margaret had come to West End Farm to do the work that the daughter of the house used to do. From this day on she did much the same work that she always did, but now she was Tom's fiancée and a prospective daughter-in-law. That would, she thought, become a real event in December, but the best laid plans of mice and men go oft awry. It was not long into August before she realised that she had missed her time of month, and she was being sick in the morning. When she told Tom somewhat timidly that their time in the hayrick was the herald to his first child, he was absolutely delighted, and quietly they told Mister and Missis that their first grandchild was on the way.

'You sly young dog!' said Mister, his eyes creasing up. 'Couldn't wait for starter's orders. Well, we'd best bring the marriage forward.'

Within a day Tom and Margaret went by trap to Dearham to see John and Nancy Adams, and whilst Margaret talked to her mother and Omega Tom asked John if he could speak to him in private.

'You want my permission to marry Margaret?'

'Yes sir, I do.'

'I'm not sir. My name's John Adams. Before I answer you I'd like to know what condition she will find herself living in if she does marry you?'

'Condition?'

'Yes. Will she have a house, can you support a wife and so on.'

'As to that Mr Adams I have a bit put away and I am paid a share of profits in the family farm while I work there. We should live at the farm at first, but I have plans to take a tenancy in another place and start up on my own breeding horses. I know well how to do it and I think there's a small farm not far from Mawbray that will be coming up soon, because there's an old chap retiring.'

'Do you love her?'

'Oh yes. Yes I do.'

'And has she accepted you?'

'I'm delighted to say that she has.'

Well then, I think it's a good step for her, but I must let you know that I am not able to provide her with a dowry…'

'I'd take her dressed in a sack Mr Adams, for I think she is gold.'

John smiled, a broad grin, 'That she is Tom. Go ahead and marry her. You have my blessing for it.'

Margaret had of course told her mother and sister the import of Tom's request for an interview and they were all waiting on tenterhooks for the men's return. The glad faces coming back through the door told them all they needed to know and there was much rejoicing and smiling as a result, especially when the younger children were told and began bobbing round in excitement.

That Margaret was expecting a child, they did not think it right and proper to announce on this day. They managed to arrange a wedding in Dearham church for Thursday 21 November, the Rev. Melrose to officiate, and Margaret would be married from home. She would undoubtedly be showing by then, but that did not matter in the face of her marriage; when the baby was born all would be respectable. There was a lot to do before November, and not least for Tom. A ring on Margaret's wedding finger, a ring with a red stone in it had led him to where he was. He was determined that when the time came, it would be a ring with a red stone in it that he would place on her finger and in a flash of inspiration it came to him that he could have one made to her exact size without her knowing it. The exact template was in a vase on her mantlepiece. Congratulating himself on his genius, he went to Over's Jewellers in Aspatria and explained his need; they willingly lent him a ring gauge for a few days; all he had to do was wait until Margaret was out.

Chapter 19

All Change at Dearham

It was plain in the household at West End Farm that Margaret was no longer a servant, was about to become part of the family, and that the family were glad of it. The routine of her life continued though, much as it had, because she had been hired to help Missis with the house and somebody had to do it unless there was a new maid. Since that was not going to happen, Margaret's bedroom continued to be above the dairy and she worked in much the same way that she had since she had arrived at the farm. However, there were differences now in Missis openly demonstrating her affection, calling her pet and kissing her occasionally during conversation which had become much freer than it had been formerly. There was no more quietly leaving after work in the evenings unless she wished to, but now found that she was expected to join her prospective family in the parlour where they read, or knitted, and played games; or indeed just talked. Margaret was also taken round to Edderside Hall to meet Mrs Sharp, who was charmed to meet her in her new guise instead of as a maid, and made her feel completely at her ease. She had entertained some fears that she might be seen as presumptive in marrying above her station, but there was no snobbery to the lady in the big house who told Missis that she was a fine lass and far too good for the likes of Tom, though this was said with a big smile, and returned by another. It transpired that Phoebe's husband Jacob was brother of Edward, who was married to Mister's sister Jane. Mister's grandfather was called John and he married a woman called Frances Barwise, a very influential family in this area, and that was where his name came from. It was one of her brothers who had built Edderside Hall; Margaret felt with some awe, that she was marrying into a dynasty and said so to Missis who laughed.

'A dynasty? Don't be silly girl. Yeomen farmers most of them, good Solway stock, though Mister's grandsire was Lord of the Manor in Bromfield and Blencogo. They're supposed to be descended from Great Barwise and that's partly why they keep the name alive down the family.'

'Great Barwise?'

'So called because he was six feet four inches tall. He lived in the Civil War time. Barwise is very proud of him and if you ask him more he'd be delighted to tell you, I am sure.'

Margaret told Missis that he had already told her some of the story in order to explain why his horse was called Richard, but her curiosity was piqued at this piece of family history, and she decided that she would ask to hear the rest of it soon.

Some arrangements had to be made for the upcoming nuptials and she found that she could have more or less free use of the pony and trap for this purpose. Tom accompanied her to Dearham for the first two visits, but her confidence in Marra and her own ability to drive him were such that she was empowered to go alone to see Omega, who had an important part to play in what was to happen. Omega's baby was due in September, so in late July and throughout August she was tiring more easily and not inclined to move about a lot in the summer heat, though desperate for something to occupy her mind and hands. Margaret's request to her that she should make the wedding dress was seized on immediately. Her sister was as good a needlewoman as herself, and cunning in the making of good clothes. The generous piece of oyster grey cloth that Missis had given her for Christmas could be put to good purpose, because it had been intended for a summer dress and was ample to fashion into something to be married in. Between them they agreed that it would be more practical to make a simple skirt but a fashionable blouse with leg of mutton sleeves; the two garments would appear to be one because Margaret, like her bridesmaids, would wear a blue sash round her waist. This arrangement, thought Margaret would also allow for a certain amount of adjustment, because although she might not be showing as too large by November, there was no doubt that measurements taken in August would not be the same by then. Omega would have to be told soon about her baby.

Whilst Margaret was conversing with her sister and safely miles away, Tom went up the stairs into her rooms and upended the little vase on her mantlepiece. Out fell the ring that he had given her from the Christmas cracker which Margaret had expanded to fit her own wedding finger. He put it onto the ring gauge that he had borrowed from John Over's Jewellers in Aspatria and found it to be size M. Taking note of this, he put the ring back then went to Aspatria, with Richard pulling the cart, to order a wedding ring, the design of which he had already seen. The most delicate matter had to be undertaken with regard to John Adams, who was insisting that he must pay for the wedding as it was traditional for the bride's parents to do so; Margaret knew very well that this would stretch his budget to breaking point, so agreed with him in the most tactful way that it had to be so.

'I understand that Father, but Tom and I take that to mean that you would pay for the Vicar and the organist. That is the wedding and all else is vain show.'

'What do you mean vain show?'

'I mean that we do it because it pleases us to, not because it is a part of the wedding. Mr and Mrs Little beg that you will allow them to decorate the church and hire a function room.'

'Decorating the church I do not mind, but the wedding breakfast we must provide.'

'I'm marrying into an old fashioned family Father. They wish to provide the Groom's cake and for my side to provide the bride's cake. It would be nice if there were some sandwiches for guests as well, but they are not worried about that, so if you and Mother....'

'We will provide the sandwiches. You have many Shortrigg uncles and aunts who may want to come if it's not too far and will no doubt be glad of something after church, though it is a working day.'

'Tom intends to take me away shortly after the ceremony and will not tell me where, but we must catch a train at Dearham Bridge shortly after two o'clock. Straight after the wedding breakfast we shall be leaving. Tom wants to hire the function room at The Ship.'

'Tom does? Why is that?'

'He knows you are Temperance, Father, and would not wish you to be involved in hiring a room in a pub, but there will be people there who may wish to buy a drink so The Ship seemed the logical place and the Blackbournes are such nice people.'

'They are; that is true. If all landlords acted as they did in refusing to serve men who'd had too much then the world would be a nicer place. I have no objection to that; it's a good thought of his. And we certainly have very little room in the house to receive guests.'

'We don't want the wedding to be swanky, so your Sunday suit and Mother's best outfit will look very smart.'

'I'm treating myself, and your mother to new hats for the pair of us. Hers is showing its age, and I have a fancy for a bowler and this is a very good excuse to get one.'

Margaret laughed. 'I have no objection Father. You'll look very good in a bowler. I also have one last request from my fiancé. He wishes to buy a present of two new suits for his brothers-in-law, so that they may act as pages.'

This had been the most difficult bit; she knew well that both Johnny and Thomas had grown out of their Sunday suits and that Father would have difficulty in buying new ones in addition to paying fees. They would have been her pages anyway, but faced with how she had presented the matter, John Adams could hardly refuse. A proud man, he would have had difficulty in allowing someone else to buy his sons' suits in any other circumstances.

Margaret felt that there was too much going on in her father's life at the moment for her to break the news that she was going to have a child. The house down the Dib was crowded, but would be more so when Omega's new baby arrived, and Bill Gannon was leaving at the end of August.

'I'm sorry to go John, but I've been thinking of it for a while. My brother-in-law's not working now after that accident, and they need a bread-winner in the house. I've got no ties and family must be looked after.'

John Adams had nodded when Bill made his announcement. Bill's brother-in-law worked at the Barrow shipyard making ships for the Royal Navy and had lost the fingers of his left hand earlier in the year when they were pinched between two steel plates.

'I'm sorry to hear that Bill, though I think I saw it coming. I'll miss you down the mine; I won't get another marra as champion as you.'

'You'll find someone just as good John, I have no doubt. It's cleaner work down there and good money and Phyllis needs me.'

When Bill was gone, Omega and her new born would move into the lean-to room which was quite cosy, if small, with its own fire and just enough space for a bed, chair and cot. However, thought Margaret, Father and Mother must not know of her condition, Omega was different; she was her sister and if she could not confide in her then there was no-one she could give confidences to.

'I have to tell you, Ommie, that you are not the only person in this room who is expecting a baby.'

If an electric shock had been put across Omega's body, she could not have been more surprised and her jaw dropped open as her eyes widened.

'Good God Margaret! How? When?'

Margaret could not help laughing, 'In much the same way as you, I think.'

'Ah. Well, that's got to be true.' Omega giggled. 'What a stupid question. Alright, tell me what happened.'

When Margaret had finished she gave a short laugh.

'So you and Tom went to a dance and you both got tipsy and ended up doing what you shouldn't have in a hayrick. Oh Margaret, and you are the sensible one; or so I thought!'

Margaret, slightly pink, 'Well we didn't know that somebody had put something in the punch.'

'I'm rather glad they did. You're going to marry a good man with prospects and improve your lot in life. And I'm so pleased you're going to have a baby too. We can promenade about together with prams.'

'I don't think there'll be a lot of time for that sort of thing. Just don't tell anyone, and especially not Father and Mother. They have quite enough to manage with at the moment.'

'Ah,' said Omega, 'I think you have a point there. Between the baby and the wedding and Bill leaving, Father's looking a bit strained at the moment. Being a grandfather once is a lot to take in. When were you thinking of telling them?'

'We thought it might be good to wait until after you've had yours. When they are in the first flush of being grandparents it might be more fitting to tell them that they have another grandchild on the way. With any luck I won't be giving too much away with my tummy size before then. You'll have yours in September and then they shall know.'

'Are you afraid?'

'Afraid Ommie? Of what? Father and Mother?'

'No. Of having the baby.'

'Yes and no, I think. I've seen them being born, human and otherwise and I know it's messy and there's a lot of pain. The pain worries me, but the baby doesn't.'

'I'm a bit like that too. It's a very strange thing to be, Margaret.'

'Having a child? Yes it is. There's someone growing inside you for months and it gives me a very odd feeling, and I can't exactly describe it.'

'Nor can I, but I know exactly what you mean.'

'It's what women do though, isn't it? It's part of the natural order.'

'I'll try and remember that when I'm screaming to get it out in September.'

'Oh Ommie! It won't be that bad. Remember when Alpha was born? Mother had a short labour and she did not make much noise at all.'

'Yes, but that was Mother's sixth child and I'm told it gets easier after the first. This is my first. And yours too. I shall expect pain and if it is not painful then I shall count myself lucky.'

Margaret ruminated on this for a while, because it was how she felt and every so often the inevitability of it overwhelmed her, though it was entirely unavoidable.

As time passes, sometimes it flies and September came around very quickly. Omega went into labour on 20 September and continued so for eighteen hours attended by her mother and Martha May a local cunning woman who was famed as a midwife for miles around among working families. People on this stratum of society could not afford doctors save in dire emergency and babies were not that, being a part of life. Mrs May had helped hundreds of new souls into the world, charged little for doing so, and in her Nancy Adams reposed a complete confidence. The cunning woman used no forceps and carried out no caesarians, but in cases of normal births she was perfectly competent; where a breech birth became apparent she would cope very well in rotating the baby, but would always advise that the doctor attend. In her skilled and capable care Omega was safely delivered of a baby girl on 21 September whereupon Mr and Mrs Adams became grandparents. John Adams then did something that for him was remarkable, for he walked up to Dearham Post Office and sent a telegram addressed to Furnival, Solicitor, Maryport, 'Mary Hannah Adams born safely.' He sent a second one to Edderside informing Margaret of the same. Let it be recorded to his credit that Omega shortly afterwards received a visit from the notable solicitor and did not grudge him a view, and a hold of the small person who was also his first grandchild; on leaving he grew quite emotional, averring that the child looked like its father.

Naturally Margaret and Tom came over to see the new baby on the very next day and were delighted, as people are wont to be on such occasions. Tom was, unfortunately once again sporting a black eye, which caused John Adams to hope that his daughter was not marrying a man given to violence.

'Oh no, Father. Tom is a very gentle man; he got that defending my honour.'

She was positively twinkling as she said it and obviously approved of whatever it was that Tom had done.

'Defending your honour? What on earth do you mean?'

'Well I couldn't expect to marry the son of my employer and everything to go smoothly could I? There's been some talk locally about Tom marrying beneath him and a certain amount of looking down at me.'

'I of course think that I'm marrying above me,' interjected Tom, 'and my Mam and Dad say so too. I'm marrying a lady.'

'Quite right too,' approved John Adams. 'My daughter is a credit to me and you're a lucky man. So what happened?'

'Tom took me into Aspatria two days ago and there was someone he knew at school there; a bully and a lout.'

'A known wife beater and tough, that I dislike and always have,' said Tom.

'He'd had a few drinks and accosted us on the pavement because he saw Tom during the election campaign last month wearing a Liberal favour.'

'Well that's not so unusual in Aspatria,' said John Adams. 'It's solid Liberal country.'

'Yes, but he was a Conservative and told Tom that he was a farmer and a traitor to his class. Tom just laughed a little then walked on ignoring him. He was out for a fight though and talking politics had not done what he wanted, so he sneered at Tom that he was not surprised he was a Liberal because he had low tastes and thought it acceptable to marry his maid who looked no better than she should be. Then he spat on the ground in front of me. Tom told him that he had nothing to say to him, because he was a well-known wastrel and a man who beat women. Then the man hit him; that was a mistake.'

'I'll say!' cried John Adams. 'What then? Did you hit him back?'

'No Mr Adams, I did not.'

'Tom's not a boxer Father, but he has done a lot of Cumbrian wrestling. He just grabbed the man and hoisted him up into the air yelling. Then he threw him on his back on the ground and knocked all the breath out of him. He was sobbing for breath and actually crying. He wanted to send for a constable, but people who saw it told him he'd got what he asked for and they'd bear witness against him, so he didn't. Then Tom told him that he insulted his girl like that again he'd put him in a box. It was quite thrilling.'

Margaret's flushed and pink face told of her pleasure that her knight had defended her honour. John Adams did not quite approve of fighting in the street, but saw that the situation was not of Tom's making, so he shook his hand and thanked him; he was glad that she was getting a husband who would look after her even in the face of such an event and not a coward who would run away. He looked into Tom's stern blue gaze and saw the smouldering determination there of a good and steady man; he was a fit match for Margaret.

'Now Father, I would like to talk with you, so would you please come for a walk with me up the Brow as you do when you like to think?'

The unsuspecting John was led up the Dib, and then up the road by Margaret who asked him gently how he liked being a grandfather.

'I like it. It's not something I'm used to yet, but seeing that little mite lying there and knowing that is the next generation of my line, well that's a good feeling.'

'It doesn't make you feel old then?'

'Well it does a little bit, but you know me Margaret. It's all about this and it's....'

'In the natural order of things,' she finished his sentence laughing. 'I knew you'd say that and I know that Mother is over the moon about it, but I thought I'd ask anyway.'

'Silly expression that.'

'Over the moon? Well everybody says it now.'

'I know they do, but I'm not fond of it. Anyway, is that what you wanted to say to me?'

'No Father. It's not. I know you're glad that I'm marrying Tom and of course you'd expect to be a grandfather again soon.'

'Well of course I expect it after a marriage. You're getting married in November, so I might be a granddad again before the end of next year.'

'You'll be a grandfather again next year Father, but I'm sorry to have to tell you that it will be quite early in the year.'

This news took a moment to sink in before the astounded John jerked out a response.

'You mean that you and Tom....?'

'I'm afraid so, Father.'

'Did he feel that he had to marry you? Because of this?'

'No, Father. Tom loves me and asked me to marry him before he knew about the child.'

'And you love him I suppose, otherwise...?'

Margaret was caught momentarily on the hop and her own answer, torn from her unexpectedly in the need to respond, surprised her.

'Yes I do, Father, probably not as much as he deserves, but I do.'

'What you are thinking is common. Love grows with time but you'll find that. I must say that I am surprised. Of all girls I know I never thought you'd be one to find herself in this condition.'

Margaret told her father that she had not intended anything like this to happen, and found herself telling him of the fruit punch and how they thought someone had put something in it that made people act in ways that they would not normally have done.

'You see why I'm temperance Margaret. That's what alcohol does. Shakespeare has it as men putting a devil in their mouths to steal away their brains.'

'You're not angry then?'

'Angry? No. That would not do a lot of good and I'm not an angry person anyway. Tom and you are a good match, though you have jumped the gun a bit. It would have happened anyway I think, and you're getting married before the baby comes. It's going to end well and if people want to chatter about it then let them tattle. I don't care about it so long as my lass is all right. Now let's go and tell your poor mother. Never mind babies, I think she might have kittens at the thought of being a grandma again, the way she's cooing over this one.'

Well before the end of October the details of the marriage were being finalised. Omega, being older than Margaret, could not break convention and be a bridesmaid, so it was determined that she should be a witness. William would be the usher and Joe would be the groomsman and witness from the groom's family. Thomas and Johnny were to be pages, and Johnny, as the youngest, would have to hand over the ring to the Vicar when asked for it; he was to be counselled that he must drop it accidentally on purpose, for the best of luck would attend the couple whose page dropped their wedding band. In compliment to Joe and for friendship, Agnes was to be chief bridesmaid, and the other was Alpha. Annie, Tom's sister could not be a bridesmaid for she was a few years older than Margaret and it was accounted bad luck for her own prospects if she acted as maid to a younger bride. Mr Melrose ran through a rehearsal with Tom and Margaret a week before the ceremony and word had been sent out. The banns had been posted by the end of October; John Adams' daughter was marrying on Thursday 21 November. It was a working day, but John was respected in the village; many would wish to attend in friendship to him and his wife.

Margaret's last night as an Adams was spent in her old room at the Dib. She was not allowed to stay up late and she had the room to herself as Alpha had to sleep with her parents in order that the bride should not be disturbed as she had to look her best for the morning. Her mind was surprisingly serene as she drifted away, because there was a certain inevitability about what was happening and her boat was bobbing along in the waters of a smooth river that bore her to where she wished to be. She actually did wish to marry Tom and had not wavered, despite what she had said when he had proposed to her. The thought of calling the marriage off had not really entered into her mind and though she had asked herself on several occasions if she was marrying because there was a baby on the way and she felt compelled, her answer had always been in the negative. She would have married Tom anyway because she had liked him enough, but now, just before the event she found that she loved him. It is true that it was not a great flame of passion that carried her away on a stormy set of rapids, but that was not in her character anyway. Margaret's nature and approach to life was much more level and the great and overwhelming force that people have described as a grand passion, was something that she would have mistrusted and shied away from. Her path was clear to her, and in her mind love was like a timid flower that grew in soil that may prove deep or shallow, but in the right conditions it would grow. Her love for Tom was growing and would grow more; that thought contented her because it felt right. She may never set the world on fire with what she felt, but it was comfortable and it fitted well with her nature.

It had rained in the night and the wind was blowing. With such changeable weather Margaret felt some dismay at the thought that it might rain when she had to go to church, but as the morning went on and the clouds scudded overhead, the sun burst through somewhat in watery gleam, and it appeared that the wedding party would not be soaked. After breakfast John Adams left to go to the church to help with the decking out of it, whilst

Mother and Omega helped Margaret to dress. Margaret's condition was not showing much and unless people looked very closely they would not notice her pregnancy; this appearance was helped by Missis who had sent a letter to Annie in Carlisle instructing her to buy a pregnancy corset up there, so that tongues were not set wagging by one being purchased closer to home. Margaret was thus cinched in and supported, but not too tightly and not to her discomfort or that of her unborn child. The skirt of plain oyster grey was surmounted by a fashionable blouse, the neck of which was closed by a beautiful old gold brooch borrowed from Missis. Her clothes were new, and round her waist was a sash of blue satin, a feature echoed in her bridesmaid. Agnes was in her white summer dress, whilst little Alpha was dressed similarly in one sewn by her mother. Just before ten o'clock John Adams came back and said that the church was ready, all the Littles were there except Joe and William, and that the place was a sight to see. Just after ten the bells of the church began to peal out. John Adams grinned and said;

'I do confess Margaret that I forgot the bells. Barwise came up to me this morning and said that he hoped I didn't mind, but he wanted bells at his son's wedding and he'd paid the bell ringers to ring like billy-oh for an hour starting at ten. I told him that I'd clean forgotten about bells and did not mind at all. He wouldn't let me pay anything for it, saying it was his fancy but I'm glad he did. It sounds grand.'

Brides must not hurry but Margaret did not wish to be late, regarding that as slovenly and disrespectful so at 10.30 am the wedding party set out for the church. Under a blue sky flecked with white cotton clouds Margaret walked up the Dib on her father's arm, immediately followed by Thomas and Alpha. At present they had no duties for she had no train to her skirt but her long veil would symbolise that and they could support the ends of it when she walked down the aisle. Omega put her hair up for her, held in place with the tortoisehell comb she had given Margaret for Christmas. Around her head was a coronet of late roses, with the veil attached, and to her dress were pinned ribbons or favours to be bestowed on the officers of her marriage later; her father already had his pinned to his lapel as did Omega, Thomas, Johnny and Alpha; Omega carried little Mary Hannah, well wrapped up against the weather. It was hoped that the baby would not be inclined to disrupt the ceremony by crying. Father wore his new bowler hat and Sunday suit, his watch and chain polished for the purpose. Mother was in her Sunday dress, her hat decked with roses too, to match the bouquet in Margaret's hands. At the top of the Dib the two boys raised up a willow arch that they had made decked with ribbons and artificial flowers over Margaret as she and her Father mounted into the gig beside Joe who grinned at her. Thomas and Johnny fixed the arch to the gig, slotting into two prepared staples, then stepped back. Behind the bride the rest of the family got into the Little's family cart which was pulled by Richard decked with flowers for the occasion and driven by William. The horses walked proudly down the road towards the mill. As they walked people got out of their way with smiles and as they passed by the entrance to Townhead Colliery a group of miners called out to Margaret, 'Good luck to you bonny lass on your wedding day,' and gave her three cheers at which she smiled under her veil and waved back thank you at them. Just as they approached Church Street a very posh looking carriage drawn by a fine pair of black horses turned into it driven by Mr Styles, the coachman from Edderside Hall. Mrs Phoebe Sharp and her husband Jacob were showing of their best for her wedding day, and when Mrs Sharp looked out of the carriage window and saw the bride driving up the road she waved and blew her a kiss. On the approaches to town people waited, some in their best clothes, friends and neighbours, who fell in behind, going to church to see the deed done. Others, not going to the church cried out 'Joy to the bonny bride,' and other good wishes, whilst overhead the bells pealed. The hour of eleven came, so the bride entered the church to be met by Mister beaming widely, with Missis on his arm blinking back tears. The church was full of neighbours, people from the village, from the shops, and people that she had known at school, all come to do her honour by witnessing her wedding. Some of them she knew were from the Shortriggs family with aunts and uncles, cousins, nephews; a lot of people had taken time off work to be here and she was glad of that as it was done for love. The church was decked with a lot of ribbon and manufactured flowers and a quantity of November roses and looked splendid.

Omega tucked herself into a pew near the church door, to enable a quick exit if Mary Hannah should start fussing. Mr Melrose stood at the front behind the altar rail. William, as usher, led the party up the aisle. First came Joe as groomsman with Aggie, the chief bridesmaid. Then came Tom with Margaret's mother followed by John Adams with the bride on his arm. All eyes turned to look at her and thought how lovely she looked. It has to be said that the oyster grey trimmed with white lace suited her very well and she was a beautiful bride. Immediately behind her were her pages, who now reached up to support her veil which covered her head and face. Alpha Nancy brought up the rear. At last she stood before the altar with Tom and Mr Melrose proceeded with the marriage as her father gave her away. A ripple of laughter came when the Vicar asked who had the ring and Johnny, who had been given it by Tom a few minutes before called out, 'I have,' and came forward holding it out most obligingly, then remembered what he was supposed to do to bring luck to the marriage and said 'Oh!' and deliberately dropped it. It was such an obvious contrivance that it could not but lighten the mood. The ring itself was of the new and fashionable type called a gypsy and when Margaret saw it she inwardly gasped at how lovely it was. It had three stars cut into the gold band and into them were set a central ruby and two small diamonds; inside were engraved the initials TL and MA 21.11.95. It was a beautiful thing and quite worthy of the wife of a prosperous farmer.

Weddings have a strange effect on many people, no matter how sternly they intend to keep their emotions under control; this is not surprising as they are significant events in peoples' lives, if at least they take them seriously. Margaret had slept well enough, but her stomach was churning with nervousness and her heart beat quite rapidly as the ceremony proceeded. Tom looked very good in his wedding suit, but rather tired as if he had not slept well. However, he looked at her and for a moment she thought he was going to wink. Thankfully he did not, of which she was glad as she would have remembered it forever. Mother said that winking was vulgar; however his moustache did twitch up at one side as he gave her a small grin. She found herself saying 'I will' and realised that for better or worse she was now wed to Tom and he to her, and she smiled at how happy that made her feel. The matter of her marriage was decided and need not be thought on or worried about again. The wedding was to be made memorable in one way though, and one which she had never expected. Mr Melrose led the bride and groom through to the vestry to sign the register and record that in the parish church of Dearham Margaret Adams, spinster aged 20 had married Thomas Little, bachelor aged 30 on 21 November 1895. The parish clerk, who knew Margaret, had already filled in the details and she noted that he had put 'Maggie' as her name. Tom appended his signature and she took the pen. She scored a line through Maggie, wrote Margaret beside it, and signed her maiden name underneath for almost the last time ever.

'You can't do that,' said the clerk.

'I've done it. That's not my name. Mr Melrose called me Margaret during the service and that's my name.'

'Quite right,' said Mr Melrose. 'It is your name. I'll have to clear this with the bishop, but it should be alright. This is just a record. In the eyes of the church you are married anyway so have no fears about that. Now the witnesses please.'

Joe and Omega signed their names and that was almost the end of the matter. A momentary leap into the future would reveal that the bishop was of the same opinion as Mr Melrose, but thought that Margaret had better signify that she had made the correction herself. So it was that on 19 February 1896 a heavily pregnant Margaret returned to Dearham church as Mr Melrose initialled the register of her marriage stating that he had corrected the entry. Margaret then initialled it MA, then underneath ML. She was glad of this, because there would be no possible doubt after of the legitimacy of her baby which was almost due.

For now though the bride and groom walked out of the church preceded by John and Nancy Adams as fitting for the bride's parents, amidst the approving looks of their friends and family, though as convention dictated all was silent and they looked neither to left nor right. In the churchyard they halted and it was then, once out of the door that people could begin to shake their hands or kiss them whilst offering their congratulations to Tom. This did not include their parents or relatives who would do this later. At the door stood a singular figure in the stout form of Mr Purvis, a local sweep who was black from head to foot with soot. She knew why he was there, so stood and waited as he swept his hat from his head and bowed; he had done this before.

'Take off your glove lass so that I do not dirty it. When King George III was on his way to his wedding a horse pulling his carriage was affrighted by something in the crowd and it bolted making the others do the same. The coachman could not stop them, but a brave chimney sweep stepped out and stopped the horses, saving the King and many spectators from injury. The King then thanked the sweep and proclaimed that he and his brethren were thenceforward to be the bearers of the best of good luck. So stand I here to pass it to you. Now give me your hand.'

Margaret placed her hand in front of Mr Purvis and he kissed it with ceremony leaving a sooty imprint on the back of it.

'Now have your maid put your glove back on and do not wash it. That's the luck of the sweeps for your marriage; allow it to wear off naturally and you'll meet with good fortunes all the days of your marriage. A sweep gives you his blessing.'

As he stepped back Margaret thanked him and Aggie unpinned a favour and gave it to him, which he pinned to his hat whilst Tom handed him a crown. Once again the bells pealed out in gladness as the rest of the congregants filed out, the last man out being the Groomsman who paid Mr Melrose the due fees before inviting him to the wedding breakfast. When this was done that clergyman followed the party outside and kissed the bride wishing her all joy of the day; then as rice was thrown in the air, showering around them Tom and Margaret moved to the gate of the churchyard. Joe brought Marra, a grey horse, which was the best of luck, pulling the gig for them to get into, but he was wonderfully decked round with ribbons and roses and Margaret smiled to see him, for if ever a horse looked happy then he did. On the back of the trap was hung a horseshoe and Margaret recognised it as being the one from her own mantelpiece at West End Farm. Turning and squinching her eyes against the grains raining down, Margaret threw her bouquet high in the air and Agnes, very cunning, did not jump as many did, but timed her leap exactly as the flowers fell down to within her reach. Many people thought that Annie was too reserved, because she did not jump at all, or even try to catch the flowers, but Margaret knew she was thinking of career, not marriage.

'No surprises there,' whispered Joe to her, which made her laugh aloud. 'I'm going to tell Mam and Dad at the wedding breakfast when I've seen you off. They'll be in a right good mood by that time.'

Slowly Joe drove the bridal couple back down through the village, and to The Ship hotel where a room was prepared, and the rest of the wedding party followed behind on the Little's big cart or with Mr and Mrs Sharp in their grand carriage. Not everybody who was in the church would be coming to eat cake. Before long the people who had walked from the church had arrived and she stood in a decorated corner of the room to receive her guests. Quite a few people had decided to attend the wedding breakfast and there were probably forty in the room; etiquette demanded that they speak to her first, and this process began with the parents. Mister actually had a tear in his eye as he kissed her.

'You make a lovely wife for my son. I could not wish for a better. I have a new daughter to be proud of.' Then he congratulated Tom as the form was, for the bride was never congratulated, the implication being that the honour of the occasion was conferred on her by the very act of marrying the groom. When this process was completed, Tom cut his cake and began to hand out pieces to his family; this was rich dark chocolate cake and very succulent. Margaret's was a light fruit cake, and this was soon shared among her attendants and family. Finally the couple stood by the wedding cake, the third and final cut to be made, and together they sliced the knife into it, completing the proceedings for this would not be eaten. After they had left the big heavy fruitcake would be cut up and put into cardboard boxes for guests to take away, or to be sent by post to distant family members or friends so that they too could partake in the wedding. It was at this point that Agnes drew Margaret aside and reminded her that time was short so they hastened down to the Adams' house so that she could change out of her bridal gown and into travelling clothes with a warm grey coat and a red hat that she had chosen to go with the mittens her mother had given her last Christmas. By now the time was approaching half past one and Joe had already placed their bags on the trap; their train was at two o'clock and they could not miss it. Margaret did not know where Tom was taking her and had been surprised when he told her that they were going away straight after the wedding breakfast, as this was an unusual thing to do.

'Just for a few days Margaret,' he had said. 'So that we can be on our own for a while.'

Some of the guests would no doubt stay on at The Ship for a time as they had pints in their hands, but the wedding was completed when Tom and Margaret climbed onto the trap once more to be driven up the road by Joe, heading for Dearham Bridge Station. Outside the station was Mr Reed the station master, resplendent in his neat uniform and peaked cap, and seeing Marra in all his finery he took in the scene at once and snapped a smart salute to the bride, like the ex-soldier he was, then offered his hand to Tom in congratulation before ushering them into the waiting room where a coal fire gave a genial warmth to the air. Within a short time the northbound train arrived and they boarded it into a First Class compartment, which quite overwhelmed Margaret, especially when Mr Reed handed her a foot-warmer. Joe and Mr Reed himself handed their bags in, and with many good wishes they were off. It could not be said that the train was one of the fastest on the system, but to Margaret, who had never been on a train before, its 30 mile per hour progress up towards Bullgill seemed like flying. Tom was very pleased with his new wife's obvious delight in watching the countryside go by, and even more pleased that they had the compartment to themselves; there were not many first class passengers that used this line, though it did have a station at Brayton Hall which was used by Sir Wilfrid Lawson MP. The compartments in this train were not heated and Margaret was glad to the foot-warmer as it was cold. At Abbey Junction there was a comfort stop for twenty minutes, which also allowed them time to have a hot tea in the station waiting room. Her mystification about where she was going increased more and more as they passed through Whitrigg and stopped at a station called Bowness. Looking out of the window Margaret saw ahead a wide stretch of water and asked Tom what it was.

'That's the Solway Firth my love, and we are going across it on the train.'

'Across the water?'

'Yes. There's a long bridge across there and we are going to Annan in Scotland where we change trains.'

'In Scotland!' her eyes flashed with a joy mixed with trepidation and her hand flew to her face.

'Yes, Scotland. Now I'm not going to tell you any more for now. It's a surprise where we are going so ask no more please.'

Like a child with a new toy she clasped the new land to her heart with glee so that she could hug it and play with it. She was going to Scotland where she had seen before over the water; Tom was so thoughtful.

'Do you know the patron saint of Scotland Margaret?'

'Yes. It's Saint Andrew. Why do you ask?'

'Well because there is another, a lady. Do you know who she is?'

'No I don't. Who is it?'

'It's Margaret dear. St Margaret of Scotland.'

Oh, how she liked that. This was the best of omens, to begin her married life where Margaret was held in such honour. A smile spread across her face and over the next few days she was to smile a lot and from then on; marriages full of smiles are happy ones.

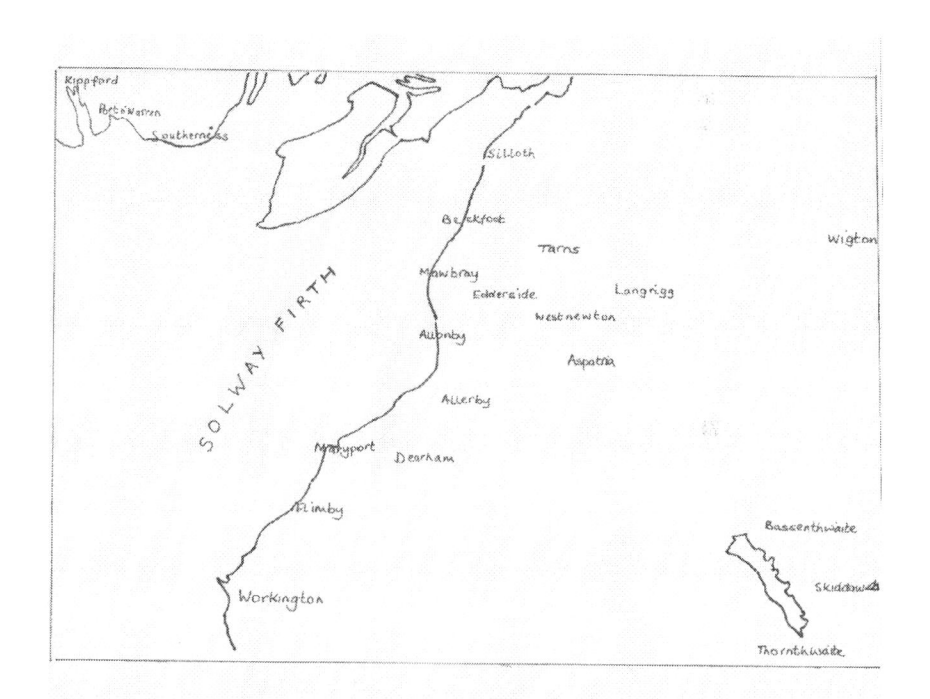

Chapter 20

A Scottish Interlude

Margaret, looking ahead out of the window at the railway viaduct running from Bowness on the English shore, to Seafield in Scotland, thought that it looked very spindly and said so.

'You have good reason to think it,' said Tom. 'In 1881 the river and the sea here froze over and formed icebergs which damaged the bridge and part of it fell down.' He laughed at her look of dismay and assured her that it was a lot safer now after it had been rebuilt, and hundreds of trains had passed over it; she need not fear that she would be involved in a repeat of the Tay Bridge horror of 1879.

'Don't worry. I've seen it and the pillars are cast iron twelve inches in diameter and there are dozens of them. Quite a solid structure.'

It has to be said that it did not look very strong and she felt a thrill of fear and also of excitement as the train slowed and began to cross. Looking out of the other side of the carriage she saw sea there too, and craned her neck out to look down. The sea smell and the chopping of the waves underneath made it a surreal experience, like being in the air; underneath the train, the distance to the water did not look very much.

'We are 37 feet above the high tide mark,' said Tom, 'And really it's not enough. Port Carlisle was not very happy when this was built because they were expecting to expand their business, but this stopped any hope of that. Even some fishing boats have to fold their masts back so cargo steamers can't get there. I'm surprised they allowed it to be built.'

'It's like going along a big seaside pier,' said Margaret.

'Yes. In effect that's what it is really, but there's no show at the end.'

'I've never seen a proper show Tom, though I've read of them, so that's a pity. I should have liked to have seen one.'

'Well, who knows what may happen? We have escaped and may do as we please, for a short while anyway.'

The train clattered slowly over the viaduct, on the right the view was up the firth where the tide was in and the land was flat, but to the left Margaret could see the blue hazy outline of the hills she had seen from Maryport and Allonby, and where she had longed to go.

'Are we going over there?' she asked.

'You'll have to wait and see!'

At Annan they changed trains onto the Glasgow and South Western railway and headed for Dumfries where once more they changed onto the Castle Douglas and Dumfries Railway. Margaret was beginning to feel that she had had quite enough of trains when shortly after six o'clock they arrived at Dalbeattie. Here, wondering what on earth they had come to this place for, Margaret followed Tom onto the platform and a porter carried their bags to the concourse of the station where Tom found the stationmaster and introduced himself. He thanked the man for something he had done, shook his hand, and asked how far it was to the Maxwell Arms hotel. On learning that it was a very short distance down the road he decided that they would walk, the night being dry and it being under five minutes; taking their bags he started off down the Craignair Street and was soon outside a handsome fronted building where he entered and asked at reception for Mr William McDowall who came and addressed him in a good brogue

'I'm pleased to see the face behind the letters sir; it's good to meet you. Now if you'll follow me I'll show you your room. As you asked, it's one of my best.'

'I'm grateful Mr McDowell, for as you know, you came well recommended.'

'I'm obliged to the station master for that; he does send a fair bit of business my way.'

'And my other request?'

'Not a problem at all sir. We were formerly a posting inn and have our own stables. The days of the coaches may have gone but we still hire gigs and phaetons to any who need them. I can have either ready in the morning.'

'Do you have a park phaeton?'

'I do sir; that would be a wise choice I think.'

'So do I, in view of the weather. I'll have that please for the whole day.'

Their room was quite large, and as he had requested a suite, they had an adjoining chamber with a bath and flushing toilet. Margaret had heard of these but had never seen one. Tom had, in the houses of some of the Little's prosperous acquaintances, but particularly in Edderside Hall where Mrs Sharp had one installed with a septic tank. This was luxury indeed. When they had disposed of their luggage they dined in a small and snug private room downstairs with a fire, before retiring to bed.

There is of course a physical side to marriage and love, which Margaret had been thinking about with a degree of curiosity and even apprehension. If this seems surprising in a woman who had been with child since June, then it has to be remembered that she had been tipsy at the time of conception, as indeed had Tom. Her memory of the event was rather fogged with some embarrassment at how she had behaved, though she was aware that she did not place it among her bad memories. There was a sense of regret that having given of herself so freely and for the first time, she had no clear memory of it and though she thought she had enjoyed it, the recollection came tinged with guilt as of eating forbidden fruit. There was nothing forbidden now though, and all was sanctioned by parents, society, the church and everyone. This time her head was free of alcohol, as was her husband's, and suffice it to say that they consummated their marriage to their mutual satisfaction to the extent that as they went to sleep Margaret reflected that if this was how things were to be, then she liked being married to Tom.

The following morning they arose late and breakfasted at eight o'clock, then went out front to where a phaeton was waiting for them. It was not a new carriage being somewhat larger and heavier than the trap that Tom drove at home, but it did have one great advantage in that it had a hood. This was just as well as there was a breeze blowing and it was raining quite heavily. However, with a hood over them and sheltered on three sides, with an oilskin cover over their knees, they were cosy and dry enough.

'You're used to horses, I take it sir?' asked the landlord.

'Man and boy,' replied Tom, 'though not usually a pair. They look well enough.'

'They are docile and biddable sir. They'll take you where you wish.'

'Kippford and Port o'Warren.'

'They will do it easily if you don't tire them out.'

'I'll take it easy with them. Don't worry.'

Trotting out of Dalbeattie, they drove down southwards towards Kippford on a road that ran along the edge of a flat and farmed area. In the distance were hills, but they were not heading for them; Margaret wondered where they were going but did not ask, aware of Tom's wish to be mysterious. The country was good pasture-land with quite a lot of clumps of trees, hedged and with a lot of gorse, not unlike some parts of Cumberland. Soon they came to a right turn where a post indicated Kippford and they drove uphill until the road levelled out again. Eventually they came to a long stretch of downhill and entered Kippford less than an hour after setting off from the hotel.

'Oh, there's the sea.'

'Yes,' said Tom. 'It's an inlet of the Solway called the Urr water where the River Urr meets the Solway Firth.'

'How do you know all this Tom?'

'I did Geography at college in Aspatria. I was good at it too. I must show you my maps; I drew loads of them.'

'And how were you able to arrange all this? The hotel, the horses?'

307

'Oh, that was easy. I knew where I wanted to take you from looking at a map. So then I simply sent a letter with a stamped and addressed envelope to the station master here and told him that I would be travelling on his railway and needed the name of a good hotel that could hire me a carriage. Once I had that it was simple to write to Mr McDowell and make my arrangements. Now we will stop here and have a look around, but we are not quite where I wish to be, so we will be going on later.'

'Don't they talk strangely up here?'

'I imagine they think that we do Margaret. That's a Scottish accent you're hearing, though I think the people round here have one of their own. I should think our Cumbrian accents would sound equally strange to them.'

'But I talk normally like everybody else.'

'Believe me Margaret, at the agricultural college in Aspatria they have people from all over. I could take you there and there would be Englishmen with accents so strong that you would have difficulty understanding a word they say. And they you. For example you asked me a few minutes ago, *'werst thew of te?'*

'Yes and you told me. Kippford.'

'Aye, and I understood it. But a Scot might not and a person from Kent certainly would not. This morning when I dropped the room key and you said to me *'I owp thew's garna put that in thys pocket cos ah divvent have wun.'* That would be entirely indecipherable to most people outside Cumberland. Yet it is the way we speak and nobody thinks any the worse of it. You take my point?'

'I do. Alright, the Scots do not have a strange accent. But they have an accent, just as we do.'

'Correct.'

Kippford was a place that perched on the edge of the sea where the road ran, the houses on one side, and a wall on the other dropping to rocks and the water. The houses were grey granite, which the area was famous for, exporting it all over the world, and some of them were handsome villas. The village was a small one, formerly dependent upon fishing, but in recent years had become a fashionable summer watering place where people would come to promenade along the seafront, admire the view and take the air. By now, the rain having stopped, that was more or less what Margaret and Tom did before returning to the phaeton and retracing their steps a way, for the seafront road was a dead end.

'I just wanted to see this place because I had heard of it as being fashionable.'

'Well it's nice, but I prefer Allonby.'

'So do I. We'll go down there as soon as we get home.'

A few miles down the road Tom steered his pair down a narrow country lane signed for Port o'Warren and drove down it between dry stone walls with well watered grassy hills studded with spiky grass and sheep. Eventually, cresting a rise, a wide expanse of sea appeared in front of them. It was the Solway again and in the far, far distance could be seen a line of distant land almost lost in the November mist. Tom pulled a small pair of binoculars from his coat pocket and offered them to Margaret, but as she had never used any before he had to show her how to adjust them.

'This is why I've brought you here. Have a look at this.'

Reaching into his pocket again he brought out a folded map and spread it out in front of her.

'That's where we are. This is the Solway and over there is Maryport, Allonby and Silloth. And if you look in that direction you might see something, though it is a long way.'

Smoke rose from several points on the far horizon, flecking the sky with different shades, whilst the Cumbrian mountains could be seen rising hugely beyond. On the vast expanse of the firth itself were numerous white sails where fishermen and cargo vessels went about their daily business.

'I can see some white smoke rising from a chimney.'

'That might be the iron foundry at Maryport though there's no way I can tell. The hills you are standing on right now are where you always said you wanted to visit. That's why I brought you here.'

It was simply said, but the eyes that said it were kind and caring. He had taken all this trouble to bring her over here simply because she had said that she had always wanted to go over there one day. In a way it was quite overwhelming, and a wave of thankfulness washed over her because he was a good man. So she decided to make him glad and looked at him with her level grey gaze and simply said, 'I love you Tom,' and it was true. It was not yet a great love, certainly not a conflagration, but the flame was alight, and as fires do, it would grow. She knew that, and so did he. To his credit he did not over dramatise the moment, but his wife loved him, so he simply took her hand and kissed it whilst his eyes did the talking. They left the phaeton with the permission of a farmer where the road ended, and strolled hand in hand down a track to the sea. In a small cove, sheltered on three sides, was a golden beach with the tide out and there they walked, quite comfortable together, any awkwardness gone for all time.

The following morning they left Dalbeattie and simply took the train to Dumfries. It was not yet time to go home because Tom had arranged for something else to happen and Margaret was quite excited because he kept hinting that it would be special. It was not common for people to go away after their wedding, so she was revelling in her feeling of freedom and looking forward to whatever was going to happen. At Dumfries their journey ended at the station itself because they checked into the very large and impressive station hotel where Tom had made a booking. It was an immense brick building with a pointed and spired tower lifting to the sky and the roof pierced by dormer windows, whilst inside, once through the turnstile doors, waiters and maids in uniform descended on them to fill their every need. She wondered if they could afford it, but Tom smiled and told her that they were not poor and she should enjoy it because it would not happen too often. The opulence of the hotel was one thing, but having arrived there in the middle of the afternoon they stayed in their room resting because Tom said that they would be up late. At seven o'clock that evening she found herself sitting in the stalls in the Theatre Royal Dumfries in a high state of excitement because she had never been to a real theatre in her life. Now, in the 100 year old theatre she was about to watch a dramatic presentation of '*Ballyvogan,*' an Irish play written by Mr Arthur Lloyd who not only was directing it but appearing in it too, with the rest of his famous company.

It would be an understatement to say that Margaret empathised with the heroine, Norah o'Sullivan, played by the excellent Miss Katty King. Norah refused her cousin's offer of marriage because the heir to Ballyvogan, Gerald McMahon, had made love to her and though he was far above her station, she had hopes of him. That made Tom look at her and smile broadly. Gerald gave Norah a locket with his portrait in it as a token of his love and his father declared that he would not stand in their way if they still felt the same after three years had passed. Some time after Gerald had gone to join his regiment abroad, a canting devious Scotsman called McCrindle, played by Mr Lloyd with pawky Scottish humour, told Norah that Gerald's father was determined to marry him to the daughter of a Major Redmond. Gerald's father appeared and denied it, so Norah determined to wait. But Gerald was shipwrecked on an Australian island with a rogue and forger called Jim Branson, a transported criminal who bore a striking resemblance to him. Branson shot Gerald and left him for dead, an action that caused great reaction in the audience who booed and hissed the villain as he deserved. Branson then made his way back to Ireland where Gerald's father had died, and the imposter took possession of his property and determined to marry the daughter of the prosperous Major Redmond. When Norah appeared and showed him his portrait in the locket, he rounded on her and accused her of stealing it, which had Margaret on her feet yelling at the scoundrel, which passed unnoticed in the audience as more than half of them were doing the same thing. The imposter called the police and was in the process of having

Norah arrested when the real Gerald turned up; recognised by his friends he was none the less arrested and thrown into jail charged with imposture! At this Margaret's indignation knew no bounds and she jumped up at a time when no-one else did and shouted, 'You absolute rotter!' at the stage before going cherry red when she realised that everyone was looking at her. At least Tom laughed loudly. In the end all was well and another ex-convict who knew Branson arrived and testified that Gerald was the real heir, Branson was arrested, and Norah married Gerald. The handsome Mr J Stewart who played both Gerald and Branson with an astonishing quick-change artistry, was admirable and the applause he received at the end of the performance was loud and full, several curtain calls having to be made.

It may be said that Margaret was impressed by her first trip to the theatre; as they made their way back to the hotel she was positively fizzing with excitement, and her head felt like it would pop. As they sat down in the hotel dining room to enjoy the dinner that Tom had bespoken for after the theatre the conversation was of little else.

'But would you actually like to do it yourself Margaret?'

'Act? Oh no I couldn't. I'm too shy for that sort of thing.'

'I can't say that I'd noticed you were a shy person.'

'I don't mean shy in that kind of way Tom. I mean that it takes something to stand up on a stage in front of a crowd of people and I don't have it, whatever it is.'

'Fair enough. It is a curious sort of thing that they can get up there and put on something that just transports an audience to a different time and place though.'

'I think it's marvellous. I really got carried away.'

'I did notice that…. But I'm glad you enjoyed it. We'll do it again.'

'You mean come here?'

'Good heavens no! We might be well off Margaret, but trips up to Dumfries will be few and far between. However, they have shows in Silloth in the summer when pierrots perform on the

312

green. They also do shows at Her Majesty's Theatre in Carlisle which is not that far, and they have the Star Music Hall, but for our purposes Workington's probably better if you like shows.'

'What have they got?'

'Oh well, Workington has the Theatre Royal, and the Queen's Opera House. Maryport used to have a music hall you know.'

'Oh yes, I remember that. Mr Russell's Music Hall. It's a good job no-one was in it when it fell down.'

'That's true. So anyway my love, if you have a fancy to go to theatre occasionally then we can do it and we will do it.'

'But there'll be a baby to look after soon and I won't be able to.'

'Haha. You don't know my mother as well as you might. Believe me, if we want to leave the baby to be well looked after, then we may do so at any time. She has been wanting a grand child to spoil for years.'

The theatre to Margaret was magic and fantasy so she looked forward to more of it; she could get quite used to this married life. The following day they took a train back to Aspatria where, Tom having telegraphed ahead, Marra was waiting for them with Joe holding the reins and with a big smile on his face.

'I went back to the Ship Inn after you left and I told Mam and Dad about Agnes and me. They were fit to bust!'

'They were angry?' said Margaret in some dismay.

'No. Quite the reverse, Margaret. Busting for joy they were and even a bit disappointed.'

'Why disappointed?'

'Well because I told them we were going to wait until next year. I think they'd have been happy to have had the wedding the following day! Anyway it's all in the open; you showed the way and broke the ice so I'm glad of it. Now give your new brother a kiss and let's go home.'

313

Chapter 21

A New Home

Back at West End Farm they found a change for in the two days they had been away Margaret's two rooms had been altered greatly. The smell of fresh whitewash and the gleaming walls, the new curtains and the double bed in place of the single told them that they now had their own establishment. A fire flickered in the grate and it was cosy and warm to come home to.

'It'll do for now,' said Tom, 'but only for now; and only to let the baby come and everything to settle. I have an eye to take a farm in my own right, but I'll save that idea for now. Don't tell Mam and Dad yet.'

Part of the newly weds' welcome home came when Missis fished in her apron pocket and brought out a telegram from Margaret's father.

'Please attend J Huff and Son Tuesday 26 inst. 2pm.'

'He wants you at the photographers. I wonder what for? But you must go of course.'

So it was that Tom drove Margaret into Maryport to the photographer's shop in Curzon Street to find John Adams waiting outside with Omega and Alpha Nancy, with Mary Hannah wrapped up against the cold.

'I want a picture of my girls altogether now, so I can put it on my mantelpiece to look at,' declared John Adams. I'm glad you look smart for it; Alpha's borrowed a necklace for the purpose and looks very pretty.'

She did indeed. Alpha's hair was very curly at the front above her forehead, but had been combed out and straightened by Mother at the back, and on the top of her head she wore a new white straw hat. Her dress was a ruched smock whilst round her neck was a massive three-stranded mock pearl necklace that Margaret thought a little old for her. Omega was in a russet coloured dress that looked very fashionable with leg of mutton sleeves and a bodice absolutely covered in intricate needlework, decorated with large mother of pearl buttons below the bust. Mary Hannah, who had the most prolific head of dark hair that Margaret had ever seen on a baby, was wrapped up in a soft woollen shawl which wound round her in several layers and looked beautifully warm. Margaret herself, though her blouse from the Aspatria Co-op was a new gingham, closed at the neck with a silver brooch and very fashionable in the sleeves, felt underdressed. Had she known she would have worn a dress but her good black skirt would have to do. Inside the shop the sisters sat looking at the camera, Margaret on the right, Alpha standing in the middle and Omega seated on the left with Mary Hannah on her knee. They did not smile, having been told not to as they did not wish to look like fools. Alpha was afraid, because she had never seen a camera before and she clutched Margaret's left hand so tightly that her knuckles showed white on her right hand for people to see a hundred years and more later, whilst the expression on her face was verging on fascinated fear. Margaret's hat, the very picture of chic, was perched so far up her head that it barely seemed to touch her hair. Omega's sat more firmly on her head, or rather on her hair, which was piled up high, but a moderate breeze would have blown it off. The elder sisters stared unblinking into the camera for the prescribed amount of time and their faces could not be read, their thoughts opaque behind a level, cool, appraising yet dispassionate gaze as enigmatic as the Mona Lisa's. Thus they sat, preserved for all time on a silver nitrate print in black and white for their posterity to wonder what they were thinking about when the image was taken.

Back at the farm that evening Margaret held a conversation with Mister that was to have consequences far into the future because she remembered what Missis had said about Great Barwise. In the parlour after dinner she reminded him that he had told her he had a famous ancestor and had named the big horse Richard after him.

'Oh yes, I remember telling you. Great Barwise he was and I am named after him. It's a name that's passed down through the family; my grandmother was Frances Barwise who married John Little back in the last age. I'm not a direct descendant of Barwise of Ilekirk, for he had none, but I'm of his family.'

'So who was he?' asked Margaret. 'I know you said he was MP for Carlisle, but what did he do?'

Mister's eyes twinkled, 'What did he do? Well I'll tell you what he did. Just let me fill this and I'll tell you right enough,' and so saying he carefully filled his pipe, rubbing flake tobacco between his palms. When he had lit it with a taper from the fire, he began his tale.

'He was born in 1601 during the time of Elizabeth 1 and inherited his estate when he was 14 and already of great strength and size. By the time he was 17 he stood six feet four inches in his stockings which is why men named him Great Barwise.'

'Not a close relative of ours then by the look of it,' interrupted Joe.

'Any more interruptions from thee lad and I'll make you shorter than you are now. Anyway there is a tale about when he was a young man and he was away from home. Ilekirk, as you may know, is in Westward parish to the north west of here. He was at Silloth on some business matter and lay at an inn at Dryholme just outside Silloth, the hour being too late for home. He bespoke himself a supper and went up to his room to change, but when he came down there were two men, notorious highwaymen, as he well knew, had taken his supper and were eating it. They did not give a rap for him, but like so many big men he was of a very peaceful disposition, so he simply sat down with a mug of ale and ordered another supper. When it came the men ordered that it be brought to their table, for they would eat it as well. Although a slow man to anger, this roused him, being hungry, and he went over and picked them both up despite all they could do, and put them onto the floor by the fire. Then he took the great poker and bent it in a loop round their necks, which held them so fast they could not stir, try as they might. In this way they were delivered to a local justice as known rogues.'

'Well he sounds like a giant,' said Margaret.

'By all accounts he was. At Ilekirk Hall there is a huge stone that he is reputed to have thrown the length of his courtyard which it would take two ordinary men to lift, and some other big round ones he is supposed to have played bowls with. They also say that he was wont to save his wife's shoes by walking over the bridge there with her sitting on one of his hands. He was married to Frances, the daughter of Sir Edward Musgrave of Hayton Castle. Richard was the MP, the first Mayor of Carlisle when Charles I gave the town a charter and served as sheriff.'

'He sounds like he must have been quite famous round here.'

'Oh, more than just round here. In the Civil war he was very active in raising money for Parliament and capturing Royalists over in Northumberland and Sunderland. In 1644 he wished Carlisle to be secured for Parliament, so persuaded General Leslie to march from Newcastle to garrison the city with 800 men. When they came almost to Salkeld, across the river they saw a host of cavalry from Cumberland across the other side to many times their own number. When he saw this General Leslie fell to railing at Barwise, saying that he had led him to a trap and that he had assured him that there would be no opposition to his advance.'

'And had he done that?'

'Yes he had, but not without reason. Barwise did not answer Leslie, but drew his sword and set his horse to cross the river, and the Parliamentary forces followed him, sword and pistol ready. On the other side of the water the Royalists saw this and they fulfilled the old saying, *veni vidi fugit*.'

At this Mister slapped his thighs and broke into uproarious laughter. Margaret, who had no Latin, was mystified, but Mister saw her face.

'*Veni vidi fugit*, lass. It means they came, they saw, they ran away; as fast as their horses could carry them. He knew they weren't soldiers, but farmers with a few weapons and good intentions so he just chased them away. The sight of him was enough. Anyway he provisioned Carlisle and held it for Parliament until 1648.'

'What happened to him then? Did he win?'

'No. That seldom happens in real life Margaret, and usually in novels. No a small bunch of Royalist rogues scaled the walls and put a pistol to his head when he was asleep, then led him in chains to Scotland where they put him in prison. Parliament negotiated his exchange from the villains who had him and secured his release, but whilst he was in the foul dungeon he contracted a fever and he died shortly afterwards. He was only 47 and had no children, but I am related to him through my grandmother. I've seen his memorial in Westward Church to an excellent and accomplished gentleman. It says:

'Below good Barwise clos'd in body lies
Whose saintly soul joys crowned above the skies.'

There you are lass; a real hero in the family. What do you think of that?'

Margaret thought about this for a moment then looked into his eyes which went solemn as he realised something big was about to happen.

'I think,' she said slowly, 'That when I have a son I shall call him Barwise.'

The pleasure of her words hit him like a poleaxe and knocked his laughter out of him.

'Oh lass. Margaret lass.'

In that house, and from that day, she could do no wrong.

The next few months went by quickly and Margaret grew in size until she was sure that she looked like a whale and wondered how people could bear to look at her. She and Tom lived in rather cramped style in the two small rooms above the dairy, which was better than attempting to have a family life of their own in Tom's old bedroom in the house. As her pregnancy advanced, it became necessary that she not work so hard, so Missis, now used to

318

having a maid, engaged a girl from the village to help her in the house, undertaking to train her herself. On 10 March 1896 Margaret's baby was born and Mister betrayed no disappointment at all as he cuddled and cooed at his first grandchild, who they decided was to be christened Annie Eleanor. The original Annie Eleanor, home for the weekend to see her new niece, was delighted with the choice, but worried about the confusion it would cause in the family.

'There'll be no confusion,' said Tom. 'We shall call her Eleanor for any formal use, but her day to day name will be Nellie.'

The advent of Nellie meant that the two tiny rooms above the dairy were too small for married life and it was time for Tom to broach the subject of moving his family elsewhere. This he did in the parlour one evening with all the family present. Mister could hardly deny the power of his case to move.

'But I need you on the farm.'

'No, you don't Dad. You need someone on the farm, but not necessarily me. You pay me an allowance from profits for the work I do. The same for Joe and William. If you didn't pay me, you could hire a man and pay him a lot less. You'd actually make money if I left and set up on my own.'

'But I'm getting on. I need you lads to carry on the farm, after me and your mother have gone.'

'You don't Dad. The eldest here is Joe and he's getting married next year. When you and Mam are gone he'll inherit. I'm sure he doesn't need two brothers round the place getting in the way. He can hire men just as you could.'

'Actually Dad, I've been thinking the same way.' This was William. 'I'd like to move out too and I've been thinking like Tom. I've got an offer to train as a quantity surveyor on the job with an old pal of mine from college.'

'Is this a conspiracy? You're all deserting me!'

'Not deserting Dad. You can't deny the sense of Margaret and me getting a place of our own now can you? We need to do that.'

'Yes, I can see that, but William too. That's a hard knock.'

'Not really. All William does is milk and work with cows. He wants more from life and not to be stuck here on a place that ultimately will not be his. Life moves on.'

'True enough. I'm fond enough of saying that myself. I'll not stand in his way if that's what he wants. There's men in the village will be glad of the work.'

William flashed a grateful look at Tom; it had been a lot easier than he thought it might have been, but the arrival of Nellie had changed everything. Mister knew that he could not hold back the flood tide of time and that matters had to play out to their natural ends. However, he went on;

'So when you and Margaret move out where are you going to be taking my grand daughter?'

Tom replied very softly. 'I'm going to rent Tarns Dad.'

'Tarns! What? That Tarns?'

'Yes Dad.'

Upper Tarns Farm was two miles away so Tom and Margaret would be just down the road; it was probably rather closer to church than West End Farm so they would certainly see each other there. They were hardly moving at all.

'Well that's not so far!'

'I know Dad, and with any luck,' here Tom glanced at Margaret, 'Your next grandchild will be born there, and the one after that…'

'What will you be doing there?'

'Horses, Dad. I'm fed up with cattle and if I never milked another cow in my life I'd be glad. I've a sum put away and I'm going to breed Clydesdales.'

'Tarns is 37 acres; you can breed a few good horses there and have hay too.'

'My own thinking exactly; if we prosper then I can rent more land and expand the business.'

'Ha! If indeed. You know the business Tom. You'll do well. You have my blessing the pair of you,' here he looked at his two sons wryly, 'and you too my lass. Take care that I see this little thing as often as possible.'

So saying he picked up his grand daughter on whom he doted, and she cooed back at him with baby noises and grabbed the end of his thumb.

'A good grip she has. She's a Little this one alright.'

Preparations now went ahead for the business of moving. In the case of William it was easy enough. He rented a house, Solway View, in Bothel which his mother helped him to furnish, and with his savings he had enough to live on, and Mr Smythe, his college friend, paid him a small wage to act as his assistant whilst he trained. In due course, they hoped to form a partnership that would be profitable to them both. Tarns Farm would be vacated at the end of June 1896 as the tenants were giving up farming and moving to Northumberland.

Margaret looked forward to her new life very much as a farmer's wife, and all her attention was focussed on this prospect; she was entirely unprepared for the letter that came addressed to her in a hand she thought she knew, at the beginning of June. Opening it she saw that it was from the Reverend Melrose, whom she had not seen since March.

'Dear Margaret. Your father has asked me to write to you as he does not wish to touch anything which will be handled by you or by anyone in your household for fear of infection. This is not an easy letter to write Margaret, but I regret to inform you that your family is the victim of a tragedy so poignant that I can hardly bear to write about it.'

Margaret quickly looked away from the writing without going further, a sudden fear gripping her. Going to the door she shouted across the yard for Tom, who came from the stables wiping his hands, asking what was the matter. She handed him the letter.

'I've read the first paragraph Tom. I don't want to read it. Can you read it to me?'

'Mary Hannah Adams was taken ill last week with measles; there is an outbreak of this fell disease in the village at this very time. It pleased God to take her from us on Monday and her soul is in heaven as I write.'

Margaret stared at Tom too dazed to react; it was Wednesday and the baby had been dead for two days. There is an unreality to the news of sudden death that many, probably most human beings are not able to comprehend. Unlike in great plays or melodrama, grief does not afflict the bereaved with a sudden loud and screaming hand. The knowledge has to sink in and the realisation to grow that what has happened is real.

'Your father has asked me to emphasise that you must not come home for the sake of your own infant. There are outbreaks in the towns and villages all round this area, particularly in Wigton...'

Margaret caught her breath. Wigton was not very far away.

'You know, dear Margaret, how difficult I find it to speak of these things in the light of my own tragedy, but if my son's death has taught me anything then it is that I must accept the will of God even when I do not understand it. This makes me able to counsel you that what you and your family feel will be accepted in time, if never forgotten.'

The Vicar indeed knew more than many what it was to grieve. His ten year old son had been killed in a most tragic accident at Maryport railway station just six days after Margaret and Tom had been married. She had written to him on her return from Scotland to tell him how sorry she was.

'Your father further says that he knows you will want to be at the funeral for your sister's sake, though he would not wish you to. He advises that if you do come you keep a safe distance between yourself and the rest of the funeral party as it is so infectious. The funeral will be at 2.00 pm this Thursday 4 June. I

also counsel you not to come, but fear that you will anyway. God bless you dear Margaret. Yours in Christ Thomas Melrose'

Now Margaret cried for the baby, for Ommie, for her parents who had lost a grandchild, and for the world where innocent children could be taken in this manner, and Tom held her while she cried. Mister's face was fierce when he heard the news that measles were all round them and he put a notice on the yard gate saying that no-one was to come in unless known and free of infection. In the event Edderside was not infected; people bought in Mawbray and Allonby, but for a few weeks avoided going to Aspatria, Wigton or Maryport. For a while they could be self-sufficient. The Littles turned out in force, all of them, for the funeral of Mary Hannah at Dearham; though Nellie was left at Edderside Hall in the care of Phoebe Sharp. Mister said that it was family and that was that. They did not go near the Adams house, but stood over to one side of the churchyard away from the graveside as the ceremony proceeded. Throughout the funeral John Adams was helping to support a tall man of his own age or thereabouts who attended in a black frock coat and silk hat, which he took off at the graveside; he wept inconsolably and seemed beside himself with grief. Mr Furnival was more of a human being than his son. The Littles talked to and wept with the Adams, but did not approach, as indeed John Adams feared they would and Margaret promised through weeping that she would visit as soon as it was safe.

It was under a cloud then, that on Wednesday 1 July 1896 Tom and Margaret with little Nellie put their bed and few belongings onto the farm cart and moved down the road to their new house at Upper Tarns Farm.

Chapter 22

At Tarns

Omega's face was a study in misery, not that it was overt or oppressive; on the contrary her presence at Tarns Farm was helpful to Margaret, because her sister was as consummate a housekeeper as she herself. Having just moved into a new home would be a stressful thing at the best of times, but Omega's help with the placing of furniture, the wielding of a brush, the hanging of pictures and even just with the washing, was a great blessing. It was not so much that her face was gloomy or tearful; this was not Omega's style; rather it was blank and something in the stoic expression of it spoke of that which was sternly repressed. Some weeks had elapsed since the death of her baby and there had been tears and grief, sobbing and even screaming in the most heart-rending way, but that was now passed. This Omega was different to any other that Margaret had ever seen and often she wished that her sister would scream or cry, because this human statue was something outside her experience. She had tried to talk to her about it, but Ommie had told her, 'I'm numb Margaret. There's nothing left. I'm just numb.' All Margaret could do was to hug her and tell herself to bide her time. It had been her idea that Omega should come to Tarns to get away from Dearham for a while; the measles outbreak appeared to have abated, so the threat to Annie Eleanor was minimal. Financially Omega had nothing to worry about as the grief stricken Mr Furnival senior had written to her after Mary Hannah's funeral and told her that he intended to continue her stipend at £3 a month until such time as she married, at which point it would cease. This could be seen as assuaging his guilt at the conduct of his son, but John Adams had preferred to think of it as a manifestation of human decency towards a young woman whose life chances had received a setback of considerable proportions. Omega was certain that she did not wish to remain idle and had aspirations to become a cook-housekeeper in a respectable house. With a good reference from Mr Furnival she could reasonably bring this ambition to pass when she felt ready and able. He had even hinted that he would be quite prepared to have her back in that capacity in his own house, but she felt this would not be appropriate, even allowing for the fact that Edward Furnival had become estranged from his father whom he had offended beyond measure. The sensibilities of the solicitor had been severely jarred by his son's behaviour with Omega, but the latest escapade had led to a major falling out. Edward had ended his advantageous engagement declaring that he did not find the appearance of his fiancée congenial to his tastes. More than this, he had thrown up university in his final year, stated quite emphatically that he had no intention of becoming a fusty old lawyer in a provincial town, and had joined the army. Having been in the cadet corps of his college for two years he had no difficulty in enlisting as a Gentleman Cadet at Sandhurst where even now he was strutting around in uniform. In all justice, it has to be said that this was a profession far better suited to his rather tempestuous nature, which was not inclined to settle, or at least not yet. Though she was, under the circumstances, very unlikely to encounter the father of her dead child, Omega turned down the solicitor's offer; she would find employment when it felt right to do so, though she was grateful to him for the financial support that allowed her the luxury of time.

Tom's work was made easier for him on the farm, as he had engaged a farm servant from Mawbray, a 17 year old lad called Joseph Hayriggs. This was very necessary with the myriad of tasks to be done around the place, because the previous tenant had not been very active in taking care of the fabric of the holding. Walls needed repairing, rotting fences replaced, new gates installed on some field entrances and the roof of the large barn retiled. Tom could not afford to bring in people to do these things so he and Joseph had to do it, no matter what the weather. His 37 acre holding was enough for more horses than he could afford, but he did not have sufficient cash to buy more than six Clydesdale mares at prices ranging between £45 and £55 each. The rest of the farm would be put to hay, and the machinery to cut it would be hired in from the Agricultural Co-operative. With what was left of his capital, a little help from his father and careful management, he planned to increase the number of horses as he bred them and sell their foals as yearlings. In time he thought he could make Tarns a prosperous and well-known heavy horse breeding centre, and for such animals there was always a brisk and ready market. Whatever else, he did not wish to have dairy cattle, stating quite clearly that he had pulled on enough teats for three of his lifetimes. To help tide away the time and cash flow until such time as his income grew to be handsome he also invested in the purchase of a Clydesdale stallion to service his mares, but also to hire out. As he told Margaret enough times until she grew sick of it, great oaks from little acorns grow, and in time she would wear silk. In vain she told him that she did not particularly wish to, being quite happy with what she had, but he always replied that some day she would think differently.

With a new baby in the house Margaret's time was pretty full and well used, so she was glad that Omega was visiting, but she was not so blind as to miss a business opportunity right in front of her eyes as August wore on, and it concerned The Tarn. More accurately, this was Tarns Dub, which is a small lake just up the hill from Tarns Farm and over the rise. Every weekend the road passing the farm had quite a lot of traffic with well to do people trotting their gigs up to take the air by a lovely expanse of fresh water, and just sit looking at the blueness of it. Tom was amused when Omega put a sign at the end of the lane with 'Teas, cakes, lemonade' on it, and lent a hand sweeping out and cleaning a lean-to into which they placed a few plank tables and chairs. The amusement ended when the first day-trippers pulled into the yard and it became plain that they were very willing to spent their halfpennies and pennies on a cup of tea or home-made lemonade, giving the farm a nice little profit on each transaction. Since most of the business was done on Sunday afternoons, it did not interfere with the running of the farm at all and another stream of income was very welcome. It was partly this, but not solely, that led to a conversation initiated by Margaret during the Indian summer of 1896.

'I've been thinking Ommie, and if you want the truth, I've been talking to Tom. We're wondering if you'd like to stay on here?'

'You mean live here? Whatever for?'

'Well, the fact is that it's very useful having you here; and you're my sister. I like having you around.'

This last remark was not merely a natural affection, as Margaret had calculated its impact quite closely during the small hours of the previous morning. Omega needed to feel needed. That she really was needed had little to do with the fact that she actually needed to feel it. It was quite plain that the transition from being the most needed person in the world to her little girl, to having no-one needing her, had hit her hard. Margaret could not replace Mary Hannah, but she could supply the need, as it was genuine.

'You mean as a sort of maid?'

Margaret laughed. 'No. Not as a maid. The fact is that you're a help; and not just with the house. There's more money coming in from teas and cakes now and I won't be able to keep it up soon.'

'Don't talk daft. Our mother taught you as she taught me; we can cope with anything round a house, anything at all.'

'At the moment Ommie, yes, but soon I won't want to, and you'd be a help.'

Margaret looked at Ommie who looked into her eyes and divined her thoughts perfectly.

'When is it due?'

'I would think about the first week of May.'

'You don't hang about you two, do you? Two years married and you'll have two children!'

Margaret smiled, 'We are greatly blessed.'

'Well that's one way of looking at it. What about Mother and Father? I pay them rent you know.'

'I don't think they'll mind, though I will write and ask them. They've got little enough space with Thomas and Johnny and Alpha, but they have taken lodgers before.'

'That's true enough and they could do again,' mused Omega. 'A lodger would probably pay more than me too. I'll write the letter to them and ask what they think, so don't you trouble. Mind you, there's one condition.'

'What's that?'

'I might be useful, but being useful doesn't pay. You'll not charge me for my room, but I pay for my own food.'

'Don't be daft. We need your help Ommie. Why should you pay as well?'

'I pay my way Margaret. My food I pay for. That's it. Take it or leave it.'

Margaret paused, 'How much did you have in mind?'

'I don't eat much because I'm not a big person, so I was thinking, say eight shillings a week.'

Margaret was scandalised, 'Eight shillings a week! Are you planning on dining on caviar Miss? Off gold plate perhaps? I'll take five and there's an end to it.'

So it was agreed, and the extra income was welcome; Omega would save money from this, and the farm would not suffer by it.

The reply to Omega's letter was not long in coming. John Adams wrote for himself and his wife, expressing the thought that the idea of Omega living at Tarns was a good one and they were not to worry about any loss of income at the Dearham household. There was a young man called William Dand who had been seeking a better place to live than the communal miner's lodge he was in, and he was pleased he could oblige him as a nice young chap, though somewhat ugly. Margaret laughed loudly when she read that last piece.

'He doesn't want you getting any ideas about the lodger, Ommie.'

'I've had it with men Margaret. I took up with someone supposedly a gentleman. If that's the best of them then they know what they can do. I'll have no more.'

Margaret looked at her sister with a long and noncommittal stare, 'We shall see.'

'No I mean it! They're trouble and I've had enough.'

Life is littered with resolutions, which human beings, intrinsically fallible, are wont to renege on. We make such declarations with the best of intentions, and in all justice it must be said that some, more saint than sinner, do manage to keep their vows. Margaret was no saint, but also no great sinner; however she knew her sister. Omega meant what she said; for now. It was a discussion best left to lapse.

The great event of the year apart from Tom and Margaret leaving Edderside, was the wedding of Joe and Agnes which took place at the beginning of October. Joe, bundled up in his best suit was red with pleasure throughout the service, beaming at his small blonde bride. She spent the ceremony smiling with a perfect delight and looked, as Margaret thought, like the cat that got the cream. As the eldest son in West End farm he had always had the largest bedroom, and as the heir, he kept it, and Agnes simply moved in. Mister engaged another milkmaid to relieve the burden on his new daughter in law though she insisted that she wished to keep working. Freed from much of the mechanics of milking, she had other ideas. She wanted to use her skills in making butter, and added to the farm income by undertaking to prepare more of it and to sell it through the local shops. As Mister was paid by quantity from the dairy in Aspatria, he did not demur at the experiment.

There is no-one closer to a woman than her sister in most cases. The sibling closeness of genetics, of ancestry, of experience is so exact that it is one of the hardest of human bonds to break. Even ties to parents are fragile, because they can be broken by neglect, indifference, domineering, by cruelty and other abuses, so to Margaret, having her elder sister living with her was a pleasure. She had someone to talk to on even terms all day long whilst Tom was out at work, someone to trust and whom she loved. In short she had company. In addition to this her hands were full with the round of housework and looking after Annie Eleanor who was sitting up on the tatted rug in front of the fire making gooing noises. She'd be walking soon and the fireguard was very necessary as she was always reaching out to touch things; fingers and hot stoves would not mix well. Despite the comfortable domesticity, however, there was a new element in everyday life that Margaret did not find so enchanting. Freed from the paternal rule of Edderside, Tom had taken to spending more time at the pub. He liked a pint or two and Margaret knew it well, but though she had been brought up temperance, she knew that many men regarded beer after work as a food supplement vital to their well-being and energy. She had heard enough of them say it, but Tom had started to go to the pub more often. He had pointed out that she was not lonely and with Omega and the baby, she would never want for company. He wished to see his marras, and have a craic with them. Also he said that it was good for pressing the flesh. Margaret was not fond of the expression, but knew that he meant that he was forging and reinforcing links with local farmers, carters, hauliers and businessmen who might wish to buy his horses in future. She could not deny the benefits that might accrue, but Tom used to go to the pub once or twice a week. Now it was practically every night. It was a good job that he had Marra; Mister had told him that he could take Marra with him when he moved to Tarns as the horse doted on him, and he had bought another for West End farm use. Marra quickly learned his way home to Tarns from the Lowther Arms and it was a good job because sometimes Tom drank so much that he was drawn home fast asleep in the back of the gig. She attempted to remonstrate with him about his drinking too much and smelling of stale beer and making a beast of himself, but he laughed at her and told her that it was what men did. If he stopped they would say that he was henpecked and unmanly; what would she have him do? She felt terribly guilty about treading on what seemed to be male territory so her resistance to his behaviour wilted in the face of this; she did not wish her man to be thought of in that way in the neighbourhood. It would be nice though, if he spent more of his evenings at home.

Monday 7 December 1896 was a day Margaret would always remember. It was, as Monday always was, washing day. As ever, washing day was hard hauling wet clothes in and out of tubs, bending over washing boards and scrubbing, using the mangle. At the end of the day Margaret's back ached, which was not unusual and she sat down gratefully at the kitchen table as Omega made a cup of tea. It had barely touched her lips before the cramps hit her stomach and she doubled over the table in pain, crying out at its sharp onset.

'Margaret. What's wrong?'

'I don't know. Something's wrong. Oh.'

'Where does it hurt?'

'All across my tummy. Oh, I think I've wet myself.'

'Let me see. No you haven't. That's blood. I think the baby's coming.'

'Can't be the baby Ommie. I'm only five months.'

Omega's hand flew to her face. 'Miscarriage?'

'I think so. Ohhhh.' Margaret grimaced with a fresh spasm of pain. 'Help. Now,'

Omega was at the door screaming for Tom and he was on the way within ten minutes galloping Marra for all he was worth down to Mawbray with the gig. Within 25 minutes he was back with Mrs Beatty, one of the local cunning women, and the midwife who had delivered Annie Eleanor. They found that Omega had removed Annie Eleanor from the room and Margaret was lying on a shakeydown in front of the fire, towels under her that were soaked with a fair amount of blood; she also looked frightened.

Mrs Beatty smiled at her, 'Now don't you worry my pet. I'm here now and you're going to be fine.'

'Do you think so? Really?'

'Yes I do. I'll not beat about the bush my dear and I think you know anyway that you've lost the bairn, but you will be all right.'

'I know I've lost my baby, but how do you know I'm going to be all right?'

'Because I've seen this before my love and far more than once. Sometimes it's just nature's way when something isn't meant to be.'

'What do you mean that it isn't meant to be?'

'Well now, that depends if you believe in God, and I do.'

'So do I.'

'Then you'll know that we don't always understand why these things happen and we have to accept them. Now it's not pleasant and we'll get you through it, but you're a young woman and you'll have other children.'

Margaret's face furrowed with pain as another spasm came.

'Right my love, just lie back and let me help you through this. Just let nature take its course. Your husband has gone for the doctor now, so let your body do what it wants to.'

The course of the next few hours were not the happiest of times, but the major part of the process came to an end during the small hours of the morning, leaving Margaret exhausted and asleep. The doctor came and greeted Mrs Beatty with an affability that demonstrated that he regarded her as a safe pair of hands, and he was well satisfied with what she had done.

'It is a natural process Mr Little, and the major part of it is over. Mrs Beatty will dispose of what needs doing and she's done well so I would not stint her reward. There are some so called midwives I've come across… well I won't describe what they do, but she's made your wife clean and comfortable and I have no fear of infection. She'll recover well.'

'Is it all over then Doctor?'

'Oh no, not all. I told you. It's a natural process and especially in a pregnancy as advanced as this one. Frankly, man to man, the situation is ongoing and there is material in the womb that nature will expel. How long that takes will vary from patient to patient; some are lucky and it's all done in three or four days, but in others it can be as many weeks.'

'She'll be right then?'

'Yes. Look after her and make her rest. She must not work at all for at least the next week and then only light work.'

'That'll be hard on her. She does graft and likes to.'

'That may be, but you must stop her.'

'I do not see a problem there; her sister lives with us and she will make her rest.'

'That's all to the good then. I will pop in on my rounds a few times just to check her over, but I don't anticipate any problems except with sleep. If she is in pain then give her three drops of this in a cup of milk. If she has no pain then three drops at bedtime so that she sleeps.'

'What is it?'

'Some of my colleagues call it 'the woman's friend' but technically it's called Sydenham's Laudanum. It's very good and extremely useful in cases such as this. When she is recovered well enough in a week or so she'll need a tonic to perk her spirits up. Go to the chemist in Aspatria where they stock Elixir Mariani and give her a dose of that. Wonderful stuff. Now I'll be about my business; I'll send you my bill later. Goodnight Mr Little.'

A house where two women have lost babies within a short period of time is not the most cheerful of places and it could have been worse at Tarns Farm than it was. Omega, though, was like her sister and made of stern stuff. Instead of allowing herself to sink back into a complementary slough of despair and grief, she assumed the role of nurse; the need to look after Margaret to some extent placed her own grief at the back of her mind, subordinated to the more immediate claims of the present. It was never going to be easy; Margaret slept round the clock, but it was not a peaceful rest as her psyche was very disturbed. When she did wake it was with a blank stare, which was very appropriate to her state of mind that told her that such a thing could not have happened. It could not have happened to her and though she knew it had, her pervading senses were of numbness and disbelief; these thoughts she could not wish away because they do not respond to rational thought; all reason bounces off them as bullets do to armour. She did not speak much at all in the ensuing days, and kept bursting into tears, sobbing her heart out, whilst all Omega could do was to hug and soothe with crooning noises.

'It's my fault, all my fault.'

'And how is it your fault Margaret?'

'I must have done something wrong. I should have stopped working and let you do more of the washday. I know you wanted me to but it's my job.'

'That's not true. There's lots and lots of women carry on with their normal work long past five months. Doing the washing did not lose your baby.'

'Yes it did. There's no other reason is there? I was lifting heavy stuff out of the tub and working the mangle. What else could it be?'

'That's like me blaming myself for Mary Hannah catching measles. You don't know why you miscarried and you never will. Nature or God has reasons; maybe there was something wrong and the birth was never meant to go full term. You don't know.'

'Well if it's not me, then it's God. Why would he do that? I don't believe that he would want to do that. It must be something I did.'

'Margaret; it's just what happens. It's all very well blaming yourself, but look at that poor woman at Edderside. You know what happened to her bairn. Five years old and tips a pan of boiling water over herself and is scalded to death. Was that her fault?'

'No that wasn't. She only turned her back for a few seconds; it could have happened to anyone. Any woman doing the cooking runs that risk.'

'Well there you are. What happened to you happens to lots of women, probably thousands in this country every year. Are they all to blame for losing their babies too?'

'No, of course not.'

'Well then, neither are you.'

This kind of palliative conversation could bring on a period of calm, but the storms of self-rage and weeping continued and it seemed that nothing could touch them. Tom tried his best to comfort her, being tender and considerate in all that he could do, but he was a man, and like the sun he shone from the east, the south and the west. He could not shine from the north and Margaret's utter prostration in the week following her miscarriage continued, changing form as time passed. After a week the crying more or less stopped, but she was plainly depressed and almost unable to eat, though Omega did her best to make her. She wondered aloud if she would ever be able to have another baby after losing this one, and no reassurances would move that thought. As the doctor pointed out, women who had a miscarriage had a right to grieve for the dead, though they had no grave, no funeral, no flowers. Eventually though, there would come acceptance and when this began, most people could move on. Thanks to the laudanum Margaret was sleeping heavily, so her body was getting rest, but her mind remained in turmoil during her waking hours. Her time for acceptance seemed to be a long way ahead, until Tom went to Aspatria and paid a visit to Pattinson's Chemist where he procured a bottle of Vin Mariani, which the chemist assured him was 'champion stuff that' and asserted that it was used frequently by the Queen and the Pope. The Pontiff had in fact bestowed a papal gold medal on this medicine which appeared on the label also. Tom looked at the label on the bottle that promised health, vitality, energy and strength, was inclined to be sceptical, but recalled that he was here on Doctor Coulthard's recommendation so took it home.

Within ten minutes of Margaret drinking the glass that he poured her, the depression lifted; her eyes brightened and she shivered, looking at the glass and telling him that it was delicious. He did not allow her to drink more than a glass though, as he had been strictly enjoined that one glass with each meal during the day was quite enough. The effects of it were quite astonishing as Margaret's colour improved, a pink mantle suffusing her cheeks and she appeared to be quite herself again. It is true that as the hours went by, and for an hour or so before each meal her mood subsided back, but the medicine definitely worked. Angelo Mariani's Bordeaux wine, which contained, did she but know it, seven and a half milligrams of cocaine in every fluid ounce, smoothed her way through the distance between her miscarriage and the time where she could begin to accept what had happened. The supply of Snr Mariani's elixir increased in the household as Omega, having tried it also simply had to get some. This emerging habit ended when the Doctor noticed the bottles on a visit and warned them against cocaine addiction; it was a medicine, not a recreational drink and they must not take it unless on advice. Between the opium at bedtime and the cocaine during the day Margaret made a remarkable recovery both mentally and physically. The propensity of the female reproductive system to repair itself is very great in young women and Margaret's cycle resumed normality two months after her miscarriage, in early February 1897. At this time she was still drinking Mr Mariani's wine, and cocaine, unknown to her, was what drove her enthusiasm in the physical side of her marriage. By early March, though she did not realise it at first, she was pregnant again and Doctor Coulthard told her to stop drinking the wine as he thought it would be bad for the baby; he also told Omega not to get too fond of it, though she continued to indulge in it occasionally.

It was on 12 February when Tom exploded with laughter as he was reading his newspaper; he had begun taking the Carlisle Patriot shortly after they moved in to Tarns Farm and it was delivered from Mawbray each day.

'My Dad's going to make hay with this! Oh dear, oh dear.'

'What? Mister's in the paper?' asked Margaret.

'In a manner of speaking he is, but not in the way that he would like.'

He handed Margaret the paper and there she read a report of the meeting of Holme Cultram Urban District Council, under which came Edderside.

'Insanitary conditions at Edderside.'

'Oh dear. You're right. He'll explode!'

They were right. When next they saw Mister, his eloquence was fit to burn paint off a wall. As the newspaper had reported a Mr Wilson of The Gale had given the council notice that unless the council took steps to stop liquid manure from the majority of farms in the village from flowing into the public pond then he would consider it his duty to report them all to the Local Government Board with a view to having the place properly sewered.

'Aye and at our expense too mark you! We'd have to pay for it, not him damn his eyes. What's it got to do with him anyway? He lives miles away up by Abbeytown. I've a good notion to go and pull his nose for him. Interfering busybody! That's what he is.'

Mr Wilson was not popular in Edderside, the whole community feeling slighted at being called insanitary.

'He says that the water in the pond is so polluted with sewage that it is unfit for cattle to drink it.'

'Well he's right there,' ventured Tom.

'Oh aye, but you know as well as I do that none of the local cattle drink from the pond. Our cattle are all in their fields where they've either got troughs or streams. Does he think we allow the cattle to roam across the public road? That pond's not used by anyone for drinking. It hasn't been since before my father's time.'

'It is in a bit of a state though, you must admit Dad.'

'It is that, but nobody here uses it. Why should anyone be suggesting that our rates go up to sewer the village? That's just daft. I know what's what here; he's been riding through and wanted to let his horse drink at the pond, when anyone could have told him better. They say it's the only watering place in the village which just isn't true.'

'Well speaking literally it is. It's the only pond.'

'Aye. But go down the bottom of each strip of our land and what do you find?'

'Fresh water from Black Dub. There's enough water on our farm just in the soil, never mind the ditches!'

'So he's painting it as bad as he can. Why? Anyway the lad's got a new job now. I've told him that no manure's to go onto the road. Rest of them can do what they want, but if anyone says we are letting liquid manure flow into the pond then they're lying.'

'So that's what Councillor Peat meant when he said that one of the nuisances had been abated.'

'Yes he did. Me. A nuisance at my time of life. If I come across this Wilson of Gale then I'll give him a piece of my mind.'

'Never mind Dad. At least you're in the paper; in a way.'

'Maybe. But it's all a bit late now. I see that they are going to make us a separate rating area and carry out drainage works. It'll cost.'

In time the council did carry out works at Edderside, but the cost was not great. The main street had a sewer dug along it ending in a large septic tank which was dug down near the pond. Each farm and house had a drain connected to the main sewer, but it ended at the tank that was emptied once a week by council workmen. The matter of water supply did put Tom into a train of thinking about the Tarns Farm supply though. His home was supplied from one well that had been sunk in a corner of the farmyard. This served all purposes and he had often thought that it would be useful and more sanitary to have a well in by the house. Now he determined that at some point in the not too distant future, he would dig a well dedicated solely to domestic use.

Chapter 23

Arrival and Departure

Omega's presence continued to ease Margaret's workload through the summer of 1897 and especially after she discovered her new pregnancy in March. She took it much easier than she had before her miscarriage, and though she cooked and did light cleaning, Omega took on all the heavy work. Margaret spent a lot of her time having conversations with little Nellie who was from the first a vocal child, and then she progressed into a very talkative one. It is true that at first the conversations did not make a lot of sense, at least on Nellie's side, but it became increasingly apparent that she liked the sound of words, she liked to communicate and liked people. Omega was of course perfectly free to organise her time as she pleased, and decided in September that she would shorten the time she took to do the shopping by investing in a bicycle. To Margaret this was rather a daring thing to do, but Omega told her not to be such a mouse. Bicycling was becoming all the rage for the modern woman, or so she asserted.

'Anyway, I've been thinking about it for some time,' she declared, pulling a newspaper clipping out of the book she was reading. It was a report from the previous year of a four day bicycle race held at the Aquarium Velodrome in London. Ladies had raced against each other and though not being allowed to ride for more than four hours in the day, the mileages were impressive even spaced over four days. Mademoiselle Dutrieu of France had ridden 785 miles and two laps to take first prize. French women had taken second and third places, whilst the British girl, Miss Blackburn, had come fourth with 756 miles. Astonishingly, Mrs Ward had come fifth with 723 miles and two laps. With this example in front of them, thousands of young women the length and breadth of the land were taking to two wheels.

'Imagine Margaret; a married woman doing that. You could too. It's quite inspiring.'

'Maybe one day Ommie, but I'm too busy having babies right now, if you don't mind.'

Taking note of an advertisement in the *Carlisle Patriot* Omega saw that Mr RT Dalton had been instructed to auction off the contents, household furniture and effects of a small hotel in Silloth that had failed; among them was a lady's safety bicycle. Persuading Tom to take her down to the sale on 10 September, they returned in triumph with her prize.

'Look at it Margaret! It's almost brand new. They bought it this year for the use of lady guests and now they've gone bankrupt. I got it for £3 and it must have cost £20 at least when new.'

'That's a lot of money to pay out. A month's allowance.'

'Well yes, but I've got quite a lot in the bank you know; and anyway it'll pay for itself in saving me time. It's a Singer Modele De Luxe and very good.'

'But you can't ride a bicycle.'

'Oh, just you watch me. How hard can it be?'

'I would think it would be very hard. You're not going to wear those bloomers are you?'

'I might! If I decide I want to buy some, and there's lots of women do. There's a divided skirt you can get called a rational costume, but I don't think I'll bother. One thing I do know and that's that I'm not wearing a corset when I ride. I've heard quite enough to know to avoid that. It's a freedom machine Margaret. It's quite respectable to ride on your own and you can go where you like.'

'Well you be careful. Just remember that poor girl who disappeared at Ullswater.'

'You mean Annie Johnston? Don't be daft Margaret. She cycled to Ullswater. Her disappearance had nothing to do with cycling. They think her boat sank.'

'That's all very well, but they haven't found her have they?'

Omega merely rolled her eyes and decided to discontinue this discussion.

340

It was not, ultimately, too hard to learn to ride. Omega did not like the idea of falling off, but she had seen women riding bicycles round the lanes often, and Mrs Melrose, the vicar's wife at Dearham, was a very keen cyclist. What they could do, she could do. The field nearest inby the farm had been closely clipped by grazing horses and foals, and it had a slight slope. Omega learned to ride by sitting, her feet splayed out on each side of the machine, and allowing gravity to take her down the slope. In this way, after a few practice runs, she found that she could balance. Once she started to pedal she did fall off, but only four times and her landing on the grass was soft. After this, her progress was rapid and she grew quite keen, shopping at Mawbray and venturing even further to Aspatria when the mood took her, coming back with the basket on her handlebars piled high with her purchases. Rational dress was quite unnecessary, though true to her word, she did not wear the universal corset when she rode. That alone was a daring step for her and the feeling of liberation it gave her was quite exciting. On summer afternoons in the following year she would take herself off to Silloth where there was a small but active lady's cycling group; quite a few of them were Suffragists too, and it was here that she first heard the name Millicent Garrett Fawcett. For Omega life was turning interesting.

Margaret's life on the other hand, got a lot busier. Nancy was born in late November 1897 and Nellie had a sister so their mother had no time for cycling or other recreations. No more did Tom. The farm was in a fair way to succeed and after he sold four Clydesdale yearlings at Wigton Martinmas Fair in November for £60 apiece, things began to look prosperous. He had income from breeding, increased his breeding stock by keeping a couple of yearling mares, had enough hay for winter feed, and had enough put by to tide them over until his establishment was big enough to stand a few shocks. The news from Edderside was entirely good too, as Agnes was delivered of a healthy baby girl whom she and Joe named Elizabeth. Mister was good-humoured about it and very happy, with one small reservation, to have three grand children.

'I can see now that the Littles are very good at producing lasses. What I want to know is when one of you's going to produce a lad? In fact as you may have noticed, I'm cracking on a bit; I've had my three score and ten with a bit added on. But I'll tell you what; the devil's not going to get me until one of you gives me a grandson. Now what do you think of that? I'll spit in Old Nick's eye and tell him to bugger off.'

This was repeated at intervals and always with a twinkle in the eye, but both Agnes and Margaret knew that Mister would like to see his grandson if there was going to be one.

William was now firmly ensconced in Bothel pursuing qualifications to be a fully professional quantity surveyor and had, by all accounts, done so well that he was the boss's right hand man. Annie Eleanor appeared every so often from Carlisle to fuss and coo over her young nieces, but was still enamoured of the idea that she was a rising career woman. She appeared to have no followers, nor interest in them and at 28 Margaret thought she was well on the way to becoming an old maid. Tom told her that it was not anyone's business but her own and if that's what she wanted to do, then fair enough; it was just a bit hard on that poor chap Metcalfe who also had not married, and for all he knew was still stuck on Annie. She had other things on her mind and in October 1897 was one of the first young women in Carlisle to join the new National Union of Womens' Suffrage Societies.

'She takes far more notice of the doings of Lydia Becker or Mrs Fawcett to heed much our Mr Metcalfe I think,' said Tom.

Margaret smiled at that because there was a lot of truth in it. She herself had far too much to do to be bothered with any Suffragists; washing nappies was much more important.

In the spring of 1898 there came one of those Sunday afternoons where the sky is blue, the sun shines, and the air simply oozes high spirits. Tom was reading his newspaper outside the back door and Omega, with a great and mysterious air, asked if he would watch the children for a little while. He agreed and asked why.

'I'm going to teach my sister how to ride a bicycle. It's about time she learned.'

'First I've heard of it!' said Margaret.

'Well, that's because I've just thought of it. Come on you. You can wear what you've got on.'

'But why should I?'

'Freedom Margaret. Freedom and freshness. Come on!'

Persuaded by her sister Margaret ventured out and followed exactly the same process as Omega had except that she only fell off once. She had very good balance and was riding the machine round the field within a few days, Omega sitting on a blanket with the children on some nice soft grass near the gate.

'Now we can go out for rides together when the weather's nice.'

'I don't know about that. My bottom's a bit sore from this saddle; and anyway I don't have a bicycle.'

'You are such a bucket of cold water sometimes! Your bottom gets used to it and won't hurt if you keep doing it. And I'm sure that Tom is not going to grudge you a few pounds for a suitable machine.'

'What about the children? I can't ask Tom to look after them while I go swanning off on a joy ride round the countryside.'

'You have a lovely mother-in-law just two miles down the road who'd give teeth to look after her grand daughters for a few hours. Missis dotes on them. All we'd have to do would be to take the cart over to Edderside and leave it there with the children. The bicycles would be on the back and we'd ride from there. Simple.'

So it was that the summer of 1898 turned golden for Margaret; Tom thought it a good idea that his wife should get away from her work occasionally, paraphrasing, 'All work and no play makes Jaqueline a dull girl; not that you're dull my love, but it would do you good to get out a bit. And since there'd be two of you it would be a kind of mutual chaperone arrangement.'

'What? Do you expect some man to try and run off with me?'

'Well they might. You scrub up quite well…'

Margaret's bicycle was new, and, like Omega's, had the new pneumatic tyres. Soon she was using it to go to Mawbray for shopping, and for pleasure rides when the opportunity afforded. Both sisters wore skirts which made cycling harder, as they well knew, than it was for men. They could have adopted the rational dress of a divided skirt or bloomers that many brave women used, but they knew the abuse that went with wearing such. Annie Eleanor sometimes put her own bicycle on the train and met them in Silloth, and she, being a forward thinking and modern young woman, did wear rational dress. Men would shout sometimes 'Get yer 'air cut,' as if she was a man wearing what they deemed to be trousers. More respectable men would make their point by lifting their hats and asking 'sir' for the address of his tailor, whilst a cheeky barber in Silloth asked her if she'd like to have a shave. One elderly woman battleaxe planted herself in front of Annie one day and told her that she was a 'forward young minx.' Annie usually just tossed her nose at men and ignored them, but on this occasion she asked the woman if there was license this afternoon to make personal remarks on a stranger's appearance.

'I have a right to my opinion!'

'Well then' replied Annie, 'I will avail myself of the same privilege and inform you that in my opinion you are an old frump!'

'Well I never did!'

'I'm fairly sure that you have!'

'How dare you; you're no better than you should be!'

'And you're no better than you are, and that's not saying much!'

The woman sputtered and had no reply and all three girls rode off giggling, Margaret and Omega admiring at Annie's daring. As they did so, a rough looking and middle-aged man in working clothes took his hat off to them.

'Bravo lass. I like your pluck.'

Annie stopped her bicycle immediately, got off and went to him.

'And I thank you for being a man, and more of a gentleman than most in this town.'

Then she kissed his cheek and returned to her machine.

'Oh my eye! Oh my eye! I hope my missis don't hear of this.'

'If she does, then tell her it was a thank you. She'll understand.'

He stood looking after her until they had disappeared down the road.

Out in the flat country and in the lanes over towards Abbeytown Omega began to sing.

'There is a flower within my heart,
Daisy, Daisy,
Planted one day by a glancing dart,
Planted by Daisy Bell.
Whether she loves me or loves me not
Sometimes it's hard to tell;
And yet I am longing to share the lot
Of beautiful Daisy Bell.
Chorus:
Daisy, Daisy, give me your answer, do.
I'm half crazy all for the love of you.
It won't be a stylish marriage.
I can't afford a carriage.
But you'd look sweet upon the seat,
Of a bicycle built for two.'
Etc.

Rounding a corner they stopped singing and halted because there was an elderly man standing astride his bicycle in the middle of the road. He was lean and looked fit, with a grey beard and a Norfolk jacket topped with a cap; he stood looking at something, or maybe into space, and tears were rolling down his cheeks. Though all were concerned, it was Margaret who spoke.

'Whatever is the matter sir? Shall we fetch help?'

He turned to look at her with brimming eyes. 'No no thank you Madam,' evidently spying her wedding ring. 'I am quite well thank you. Quite well.'

'I must beg to differ; it is not usual for gentlemen to be found crying in the road.'

'I am quite well I assure you; just overcome a little. I will be all right in a few moments.'

'Whatever has caused you this distress.'

'Oh it is not distress. No no; you misunderstand.'

Seeing their collective puzzlement he made a gesture with his hand.

'I shall explain; I am a cobbler and I live in Carlisle. Six days a week I labour in boots and leather and a dark shop in the middle of brick and stone and cobbles. Today I have release from that prison and I rode out to this green and sunny place. Now tell me, did you ever in your life see anything more beautiful than that? There's the hand of God in it and that made me stop and cry with the loveliness of it.'

At this he pointed to some bunches of violets glowing in the hedgebank. Margaret looked hard at the violets, to her and the other girls a commonplace in their environment.

'No,' she said softly, 'I never did. You're right. They are beautiful.'

He was not the only urban dweller they met on their rides. One woman was fascinatedly looking over a fence one day and hailed them with the cyclist's comradeship that was so widespread then and asked, 'Can you tell me please what those black things are?'

'Well yes,' said Omega. 'They're cows.'

'No not the cows; I know what cows are. I meant those black things.'

The three young women had to look very hard until suddenly Annie twigged what the problem was.

'Oh it's the clouds. That's the shadows of the clouds going across the hill.'

'I've never seen such a thing; just imagine. Cloud shadows!'

'You must live in a town.'

'I live in the centre of Carlisle.'

The bicycles were put away towards the end of September 1898 as the weather drew in. There would be no more pleasant country rides for Margaret for quite some time now because towards the end of the year she found that she was expecting another child. This one was big and Tom was confident that it was going to be a boy. It turned out that he was right. Margaret's son was born in the afternoon of Sunday 16 July 1899. Joe Hayriggs was sent post haste to fetch Mister and Missis and he did so very quickly, mounted on his own bicycle, an old machine with solid rubber tyres on which he seemed to flash around the lanes. Soon the cart from West End farm arrived with Mr and Mrs Little with Joe and Agnes too.

Missis said as she came through the door, 'We had the cart standing by when you didn't come to church this morning. We knew the time must have come.'

Mister was bubbling with the new event.

'The first boy born in this family since William in 1867 and my first grandson.'

Mister was quite overcome to hold the small bundle in his arms.

'What's his name going to be?'

'You've forgotten Mister. You know his name.'

'Still calling me Mister,' His eyes twinkled. 'Yes I know his name well enough; I was just checking you hadn't changed your mind.'

He offered the baby a finger and a tiny hand clenched round the end of it.

'Hello Barwise Little. There's two of us now. That's going to confuse folk a bit.'

The arrival of a new Barwise seemed to put life into the old one. At 75 he was still very active in the workings of his farm, but he seemed to gain a new lease of life with the arrival of the baby.

'You leave it to me Tom. I'll go home by way of Rowks and tell Mr Bardsley the news. We'll set a christening date for about a month's time and let the whole world know. You can use the lad's old christening robe and we'll have tea sandwiches and cake at home. Oho, I'm that pleased I could skip like a lamb!'

Glad preparations went ahead for the next few days. Omega and Joe were to be God-parents and though the christening was always free, Mister declared he would make a gift of money to the church in thanks for his grandson. His enthusiasm knew no bounds and to tell the truth he worked too hard and his

348

rejuvenation did not serve him well; to expend the energy of a young man when you have an old body is not always advisable. Six days after the birth of young Barwise, on Saturday 22 July, Joe appeared at Tarns Farm in the afternoon and found Tom in the barn. His face was downcast and he appeared to be holding back a great emotion inside himself.

'Why Joe. What's up with you?'

With difficulty Joe dragged out the words,

'He's gone Tom. He's gone.'

'Who's gone? Whatever are you talking of?' A fear seized Tom, but he could not say it.

'Dad's gone. He's dead. Dad's dead.'

Gradually Joe managed through misery to tell Tom and Margaret what had happened. It was a simple enough thing. Mister had been his normal self when he got up that morning, and energy seemed almost to flash from him. Normally he let Joe or one of the hands take the milk churns out in the morning, but this time he had ordered the cleaning of the stable and told Joe that he'd give him a hand with the churns. Joe pleaded with him not to strain himself, but the old man told him not to talk wet, and with a practised ease he rolled two churns out to the gate one after the other.

'When he'd finished he said to me that he felt better than he'd felt for years, fit as a flea. Then he spotted that his bootlace was loose, so he bent down to tie it. When he stood up he smiled and told me to hold on because he felt a bit giddy from standing up too quick. He was looking at me smiling, then his face just went blank and he fell over. I caught him before he hit the floor but he was gone. Just gone.'

The doctor had been sent for, but it was clear even before he arrived that Mister had died instantly and all he served to do was confirm that a massive stroke had carried him away. He could only offer the comfort of telling the family that Mister would not have felt a thing, and indeed would not have known what had hit him. It was as if God had reached out with a finger and switched him off like turning off the gas or snuffing a candle. The death of a parent is a thing that human beings must face if they are lucky, or unlucky enough to live long lives. It is in the natural order of people to die and to give way to the next generation, but in many cases, however part of life it may be, it is not an easy matter to accept. In the case of Barwise Little, the family were stunned by the suddenness of it. He was a patriarch, a well-respected man, a prominent member of the community and on the committee of the Longcake charity which did much for religion and education in the area. Almost he had an aura of permanence to him, rooted deep in the soil of the Solway Plain like his father and his father before. His passing was of great moment to his community.

They buried him in the churchyard at Holme St Cuthbert which he called Rowks all his life, and in a grave near his parents. The church was packed full of his neighbours and the congregation was a roll call of the Plain families; Ostles, Osborns and Sharps rubbed shoulders with Hodgsons, Wises, and Hollidays. John Adams and his family came up from Dearham, greatly upset for they had taken to Mister. The service had almost the feel of a gentry funeral as the choice of first hymn insisted upon by Missis was one of Mister's favourites; this was Charles Wesley's great and solemn 'Jesu lover of my soul.' The coffin was carried out to 'What a friend we have in Jesus' and thus far all was conventional. However, when the coffin was lowered and the clods were thrown Joseph stepped forward.

'My father was a Cumbrian and a Cumbrian to his marrow. He said on several occasions that he wanted his friends to sing John Peel over his grave because he'd hear it and it would make him glad to have you go off blithely. That might seem odd to you but it's what he wanted, so I'm going to do it and I'd be glad if you joined in. I've got Billy Hetherington here with his squeezebox so let's give him a rousing send-off so that he can hear it up there.'

Tears rolling down cheeks Mister's sons began to bellow out the words of the old song, joined by everyone present who were greatly affected and then the crowd, for such it was, began to disperse, some to go back to Edderside Hall where Mrs Phoebe Sharp had arranged for refreshments and to offer their condolences. Strangely, the singing of John Peel removed much of the pain of the wake because all were convinced that it was the right thing to do because Barwise had wanted it and it would have made him glad.

In the midst of life there is death, but it is also the other way round. There was a baby who had not yet been christened and three weeks after his grandfather's funeral young Barwise received his name, baptised in the font of the same church. A family, prostrate with the scale of their loss, found much comfort in new life, as with the spring, replacing old. Life goes on after someone has died, and so did West End Farm. Missis was now the farmer, though in practice Joe ran the business and would, eventually, inherit the tenancy. The world moved on also, a war broke out in Africa and a new century was just ahead. Once grief was tolerable, a good future seemed to wait for Tom, Margaret and their children; such was their hope, as is the hope of all rational people.

Chapter 24

The Well

On Saturday 11 November 1899 Tom and Joseph set out with four yearlings for Maryport Martinmas fair and high hopes of good prices at auction. Margaret took a holiday from work, leaving Omega in charge of three infants, sure in the knowledge that Nellie, Nancy and Barwise were in good hands. Fleming Square was packed with fair goers and, as usual, the activities spilled out into the surrounding streets. The journey to the market was slow and they started early with the young Clydedales strung to the back of the cart, Tom and Joseph Hayriggs marching beside them to keep them steady, whilst Margaret drove the cart pulled by Marra who had migrated with them from West End Farm to Tarns. Prices for horses were sky high and Tom was positively chortling when he secured £90 for each of them, leafing through banknotes with a very happy grin on his face.

'I knew it Margaret. I just knew the prices would be good, but I had to catch it now. War is always good for the price of horseflesh. We could live on this for a year if we had to, but we won't have to. Good times are coming, my love, for we are getting prosperous.'

He looked very young sometimes, so long as he kept his hat on, and Margaret thought he looked like a schoolboy who had pulled off some adventurous jape and got away with it. Nonetheless, when Tom pulled his cap off and dealt with purchasers or other businessmen he looked quite formidable with a fierce moustache and that piercing blue gaze that shot through like steel. She had seen pictures of the famous soldier, Kitchener of Khartoum, who had been ennobled earlier this year for his victory in the Sudan, and thought their look was quite similar. His enthusiasm was infectious, but he was right though; war was good for business and if he continued to make profits like this then their future would be secure. In his more optimistic moments he dreamed of putting enough money away to buy the farm if he could, and cease being a tenant. It was just as well that they were making money, because Margaret was expecting her fourth child; if this continued then she might end up with not so much a family as a tribe, or so she sometimes thought.

When Tom had finished his horse trading he and Margaret left Marra and the wagon in charge of the boy and sauntered down Crosby Street to shop for a few items and peer into a few windows. Maryport's shops had a much wider selection of goods than was found in Mawbray or Allonby and it would have been remiss of them to have missed an opportunity to gaze at things together. As they came down to the junction with Senhouse Street, they could go no further as a crowd was lining the road on both sides all the way down to the harbour and up towards Curzon Street as far as they could see. Obviously, something was about to happen which was worth the seeing.

'What's happening marra?' asked Tom of a man standing in front of them.

'Irish volunteers for the war. They've landed in the harbour and they're going to march to Whitehaven.'

'Why did they not land them at Whitehaven and save them the walk?'

'I don't know. Maybe they want to drum up some support. Crowds always like a parade.'

There was a muffled sound down the road and they discerned drums and fifes playing Liliburlero heading towards them. Soon a man came riding down the street on a white horse, so well controlled, and behind him a long column of men in uniform marched in relentless fashion, rifles over their shoulders and grim looking faces, most of them with a fine moustache.

'Well, I would think those Boers would be fools to tangle with them!' said Margaret, then she joined the rest of the crowd in cheering the warriors on their way. 'Mind you, I prefer soldiers in red myself. They look so much smarter.'

'Yes they do,' agreed Tom, 'but they make splendid targets too. Our boys found that out in the first war against the Boers; they have some fine marksmen so there's no point in standing out and making yourself obvious. Those dirt coloured uniforms are better for what they're going to do.'

'I hope that they win.'

'What a thing to say Margaret. Of course they'll win; the British always do.'

'I wish there didn't have to be a war.'

'There doesn't, Margaret. If our party were in power there wouldn't be one. This is all about Tories and empire building. Basically, Mr Cecil Rhodes is trying to take over someone else's country and they are doing what we would do.'

'I beg your pardon!' said a man on Tom's left. 'What do you mean by that? We have to teach these scoundrels a lesson. They started it.'

Tom turned to look at him with a steely gaze and, as often happened when he looked at someone, the man visibly quailed.

'I was having a conversation with my wife and it is of no concern to you that I can think of.'

'But you are against the war. Don't you support your queen and country?'

'I do, but not in the way that you do. You have your opinion and I have mine. I suggest that we leave it at that.'

'You're a Liberal aren't you?'

'I am. What of it?'

'I think you should all be ashamed of yourselves for not backing your country and her soldiers.'

'I do back the soldiers in that I do not think they should be put in harms way without good cause and I wish them well. I do not agree with the men who have set them to this particular task. The South Africans have been left with little choice but to do what they did. We have engineered this war for the gain of rich men and some of these men will die for that. I take it that you support Lord Salisbury?'

'That is correct.'

'Well then, sir, we have nothing more to say to each other, for I do not think as you and never will. I dare say that you think the same and I see little profit in bandying in the street, so I will wish you a good day. Let us go home, Margaret.'

Although she had said nothing, Margaret had watched this altercation with a small frisson of fear and quite a lot of interest. The two men had staked each other out in hostility and she had thought that they were about to come to blows; it was plain, however, that the other man was afraid of Tom and somehow, in an atavistic primitive kind of way, she liked that. Her man could hold his own. Whatever the arguments for or against the war in South Africa, events in December 1899 changed life at Tarns Farm for ever for Margaret, but rather more for Omega. The British had been outnumbered at first, but as the weeks went by troop reinforcements arrived in great numbers and the military commanders grew over-confident. The Boers, or so they thought, were good at mobile guerrilla warfare, but faced with a modern fighting force in conventional battles, they would quickly be conquered. On 15 December General Buller attempted to relieve the Boer siege of Kimberley by crossing the Tugela river with 21,000 men. Eight thousand Boers faced them under Louis Botha and they were armed with Mauser rifles supplied from Germany. Buller was repulsed with the loss of 145 dead and 1,200 missing or wounded. The telegraph cables brought the news to London and thence to towns and villages across the country where it was received with a stunned disbelief; Britain could not be, must not be defeated. People began to follow every bulletin and newspaper report with avid interest and particularly in the sieges of Kimberley, Ladysmith and Mafeking. So it was that Omega received a letter from Mr Edward Furnival Snr on the morning of Christmas Eve.

'Dear Miss Adams, This is not an easy letter for me to write, as you may well imagine, but I have received news from South Africa which I feel that I must impart to you. My son was with his

regiment at the battle of the Tugela River and he fell at the head of his men. It is my understanding that as his column approached the river they received fire from the bluffs on the other side, which they had expected, but that the Boers had dug trenches across the river at the base of the slope and these were unobserved and a complete surprise. Edward attempted to lead his men in a charge across the river, which is not deep, and was killed by a single bullet in the act of doing so. The colonel of his regiment states in his message that he behaved most gallantly which I was glad to read. You must appreciate that this is news which I had feared since he joined the army in the first place and against my wishes; it is a most hazardous profession and I deemed it ill advised, though he would do it. Now that he is gone I would like to say that I deprecate greatly his behaviour towards you and hope that in some way the selfless manner of his death may atone for his actions and that you may find it in you to forgive him. Yours sincerely, E Furnival'*

Margaret watched Omega as she read the letter and she shed a tear, then wiped it away.

'There's nothing to forgive, but if there is then I do. He did what men do, but it takes two and I wanted him to. I didn't try to stop him and I don't blush to say it. Now he's gone and got himself shot the poor silly man; and what for?'

Margaret gave her a hug, but Omega shook it off.

'No. No, I'm alright really, but it decides me.'

'What does it decide?'

'What I've been thinking for some time Margaret. It's almost time for me to move on. It's very nice living here with you and Tom, but it's not moving me on anywhere. I need to live my life.'

'But we love having you here. You are so useful.'

'Yes I know; and I needed that badly when Mary Hannah died. But time passes, my love, and I have to get on with things. Sometime in the next few months I shall be looking for a place for myself and earning a living.'

'But you can get by with what Mr Furnival pays you.'

356

'That's another thing. I don't want to. He's been very decent and very sweet to do what he's done, but I want to earn my own bread. When I have a place I shall stop taking his money with a heartfelt thanks, but I don't want him to be keeping me.'

'But what am I to do Ommie? Three children and another on the way.'

Omega thought about this very hard and then said, 'Very well. I'll concede that I would feel very bad about leaving at this time with another baby coming, so I will stay for now, but put you on notice.'

'What do you mean "notice?"'

'I can see that it would be best for you if I stayed a while longer and it's not fair to run out on you now with a baby due, so I will stay for this year, but that's it. One year from now I shall be looking for a place. It'll be a new century and a new start, not just for me, but for everyone.'

'I'm glad you're going to stay this year, but there really is no need for you to go at all, you know. The situation will not change even in a year. What will I do without you here?'

'Hire a girl Margaret. There's plenty of them to be had and you can probably get one all found for £4 a half year if you ask in the village. You've said that the farm is doing well, so you should be able to afford a help.'

This was true and there was no denying it. Nothing they could say would dissuade her and they could see why. Omega was in a kind of stasis, stuck in a place that had been an oasis when she needed it, but now she wanted to go out into the big world and fend for herself. This is what human beings do and eventually they had to acquiesce in their hearts as well as their mouths; she was right and it was good of her to stay with them for this one year. It was time to grow and she had given them plenty of notice.

New Year 1900 came and went with visits and cards and the first few months of the year were marked by cold, but not a lot of rain. As her pregnancy advanced Margaret partook of a fever that gripped the entire nation in the early part of the year and its name was Mafeking.

From 13 October 1899 this small South African town with 2,000 British soldiers in it was besieged by 8,000 Boers and the matter should have been settled very quickly. However, it was not, and for some reason, although there were other similar sieges going on, Mafeking gripped the nation's imagination. It is possible that this may have had something to do with the Prime Minister's son being among the besieged officers, but reports from the town which managed to get through focussed attention on Colonel Baden-Powell who commanded the garrison. He appeared to be a most gallant gentleman with all sorts of devices and ruses to thwart the Boers and he soon become a national hero. Tom's position on the war was quite clear, and he stated repeatedly his opposition to it, but in the matter of the common soldiers, he was all for them, and did not wish to hear of them being defeated, though he thought they should not have been sent there. Like most of the population they read the reports in their newspaper of what was going on, and the 217 days of the siege seemed to be almost as if they would go on for ever. Whatever happened, no-one wanted the Boers to defeat the brave defenders and their redoubtable commander and on 18 May when the news came through that Mafeking had been relieved the previous day, the entire country went mad with joy. Young Joe Hayriggs came dashing in with the news.

'Mawbray's going mad Master. Flags are out everywhere and they're building a bonfire for eight o'clock tonight.'

In the distance could be heard noises; guns boomed out over on the range at Silloth whilst massive combined noise of hooters could be heard though whether the wind was carrying the ship noises from Maryport or Silloth docks they could not tell. Far to the south a huge plume of smoke could be seen where miners at Whitehaven had dragged sleepers and tar from their pitheads and built an enormous fire. No work was done that day and Tom drove Margaret in the gig down to Mawbray with the children that night so that they could see and remember the celebrations. There was a lot of drink being consumed and someone had procured fireworks, which set little Nellie's face aglow with wonder. Nancy, who at three years was showing signs of being a most determined character, although very small, had to be prevented from walking off on her own far too close to the fire, whilst baby Barwise, snuggled up in a soft blanket, slept through the whole proceedings. Mawbray Band of Hope were there in force, though they drank no alcohol of course, but their musicians set about playing patriotic airs and they sang *Hearts of Oak* with gusto then one of Tom's favourites, *Britons strike home*, which though old, was well beloved at times like this being a stirring and martial air:

> 'Britons, strike home!
> Revenge, revenge your Country's wrong.
> Fight! Fight and record. Fight!
> Fight and record yourselves in Druid's Song.
> Fight! Fight and record. Fight!
> Fight and record yourselves in Druid's Song.'

Mr Bookless stepped forward and sang *Private Tommy Atkins* to great applause; and then all joined in with *Soldiers of the Queen* and many others. The national anthem burst out several times during the course of the evening, begun spontaneously by people who would not seem to tire of hearing it, but nobody minded. The forces of Victoria the Good had been victorious and that was all that mattered. One of the girls from the village was among the crowd dancing round the fire and Tom knew her as Ettie Jefferson and that she had just turned fourteen, so he had a word with her mother. Ettie was indeed to be looking for a place shortly and Mrs Jefferson was delighted that she could fill the new post of scullery maid at Tarns Farm. That Ettie could live at home and start at £3 the half year, yet eat three meals a day at Tarns was especially pleasing, since she lived much less than a mile from the farm in Rowks. The Littles went back to Tarns content and sleepy; the load would be lessened for both Omega and Margaret.

Just after John was born in June Tom told Margaret that he was going to dig the well that he'd been putting off for so long. Four children would need a lot of providing for and if he didn't do it then it would never get done.

'Couldn't you just get someone in to do it Tom?'

'Why pay good money for something I can do myself?'

He had a point, and so it was not long until a wagon came trundling up the road from the iron foundry in Maryport with a huge cast iron ring, the hole about three feet in diameter, weighing several hundredweight on it. The two men with it set up a sheer legs next to the wagon and with the help of Tom and Joseph swung it onto the ground on a place in the yard not too far from the kitchen door which had been judged suitable for the well. When they had gone, Tom looked at Joseph.

'There's no point in hanging about. Let's get started. I'm digging. You're carting. The bricks should be coming from Dearham today as well.'

Setting to work with a spade Tom excavated the earth from the centre of the ring to a depth of about a foot, putting it into a barrow which Joseph then took away to dump then called Margaret out to watch; she came and stood, nursing the baby at the same time. With the air of a conjurer he worked his way round the underneath of the ring with a small mattock and gradually chopped the earth away from under it. He worked methodically in a circle, not wanting the ring to tilt, and gradually the ring began to sink into the ground so he increased the amount of earth he was removing from under it. The whole process did not take very long and when it was done, the ring sat in a hole a foot deep and pretty level. Shortly after this a dray arrived with 1,500 well-baked bricks from the Dearham brick works which had to be lifted and stacked near to the hole. By this time it was getting late, but Tom would not stop.

'If I don't get the first courses done today I'll have to do it tomorrow and lose a day of digging. Joe, you'd best knock up the first load of cement.'

By the time he had done, Tom had laid three tangential double courses of bricks end to end in a circle. Then he told Joseph,

'This is work for afternoons and I don't want to hurry it. The water table goes lower in July and August so I want to go as deep as I can during the low period. That'll give us more water to draw on as it fills up.'

'How far do you think you need to go, Master?'

'Not far I think. Water tables are quite high round here. I figure on fifteen to twenty feet.'

As the days went by the hole got deeper and deeper, and as Tom kept saying, it was hard graft. It was perfectly safe, for as he went down each afternoon the brick lining that he was laying down had set into a well-lined shaft, but it was only three feet wide. He was working with a crowbar to loosen the clay and loading it laboriously into a bucket, which Joseph would then haul up and dispose of. He could not get out of the shaft while he was working for when he had descended, the ladder had to be taken away to give him space to work. It was also a good job that the weather was fine, because there was enough light to come down the shaft to see; he could not have a light down there because it was hard enough to breathe anyway and the flame would burn the air away more quickly. One afternoon he was undercutting the ring yet again when his light almost disappeared.

'Joe get your bloody head out of the way you fool. I can't see.'

'Oooooh, Daddy. Divvent dig too deep or't paddicks'll get thee feet.'

'Nancy. What are you doing up there sweetheart? Get back from the hole; I'm coming up. Joe!'

Within a few minutes Joe had the ladder down the well and Tom was out.

The little girl was waiting for him, sucking her thumb and with wide eyes. Tom swept her up into his arms.

'So you think the paddicks will get my feet do you?'

'Yis, they will if thee go too far down.'

'Margaret!'

Margaret's attention had been taken by the baby, 'I needed to change John's nappy. I don't know how she got out.'

'Where's Omega?'

'Down to Mawbray shopping nigh on an hour ago.'

'Ettie! Did you leave the kitchen door open?'

'I'm sorry master. I had to get some eggs from the barn and I must have missed putting the latch on properly.'

'I see. Well if my daughter pitches head first down the well, what would you think of that?'

Ettie burst out crying. 'I'm sorry Master. I didn't mean it to happen. I wouldn't like that at all to happen to dear little Nancy.'

'Aye well, if it happens again you'll get your marching orders if I don't pitch you down after. You've heard me tell you all to keep the kiddies indoors.'

'It won't, I swear.'

'No harm done this time. No more carelessness on the door though.' Now Tom burst out laughing and said to Margaret, 'She's worried the frogs will get my feet if I dig down too deep. Where did she get that idea from?'

'She saw a frog in the garden the other day; she thinks they're some kind of monster that eats things like toes, but I don't know why.'

Tom was amused by the thought of feral frogs attacking his feet in the well, so the small incident became family legend, referred to many times over the years.

One Sunday afternoon John Adams turned up at Tarns Farm on a bicycle with young Thomas to everyone's surprise. He protested that he might be an old dog but he could learn new tricks still and that since Thomas had wanted a bicycle he had obtained one for himself and they had learned to ride together. With a professional interest, he examined Tom's well.

'How far down are you now? I'd say about twenty feet.'

'That's exactly right. How did you know that?'

'I've been digging for most of my life Tom. You're sinking a shaft and it's the same principle as building a mineshaft. How far do you reckon you'll have to go?'

'I think not much further. I'm standing on damp now so I think another five feet or so should do it.'

'Well it's a fine piece of work. If ever you are short of a job you come and see me and we'll make a miner of you. Who knows, you might have missed your vocation.'

That made them all laugh, as it was such a very unlikely prospect that it seemed ridiculous.

'Really I would have thought that if you heard of any jobs going it would be Thomas who would get them,' said Tom with a glance at the boy. He knew that when Thomas had left school three years before he had been given a surface job helping a banksman at Crosshow Pit.

'No. I don't want Thomas down the mine if I can help it,' replied John Adams. 'There's too much of lung disease about in my profession and I've been lucky. No, I've just managed to arrange something that has pleased me and the lad very much.'

'Oh aye, and what's that?'

It was Thomas who replied, 'I'm an apprentice Tom. Father got me a post with the engineer on the pump engines.'

'What does that entail? Shovelling coal?'

'No. Mr Sykes is in charge of maintaining the engines for the pumps and the winding gear. It's a mechanical task to do with how the engine works, so if it breaks down or something goes wrong then he's got to fix it and make it work again.'

Tom looked at Thomas with raised eyebrows. 'Well now that's a plum job and one with prospects. I'm very pleased for you young Thomas Adams; let me shake your hand. My brother-in-law is going to be an engineer. You've done well there. Prospects are good I should think.'

'They are that,' beamed Thomas shaking Tom's hand. 'So as Father said, if you ever need a mining job come and speak to him.'

In due course Tom went down a further five feet and by that time the iron ring had water up to the top of it one morning. He bailed it out, Joe pulling the water up as fast as he could and Tom worked flat out to sink the ring another foot. In the end he had to bail out again to set the last three courses radially for more strength to support the shaft. Lastly, Tom dug out the centre to a bucket's depth and came up out of the new well with an air of triumph.

'One more time down that hole Margaret and I don't care if I never go again.'

'Why do you have to go down at all? All you need to do is put a windlass and bucket at the top.'

'No. That's from the middle ages. Our well is going to have a proper pump and there's one in the barn just waiting for tomorrow.'

So it was that an iron pipe was fixed down to below water level and emerged on the surface. A small wall was built round the well head to prevent people falling in and the well was covered with a wooden lid knocked together with planks. Finally a rotary pump was fitted to the pipe and Tom primed it with a jug of water from the old well. To Margaret fell the honour of turning the handle and to the cheers of all around a stream of clear water gushed out into the bucket underneath. This was summer and the water level was quite low as the year had been dry, but July had brought a heatwave. The average level of water in the well in after years proved to be four feet so the domestic water supply was assured, closer to the house and not shared by the beasts.

August also brought a house guest in the shape of Tom's sister Annie Eleanor, who had come to spend some time with her brother and his wife with her beautiful nieces and baby nephews. Margaret looked at her bending over the cot where little John lay making baby noises and detected something that to many eyes would not have been obvious.

'She's broody Tom.'

'That one! Not very likely I should think. She's one of those new modern women Margaret. Career is all that's in her mind I think.'

'No, I don't think so. She's getting on now you know; she's 30 and time is limited for a woman who wants a family.'

'That's all right then, for I don't believe she wants a family. She's a supervisor now and wants to rise in the telephone company.'

'We will see; if I'm not very much mistaken I think her mind may have gone through a change. Two of her brothers have married and have children. She might be feeling that her chances are passing her by.'

Tom's sister Annie might have been, but it was Margaret's thoughts that were vindicated in church on Sunday. As the congregation sang the first hymn, Annie deliberately turned her head across the aisle and looked into the eyes of John Metcalfe, still a bachelor at 32, who had been looking at her as he always did. What messages were carried in that prolonged look were known only to them, but she captured his gaze, held it, and smiled at him faintly. A look of disbelief came over his face and then all expression drained from his features. Margaret saw it and thought that had Annie crooked her finger and said, 'Come hither,' she could hardly have made a more obvious invitation. In the churchyard afterwards their conversation was animated, John Metcalfe's face lit by great emotion, and they parted expressing the intention of seeing each other soon and on most cordial terms.

After midnight Margaret awoke as she often did at the slightest noise, but this time it was not one of the children that had caused it. Stone against glass had made a sharp rap sufficient to bring her to consciousness, but the soft creak of the slightly loose board on the stairs told her that someone was going downstairs. Taking very great care not to waken Tom she went over to the window and very cautiously looked out. There outside the kitchen door was John Metcalfe and as she watched, someone opened the door and let him in. Annie was night courting. Margaret stared into space for a moment thinking, then smiled and went back to bed; he'd be gone by morning. Although in her mining community where a great number of people were conventionally religious, and this type of courting would not be countenanced, it was very common among the rural folk. Down in the kitchen, Annie, being a Cumbrian girl of long descent and very traditional, placed in front of her visitor a bowl of cream and sugared curds, the symbols marking the beginnings of courtship. She did not take him to her bed that night, but on the third. It would not do to seem to be too eager. Life went on at Tarns Farm much as usual in the cutting of hay and corn, and the rearing of horses, but when Annie Eleanor left to go back to Carlisle, though she did not know it yet, she was, and by her own design, with child. John Metcalfe, thought of as a dour man locally, was transformed into a man of smiles and humour and many wondered at it, though others guessed that the cause of it was a woman.

When Annie Eleanor had departed for the bright lights of Carlisle and her telephone exchange, life settled into a routine enlivened in September by the commencement of a national election. Sir Wilfrid Lawson, the local MP was a very prominent anti-war speaker in Parliament and opinion in this Cockermouth constituency was very polarised. Tom and Margaret were solidly for Liberal and approved of almost all he said. However, Lawson had alienated many with his criticisms of the government, the clergy, the newspapers and most of all, Lord Kitchener who had made a bloody slaughter of primitively armed people in the Sudan at Omdurman in 1898. He had denounced the war, favoured the Boers whom he avowed were only defending their land against British aggression and had joined numerous anti war committees, including one called "Stop the War." There was one thing that Margaret heartily wished that Tom would emulate Lawson in, but it was the issue on which her husband strongly disagreed with Lawson about; this was Temperance. Although he was not elected on a Temperance ticket, Lawson was probably the strongest speaker in favour of Temperance in Parliament at this time. Margaret well knew this for she had heard him speak with passion on the subject several times in Dearham. Tom was solid that a working man deserved beer at the end of a day and particularly in the summer when he sweated a lot; it was only sensible to put back what he had lost in perspiration. This was why he still spent many of his evenings at the Lowther Arms, though by no means all, but it made her unhappy that he drank what she saw as too much. This was, abidingly, the only tension between them because he was an excellent husband, a good father and they were provided for very well; it made her feel guilty that she might be seen as grudging him his beer, but it made no difference to him, as he still went, though he did not get drunk very often. Sir Wilfrid lost the election and the Conservative candidate John Randles went to Westminster in his stead.

When the new century arrived in 1901 all looked positive for their future except that Omega's year being up she persisted in her determination to leave. She had found herself a place through a newspaper advertisement in Workington with a Doctor Spedding and his wife as cook-housekeeper. In this house she was to have £25 a year and this being a larger house than Mr Furnival's, she had her own parlour and bedroom downstairs. She would also have a young scullery maid and a parlour maid under her who were used to hard work; she was happy once more to be going to live in a town. Life on the farm was very nice, but there was so much going on in towns that it would be more interesting.

Chapter 25

Crisis

Then the news from London came like a hammer blow on 22 January; the Queen was dead. It had been known for a few days that she was ill, but most people had not known why. In fact a series of strokes carried her away at the age of 81 after 64 years on the throne. Most people had never known any other monarch and the news hit them very hard, many feeling that they had lost a close relative of their own. At Tarns Farm it was no different to most other places and when Ettie shook her young head and came out with; 'Our poor old queen. We shall not see her like on the throne again,' a phrase she had obviously heard elsewhere, Margaret just sat down at the kitchen table and bawled her eyes out, but she was not unusual in this. A mention of the Queen was enough to set a tear in Tom's eyes also and even people with hardly two halfpennies to rub together mourned the loss though the Queen had never done anything for them. Margaret spoke to Snuff Tom, a local shepherd passing in the lane, 'This is sad news about our Queen,' he said in halting tones and passed on his way shaking his head with sorrow. People's voices hushed and their eyes brimmed, calling her 'Victoria the Good' and 'The Mother of her people' whilst retelling stories they had heard of her charity and her kindness. A mood of gloom and loss pervaded everywhere that lasted after the Queen's funeral on 4 February and rose only slowly with the proclaiming of Edward, Prince of Wales, as King Edward VII, who would be crowned later in the year.

Sunday 31 March though was a day for the family records, because Tom had never had to fill in a census return on his household before. The blue forms for the national census had been brought round and the law of the land made it clear that the householder was responsible for filling it in. The enumerators would be collecting the forms in the next few days and it had to be accurate and free of frivolity. This caused great scratching of heads at Tarns Farm because Omega was leaving for good on the following morning; should they count her or not?

'I don't think I should set your name down here,' said Tom. 'If you're gone in the morning and they come to check who lives here then they won't find you here.'

'That's very true,' rejoined Omega, but Dr Spedding will be filling his form in tonight as well and I won't be on that one either.'

'What's that got to do with it?'

'Well if you don't put me on the form Tom then officially I won't exist. It'll be like I'm a non-person and I'd far rather be listed on the census than not. What do they want to know anyway?'

'Name, sex, age, profession or occupation, condition as to marriage, relationship to head of household and your nationality. They also want to know if you're blind, deaf, dumb or an imbecile.'

'An imbecile! I'm not an imbecile.'

'No-one's called you an imbecile. They just want to know if people are imbeciles.'

'What on earth for? That's a rather impertinent thing to be asking perfect strangers.' Here Omega tossed her head with indignation. 'In fact I've changed my mind. Don't set me down there. Asking people's sex and occupation and how old they are! That's just being nosy.'

'Right; so you don't want me to set you down as living here?'

'No, I do not. I don't live here anyway. I've just been staying here and there is a difference there. If I'd left yesterday there would be no problem and I nearly did.'

'Aye there's some truth in that, but as head of household I am supposed to put all residents at this address down here, on pain of a fine.'

'In that case your house guest is going out for a walk. I'll be half an hour. Is that long enough?'

By the time she returned Tom had filled out the census form for himself, listing his occupation as Farmer and added Margaret and his four children. Omega was not on it; early in the morning Tom trotted her down to Aspatria where she took train down to Workington and her new life. Her letters began to arrive within a few days and she took care to write once a week describing what the large town she had decided to live in was like. It was very different to Maryport, which was quite a compact though very busy community and the letters made Margaret feel quite envious when she spoke of the large numbers of people, the busyness of the place, the street lighting, the numbers and sizes of shops and all the interesting things that were going on. Clearly her excellent references from Mr Furnival had secured her a step-up in life of exactly the sort she had wanted. Omega's departure for fresh pastures had made Margaret sad at the time of her going although her life was very busy of course with four small children to care for, but a good maid smoothed her way a great deal; she took little notice of what was going on in the outside world.

Life is full of tempests and storms and it is only a very lucky few who can make it through their journey without encountering some. It might have seemed to Margaret and Tom sometimes that their futures were assured, because they were doing what farming families had been doing on the Solway Plain for centuries. In particular, they were doing what the Littles had done for centuries, and it seemed as unalterable a way of life as the course of the stars in the heavens, so the crisis of their lives came upon them without notice. It was on Thursday 4 April that Joe Hayriggs arrived at work, and, as was his usual practice, went to take some hay for the Clydesdales. He came running into the kitchen where Tom was having his breakfast in a rare old state.

'Master there's something wrong with the horses.'

'What do you mean wrong with the horses? Which horses?'

'Most of them. I think they're sickening for something.'

'All at the same time? Very unlikely. Let's go and have a look.'

When they arrived at the field where most of the Clydesdale mares were Tom saw a sight which made him thrill with horror because Joe was right; most of them were acting as if they were sick. Some were rolling on the ground in evident distress; there was drooling of saliva whilst some were turning their heads to look at their own flanks whilst apparently having difficulty swallowing.

'It looks like a mass attack of colic.'

Tom was fighting down a rising tide of panic; almost everything he had was invested in these horses. His father had advised him that he should diversify, but he had not wanted to keep cattle and was certain that he could make a success of a horse farm. Having all his stock fall sick at the same time with a potentially fatal condition was something that had never occurred to him. Within a few minutes he was in the trap and trotting Marra briskly off to Aspatria and the office of Henry Thompson, the veterinary surgeon. He was not the cheapest vet around, but he was the best and at the cutting edge of his profession. Tom had come across him when he had attended the agricultural college where Mr Thompson had given lectures on several occasions; he had also known his father. At a time like this, none but the best would do. Thankfully Marra was not affected by whatever was ailing the Clydedales, so he made brisk progress and to his relief found the veterinary at his desk. It was not long before the expert got on to his own horse and soon was examining the Clydesdales.

'It's not colic Tom, or at least not a normal colic. The symptoms are different.'

'But what can I do Mr Thompson? Can it be cured?'

'I don't know and that is a fact. It's beyond my experience, but you are right; there are some similarities to colic, so I'm going to treat them as I would for colic. I have not got what I need here, but I take it you have some drenching bottles and tubes?'

On Tom's stating that he had a few the vet told him to send to his neighbours and borrow some men who knew horses and set off back to Aspatria; he came back in his gig a couple of hours later with some large containers of liquid, some bottles, funnels and tubing.

'This is a drench to purge and I use it as a standard remedy. It's two ounces of turpentine, one ounce of methylated spirits and one pint of raw linseed oil and it might clear them out if it is colic. In addition, I want soapy enemas of about two gallons administered to each of them, so let us be about it.'

Tom owned thirteen Clydesdales in all at this moment, being six mares, six foals and one stallion and they were all sick over the next few days. Even with the help of the four men who came from his neighbours, it took all day before the drenching was done for the horses resisted. It was easier on the following day because the horses were weaker and did not resist.

'It's not having the effect that I wished to see Tom. I did not think that it was colic and I still do not. However, we will repeat the drenches with half the amount of linseed oil.'

'Is there nothing else that may be done, sir?'

'Nothing I'm sorry to say, my boy. This is something beyond my experience and all I can advise now is that you pray. Are you insured?'

Tom was not insured and did pray, and Margaret joined him. He looked bewildered and gaunt from lack of sleep, but all his watchfulness was to no avail; over the next six days every single Clydesdale died. One by one they had to be dragged across two fields to an old quarry by Marra, who was the only survivor and not happy at the work he was doing. When the last was dead Tom and Joe dug earth and threw it over them; then Tom went home, sat at the kitchen table, put his head down on his arms and cried like a baby. All Margaret could do was put her arms round him and cry as well, but there was nothing that she could say to ameliorate his grief for she knew the score. They were ruined, because Tom could not afford to restock the farm with horses. They had some small amount in the bank so they would not starve, but as a horse breeding business, Tarns Farm was finished and they would have to leave. Of course, she discussed with him

373

on several occasions what they might do and one of the things she had suggested was asking Missis for help but he would not.

'I know well that West End Farm turns a profit, but it's really Joe's and he has a family now. It would put a strain on them to lend me any amount of money to restock the farm and there is no guarantee that this will not happen again. And whatever else I do Margaret I don't want to go back to dairy farming. There's more to life; there must be!'

Margaret's bewilderment at the sudden turnaround of their fortunes was the mirror of Toms and when the last Clydesdale had died she sat facing him across their table with a face as pale and anxious as his own.

'What do we do now Tom?'

With a visible effort to collect himself Tom sat up and faced her with much of despair in his eyes.

'We'll have to go Margaret. We're done here and we'll have to leave.'

Although she knew it already, she sat stunned at the dashing of all their hopes, their dreams and the end of their hard work; he had said it and it had to be so.

'But I don't want to leave Tom. I want to bring my children up here where life is good and clean.'

'So do I lass, but we've got no choice have we? What else is there to do?'

Now it was his turn to comfort her as she cried; she had married the master's son and he had set up on his own. Her children had been born here and all her future was vested in being the wife of a prosperous farmer. Now all was turned to dust, so why should she not cry? Why should she not grieve? Their new life was dead in its cradle and they would have to find another one if they could. At the back of her mind, though she pushed it away, she was frightened; she was a grown up and knew that the world was an uncertain place, but human beings do cling to their certainties. Life at Tarns and her future there had been the rock she clung to, the safe place she wanted to live in for the rest of her life, but now, like the cloud over the distant fells in the morning, it was gone, evaporated as if it had never existed.

'How long have we got?'

'I've paid the last quarter rent up to the end of March, but it's paid in arrears. Next lot is due at the end of June. If we get out as soon as we can and they find another tenant then they might give us some back though I doubt it; if they do I think we might be needing it. There's a few empty places in Westnewton and I'll arrange to rent one while we think what to do next.'

His thinking was impeccable; there was no point in maintaining a lease on a farm that he could not turn a profit from. The practicalities of what had to be done soon occupied his mind; always a busy man, he did not rest idle but set about doing what had to be done. First he let it be known that there would be a farm auction on the afternoon of Saturday 4 May and engaged the services of an auctioneer from Hopes in Wigton, a new company but with a good and rising reputation. The furniture they wanted was kept in the house, but Margaret and Tom watched as tack, saddles, carts, hoes, spades, picks, shovels, crockery and all that was necessary to keep a farm going, was sold off, often at knock down prices. When it was done Tom paid off Ettie and Joseph Hayriggs what he owed them with a small bonus by way of thanks and bade goodbye to the last servants he ever employed. The following day Tom took Marra and the trap down to Edderside in the morning where he handed him over sadly for the pony was to once again form the farm transport there; where he and Margaret would live was no place for a horse. His brother Joe and he returned on the largest cart they had, and all their worldly goods were stacked and tied onto this vehicle. There was not much as they had sold most, so with a weeping Margaret and four silent children, Joe driving and Tom walking beside they left Tarns farm for good and moved slowly down the road to Westnewton. Tom had rented a cottage set back from the road; he had just under £150 so had no immediate necessity for employment, but needed time to decide what to do. Ultimately he would be able to find some sort of job, and of that he had no doubt, but he did not know what to do at all; a man in his mid thirties whose business has collapsed and who has a wife and family to support has to consider his options. Another factor was that Tom was well known in the immediate area; there was a lot of sympathy for him in his trouble from the neighbours and people he had known all his life, but he could not bear to appear to have fallen so far in their eyes. He began to keep up appearances and in his case it took the form of carrying on almost as if nothing had happened; this was just another stage in his prosperous life. Very well, he had had a setback, but it was only a temporary difficulty and in the end it would be resolved and all would be well again. It is also true that he was unemployed, stuck in a small cottage in a tiny village and no idea what he was going to do next. Margaret was not unemployed and never bored; with four children round her all day and night she had more than enough to do. Tom though was bored and full of schemes to make things better; his refuge was the pub. This is to use a euphemism for Tom had learned to ride Margaret's bicycle and just under four miles away in Allonby was an establishment known as the Spirit Vaults. It was more a grog shop than a pub and although Tom went there, he said, to press the flesh and chat to useful people, he actually went there to get drunk. The Spirit Vaults did not sell beer or wine; in fact it sold only one thing and that was rum; in the centre of the room was a large rum barrel and the clientele was of the rougher sort, sailors and fishermen. In short, it was not the most respectable establishment for Tom to frequent, but he did not care. At first he would manage to come home and wake with a thick head in the morning. Margaret would attempt to talk to him but he would not listen, making a drunk's excuses about needing to see his friends and to socialise, that she did not understand being a woman and to stop nagging him. In days of old, men would use a scold's bridle or so she had learned at school, to stop their wives using a sharp tongue and she'd better watch out or he'd get the smith to run one up. It was hard for Margaret to watch the deterioration of her husband's behaviour and morale, and she did not know what to do about it. Part of her understood his misery; Tom had been a hardworking farmer and now he had lost everything. But the drink was no solution and would lead nowhere except to no good. He was becoming careless of his appearance and she feared that if he spent much more of his time drunk then he would get a name and be ridiculed as the local sot.

When a man decides to go to his own particular hell it is very rarely that he can be stopped. There seemed almost a logic in Tom that if he was going to reel home to be scolded, then there was little point in troubling to come home at all. Why should he trouble when he could stay with a bunch of good fellows drinking, smoking, singing, playing cards and darts and having a jolly good time? Why bother to go home and bandy words with an angry woman? Poor Margaret; of course he loved her, but she did not understand. How could she? She was a woman and he was a man and he did manly things like getting drunk with his marras. He spent quite a few of his nights in a hayrick, in a barn or even under a hedge. When he was sober in the afternoons he might have noticed that he was running through their store of money with his rounds of drinks and losing small amounts gambling, but he did not. Margaret did though; their money was kept in a lockable wooden box under their bed and she checked it every day, getting more and more alarmed as the amount decreased and at last she decided to have it out with him, though perhaps she could have left it to a better time than she did. One morning Tom woke up in bed with a thick and pounding head, feeling sick in his gut and generally with the disposition of a grizzly bear roused from hibernation; he had taken so much rum the previous night that he was still drunk, which Margaret did not realise.

'Tom we need to talk about money.'
'What about money?'
'We seem to be getting through it rather quickly.'
'Have we enough to buy food and pay rent?'

'Well yes, but I can run a very nice household indeed for £2 a week though I usually spend a lot less.'

'What's the problem then?'

'We're spending about £3 a week. If we carry on at that rate then we'll get through our savings very quickly. Too quickly.'

'So make some economies then. Stop spending so much.'

'I'm not spending too much Tom. I run a very efficient house and with food and every thing I'm getting by on £1.4s a week. The rest of it is going on drink.'

'So you object to me having a drink.'

'I never said that, but you are drinking too much Tom. Getting drunk every night is something I never expected to see.'

Tom sat up with an angry face.

'So I'm a drunk am I?'

'I would not call you that, but if you want to know then it's what people are saying about you.'

There was a silence at this point and then he demanded with a sense of simmering and rising anger,

'What are they saying about me?'

Margaret paused for a moment and looked at a face which was flushed and angry before deciding that honesty was the best policy.

'Some of the neighbours have been saying they felt sorry for me being married to a man who drinks too much. They see you come home and they talk about you.'

Margaret's face was red now with shame but she went on.

'I never bargained for being married to a drunk, Thomas Little, and I thought better of you. My father brought me up in a temperance house and though I knew you liked a drink I hoped you'd display some moderation in your habits.'

'Moderation? You want moderation? I go out for a wee drink with my pals and I come home to listen to you blather on about me being a drunk. So tell me, when the neighbours talked about me being drunk did you defend me? Eh? Did you defend your husband's good name or did you agree with their damned lies and gossip?'

'It's not lies and gossip Tom.' Margaret threw caution to the winds. 'Take a look in the mirror at yourself, Tom, and tell me what you see. Do you see red rimmed eyes, sweaty forehead, a man unable to look me in the eyes; a man who sleeps off a drunken stupor until eleven o'clock each morning instead of looking for work. That man has a wife and four little kids to provide for. Lies and gossip! Just look at what you've become and be ashamed of yourself.'

'Ashamed of myself?' The rage mounted in him. 'As ashamed as you are eh? My wife is ashamed of me? Well bugger off you nagging bitch and stop bothering me.'

At this he lashed out with the back of his hand across her face and though she saw it coming and avoided the full force of it, the hand caught her a glancing blow across her left eye. She put her hand to her face and stared at him in utter disbelief then turned and left the room. Tom looked after her and grunted, turned over and went back to sleep.

When he awoke some three hours later the house was very quiet. He sat up in bed and called out, 'Margaret!' Since there was no answer he got up and went to the bedroom door; all was quiet. Looking in the children's room he found no-one, so he went downstairs and found that the house was empty, so he began to look in drawers and the cupboards. Two large bags had gone, all the children's clothes and all of Margaret's. It was when he saw that the black and white cat was gone from the mantelpiece that he realised that Margaret had left him. He did not know where she had gone since there was no note, but he guessed that she had gone to Dearham. His head still being thick he decided that he would think about what to do later. He did not want to go to Dearham, for there lived a man of 50 or so who had been a coal hewer all his life and who was very strong; maybe there was a way round this problem and after all John Adams was not a violent man. He was notable for his quiet and reasonable disposition and surely there must be a sane and civilised way to sort things out. His dinner that night was bread and cheese and the grog shop held no attractions for him so he went to bed at a reasonable hour where he lay awake thinking for hours, before falling into a not very restful sleep. Latterly the thoughts were of sorrow and remorse.

When Tom woke up and went downstairs the next day John Adams was sitting at the table dressed in his Sunday best. He looked so peaceful and calm, his hair now gone white and a fine beard the colour of pure snow, yet as Tom stepped into the room John Adams got up and without the least sign of passion knocked him to the floor with a blow to the head.

'My daughter has a black eye as the payment you gave her for her love. Now you will have a black eye so the principle is repaid. I think I owe you some interest though. Will you have it now or will you stay down there?'

Tom shook his head and stayed on the floor.

'My daughter left her house last night with two heavy bags and dragged them down to the main road with two bairns, where she left them sitting. Then she came back to this house and carried two infants down to join them, and all the while a drunken sot was snoring off his latest binge in the room upstairs. The kindness of a passing stranger with a farm cart going to Aspatria took her to the station and from thence to me.'

Tom said nothing but lay where he was, and felt his face go red.

'What kind of man are you?'

'A bad one. I hit my wife and I am sorry for it.'

'Drunken bully. Wife beater. My son-in-law.'

'I'm sorry Mr Adams. Truly I am.'

'That cuts no coal. Why did you hit my daughter?'

'I have no excuse. I hit her because of what she said.'

'That you were a drunk. That you were drinking the money away that would support your wife and family. That the neighbours thought you a sot?'

'Yes.'

'And yet withal it was the truth.'

'Yes.'

'So what are you going to do about it?'

'I don't know. Turn over a new leaf I suppose, but I don't know what to do. Will she see me do you think?'

'She might see you though I tell you plainly that my daughter will hold a grudge. She gave herself to you, bore your children and trusted you. She doesn't trust you now.'

'What does that mean though? For me? For us?'

'Frankly, if there was a way she could do it right now I don't think you'd see her for dust. That slap you gave her has almost destroyed her love for you and your behaviour this last few weeks has shown her a man she does not like. If divorce was possible for the likes of us then she would leave you.'

'For one slap?'

'One slap is enough to shake the universe as far as a woman's love is concerned Tom. She remains married to you because that is how it is, but you can expect nothing else. She will not live with you.'

'Then where can she live? Not with you for your house is full.'

'That's true, but if you look in your box you will find the answer to that. You can get up now.'

Tom looked in the money box to see that most of the cash in it had gone.

'She decided to take a third for herself, a third for the children and leave a third for you. Under the circumstances that seems to me to be fair and reasonable. I am going to install her in a house that's for rent not very far from us and she and the children are quite safe.'

'May I see her?'

'You may not. You might have noticed that my son Thomas is a big strapping lad. Also there are some people living round Margaret who have known her all her life and who are incensed by her black eye and how she got it. If you show your nose in Dearham at the moment then I cannot answer for it. I tell you plainly to stay away.'

'So what am I expected to do? My wife has run off and I want my children. The law says the children are mine.'

'Oh you may go to law if you wish and maybe, just maybe they'll give those innocents over to a drunk. Maybe not though. I would advise you on a better course and be guided by me.'

'And what guidance will you give me Mr Adams?'

'That in one month I will come back to you. I will expect you to be sober and not having drunk any alcohol. I will know this because I have found a way to know. If you are sober and have refrained from alcohol then we will have set the terms on which I will talk to you. It may be possible by then to bring about some settlement to this problem between you and Margaret; or maybe not. I have something in mind.'

John Adams looked at Tom with a straight and level gaze that went right through him and the younger man looked away in shame.

'Do we have an understanding?'

'We do.'

'Then I shall see you one month from today. And remember, if you slip, I shall know and I shall pay you the interest I owe you.'

With that, he turned and left to go home. For Tom a long month began in which he did a lot of thinking and a lot of reading; and even though he went to neither pub not grog shop he could not escape the idea that he was being watched. Was that girl looking at him across the road? Did those curtains twitch? Was the old man next door keeping an eye on him? He did not know which of the people around him might be a spy for John Adams, but he was sure of one thing about Margaret's father. He had spoken, and he never told lies.

Chapter 26

The Penitent

Margaret's children were safe and so was she and that was the thing that had been uppermost in her mind since her husband had hit her. Nothing in her upbringing had prepared her for the man she loved blacking her eye; although Father administered corporal punishment to his children with a belt when they were small, he did it reluctantly, with thought, and, as she thought, with justice. When she married Tom she knew that he liked a drink, but that was true of many men, and though she had been brought up in a house of abstinence she had accepted it as a part of him that was at least moderate and tolerable. She had watched his behaviour over the last few weeks with a mounting level of horror as he spiraled downward into drunkenness every night, so obviously drowning his sorrows in alcohol, yet apparently making himself ill in the process. It had not been pleasant waking next to a man with a pasty face, red eyes, a patently thick head and a whiplash temper that was getting worse. It was perhaps as well that since the loss of the farm, the physical aspects of marriage had wholly ceased. She had done her best to support him in his time of stress and need, but nothing she could say had diminished the amount of his drinking. When they were at Tarns there was a certain amount of amusement to be had from the fact that sometimes he only made it home because Marra knew the way, and when drunk he had at least been funny and affectionate. His deliberate drinking to get drunk had changed him, and he was whittling away at their savings. Finally she felt that she had no choice but to have the matter out with him. When he had hit her she did not at first believe it, finding it impossible to take in; when he turned over and went back to sleep, her stunned feeling very quickly turned into fear as she looked in the mirror and saw her eye changing colour; she did not wish to be there when he woke up and particularly she did not wish the children to be there either. That was why they had to come with her. Margaret was no fool and she had lived in a mining community all of her life. She knew of men who beat their wives, and their children. That was not going to happen to her little ones. There was thought of her own safety too and she did not have time to think it through, but she had seen those poor women round her village who bore the marks of their husband's fists. All through her teen years she had thought to herself that she would never be one of those and would not accept it; it had never entered her mind that Tom would hit her.

There was also the question of her father. John Adams had very definite views on the relationship of men to women. A man of his time, he held firmly that there were things appertaining to women and things appertaining to men, and he was no more than traditional in this. Every day except Sunday he laboured hard at the coal face to feed his wife and family. His wife made the home, cooked the meals and looked after the children. There were other duties that he considered to be in the manly sphere which required muscle round the house, and in the disciplining of his boys, but in all this he had contempt for wife beaters. He held that though operating in different spheres, men and women were equal and that a man who used his superior physical strength to get his own way was less than a man, but more animal. To him God had given men and women brains and they were one to the other as helpmeets and companions through life. For the one to use violence to the other was a contemptible thing which detracted from the dignity of man and was offensive to all moral considerations. It was the most natural thing in the world that Margaret should seek his protection for herself and her children, and when she arrived at his house she had it immediately as an invisible shield settled over her and she knew that whatever happened she was safe. There was no room in her father's house for such a number as she brought, but happily one of the small cottages on Row Brow was vacant and the landlord lived locally. John obtained it at three shillings a week and Margaret could sleep there with her children in some comfort. It was not necessary to equip it as a separate household because they could eat, wash and perform all the other functions such as laundry, in his house. For the moment they had to sleep on shakey-downs on the floor, but there were enough blankets in the Adams household to supply their needs.

When Margaret had arrived from Dearham Halt with a discoloured eye, two bags and four children, he had taken in the scene immediately as she knew when she fell weeping into his arms. John Adams was not a man to show his anger, but a fire took light behind his eyes at that moment; someone had hit his girl and would be paid back what he had given. This he did not say to Margaret of course, but busied himself with the practicalities of the situation as men do, and passed Margaret over to her mother to talk things through, but in truth Margaret did not know what to say. Tom was her husband and her mind was torn for the intervening miles had brought the thought that she should not have left him, and that her place was with him. The question arose of whether or not she had brought it on herself by raising her concerns at the wrong time; had she deserved it by 'nagging' him. Her mother told her firmly that she had not, whilst her father snorted at the idea and stated his firm conviction that nothing ever justified a man hitting a woman. Her confusion was a mass of conflicting thoughts; the man she loved had hit her. Her children needed their father; but what if he hit them? Could she trust him near her or them? Was she betraying her marriage vows wherein she had promised to love and obey for better or worse? Yet her vows had made no mention that her husband might beat her. For the moment the matter was left in the hands of her father and he, as was his habit, strode off, she thought up the brow to think matters through. In fact he had gone up into Dearham village to speak to Robert Steel the colliery manager. When he came back he announced that he would go to see Tom for he had a mind to speak to him, and Margaret should rest easy and have a holiday for the moment for she had been through a lot.

In Westnewton Tom suffered. After John Adams' visit his mind went through tortures of remorse, because in fact it was the drink that had impelled his hand. He knew that, but he also knew that it was no excuse because he had been brought up to respect women. Now he had hit his wife, an action that sober Tom found contemptible, and nor was he the only one. The news had reached West End Farm and Joe had brought the message from his mother that if she saw him before he had made up with our lass and apologised, then she'd give him the flat of her hand. More than that, if he ever raised his hand to a woman again then he was no son of hers; Tom had winced at that. What he had done went against all his education, his normal temperament and most of all, his own moral code. He did not even like to think of what he had done for the waves of shame it brought on him and he knew that if he had been a sober man then he would never have done it. The worst thing was the loneliness; he loved Margaret and he missed her; it was, he reflected more than once, as if his right arm was missing. The other component of this was that he was a family man and was used, had been used for years, to having small children round him whom he doted on. He missed Nellie most of all; his first born, so feisty and with such a mind of her own. So many times he found himself wishing with all of his might that he could somehow go back in time to that minute and stop himself lashing out, but as with all of us, he was stuck in a material world where the laws of physics do not allow for such events. So he could not see Margaret or the children; he could not go to West End Farm where his mother was angry at him and he was marooned on his own.

Missis was not happy with another of her children at this time, though her annoyance was a tempered one, somewhat sweetened by the arrival of another grandchild. Annie Eleanor had arrived home in March of 1901 having quit her post at the telephone exchange and thus lost her lodgings in the women's accommodation. It would not have done for her to stay for although she was not large in her pregnancy, it was nonetheless obvious. She occupied her old room as of a right and in answer to her mother's queries about the father of her child she replied that she was not going to say who it was.

'But don't you think you should marry him?'

'Not necessarily. I have not decided yet if I want to be married. Really Mam, this is the twentieth century and I'm a modern woman. I don't know that I want to be married yet. I haven't had time to think about it.'

'Well don't you think you should? You tell me the baby's due in May; don't you think you should be married by then.'

'Not really. I told you I want to think about it.'

'But if you don't marry the child will be a .....'

'Bastard Mam. You mean bastard. It's just a label. You know as well as I do that many children round here are born out of wedlock and nobody cares a whit about it.'

'But how will you support yourself? I hope you don't expect us to keep you.'

'I don't. I can pay my way. Mam, I've been earning good money for years and living in. I've got quite a lot in my savings so I'll pay you what you want for my keep and give a hand when I can, while I think about what to do next.'

Missis knew very well that on the Solway Plain this was not uncommon, though it often ended in tears if the mother had no means of support. If Annie Eleanor could support herself then she was no worse and certainly a lot better off than many local women.

'But does the father know? What does he think about it?'

'Of course he does. I've told him; and I've also told him to stay away from me while I think. If he knows what's best for him he'll do as I say, for if I find that a man cannot fall in with what I want in this, then it will tell me a great deal about him and not to his credit.'

Her baby was born in May and christened Ann Little for Annie Eleanor remained serenely unmarried and in no hurry to change her status. At West End Farm the identity of her baby's father remained a mystery and when Annie Eleanor was asked if he had seen the child, she replied that he had; she had taken to driving out with Marra on Sundays to visit him and no-one observed where she went or who she met. He was a good man and was staying away because she wanted him to, while she took her time to think.

'How long are you going to think?' grumbled her mother.

'How long is a piece of string Mam? When I decide what to do, that will be it, one way or another so I'm going to get it right. Have some patience.'

Faced with this obduracy, all Missis could do was grumble and look cross; Joe and Agnes, now expecting another child, did not mind what Annie Eleanor did so long as she was happy about it. However, her daughter was going through a great mental turmoil with two halves of her mind at war with each other. She had given John Metcalfe a particular book to read for she wanted him to understand her. Luckily for him and perhaps for her, he was a man of flexible mind and he read *'Jude the Obscure'* with it wide open. So it was that the moment to change both their lives came even before he had finished reading and their conversation, though not conclusive, was ultimately decisive.

'The way I'm reading this Annie is that you and me are like this Sue and Jude. She has his children and won't marry him because she wants to be free. Is that right?'

'Yes. That's about it. I don't want to be tied and stifled. To be a farmer's wife, chained to the stove and the routines like my mother; to me that looks like prison.'

'Yes I know that, so let me be quite clear. You love me in the same way that I love you, but you won't marry me. Is that right?'

'More or less; I want to be free.'

'Well let's be clear again because this is important. I know that you read a lot of stuff on women's suffrage and rights, and that doesn't bother me because as you know I agree that women should have the vote, but this free love thing is bothering me.'

'In what sense does it bother you?'

'This Thomas Hardy and others of his ilk like Mr Wells and Mr Shaw that you've been reading; they also speak of free love and marriage being like a prison. Does that mean sleeping round with lots of other people?'

'To them I think it does, but not for me. That's a personal choice and it's not something I want.'

'I'm glad of that, because I don't like the sound of it. Frankly I may be a little old fashioned here, but they are men and they seem to be inventing excuses to me so that they can justify what sounds to me seedy. That may be small minded of me but I can quite see why this book has caused a lot of fuss. In the future I think it might happen that men and women are able to live together and have children without marrying, but in this day and age it would mean ostracisation and a lot of misery. This book is quite a grim little tale.'

'I don't agree that it's seedy John and I think that if women want to sleep around and not be monogamous, then they should be able to just as men do. But that's not the issue because I have never wished to do that.'

'So what stops you from marrying me is that you wish to be free from the chains of being a farmer's wife. It's not the notion of marriage you object to but the drudgery and boredom and servitude that it implies?'

'Yes I think so. Yes. It's not the life I want. I don't want to follow in my mother's footsteps; it's not me.'

'But I seem to be the man you want? You don't find me repugnant but quite the reverse. And I'm a farmer; but I love you and you love me. And you want to marry me, but you don't want to marry me.'

Annie Eleanor nodded glumly, 'I can't see a way round this John. Can you?'

She expected him to say that he could not and to agree with her, but to her surprise he grinned broadly and took her hand, kissing it.

'Why then all's well if you would not contemplate infidelity, for I'm inclined to monogamy and you are not inclined to be otherwise. You can marry me and be free too.'

'How on earth would that be?'

'Look at me Annie. I'm clean and nicely turned out am I not? Well fed and looked after?'

She had to agree that he was.

'Now how do you think that a bachelor man in his early 30s manages that eh? I have a good farm; I employ men on it and work myself. But in the house I have a cook-housekeeper of 52, and a skivvy to work under her. I get all the benefits of having a live-in housewife for she bakes and cooks and preserves. I don't need a wife to do that for me. I don't need to set you in chains to be married to you. Marry me and be my wife and I don't mind what you do else. Run a shop in Maryport, start your own business, agitate for women's votes. I don't mind.'

Here he got down on his knee.

'Marry me and be my equal, for I truly think that a good marriage sets you free. What do you say Annie?'

She looked at him in some confusion.

'You're being a bit premature John. I need to think about this before I answer. I will answer you, but not yet.'

With that he had to be content, but told her that he would wait until Hell froze over if necessary, but would prefer an answer a little sooner if possible.

Back in Westnewton, about a week after John Adams' visit, the postman called as Tom finished his breakfast and to his surprise handed him a thick envelope. When he opened it, he found a book called *'The Teetotaler's Companion*' and there was a slip of paper marking a page in it. When he opened it, he read underlined in pencil:

*'Many are the homes strong drink has curs'd
and many hearts that are sad.
Were happily though HIS efforts blessed,*

390

Despairing souls made glad.

But ah! How frail is sinful man,
Soon are his glories fled.
Now he's happy, virtuous sober;
Now to virtue dead.

Soon alas! We were forsaken,
Home and hearth despised - forgot;
And our sire, strong drink pursuing,
Sought ruin in the pot.

Saw he not his wife's deep anguish?
His children's tears, and ne'er relent?
Who can tell how great his suffering?
Paint the miseries that he felt?
When restored to sober reason,
By that couch he humbly knelt?'

Further on, he read with horror a passage double underlined in another set of verses:

'*Who beats his wife, an a' that*
Be nothing but a rascal boor.
And half a man for a' that.'

Then Tom just howled, for whoever had sent it, and he guessed who it was, knew that it was true and just how to touch him on the raw. And so he read the book; he had little else to do. Then he thought; and thought some more, until at last he knew the price of the way back and decided there and then that he would pay it. From the start of the month set by John Adams, as instructed, he had taken no drink. To his surprise he found it easy; having decided to abstain from alcohol because he was being forced to, he ended by having some pride in his own forbearance.

In the middle of the afternoon of 29 September, it being a bright Sunday Joe turned up with the large Edderside farm cart, riding in company with John Adams whose bicycle was on the back. Tom's month had expired. John dismounted the cart somewhat stiffly.

'Riding a bicycle and then a cart do not agree with my joints today.'

Then he looked Tom straight into the eye and Tom flared cherry red.

'You might well blush. Did you get my message?'

'I did.'

'Did you understand it?'

'I did.'

'And will you pay the price?'

'I will.'

'I knew you would. No you don't have to make an oath to me. You know where that's due. Now that being the case, let us get your stuff loaded.'

'Loaded?'

'Oh aye. I knew you'd pay the price so I came prepared. Your place is not here, but with your family. You're to come with me to Dearham.'

Tom's mood soared and his face lightened.

'Don't get too excited. You can see them, but you're not sleeping in their house. Things take time to heal and you've got a long way to go. Your children miss you, and you will be near them and can see them every day.'

Tom swallowed, 'What do you mean?'

'I mean you can't expect to share the bed of a woman you thumped in the face a month ago as if nothing had happened. You sleep in the lean-to at my house. You get to see your wife and family, but when you get into her house is up to her; you will have to win that. If you can. That's it. Take it or leave it.'

Tom swallowed hard, 'I'll take it.'

392

John Adams looked into his eyes and said, 'You'd be a damn fool if you didn't.'

It did not take the three men long to load the household onto the cart once more and before two hours had passed they were moving slowly down the road heading for Dearham.

'Now,' said John Adams, 'I want you to listen very carefully to me. I said I had something in mind when I left you a month ago; well I do. How would you like to work with horses again?'

'Well I would, of course,' said Tom, 'But I can't afford to set up breeding again.'

'You wouldn't have to. That's not what I meant. I can't put you in the way of a business or riches, but I can put you in the way of a job if you are interested in it. You don't have to stay at it, but it will pay you four shillings and sixpence a day. At one pound seven shillings a week you can support a family with careful management until you get something better.'

'You mean I should get a job?'

'Well most people do, boy. Do you think you should not?'

'No. I'm used to hard work. It's just that I've never worked for an actual wage before. I had a share of West End profits and then I worked on my own account.'

'Needs must where the devil drives. You need employment and a wage. It's not much but you can live on it with careful management; and my daughter knows how to do that.'

'What job is it?'

'Putter down my pit.'

'Down a coalmine! What's that to do with horses?'

'Quite a lot. A putter is someone whose job it is to pull or push truckloads of coal from the coalface to the lift where it can be hoisted out. It used to be done by children years ago, but now it has to be a man.'

'You want me to do a child's job?'

'No I don't. It's done by men with ponies now; little horses about three feet tall. They drag two or three tubs of coal where a child could only do one. It's more efficient.'

'You have ponies down your mine?'

'Aye we do. There's six of them and you'd be working with one. I had a talk though with the colliery manager and I've told him a bit about you. He knows you are a horse man and he's interested.'

'Interested in what?'

'Well you see each pony has a man to work with and that man rubs him down and sees that he gets enough to eat; and he cleans out his stable.'

'Where are the stables?'

'They're underground too. There are stalls for them and they get fresh straw and good food. They're well looked after and all the men are very fond of them.'

'Don't they ever get out?'

'Oh yes. On holidays and during the week's break in summer they do, but most of the time they're down the mine.'

'That doesn't sound good or natural for horses.'

'Well they don't seem to mind. Anyway the men who run them are all colliers you see.'

'Well they would be.'

'Don't be obtuse young man; are you really not seeing my point?'

On Tom's shaking his head, John Adams went on, 'There's not one of them knows much about horses. Mr Steel says that if you stand a month's trial then he'll offer you the post of ostler at five shillings a day. You'd then be in charge of overlooking all the horses at the pit.'

'What would that involve?'

'I think he has an eye to have one man look over their welfare and to keep them up to scratch, but a man who knows what he's doing.'

'You say there are six of them?'

'There's eight all together. Two larger ponies pull tubs on the surface into the sidings to make up train loads.'

'Shunting with ponies?'

'Exactly so – they're a lot cheaper than a steam engine and quicker too.'

'How can a pony pull such heavy weights?'

'They're on metal rails, Tom; far less friction than on a road; if a man put his shoulder to a line of wagons he can probably shift it himself. It's not hard for ponies. The big question is, do you want the job?'

'I'll take it. I'm not doing much else at the moment. Thank you.'

His meeting with Margaret was less communicative. When they arrived at Row Brow the furniture had to be fitted into place in the little two up and two down where her father had installed her, but before that happened they were tactfully left alone in the front room where they stood facing each other, though Margaret would not look at her husband, standing with her face down.

'I'm sorry Margaret. I should not have done what I did and I will never do it again.'

The silence hung like a great pall over the room.

'I was in drink and not in my right mind. I will never do it again.'

'How do I know that?'

'I swear that I will never hit you again.'

'Why should I believe you?'

'I will swear it on the bible if you wish me to.'

'You hit me, you bully.'

Tears came into Tom's eyes, 'I know I did and I would rather cut my hand off than do it again.'

'Words Tom.' Now she looked at him, two grey gimlets straight into his eyes.

He blushed scarlet and looked away from her, unable to meet her anger. Then she asked, 'How do I know that you won't get drunk again and decide in a fit of drunken rage to hit me again or the children?'

This was his cue and he stood in the place where John Adams had brought him to, so he took it. Reaching out and taking her hand he said, 'I have been off drink for a month now and I swear to you that I will never take another drop of it in my life.'

She looked at him with a blank face.

'Margaret, I've been a fool and I allowed my fondness for drink to get the better of me after the trouble we've been through. We've lost our farm and our horses. I don't want to lose my wife and family too. I don't want us to lose everything. Please forgive me.'

'You haven't lost everything. You still have a wife and a family, but you have done such damage, such awful damage.'

'I know. I'm sorrier for it than you know. What must I do to make it better?'

'Exactly what Father has arranged. I'm not sleeping with you Tom; you knocked away the foundations from us and I don't want you near me in that way. You sleep down the Dib though you can be round during the day and for meals; the children need their father. You go to work and stay sober; give it time and we shall see.'

With that he had to be content, though he was not happy about it. He had a household once more, but did not sleep in it. He was treated with a guarded tolerance by the Adams family because he had hit their daughter, but among the neighbours he got black looks, as Margaret was well liked and he was a wife beater. Overall it was a question of trust and he had forfeited it all, so his presence was on sufferance, the situation uncomfortable. One thing he did that was significant towards his redemption was that he accompanied John Adams up to the Temperance Hall and there he took the solemn oath before God known as the Pledge, that he would abstain from alcohol all the rest of his life. He signed the certificate binding him to his oath and it was witnessed by the Vicar and John Adams; then he took it home. Margaret took it from him and hung it on the wall above the fireplace.

'That's the first step back Tom. You've made me proud, which I haven't been for weeks. Now do it some more.'

A great many more steps would be needed before she was prepared to forgive him as he wished.

Chapter 27

The Ostler

Tom accompanied his father-in-law the very next day to Crosshow pit where he descended the shaft for the first time and was introduced to his pit pony Tyan. The moment he heard the name of his animal he knew that the others were Yan, Tethera, Methera, Pimp and Sethera and laughed to find something down this hole more associated with the counting of sheep in open fields.

'They might be little,' said John Adams, 'But they're strong and sure-footed on the mine floors. Where there's rails they pull three tubs, but we only ask them to do one where there's none though in some pits they pull two. Most of the lads are very fond of them for they save us a lot of work, don't you my little marra?'

Here he produced a paper bag and the pony nuzzled forward.

'Alright lad, here it is, but only one mind you,' and he gave the pony a peppermint.

To Tom's querying look he smiled.

'You'll find it best to give your mouth something to do to keep it shut. Dust you see. It's better if you breathe through your nose. A lot chew tobacco, but I prefer peppermints or aniseed balls. Now, George here will show you how to dress Tyan and you can go with him for your first loads.'

'I know how to dress a pony.'

'I know you do, but the harness is smaller and maybe stranger than what you're used to. Just show him anyway, George.'

'Right. You put the braffin over his head with the reins attached and then these limmers over and under to keep the braffin in position. You see how it's shaped like a wishbone and the horse goes in the middle. Now you take the ends of the limmers and put them together; see these holes? Well you line them up with this staple on the tub, put this iron peg through from above and Bob's your uncle, it's ready.'

'Well that's simple enough,' said Tom. 'How do you stop it running into the back of the pony on a slope?'

'Most of our roads are level enough, but see there's a little brake on the back that you can apply if you need to; and if you need to stop very quick then use the sprag there on the side.'

'Sprag?'

'Yes – that piece of timber. Just shove it between the spokes for a quick stop, but mind you don't get hit by it, or you'll feel it. Now let's be off.'

And so Tom followed George Ritson down the tunnel, he leading Tyan and George leading Pimp, each pulling an empty tub for there were no rails but a fairly level rough floor. After half a mile or so they came to the end where a half naked man stood nearly upright waiting for them.

'About time. I've been standing here five minutes waiting for empty. Now let's get on with it.'

'Alright, alright. Hold your horses; we're doing our best, said George, 'You put the right tabs on?'

'Of course I have! What do you think I am?'

It was essential to ensure that the right tab was put on each tub, for the miners were paid for each tub they filled; nothing could so easily cause trouble as another man's tab being put on your tub.

Tom saw that to his left was a smaller tunnel and that the tub had been pushed out by the waiting man. George uncoupled Pimp from the empty tub, attached him to the full one, and dragged it partway back along the tunnel. Tom waited as a second full tub was pushed out into the main tunnel, then he too swapped it for his empty one. As far as the mining was concerned, this was his job.

He and Tyan pulled the tub back to the main shaft where the cage came down, shoved it in to be sent to the surface and then set off back with an empty tub.

After nine hours of doing this, his shift was over and he washed Tyan down from a stream or gutter of water diverted from the pumps. This was not the same water they drank as that came down fresh in tubs from the surface. There were tubs of it throughout the workings for the ponies to drink from. When Tom had dried the legs of his pony he had to give him a feed, which was the second of his shift because he had a nosebag partway through and it was the same rich mix. While Tyan fed Tom commenced to groom him, which also had to be done at the end of every shift. He did feel rather sorry for the ponies at first for when he went up the shaft at the end of the day, they stayed down, but it was explained to him that it was better to leave them down. If their eyes were used to the dark then taking them up too often made them reluctant to go down again and they grew discontent.

They did go up several times a year and were retired at the end of their working days, for all the miners were very fond of them. Tom had seen the evidence of this with his own eyes for Tyan on his way through the workings would be offered bread crusts, apples and bits of cake which were cheerfully snaffled up by the pony who expected them as his due. One day he even got Tom into trouble when he passed a man who had leaned back into a manhole in the side of the tunnel to let him pass; the pony made a lunge and bit at his pocket from which came a crunching noise.

'Hey! Your bloody pony's had my apple!'

'Sorry marra; he must have smelled it through your pocket.'

At the end of the day he met John Adams at the pit head and they both walked home to the house down the Dib. In the lean-to scullery Nancy had the set pot already boiling and the tin bath out in the kitchen; as householder John always had first bath, but this was his prerogative and Tom did not mind. Then he was free to go up to the small house where Margaret was with the children and sit with them until bedtime.

'Daddy, why don't you live with us any more?' asked Nellie one night soon after he had started work.

Tom looked at Margaret who looked back, and then he said, 'It isn't convenient right now sweetheart.'

'What's convenient?'

'Something grown-up. I'll tell you when you're older.'

This at least wrung a wry smile from Margaret, but she did not budge from her position. He had demolished the trust between them and it had to be rebuilt; he knew that, and in some way, though it pained him, he approved. The old and troublesome year went, and a new one came in. Tom was going back for his first shift after the New Year, hoping that 1902 would bring him something better than 1901 had, when his good luck fairy stepped in. Robert Steel, the colliery manager was waiting for him and called him into his office.

'Mr Little, as you might know, we have not had an ostler in this mine since it reopened, each man looking after his own pony, but it's been a bit remiss of me and I am minded to appoint one. How would you feel about taking on the duties?'

'Well sir, if you will tell me what they would be then I could say if I could carry them out, though I think I could.'

'I like your caution though I am in no doubt as to your fitness for the work. You're an educated man and you used to be a farmer, well used to horses. Very well. The duties would be to look after the ponies and the horses on the surface. You would groom them, you'd keep them trimmed, look to their health and get them shoed when needed by the blacksmith. You would see them cleaned out and their bedding changed regularly and muck them out. At the end of each shift you would check them for injury and treat minor ailments with such lotions and liniments as you felt appropriate, and administer medicine where needed. You'd feed them and make sure that they had a nosebag feed halfway through the shift and likewise ensure that water tubs are placed throughout the mine and replenished. You will keep a pony book and records of each beast; and you would operate a rota of work so that no pony does more than two shifts in a row. I will not have my ponies dropping from exhaustion. You would be responsible for their welfare overall, and if you say that a pony is unfit to work a shift then no-one may over rule you. It's a lot of work Mr Little and quite a responsible position as I'm sure you can see.'

'I certainly can. Would I also be pulling tubs as now?'

'No; I think not normally. You'll have quite enough on your plate and the men will be glad to be relieved of the grooming and so on at the end of the shift. You'd also have to come in on Sundays and when they are all on the surface for holidays.'

'This includes the surface ponies?'

'Yes it does, so I'm offering you the job at five shillings a day which is about the same as I pay an average coal hewer. I'll also put one of the young lads to help you and he can learn from you. Do you accept?'

'I do sir, and thank you. I appreciate the opportunity.'

'I'm sure you do, so let us shake on it and I shall spread the word that you are commencing your duties immediately. One last thing.' At this Mr Steel reached into his desk drawer and pulled out a gun. 'This stays in here, but it is for your use. Here is a key to this drawer. If any poor creature is in such a state where they have to be put out of their misery, then it will be your duty to do it. I trust that meets with your consent?'

'It does,' said Tom. 'I can do that if need be.' So saying, he attached the key to his watch chain.

'Oh and you'd better have this,' said Mr Steel hauling out a sack.

'What is it?'

'Ah well we are plagued with rats and mice because of the horse feed. I ordered a few traps so if you bait them and set them round the stable areas we might reduce the nuisance somewhat.'

Tom had a responsible position and a wage, which, by the standards of the area, was a good one. The difference to him, to his manner, to his morale, was astonishing. From being a drunken farmer down on his luck with no prospects, and having lost everything, he now had a wage, some status, the respect of an employer and was slowly winning his way back into the affections of his family. 1902 was looking to be a good year for him.

Across the other side of the village there was trouble. Fifty men working on the Lick Band seam in the Lonsdale Colliery went on strike when their rate was reduced from 2d a ton to 1.5d. This was not unnatural and the directors did not blame it, as many might, on the rise of socialism and the new Labour Party, or even on Syndicalism, which gave so many employers bad dreams. They simply called a meeting and explained that the world price of coal was falling. If they did not drop the price on that seam then the colliery would run at a loss and they would have to close. A deal was struck and twenty of the men, who lived in other places than Dearham simply left and went to other pits where the rate stayed as it was and the geology was more friendly to profit. For the moment, the rate in the Lonsdale stayed the same, but as an augury for the future it might have been seen as not good. The Crosshow Colliery however, by dint of being a co-operative, enjoyed much local support and had a healthy landsale take; they also benefited by selling coal to the Dearham Brickworks. Their rates stayed good and 1902 was a year of profit, despite world figures. They produced 31,000 tons of coal in the year and were sufficiently profitable to pay off £1,000 worth of debentures. The Maryport Industrial and Co-operative Society had got its money back, kept a community going, and made profits on the brickworks and the store in Dearham. The rather heroic venture of 1894 was looking like a runaway success.

For John Metcalfe it was also looking like a good year. He had woken up on 1 January as the sun was coming up to someone banging on his door, and when he opened it, Annie Eleanor stood there.

'Will you marry me?'

'Aren't I supposed to be the one who asks?'

'No. That's just convention. Be careful if you think that way or I might not ask again. Will you marry me Mr Metcalfe?'

John's housekeeper came up behind him in dressing gown and curling papers with her mouth open at this breach of male-female protocol, but he didn't care. He gave a great laugh and scooped her up in his arms while he shouted,

'Yes I will, just try and stop me.'

'You meant what you said? I'll be free?'

'Of course I did. I'll marry you as my equal. You can come and go as you please, start a business, lead a suffragist society, fly in a balloon or stand for't council as women may do, but don't you ever dare cook me a meal or wash my clothes. That's Mrs Hayston's job. I love you Annie and I always will.'

'And I love you and always will; and my daughter needs a father. You showed me a mind that's open and free to find its own way and I don't think there's another like you. But never put fences round me John, because I won't abide them.'

And so it was agreed that this longest of Solway Plain courtships was over; the wedding took place at the church at Rowks and after all Annie Eleanor become a farmer's wife, though not in the way she had always dreaded.

As the months went by Tom grew more proficient in the care of his charges, and as Margaret liked horses he even took her down the shaft with him one Sunday when no coal was cut, to meet Tyan and the others. When the ponies came up for Easter weekend he took Nellie and Nancy and set them upon the small horse's backs for a ride; it was clear that he liked the work he was doing and had turned a corner. No drink had passed his lips and he showed no sign of wanting any either. Margaret was warming to him again and he found that he was able to put his arm round her and she did not, as when he first arrived in Dearham, shy away, shrugging him off. He was also getting to be well liked by the people around as word spread of his being a good worker who grafted hard and who was pleasant to everyone. The hostile expressions of the neighbours had changed as there was general agreement that it was nice to see him and Margaret back together again. Still he slept in the lean-to down the Dib and the marital bed had single occupancy in the house up the Brow. It dawned upon him slowly that he had to do more; that marriages are things that have to be worked at and in this one, there was something that was lacking. On Monday 12 May 1902 he decided upon a further step towards reconciliation and asked her a question.

'Will you walk out with me tomorrow Margaret?'

'Walk out with you?' She smiled, 'It's a bit late for that. We've been married coming on for seven years.'

'I'd like to walk out with you tomorrow. It's an anniversary. Will you come?'

'Don't be daft. It's not an anniversary. We were married in November, remember?'

'I know that. What I meant is that it's 15 May tomorrow; the anniversary of you arriving at our farm, in 1894.'

'So it is! Fancy you remembering that. It seems such a long time ago.'

'That's because it is. So will you walk out with me?'

'Yes. I will. Where had you in mind?'

'Maryport, Margaret. We're going to the theatre.'

'Now I know you've gone mad. There's no theatre in Maryport; it fell down as you may recall.'

'You leave that for me to worry about. I'm on early shift tomorrow and I'll be home no later than four o'clock. We'll have our tea early and then we'll go. Dress nicely and look your best; you're going out on the town.'

Thomas Adams had been detailed to baby sit, but it was his mother who spent most of the following evening looking after her grandchildren. Tom had finished work and changed into one of his suits left from a more prosperous time, and he and Margaret had walked up into Central Road in Dearham, him being so mysterious that Margaret found herself hoping that he did not have it in mind to walk all the way to Maryport. To her pleasure, when they reached the Sun Inn there was a twelve seater wagonette standing there with two large and placid horses harnessed to it, and Tom assisted her up into one of the seats. Supported by two poles either side of the driver's seat was a sign which read 'Totten's Theatre'.

'Where on earth is Totten's Theatre? I've never heard of it.'

'They're a traveling theatre company Margaret. They tour all over the place and tonight they're at the Athenaeum.'

'In Catherine Street? I've never been in there.'

'No more have I, but I hear it's huge.'

'What are we going to see?'

'From what I can gather it's a sort of Music Hall, not one production but many different turns from all sorts of folk. I don't know what's on the bill, but we shall see when we get there.' He paused. 'You might remember I said we should go to the theatre more often, but we never have.'

Her eyes showed their approval. 'I think so too. How do we get back?'

'Same way we're going. The wagonette leaves fifteen minutes after the end of the show. We'll be back between eleven o'clock and midnight.'

'But are you not on early shift tomorrow?'

'Yes I am. Up at five and off, but I don't care. It's an important day.'

The two big horses made short work of the gradual climb out of Dearham, then positively flew the two miles downhill into Maryport. Soon they were getting out of the wagonette outside the door of the great Athenaeum Hall and above the doors of this 650 seat auditorium the showman, Mr Totten, had caused great flambeaux to be placed and they flared most romantically in the dusk.

'Can we afford this Tom?'

'Of course we can. You forget; we have money in the bank; we did not quite lose everything Margaret. There's a little nest egg put away which we may tap occasionally, though we live on my wages.'

On the wall outside was a playbill promising much delight and so they found when they entered the auditorium because the place was packed full and very noisy. Tom had purchased seats in the wagonette which included a reserved seat for each passenger and to this they were conducted by a gentleman with a flowered waistcoat and a waxed moustache who bowed them in and spoke ever so well. They were only three rows back from the stage and to the side of them was a kind of pulpit from whence a Master of Ceremonies soon made his presence known and introduced the first act. As the raucous assembly fell mostly silent, Miss Lettie Horlick, a nice looking young lady came on and sang '*After the ball was over*' with a sweet voice and a lilt to her tone which made her irresistible to her listeners who joined in with the chorus most enthusiastically:

'After the ball was over, after the break of morn.
After the dancers leaving, after the stars are gone;
Many a heart is aching, if you could read them all,
Many the hopes that have vanished, after the ball.'

This was all well until the last verse when Miss Horlick suddenly took on a rather roguish expression and sang:

'After the ball was over, Bonnie took out her glass eye.
Put her false teeth in the water, hung up her wig to dry,
Put her false leg on the table, laid her false arm on the chair,
After the party was over, Bonnie was only half there.'

Needless to say, as Miss Horlick left the stage there was a huge roar of approval and prolonged cheering, especially from the cheaper seats up in the gallery. This set the tone for a most enjoyable evening. There followed nineteen other 'turns' and though it would be otiose to number them all, they included a magician who really did pull rabbits out of his hat and saw a lady in half, a juggler who threw fiery torches around, and a contortionist who seemed to be made of rubber and could squeeze himself into boxes that were impossibly small. For the men though the most impressive turn of the night was Stromboli the strong man. He came on dressed in a white body suit with a broad black belt round his middle as two assistants rolled a huge set of dumbbells onto the stage. He was a big man with a very fierce moustache and carried an iron bar that he stood with in the middle of the stage and bent it. His eyes bulged, his face turned red and the veins stood out at his temples as he made the inch thick bar into a U shape. This was too much for some in the audience who took to their feet shouting words like 'Rubbish' and 'Fake'. In response to this Stromboli looked at one of them and beckoned him up on stage. To the jeers and ribbing of his friends the local man went up as an assistant handed another bar to the strongman.

'You're right,' he said to the heckler. 'I was faking.' Then he bent the new bar round the man's neck with no apparent effort, crossing the ends so he could not get his head out.

'Hey – let me out of this.'

'But it's fake,' said Stromboli. 'You'll have no trouble with that. Get a couple of your mates to open it up.'

So he did. Some of his friends came up on stage and tried to open it, but with all their might and main they could not. By this time the audience were firmly on Stromboli's side and laughing at the hecklers. Eventually he put them out of their misery by opening the bar and releasing his victim. Then he took mercy on them by allowing them to help him. They sat in a chair each, suspended from a long iron bar which Stromboli lifted into the air, then held it there by one hand. The obvious strength of it brought much applause.

For the women however the best turn of the night came from the star of the show who was Vesta Tilley. She performed dressed as a foppish young man and sang three songs whilst she cracked jokes at the expense of men in between them. She did it so well, exaggerating the worst manners of men that the female audience loved it and saw her as a symbol of what they would like to do and say if they dared. The men loved it too because they saw themselves in 'him' and so she brought the house down, especially when she sang the relatively new song that had become her signature, *Burlington Bertie*. It was a wonderful evening full of laughing and escape, and as they trundled home in the wagonette Margaret held Tom's hand and said, 'Thank you. That was lovely. We must do it again.' They were deposited at the Sun Inn and arrived back at the top of the Dib at 11.30 pm. As Tom said goodnight to her, Margaret held his hand and stopped him.

'You hit me. Bully.'

'I know. I never will again.'

She swung her hand round with great force as if to slap him, then stopped just short, then lightly, almost impalpably, slapped his cheek.

'I know you won't; and now I have returned it. Goodnight Tom.'

Then she kissed his cheek and went up to her own door.

'Goodnight sweetheart,' said Tom. Then he smiled broadly and went down to his lonely bed in the lean-to.

Chapter 28

Trapped

Omega Adams was content and indeed happy; this was notwithstanding a certain and almost impalpable melancholy in her look which is often found in the eyes of a woman who has lost a child, but not so that a casual observer would see it. Her wellbeing stemmed from the position that she had obtained in the house of Dr Spedding. Unlike many general practitioners, he prospered and, unlike many of his profession, he did not have to work in poor industrial areas and accept payment in kind. His reputation was such that his patients were of the well to do classes; this was not to say that he had to trouble himself with anything so mundane as the collecting of fees. That was done by Mrs Spedding, who had an office for her administration work up on the second floor of their large house in Church Street. His fees enabled him, his wife and their two daughters to live very well and he even carried out duties *pro bono* in the Workington Infirmary up the hill at the other end of town. Such was his reputation and success that Mrs Spedding did not have to trouble herself with housekeeping, neither with the raising of her girls. Miss Elspeth Spedding, an unmarried cousin of the doctor, lived in and acted as the governess, teaching them in the schoolroom, and instructing them on how they should be. Omega at 29, with a glowing reference from Mr Furnival, the well known man of law, was an exemplary cook/housekeeper, who ran her budget well, and had charge of Mabel, the parlour or upstairs maid and Betty the scullery maid. Dr and Mrs Spedding also called her by her own name, and indeed did so with a sort of cachet that gave her and them pleasure; Mrs Spedding's expression was always pleasantly amused when visitors' eyes arched at her giving instructions to 'Omega'. The days of being 'Jane' were long behind her. In truth, the house could have used two upstairs maids because there was a lot to do, but nonetheless Mabel kept it well.

The house was large and old, having been built in the reign of Queen Anne, and it stood where was a bank, at the top of which was High Church Street and at the base of which ran Lower Church Street. If one wished, one could enter the house by the large front door on the street at the top of the hill, and leave by the back door onto the street at the bottom of the hill. To the western side of the house was a high wall bordering the rectory of St Michael's Church, where a cobbled path ran steeply down the bank and past a high wooden gate sealing the bottom yard of the house. Omega's 'suite' was here in the basement. She had her own sitting room which was quite large and looked out onto the cobbled yard with its gutter. Through a door was her bedroom. Next door to her was the kitchen, also large, from which a door led into a very dark room with no windows, dug into the hill; this was the store-room. Also opening onto the yard was a scullery. Through the other side of the kitchen, a door led to the other rooms in the basement of the house where the other maids lived in bedrooms whose windows were barred. The only way they had of leaving or entering was by the yard door, which meant that Omega could keep an eye on what was going on. Downstairs was comfortable and much to her liking.

However, upstairs to her eye was magnificent. The first floor up was on a level with High Church Street where large and high rooms opened out from a beautiful marble tiled passageway. The walls of the passage were of scarlet patterned wallpaper above creamy lincrusta whilst each room leading off was furnished with massive pieces made of oak, rosewood and walnut. Omega particularly liked the music room where a piano stood, marvelously carved with cherubs and grapes and little faces; then there was a nursery, a library, and a billiard room where Dr Spedding liked to bring friends to smoke and drink. Her board and lodging were part of her salary so she hardly spent any money of her own, which meant that her savings were mounting well. Every Saturday she had the afternoon and evening off after luncheon, for Dr and Mrs Spedding dined out, though a couple of times a year they entertained, in which case Omega had Sundays in lieu. On such occasions she had power to hire in extra servants to cope with a large dinner party. She had a great deal more authority than this because the power of purchase had been delegated to her; it was she who dealt with butcher, baker, fishmonger and the multitude of tradesmen and delivery men who came to the door. They in turn were anxious to solicit her business and she found it becoming rather lucrative to have small 'considerations' put her way occasionally, in order that the giver might continue to be favoured over the many similar tradesmen in the area. It was actually fun to buy stuff and not have to pay, for all the bills went to Mrs Spedding who did not demur so long as Omega stayed within the figure she had been told, and that was generous. The most valuable thing that she had though, was time. With a scullery maid to fetch, peel and carry, Omega could go out with no need to account for what she was doing; and she did some shopping herself. She frequented Hagg Hill market, just along Dora Crescent for much fresh produce, but sometimes took herself uptown to the Buttermarket, along Oxford Street and up to the meeting with King Street where stood the old covered counter where farmers' wives sold the best from their dairy. The town itself, she grew fonder and fonder of; the strange burned matches smell to the air, the way the rain hissed off the canopies of the gaslights at night, the steam and smoke that puffed up from the trains at Central Station and the glare at night that lit up the sky over the Solway towards the steelworks at Moss Bay. As to her personal life, she had certainly meant what she said to Margaret, and no men figured in her comings or goings. Happy to take life as it came, she had formed friendships at her church with a small number of women who did similar jobs to herself, and her social life, such as it was, made her happy. She liked going to shows sometimes at one of Workington's Theatres, even, occasionally, the Opera House, but never in the stalls for fear of embarrassing the Speddings. The high spot of her years was when the Speddings went away on vacation for a whole month in August, often to France or Switzerland. Then she imagined herself the lady of the house who could come and go as she pleased, and hosted parties of her friends in her downstairs realm, presiding over tea and petit fours as if to the manner born.

Omega's letters to Margaret in Dearham made her younger sister quite envious that she was so foot-loose and free. Compared to Omega's lively and interesting existence, life with four small children seemed very dull and humdrum, though it had become easier since Nellie and Nancy had started at Dearham School, where she had attended herself. John Adams had kept his children at school long past the time when many parents would, because he had insisted that they would pass the examination for Standard VI before they left. These standards did not correspond to chronological age and both Omega and Margaret had not left until they were thirteen. Margaret thought that her children would follow a similar path, though she knew that life was full of uncertainties. Chief among these at this particular moment was that she was not quite sure yet if she wanted to take her husband back fully into her affections. Part of her wanted to, because Tom was clean, sober, hard working and a good father; moreover he loved her and she had begun to trust, and to love him again. It was on the point of whether or not that was strong enough to stand his being back permanently that she was not quite sure.

On Friday 4 July Tom was at work not far from a long wall on the two yard band; he had taken Tethera down there with a container of fresh water to replenish the drinking tub set there for the ponies. As he bailed the contents into the tub there came an explosion from the coalface and a cloud of dust and smoke billowed out from the entrance to the workings, accompanied by screams of pain and an ominous rumble. In response to the cries for help he immediately ducked his head and made his way to the end of the first stent where an injured man lay with his leg under a fall of coal.

'Hello Jack; can you speak to me?'

Eventually the dirt covered man who was in obvious pain, managed to speak, 'Tom; please Tom, you've got to put those props up.'

'What do I do?'

'Take that flat plank bit and put it up on the roof; now put a prop under each end of it to hold it up. Good. Now use that hammer and knock them as vertical as you can get them. That's fine. Now do it again over there.'

'You think the roof might come in?'

'I don't know but best to play safe.'

'Is your leg broken?'

'I think it is. Can you get me out of here?'

'I'll try. Hang on and I'll pull you.'

Just then, back down the way he had come, the roof fell in, trapping them both.

'Damn! I thought that might happen. Now we'll just have to wait.'

Tom fought back a rising feeling of panic and asked the obvious question,

'Has this happened to you before?'

'Twice afore now. Dug out both times, but I hated it anyway.'

'I don't blame you. Are we safe? I mean with the roof propped up?'

'Well for now, but I can't guarantee it after that explosion.'

'What happened?'

'It was Fred Dixon my marra. He put a shot of gelatine dynamite in and it didn't go off. He thought that the fuse must have sputtered out and he went back to it though I told him not to. He lit a candle too, to get a better look. It went off with him right by it and I think he had more sticks in his pockets.'

'I thought candles weren't allowed. You think he's dead?'

'Hells Bells, marra; I think he's blown to bits; dead is putting it mildly; he's under that lot. Yes; he said he couldn't see enough with the lamp and put candles in his socks.'

By the light of his lamp Tom looked at the fall of coal further up the face and knew that anyone under it was beyond human help. A man had taken chances with his life and the lives of others, and his luck had run out.

'Shall I start to dig us out do you think?'

Jack Aitkin looked alarmed, 'No! No don't do that for God's sake. Wait for the rescue men to do it. They'll do it with props and plates and get us out. You're not a miner and there's not enough stuff here to make any sort of proper support or packing. We wait.'

'Well can I get this coal off you?'

'No. Leave it until it can be done safely.'

From the other side of the fall, along the coalface a voice, muffled and barely discernable shouted.

'Can you hear me over there? Anyone there?'

'Bill. Is that you?' shouted Tom.

'Aye it is. Are you alright Tom?'

'I am but I've got Jack Aitkin in here and he's hurt.'

'How bad?'

'Broken leg I think, and he's part buried. We can't get out the other end either.'

'Aye we know that. It's pretty sound this side so we're going to come and get you from here. How many of you are there?'

'Just the two of us.'

'Alright Tom. We're fetching stuff down from the surface now. I think there's only about five or six feet to clear. It's got to be done carefully though, so it'll be a few hours.'

'Can someone take Tethera back to his stall?'

'Already done. The fall is restricted to the longwall; he was a bit spooked but he's fine. Just hang on, marra. We'll get you out of there.'

'I think you'd better put that lamp out Tom. We don't need it and there's not that much air in here. We don't need to burn it off. They're not far off or we wouldn't be able to hear them but we still need to breathe.'

Up on the surface the steam hooter on the winding gear engine had sounded out an alarm across the little valley between the colliery and Dearham village. It could not be heard very loudly at Row Brow, but John Adams came pelting and out of breath, banging on Margaret's door with the news that Tom was trapped. So it was, with that awful paralysing fear rising in her throat, that she dropped everything, leaving her mother to pick up what she had been doing, to run, to walk, to pant her way to the Crosshow pithead. There, with rising and bitter sharp anxiety, she stood, as impotent as any of the other waiting women and children.

Down in the dark the rescue men inched their way tenderly forward, not content with spacing props, but building a continuous tunnel of props and plates as they carefully removed the fall. For Tom and Jack Aitkin it seemed to take an age as they waited in a place that was becoming hotter and stuffier by the minute, sweat pouring off them, and each shallow breath seemed less satisfying to their lungs. Occasional rushes of coal from the roof caused delay, but patient work brought its reward and after three hours they managed to get through and Tom crawled thankfully out into the inbye tunnel. As he stood up, breathing in a now plentiful air, relieved men pounded his back.

'You can call yourself a miner now, marra.'

'Are they bringing Jack now?'

'Not yet. We have to go forward a bit before we can get the fall off his leg. Now just go along with Cecil here and get to the doctor.'

'But I'm fine.'

'Just a check-up Tom. That's all.'

Black from head to foot, Tom emerged from the cage blinking into afternoon sunlight, to be nearly knocked flat by his wife who eluded the men supposed to be keeping a cordon away from the lifting gear.

'Margaret, you're getting filthy.'

It was a prosaic enough thing to say to her on the occasion of his resurrection, but when the weeping bundle that gripped him tightly turned her face up to him, it was nearly as black and streaked as his own.

'I thought I'd lost you.'

'Well you haven't Margaret, my love. I think you'll have to put up with me for a while longer.'

'Oh I hope so. I do hope so. A long while Tom.'

'Well I'll see what I can arrange.'

After a brief checkup with the doctor and answering a few questions, Tom was allowed to walk home, and just as he was about to leave they brought Jack Aitkin out on a stretcher. Fred Dixon came out later, what was left of him and they put the remains into a coffin, which was nailed shut to spare his family.

Life is short and the young do not know this. The awareness of the fragility of existence, and knowledge of how brief its span is, comes with maturity. When it does, it often brings a great enhancement of how precious time is. Events where death is near, even breathing down a person's neck, have the capacity to bring a sharp catharsis where all lesser considerations are swept away. For a brief time Margaret thought she had lost her husband, and in the emotion of that potent loss, she had realized that she did not wish to lose him in any way. Like Lazarus, he had come out of the ground, risen to redemption and new life and she wished to be part of it. That night Tom slept with his wife in the house on Row Brow, and for the rest of their time together he never slept anywhere else.

It was the middle of August before Margaret realized definitely that she was expecting her fifth child and when she broke the news to Tom he was pleased, though others in the family were more grounded about it.

Annie Eleanor asked her, 'Did you want another child Margaret?'

'I wasn't really thinking about it Annie. It's just what happens isn't it? It's what we do.'

'Oh no. Not me; I don't do that.'

'But you've already got a baby. Don't you want any more?'

'Yes I'd like another, mostly because I'd like a boy. But that will be it. I've no intention of sacrificing my life, my hopes, not to say my nipples to an endless chain of squalling pups.'

'But how will you….?'

'How will I stop it? Oh come on, Margaret. This is the twentieth century for heavens sake. If I don't want babies then I won't have babies.'

'Do you mean you'll stop John from… paying you attention?'

An obvious look of disbelief crossed Annie Eleanor's face, 'You mean you don't know Margaret? You really don't know?'

Margaret's face was pink with embarrassment, because there clearly was something here she did not know and she hated being in that position.

'Know about what?'

'About birth control you silly goose.'

'What's that?'

'It means that you use a device to stop becoming pregnant.'

Margaret had heard nothing of birth control devices during her upbringing, for there was no-one to tell her. It was true that she had heard some scurrilous rumours from other girls in her late teens, but it was all seen as something forbidden, 'dirty' and not to be spoken of. Nonetheless, other considerations had come into her mind because she was quite aware that Tom and she were not facing the prosperous future that they once were. There were many people who had larger families than theirs, but the more mouths that needed feeding, the more money was needed to maintain them. Her natural curiosity impelled her to ask more, so she listened with a kind of prurient fascination as Annie Eleanor told her about her 'womb veil'. This was apparently a diaphragm of rubber; Margaret sat almost with open mouth as Annie Eleanor told her how it was used.

'It's called a 'Duplex' and they make them in Germany. I got mine by mail order.'

'But where from? How did you know about it?'

'I read Suffragist literature Margaret; perhaps you should too. There are many women writing about how we can take more control of our own lives and what we do than we have right now. I got the address of a company in London who import them and I sent for one which I use. John knows all about it. Anyway it does not always work, though if you follow the instructions it does.'

'Does he mind?'

'No. He sees the sense of it. Anyway it's not his decision to make is it? It takes two to decide something like having a baby.'

This also was a novel, even alien, thought to Margaret and she resolved that she would talk to Tom about it in due course; and when she could pluck up the courage.

It says a lot about the humanity of the colliery managers at Crosshow Pit that they tided over the Christmas and New Year before they made their announcement. Although their Landsale coal was shielding them from complete failure, the world price of coal had fallen markedly at the end of the year. The problem was over-manning in the British coal industry, which employed one and a half million men throughout the country and was easily the biggest employer. Russia was industrialising fast, and particularly in their Polish coalfields they were using fewer men and more machinery to cut coal. They also used more modern methods of mining, so that the huge pillars of coal left in many British mines to support the roof of the workings were not a feature of their work. The same was happening in the US, and coal much cheaper than British was flooding onto the market. In round terms Britain produced about 190 million tons of coal a year of which about 100 went for domestic use whilst the rest was exported. It was the exports that were suffering, so the Crosshow managers discovered that they were losing money. They had to shed fifty jobs. Some men went willingly enough because such events were not uncommon in coalfields, others not so. There was plenty of employment about at the Dovenby pit, Bullgill, Flimby, the Lonsdale, or even further afield, but the pay rates would be lower and would not improve because of the structural inefficiency of the industry. Tom was not affected, the services of an ostler being imperative in a mine where horses worked, but it left a bad feeling across the village. It did not help that Mr Melrose had moved on to a new parish and the new vicar was not as well known or as influential as he had been, so there was no intervention to save the jobs of parishioners this time. Crosshow Colliery continued to mine coal until May 1903, but had the workers there been able to read the mind or the expression of Robert Steel, then they might have had cause to worry. The company could not get the price it wanted for its coal and the other local collieries were undercutting its business because they paid far less in wages.

Life for Margaret and Tom was one of plenty at the beginning of March 1903 when John Metcalfe turned up on a cart from Allonby with Annie Eleanor and they were both very mysterious about something under a sheet in the back.

'Just give me a hand to get these in and then I'll tell you all about it,' said John.

When they had brought three wooden cases into the house, he explained.

'This is salvage I think, by the laws of the land, but the police have confiscated a few cases from people who had it, so just keep quiet about it will you?'

'Why whatever is it?' asked Margaret. 'It's not stolen goods is it John?'

'Why no Margaret; I wouldn't do something like that. No it's stuff that was washed up along Allonby bay from a ship that was wrecked there. Cases of canned fruit and canned salmon. I've got loads of it in an outhouse, so Annie thought you'd like some with all the mouths to feed here.'

'Is it nice stuff? I mean not spoiled?'

'No it's champion stuff; we've had tinned salmon till I'm near sick of it this last few days. The fruit's nice too; it's all American from California.'

Tom asked, 'What ship was it?'

'It was called the Hougomont and it was driven ashore in the gale on 28 February.'

'It was very exciting,' said Annie Eleanor. 'The Maryport lifeboat came out and the ship was driven up onto the sand. Lots of folk came out to help the crew ashore.'

'Any lives lost?'

'Not one. The ship was pushed right up the beach opposite the Grapes and all the regulars came out to help them ashore. They've been looked after in peoples' homes.'

'It's fair salvage,' said John. 'There were thousands of cans and cases washed up all along the beach. Everybody's got some, and it's all cleared up. Why waste it? As far as I know, it's the law of the sea and fair game so we brought you a share. Why not?'

'Why not indeed? I entirely agree with you. Looks like salmon for tea Margaret.'

That was the only luck that they had in the first part of the year; events beyond their control were moving to change their lives forever, and they soon began to see them.

Chapter 29

The Light over the Solway

Rumours started to fly among the 150 men that were left, and they proved to be more than mist at the end of May when Robert Steel called a pithead meeting and announced that the money had run out. He would pay them off at the end of the week, but there were no funds to continue cutting coal after that because he had nothing to pay them with. To the fallen faces and groans he offered hope. There was to be a meeting at the beginning of June when the Maryport Industrial Co-operative Society would discuss the matter. The closure might, until then, be seen as a temporary lay-off; needless to say, this welcome codicil to his announcement came as a shot in the arm. The Co-op had intervened before back in '94 and surely would do so again, for the same reasons as had appertained then. Mercifully they did not have long to wait.

The Co-operative Hall in Maryport on the evening of Monday 1 June held a meeting attended by members only and chaired by Mr Fawcett. There was a number of items on the agenda, but all attending knew what the main topic of discussion would be, and it was not too long before its turn came; Mr Fawcett moved to present a document which he had in his hand.

'I wish to put before the committee a petition I have received today from the miners at the Crosshow colliery. It calls upon us to consider ways and means of keeping the colliery, open for the good of the community in Dearham and for the mutual benefits that it gives to us and to our customers. The considerations they ask to be taken into account in support of this request are much the same as were made so effectively in 1894 when we did indeed make it possible for a colliery to maintain employment in that area. It is signed by all the men working in the mine and I wish to place it here for your consideration.'

A period of silence followed during which there was some clearing of throats and a few feet being shuffled, so Robert Steel broke the silence,

'If you please Mr Chairman, I should like to say a few words in support of this petition if I may be permitted to speak.'

'You may Mr Steel. I know that there are many people in the room who have made themselves familiar with what has been happening at the Crosshow Pit, but we would be glad to hear what you have to say.'

'Thank you sir. It is not necessary I am sure, for me to give further voice to the commercial arguments to be made in favour of supporting the continuing existence of the mine at Crosshow. I do wish to point out, however, that it has, on the whole, been a very successful venture. Over the last eight years we have produced and sold a million and a quarter tons of the best quality coal; the money generated from these sales has paid off our debts, paid aggregate wages of nearly £40,000 and kept alive a community that has demonstrated its gratitude by buying many of its supplies from the Co-operative. Until recently we were showing a healthy profit and it is only the sudden drop in the market price of coal that has put us into these straits. The mine is far from exhausted; there are many years of good quality coal still down there waiting to be extracted. If the financial strength of the Co-operative can tide us over until better times, then I can see no reason why we should not soon show a profit as we did for most of last year. On behalf of the men and management at Crosshow, I ask you to do so.'

Another awkward pause followed, but finally it was broken by Mr Thomas Edwards, a leading member of the Co-op who had held office on the committee several times over the years.

'I don't find this easy, but I know there's many of you think the same as I do, so if no-one else is going to say it, then I will. I do not support this proposition.'

Steel listened with an impassive face, but noted that there had been no gasps of surprise from the audience; it was clear that many, if not most, were of the same opinion as Mr Edwards, who now continued,

'I have to point out that over the last eight years, the Crosshow Colliery made a loss for three, broke even for four, and only made a profit in one and that was last year. Now I know you'll say that it could continue to do so if we put more capital into it, but I do not agree with you. Things have changed since 1894. Then the price of coal was high and now its low. Much of our coal is hand hewn and with all respect to you sir I do not see how we can make it cheap enough to compete with foreign coal in the world market. I'm sorry to be obvious Mr Steel but there's some pits are going to have to go to the wall and that seems to be unavoidable. The Co-operative Society ploughed money into that colliery, and, fair enough, we've got it back; at the same time the shop's been doing well, but can you, a man of your experience, put your hand on your heart and tell me that this is going to change for the better? Can we compete against Polish and American prices?'

Steel pursed his lips, looked at Mr Edwards, and shook his head. The economics were simple and clear.

'We have free trade in this country,' continued Mr Edwards, and while to some extent we enjoy a protected domestic market, it's becoming saturated and the only way to make coal more economic as a business, is to lower wages to such a level that men would not be able to support their families. Believe me when I say that I think this is going to get worse in the next few years.'

There were murmurs of agreement around the room, though quite a few disapproving noises.

'What we have here is nothing more or less than a request to take over the colliery and run it as a business. Very well, as a local businessman I see two cases. One is that we support the colliery and buy it outright. That way we support our neighbours in time of need and go down in a blaze of glory when it soaks up our money too, because I tell you straight that the price of coal is not going to recover any time soon. The other course would be to put more money into running it as it stands and I cannot see how we would get it back. So how would we explain the loss of their money to our members?'

Here he paused and looked round the room seeing glum faces and tight lips.

'I'm sorry, I truly am, but my business sense tells me that this is a literal money pit and that in our members' interests we should not entertain the idea of taking over the Crosshow Colliery. I move to a ballot on this among the members here present by show of hands.'

The matter being put to the vote the petition that the Co-operative Society buy the colliery was defeated by 39 votes to 29. Robert Steel protested that the last time this was thought on, the matter had been put to the full membership, but the feeling of the meeting was against it as Mr Fawcett explained.

'You may be sure Mr Steel that the feeling in this room is indicative of the feeling among the wider membership as I can well attest. In 1894 the Society took a risk for the sake of wider benefits that might accrue. This time there will be no benefits and all we see here is loss for our members. I'm sorry but I cannot advise them to this course and there is an end to it.'

The Crosshow colliery was closed and the shaft was capped whilst its equipment was sold off and 150 men were thrown out of employment. The ponies were all sold off as well and Thomas bade his charges farewell with something of an ache round his heart. He knew that they would be well looked after in Flimby where they were bound, but he had been fond of his shaggy little charges, each one a character on its own. The effects on the village were not as bad as feared because conditions had changed as regards transport. A regular workman's train now ran up the line early in the morning to Bullgill and Aspatria from Dearham Halt, and to get south another ran down to Flimby and Siddick; the reverse applied in the evenings. In addition, to this the colliery on Broughton Moor was taking on a few men because wage rates had dropped and they thought to improve their viability by increasing production; volume would swamp any threat of imported coal from Poland, Germany or the US. Dearham was not going to become a ghost town by the closure of the Crosshow Pit.

John Adams was not long unemployed because he had decided on a change of career. At the age of 53 he recognized that he was past his best as a face worker, so hearing of a job as a banksman at the Lonsdale Pit he applied for the post and got it. By many standards his work would have been considered hard, but in comparison to what he was used to it was light. It was his task to take tubs of coal from the pit-head and place it into the tippler which turned the contents of a tub onto a moving belt for the sorting shed. Thomas could have had a similar surface job, but he thought that accepting such a position would be an irrevocable step because he needed the wages to support his family. The closure of the Crosshow Colliery had provided time for him to think what to do next, though not without some agonies of mind.

'I'm sorry that it's come to this Margaret; and most of all I'm sorry that I've brought you to this.'

'What do you mean 'this' Tom? I'm quite happy. What do you mean?'

'Well look at us. You married me when I was quite prosperous and then we had our own farm and things looked good. Now we've lost all that and we're living in a two up and two down with me unemployed. Even if I can get a job it's not going to pay that much. We've come down in the world and you'd be more than human if you weren't disappointed by it.'

Tom was now subjected to that grey level stare that he knew so well, but Margaret didn't say anything.

'What are you looking at me like that for? You know it's true.'

'Actually Tom, it's not true.'

'To me it is. What do you mean it's not true?'

'You look at things in such a black and white way Tom though I do love you very much. I think that women have a better way of looking at situations like this and if you could understand how it really is, then you'd be a bit happier.'

'Oh now you're going to have to explain that to me, because I do not understand what there is good to see in this.'

'That's because you're not looking. Tell me; who am I?'

'You're Margaret, my wife. What sort of question is that?'

'It's a very good one. Yes. I am Margaret, your wife. I was born in a house one minute from where I stand. My father is a coal miner. I went to school here and my family are all round here. Now tell me, do you think I've come down in the world?'

'If you put it that way then no, but you had a bigger house and a servant....'

'I don't care about that Tom. That's just things; it's what life throws at you and you have to take the rough with the smooth. I'm quite happy thank you very much; I'm here where I was brought up. I live as my father and mother and friends and neighbours do. Do you look down on us for how we live?'

'No. Well; no.'

'Well then I certainly don't see myself as having 'come down' in the world and if you don't look down on us here then stop saying it or you'll look like a snob. Are you a snob Tom?'

Here she put her arms round him and looked at him with a twinkle.

'No I'm not a snob, but I can't help feeling that you deserve better.'

'Better than what? I have a husband who loves me, four well-behaved children and another on the way, a roof over my head, a little money tucked away and food in my mouth. I'm quite comfortable thank you very much Master Thomas.'

That put a smile on his face and he kissed her on the top of her head before she continued.

'My husband works very hard for his money and though he's out of a job right now, he won't be for long because he's a grafter who knows he must work for a living. We shall bide our time for a while, live upon what we have with the help of my family, and eventually you will get another job.'

'Aye, but where. There's nothing round here; 150 men lost their jobs and anything in this area's being snapped up just like that.'

'Then we'll just have to move.'

'Yes I agree, but where to?'

'The logical place is Workington.'

'Workington. Why?'

'Because it's booming Tom. Don't you listen when I read Ommie's letters to you?'

'Yes I do, but I hadn't thought of moving there. It's a town; I've never lived in a town.'

'Well if there's jobs and money there, Tom, you might have to start thinking about it.'

'It's at least seven miles away; how am I going to get to know of jobs if we're not down there?'

'That's easy enough; I shall ask Omega to keep her eyes open for anything that comes up.'

A letter to Omega was followed two days later by the advent of none other than that lady in person and in a high state of urgency.

'I've begged time off to get here, Tom, and I've said I'll be back by tonight, so I want you to get your coat and come with me now.'

'Where to?'

'Dearham Halt and then to Workington low station. I got Margaret's letter and I asked Mr Harrop this morning if he'd got any vacancies for a horseman and he said yes. You could have knocked me down with a feather, but he asked me who I was asking for and I said you, so he told me to go and get you now; he's got a post he needs to fill and there's a few interested in it. I got a cab from the station and he's waiting. Hurry up. I'll explain on the way.'

It appeared that Moss Bay steelworks had a large area of railway sidings and lines within the works and that a man was needed to work on them as a member of a small team of platelayers. There was more to it than that though; several steam engines were employed on various jobs round a large area; some went up the slag bank to dump molten slag on the edge of the sea. Others ran down to the harbour with finished railway lines, which were the plant's main product, and others ferried wagons of ore. However, there were two Clydesdales that were used to shunt small loads round and help make up trains when it was not worthwhile summoning an engine. Mr Harrop, the manager, wished to kill two birds with one stone because one of the men looking after these horses had been killed when he slipped on a ninety degree corner of a wall and fell into the path of a train. The man who got the job would be taken on as a plate-layer, but would have the responsibility of looking after one horse and using it to shunt when told to. Soon she had him in front of Mr Harrop, who explained what he needed and concluded after a talk,

'So basically you'd be working under the instructions of the yard master and if he wants you to shunt then you shunt. If he wants you on a gang to lay and shift rails, then you do that. From what you've told me you're used to hard work and you look in better condition than the other applicants who to be quite frank look a bit scrawny to me. You've got some education too so you'll learn fast. How old did you say you were?'

'I'm 39,' said Tom.

'That's a good age. Old enough to be mature and know what graft is, yet young enough to be able to do it. Right then, give me your hand on it for you've got the job.'

Tom got home late that night and walked from Dearham Halt, but he smiled all the way; he could not stop smiling when he walked through the door for a kiss.

'You got it then?'

'I did.'

'How much?'

He looked at her with a big grin.

'Two pounds a week.'

'Tom! That's good.'

'Yes I know. It's more than they get on the mainline railway, but the steelworks is doing well. They supply all over the world and they pay good wages. We're moving to Workington, bonny lass.'

'We'll have to find a house.'

'I've done it. Omega told me where to go so I went to the rent office of Curwen Estates. They own most of the town and I've rented a house for us to live.'

'What's it like?'

'I don't know; I wanted to get back, but the agent told me that it's a good house in a terrace. It's got its own water, flushing toilet, back yard and scullery; and for four shillings a week I wasn't going to grumble. If you don't like it we can move, but it'll do for now.'

'I really think you should have looked at it first; don't you think so?'

'I told you; I wanted to get back. I liked the agent and he told me it was a good house. I thought I'd come home and give you the news and take you there tomorrow to have a look. Your mother will see to the children.'

'You're such a man sometimes!'

'I know it well, but I have the key in my pocket; we shall see it tomorrow.'

55 Devonshire Street turned out to be a mid-terrace house whose street door opened into a passageway. Part way along it was a door on the left that led into the front parlour. A fireplace was set into the back wall.

'This is to be where we shall sleep,' said Tom, 'It'll be quite cosy.'

Turning left out of the sitting room they passed the foot of the stairs into a much larger back room and it was apparent straight

431

away that this was where the family would do most of its living. A black range oven and cooker was set into the wall with bright brass knobs on it.

'The agent told me that it has a back-boiler plumbed to feed this.'

Here Tom moved through a further door and down one step into a scullery to where there was a work surface and hinged it up to reveal a white enamelled bath.

'Well that's rather luxurious!' said Margaret. 'At least we shall be a clean family without much effort.'

'Apparently the previous tenant was a blacksmith and he liked to get the dirt off with ease and couldn't be bothered with a tin bath.'

'You won't find me complaining about it,' she replied with a smile.

A door led out of the back room into a concrete rendered yard where on the right were the scullery window closest to the house, and a coal-shed near the back gate, which in turn led onto the lonning behind the terrace. Coal could be tipped into it straight from the lonning. It was a clean swept lonning, which demonstrated a certain amount of civic pride by the neighbours.

Up the stairs were two rooms, one to the front and one to the rear of the building.

'Boys in one room, girls in another. It's going to be a bit crowded, Tom.'

'That doesn't matter as long as they behave; and they will behave.'

'I don't doubt it. Could we not have got something bigger?'

'We could but that would cost more. You'd have less to spend on other things. The question is - will it do?'

'Oh yes it will do. I was brought up in a house smaller than this one. It'll do well enough - at least for now. It's fine Tom; we can live here and there seems to be a lot of good stuff round; schools, a hospital, and I like the look of that big church up the road.'

'St John's? They say it's quite spectacular inside. We'll have to look.'

What is needful in human life is probably not wealth or luxury, but health, love, enough to eat, to drink, a roof and warmth. We strive to be comfortable in our existence, but there is no guarantee that we ever obtain it. The old idea that man enjoys inalienable rights such as life, liberty, and the pursuit of happiness is often misunderstood. No one has a right to be happy; they have a right to pursue that which makes them happy, but of course they may never attain it, for life brings no guarantees save the two inevitabilities of death and taxes. Margaret and Tom were part of a process that swept hundreds of thousands of people off the land and drew them into cities to work at things they never dreamed of. This is not to say that they were victims, but rather that they were part of the tide of life which picks all men and women up like flotsam and jetsam at various times and deposits them where it will. Where they had washed up they had a right to feel that they were lucky and that it had even made them rich for they had a place to live, the means to earn, and a community in which, along with thousands of others, they could even flourish to a degree. So they moved their family and their goods into Devonshire Street; from this haven they could watch the years march by and nurture those who would inherit their earth. Had they but known it, they would also watch the coming to fruition of forces that would sweep away the world they knew, and change all their certainties into dust on the wind.

In the back yard that night Tom and Margaret stood amazed as a great white light lit up the sky towards the sea. Then the light over the Solway flared red, green, violet, magenta and again vivid bright white as the great Bessemers at Moss Bay steelworks roared their volcanic fury into the atmosphere and heralded their arrival into their new home like celestial fireworks welcoming a queen. With this, the collier's daughter was content and the future beckoned, full of hope.

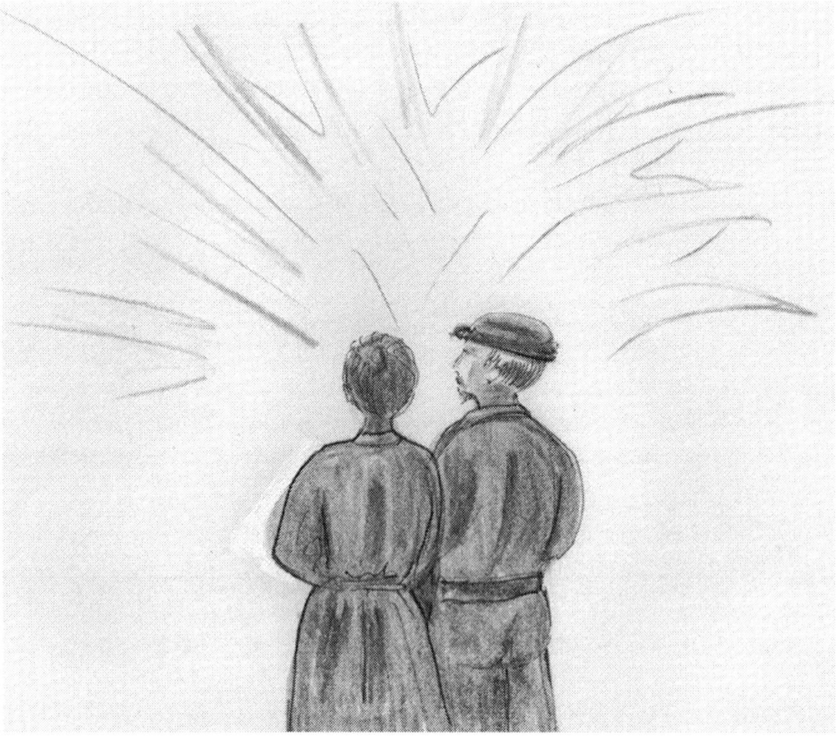

Family Tree of Margaret Adams and Thomas Little

Nancy Shortriggsm. John Adams 1847 — 1850

- John 1871(d)
- Omega 1873
  - Mary Hannah 1897(d)
- Margaret 1877
  - Annie Eleanor Nancy Barwise
  - 1896 1897 1899
- Mary 1879
- Nancy 1880
- Thomas 1883
- John 1886
- Alpha Nancy 1889

Ann Roper m. Barwise Little 1829 — 1821

- Joseph 1857(d)
- Joseph 1860
- Thomas 1864
- William 1867
- Annie Eleanor 1869

436

Glossary

Adit	Horizontal passage leading into a mine
Barwise	Old Solway Plain family name, pronounced 'Barras'
Bessemers	Vessel through which air is blown to purify molten iron
braffin	A form of horse collar
Butty	Shift overseer in a Victorian colliery
Craic	Chat
Doggy	Assistant to the butty
Foal	A junior putter
Gowks	Fools
Haud	Hold
Inby	Field close to the farm buildings
Inbye or Ingang	Tunnel towards the coal face
Judd and Jenkins	Coal that has been undercut and is ready to be brought down
Lanthorn	Victorian spelling of lantern
Limmers	Straps on a horse harness
Lollicker	Tongue
Lonning	Lane or back alley
Maingate	Mining tunnel formed in advance of the Longwall
Marra	Mate or pal
Paddicks	Frogs
Pattens	Wooden platforms strapped on to raise and protect shoes
Putter	A person who pushes tubs of coal from face to shaft
Rippers	A miner who removes rock, not coal, to enable coal to be hewn
Sprag	A crude brake composed of a length of wood

Werst thew of te? Where are you off to?

I owp thew's garna put that in thys pocket cos ah divvent have wun.
I hope you are going to put that in your pocket because I do not have one.

Printed in Great Britain
by Amazon